Storms & Sacrifice

Storms & Sacrifice

DOMINIC N. ASHEN

4 Horsemen
Publications, Inc.

4 Horsemen
Publications, Inc.

4 Horsemen Publications, Inc.
1497 Main St. Suite 169
Dunedin, FL 34698
4horsemenpublications.com
info@4horsemenpublications.com

Edited by Tilda M. Cooke
Cover by Oxford and VW

Library of Congress Control Number: 2021944766

Print ISBN: 978-1-64450-342-3
Hardback ISBN: 978-1-64450-343-0
Audio ISBN: 978-1-64450-340-9
Ebook ISBN: 978-1-64450-341-6

Table of Contents

Map Key

1. V'rok'sh Tah'lj
2. Holbrooke
3. Bridgeport
4. Pinewater
5. Goldbury
6. Northern Patrol Camp
7. Eastern Patrol Camp
8. Western Patrol Camp
9. Southern Patrol Camp
10. Temple of Zeus Ruins
11. Gul'fam Bridge
12. To Pákannon
13. To Kiz'urngor
14. Emerald Hills
15. Durgash Forest
16. Shad'rok Springs
17. Kar'guk River
18. Marfu River
19. Trou-gah Creek
20. Lake Ulgan

AVURAL UG'DOL
(TURTLE ISLAND)

Nova Mundus

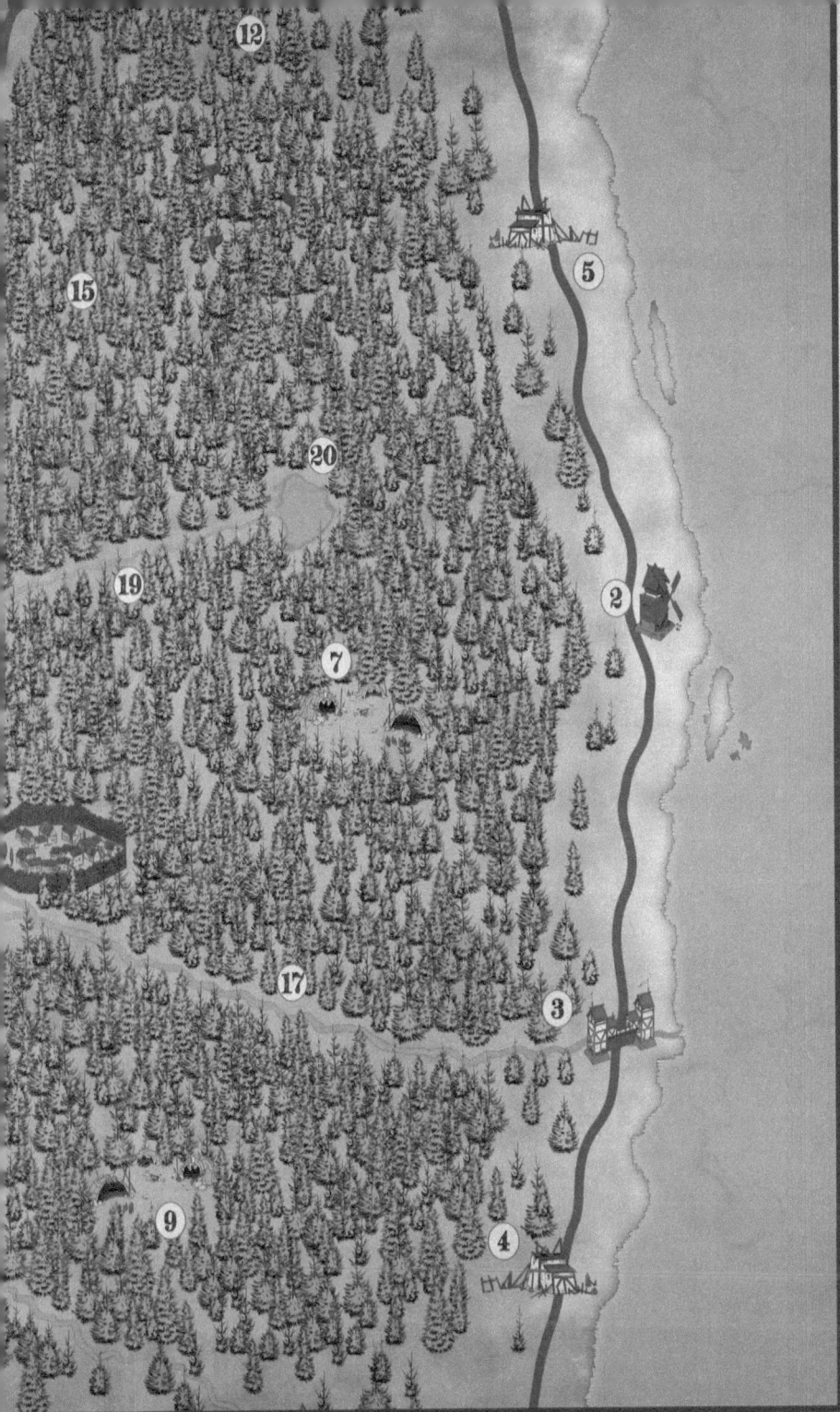

Dedication

To Jay, one of my first readers and someone who has always encouraged and pushed me for more. Good boy.

Chapter 1

"*Y*ou look good."

"You look better."

"...Sorry." Adam's words make me grimace. *Knew I shoulda dressed down more for this.*

"Come on. You know I didn't mean it like that," he huffs from his spot across the table and smiles. "I'm glad you're doing good. We've heard some rumors, and I've been worried."

"Yeah. Like is it true that after you lost the fight to that big guy he fu—*oww!*" Nate rubs his side where Adam's elbow hit him.

Adam glares at the mage to his right before turning back to me. "Seriously though, David. Is he hurting you?"

"No, really. *I'm fine.* Better than fine, all things considered." I smile back, trying to hide any discomfort over the topic. I can only imagine what they've heard—and how much of it is true. "I'm more worried about you guys in here."

It's Astraday, which is visiting day at the Yash'ak Cr'hol Labor Camp. I've been worried about my friends and where they've been held since we were first arrested, and this place was no different. Even though Khazak assured me that everything would be fine, that this place was better than an actual prison, I still needed to see it for myself. So, before my first visit, he arranged for a brief "tour" of the camp for me. It's actually…pretty nice. I mean it's still a jail, but it's also basically just a bunch of boring buildings behind a big fence.

It almost reminds me of the knight academy; everyone's wearing a uniform, the prisoner's rooms look more like dorms than cells, and half of them leave during the day to work—where they earn *actual* money. From what I saw (and smelled), the food doesn't even seem half bad. Khazak told me the place is named after one of the city's first rangers, and that the term "labor camp" is a holdover from when this place was an *actual* camp, when most of the city was still made up of tents. All the more reason I think they need to change it; labor camps are something *very* different where I come from.

This is my second time here, my first being last weekend when I saw Liss and Corrine. Thanks to Khazak pulling some strings, I'm able to sit with two of my friends at a time. After I get patted down by one of the guards, they bring me to a large room filled with tables where they're already seated. They've got the prisoners split by gender, and since Adam insisted the girls go first—which is a very Adam thing to do—this week I get to see him and Nate.

"We're alright. It's not as rough in here as you'd think." Adam gives me a small smile. "The food's not that bad, and the beds still beat sleeping on the ground outside. They say we're earning some money while we're in here, too. They've got me and Liss working construction, so far just helping to build homes in the poorer parts of the city. It's mostly moving materials around and holding them in place while the mages do their thing."

"What about you?" I ask Nate, more out of politeness than actual interest. When I was here last week no one had been assigned a "job" yet.

"Corrine and I have been hard at work transcribing books." He flexes his hand like it hurts. "If they'd just let me use my magic, I could have the whole thing done in a few hours but *nooooo*..." On both of his wrists are small metal bracelets, the same as I saw on Corrine last week. They're long-term versions of the city's anti-magic bracers, lighter and unconnected to make it easier to move around and work while still cutting off the wearer from their magical abilities.

"What about you?" Adam ignores Nate's whining. "What does... Ironstorm, is that his name?" *Yep.* I nod. "What does he have you doing?"

"Actually, I'm kinda...working with him and the people who arrested us." I scratch my head, feeling embarrassed that I'm basically working with the enemy. "It's not all that different from what we did back at the academy."

It's been about two weeks since I started my "job" with the V'rok'sh Tah'lj rangers as Captain Khazak Ironstorm's assistant. I wish I could say it's been an interesting two weeks, but sadly after the investigation we had my first two days, it has been incredibly boring. Khazak—or Sir, as I sometimes know him—wasn't kidding when he said a big part of his job was filling out paperwork; he spends *most* of his time in his office doing that.

"Isn't that kind of weird?" Adam sounds surprised. Understandable, given one of the main reasons we left home was the work we were doing as part of the Northlake Academy of Knighthood—you know, real honorable knight things, like arresting protestors or protecting rich people's property. "It's a lot more boring than it sounds. The most exciting thing that happened last week was helping an old lady find her dog." She was thankful, at least. "Check it out though." I bring up one of my arms and flex. "They've got a gym."

Just because Khazak has to do a lot of paperwork doesn't mean I do, unless you count the whole "trying to learn a new language" thing. When he's not making me work through my *Learning Atasi* book (which is going...alright), we manage to break up the boring downtime with some fun activities. Not like *that* (Well, except this one time we were stuck there kinda late...). I just mean there's been plenty to keep me busy.

Not only do I have a gym to workout in now, but a few days after I started, they tore down the old cells in the yard and converted the space into an outdoor training area. When I can convince Khazak or one of the other rangers to join me, we'll spar back there. It's mostly hand-to-hand stuff, which isn't really my forte against a bunch of muscled-up orcs, but there's been a few times where I've gotten to wield a sword again. I even got my own work-issued shortsword! I know it's only been two weeks, but it already feels like I'm starting to bulk back up.

"You'll be back to your old self in no time." Adam grins.

"Working out won't make you taller, David," Nate snarks.

"So anyways," I push past him, "if you see the girls, can you let them know I won't be able to make visiting day next weekend?"

"Why? Everything alright?" Adam tilts his head.

"Yeah, just gonna be spending the week in the woods." That's what Khazak told me a few days ago.

"You're just...going camping?" Nate squints his eyes.

"No, it's this ranger thing. Every week a different group goes out and patrols." It was one of those patrols that caught and arrested us. "At the end of the week, a new group comes in and takes the old one's place. They rotate every four weeks or so, and we leave tomorrow for our turn."

"Huh. Yeah, I'll let 'em know. Have fun." I cringe inwardly at Adam's use of the word "fun," realizing that I basically just bragged about going on a camping trip for a week while they sit in jail. "If there's one thing we actually got good at in the last couple of months, it's sleeping outside."

"Did you have a nice visit?" Khazak asks when I return from the visitation room now that the hour is over. He's been kind enough to give me privacy when I meet with my friends.

"Yeah, it was good to see Adam." It has sucked to not have my best friend around to talk to about...*any* of the stuff that's been going on. "He's in good spirits, but he's always been pretty good at hiding when he's unhappy about something."

"What about your other friend?" He's still learning their names.

"Nate? He's fine. And I told you, he's not my friend." I refuse to acknowledge that dick as anything more than an acquaintance. "Thank you for bringing me."

"Of course." He reaches over and squeezes my shoulder gently as we walk.

Unlike work, things between Khazak and me have been anything but boring. Not that the excitement has reached anywhere near the levels of crazy drama that first week held. Would you believe I only managed to get spanked *once* last week? It was my own fault. I let Ragnar, Khazak's half-orc, half-elf best friend, talk me into pranking Khazak by swapping his regular ink for some that turns invisible fifteen minutes after being put on paper. He didn't notice until he was writing a particularly long report and the top started to vanish before he had reached the bottom. He said he spanked me once for each field he had to re-fill out on each form. I didn't keep count, but it felt like it.

Outside of that, things have been great. You'd think after almost three weeks of waking up next to and spending the entire day with someone, I'd be sick of him, but we've been getting along swimmingly. Even when we do start to grate on each other, I'll just go for a run around the city or hit the gym at the station for some "me" time. There's not a whole lot to do around here aside from eating, reading, and exercising, but he always manages to find something to keep us occupied. Which is sometimes me. Safe to say I think I'm getting kind of good at *that* kind of stuff.

"Ready to pack for tomorrow?" Khazak asks when we arrive back at the house.

"Yep. Do you have a bag I can use?" I'm gonna need a lot of clothes for a whole week. "And do you have an extra bedroll?"

"Mine should be big enough for the both of us." Khazak walks down the hall, turning into the spare room with me following.

"Your bag or your bedroll?" One of those makes more sense than the other.

"Both." He opens the closet and pulls out a large bedroll attached to a sturdy looking leather backpack.

"My clothes are gonna fit in there?" It's sizable but so is he—as are his clothes.

"No, this is filled with tools and supplies." He slings it over one shoulder. "I meant my other bag."

I look at him skeptically, assuming he's talking about the pouch he carries around when we go out. I've had my suspicions that there's more to that bag than meets the eye, but I haven't gotten confirmation. He snorts at the face I'm making, bringing his camping supplies into the bedroom and motioning for me to follow.

"This bag is much larger on the inside than it appears," he tells me after placing the bedroll on the floor and grabbing his other bag. He turns to one of his clothing chests and grabs a large stack of shirts and pants, a pile larger than the bag itself. I then watch as he proceeds to put all of them into the bag, which bulges out a little, *maybe*. Not nearly as much as it should—it should have burst by now.

"I knew it," I whisper to myself. *Magic bag.* I've seen them before. Well, I've seen one before, once. "Where did you get that?"

"A port city in the north." He motions me over, holding the bag open so I can peer inside. "My sister and I made the journey there together. It is known as a 'spacious satchel.' I've had it over a decade."

Looking in the top of the satchel is weird. It's pitch black, like a void. I'm almost scared to put my hand in. "How does it work?"

"After you have put something inside, you simply need to picture it in your mind as you reach in to retrieve it," he explains.

I give it a shot, picturing one of the shirts I just saw him put inside. The inside of the bag feels cool as I insert my hand, and suddenly my hand feels full. Pulling it out, I can see that I'm now holding the shirt in question. I repeat this with another shirt and a pair of pants. Then I try inserting my entire arm, touching the bottom of the outside of the bag with my other hand at the same time and ignoring the smirk I receive for my antics.

"That's awesome." I would love to get my hands on one of these myself. It would be *so* useful for traveling. Not only does it give all that extra space, but anything inside is basically weightless. I could carry all sorts of equipment and loot in that thing.

"I trust this will suit our needs, then?" He hands me the satchel so that I can start adding in my own stuff.

"Perfectly, Sir."

Khazak and I leave for the patrol the next day after lunch. We're both in uniform, him carrying the bedroll and supplies while giving me the weightless bag holding our clothes and other items—I packed a couple of books in case it gets boring. He wasn't going to let me carry anything else until I convinced him to at least let me hold his bow for him, so I have that strapped to my back with my sword scabbard.

The guards open the gates for us when we approach through some mechanism I don't see, but I'm willing to bet is magic. They both salute the captain as he passes through, closing the large doors behind us once we are on the other side. Immediately, we are greeted by the sight of the forest. As we make our way forward, the trees around the city walls look larger than the rest, covering the wall hiding the city behind it. Their height seems to even out to normal levels fairly quickly as we move away, and you probably wouldn't even notice if you didn't know what you were looking for. More magic or just good landscaping?

The forest is quiet aside from the occasional bird chirping or squirrel rustling the leaves. It's so peaceful and untouched, despite the fact that there's a city not even a mile away. There are no paths—that would probably defeat the purpose of the city being hidden—so it feels a little bit like we're just wandering randomly through the woods. Khazak seems like he knows where he's going though, so I don't question it.

"Do you know where we're going?" Okay, maybe I do. "I mean, are you doing this from memory, or is there some kind of trail I'm not seeing?"

"Afraid you might get lost?" Khazak muses as he looks over to me.

"No... Maybe." *The last time I was out here I ended up getting arrested so...*

Khazak laughs and pulls me up to walk alongside him. "At this point, I could probably get to the campsite blindfolded if needed, but there are landmarks. Remember that large tree we passed a short while ago?"

I nod. "It looked like some of the branches were bent strangely." Almost twisted together.

"We left the city through the west gate and walked two kilometers until we reached that tree." That's around one-and-a-quarter miles—my twin brother Michael would be proud at all the math I've been doing lately. "Then we turned northwest and have been walking another two kilometers looking for...*that* rock formation."

He points to a pile of mossy boulders coming up on our left. The smooth surfaces tell me they've been here a while. The largest of the boulders sticks up from the center, almost making the pile resemble some sort of throne.

"From here it is another kilometer north until we reach a stream with a fallen tree spanning it, and then after a short hike northwest from there, we will be at the camp." Khazak marches forward confidently as he speaks.

I nod, glad for the instructions. I'm not actually worried, but if for some reason I *do* have to make it back to the city on my own, at least I know how. I try to pay attention to how long it takes us to cover a kilometer at our speed; it'll mean less math to do in my head later. I keep my eyes peeled for the stream in question, though I figure it will be pretty hard to miss. Unless the direction we're going is completely wrong, we'll have to cross it eventually.

I end up spotting the fallen tree before the stream. It would serve as a very useful bridge to cross if the stream wasn't little more than a trickle. I barely have to jump to get to the other side. When we're both across, Khazak leans back against the fallen log with his hands clasped in front of him, waiting for me to tell him where we need to go next. *Easy.* We were already walking north, but I look up at the sun's position just to verify.

"Camp is that way." I point northwest from our position.

"Lead the way." He pushes himself up.

"Oh, is this my job now?" Despite my words, I start walking in the direction of the camp.

"Merely testing your skills," he defends as he follows.

"Uh-huh. You just wanna stare at my ass." I've gotten a lot more confident in the flirting area (at least with a guy).

I hear a thoughtful hum from behind me but no denial. *Yeah, he's totally looking at my ass right now.*

We're only walking for a couple of minutes when I feel Khazak's hand on my shoulder. "Wait." He points ahead of us. In the distance, I see a figure walking away from us: a person. An orc. Must be one of the other rangers headed to the campsite.

Khazak lets out a noise from my left, something between a growl and a bark. It's not loud, but it does make me jump. It also makes the orc ahead of pause and turn around, returning the noise and throwing an arm up to wave when they see us. They start walking back to meet us halfway.

"You didn't just say something, right? That wasn't a word?" *Otherwise, learning this language is going to be even more complicated than I thought.*

"No," he chuckles. "Just a signal."

Once we get closer, I recognize the orc. Not just from the station, but...shit he's one of the orcs I fought in the ruins. The one who was slightly burned before I feinted his attack and uh, kicked him. He's a little shorter than Khazak, and a little chubbier, with medium length brown hair and a beard but no mustache. His left tusk is gold, either plated or replaced, and his arms are covered in tattoos, *way* more than the crest on Khazak's chest or the bands on his upper arms, probably more than I've seen on any other orc so far. *Shit, what was his name?* Ranger... Bighands. Nope, that's not it. Widefingers? No, wait it's— "Deepfist!"

Both orcs turn to look at me for my sudden outburst.

"That is my name." The ranger in question leans in and leers at me, winking. "Maybe one day I can show you exactly *why* they call me that."

"I—I—" I stammer, the implication of his words making my body flush immediately. Khazak had mentioned something about fists in passing the other day, and my morbid curiosity made me press him for the details of what exactly "fisting" was.

"Wow, Deputy Rockfang was not joking. It *is* easy to rile him up." Deepfist pulls back, a smirk on his face.

"If you are quite done," Khazak chides, but there's no irritation in his words. *Probably just mad he didn't think of it himself first.*

We resume walking toward the camp in silence. Comfortable for them but awkward for me.

"I'm still really sorry about the day in the temple ruins!" I blurt out after another minute or two.

Deepfist tilts his head at my second outburst. "No need to worry, kid. You are practically one of us now." He smiles. "Besides, I was mostly over that once I saw you give the captain just as much trouble in the arena. Not bad for a human."

"You were at the arena, too?" I really shouldn't be surprised by that anymore.

"Pretty much every ranger not on duty was there," he states like I should already know. "And the rest of the force was told the story in *very* graphic detail."

"...Great." You'd think after working with them for two weeks, I wouldn't still get embarrassed learning someone was a witness to my *very* public fucking, but here I am, feeling too warm in my clothes. Going forward, maybe I should just assume anyone new I meet has already seen or heard about me having sex.

"Hey, I said I was impressed. Most of us were." *At least they're not dicks about it.* "Call me Arik."

"...Thanks Arik." Khazak gives my shoulder a squeeze as we walk. I'm looking ahead for signs of the camp, but all I see is more forest. Did I send us in the wrong direction? No, Deepfist was going this way too. Where the hell are we?

I jump back when a few yards ahead of us an orc just *appears* out of nowhere. Both orcs I'm walking with pause, but it's more because of my reaction than the orc who apparently knows how to teleport. She's dressed like a ranger, so I know she's no danger, but *fuck*. The new orc waves at us as she passes, giving me a funny look but walking past as if nothing strange has happened.

"I forgot to tell him the campsites are camouflaged." Khazak's voice is full of realization.

"That would do it." Deepfist chuckles.

"What the hell was that?" They must have pretty fucking good camo around here.

In response, after walking forward a little farther, Khazak sticks his arm out ahead of him, and everything up to his elbow disappears from sight. Oh, "camouflaged" with magic. It's not something Nate or Corrine can do, but it's a pretty common practice to protect a campsite from wild animals—or other intruders—when traveling outside. With another chuckle, Deepfist walks forward past Khazak and vanishes into thin air. Khazak tosses his head in the same direction, and as I walk over the threshold with him, a campsite appears where before there were only trees.

When my friends and I were first told there were "orc camps" in the area, this is a little closer to what we pictured. Around a large central campfire are several tents, eight total with two on opposite sides that are much larger than the rest. One of those is open air, and I can see four orcs congregated at a table under it. Deepfist is over near one of the smaller tents, probably putting away his things, but Khazak leads us over to the group.

"Captain." A female orc dressed a little more officially than the rest—more like Khazak or his deputy Ragnar— stands and salutes on our approach. Which around here is done by clasping your fist over your chest. With black hair and brown eyes, she is as tall as the other orcs I've seen. Her left tusk is shorter than her right, like it was damaged, and the top has been smoothed out. She's got a short, cropped haircut, honestly not that unlike Khazak. It suits her.

"Deputy Captain Keenguard." Khazak returns the salute. This is his second deputy, the one that works out of the other ranger station. "Here to relieve you. Anything interesting to report?"

"Just another quiet week in the forest, sir." She doesn't sound too upset by that. "Afraid you had all the fun out here three weeks ago." Her eyes fall on me. "This must be David."

"I do not believe you have had the pleasure of meeting him yet." Khazak half-turns to me. "David, this is Deputy Captain Morgal Keenguard."

Morgal holds out her hand to me, and I reach for it, only remembering a split second after she grabs my wrist that they do handshakes differently around here too, and I'm pulled in for a quick hug, her other arm slapping my back. *Oof.*

"Nice to meet you, David. Sir." With another salute, she hoists a large bag over her shoulders and makes her way out of the camp. I see the air around the camp's border shimmer as she passes through, the air snapping back into place once she's on the other side.

"Let me show you where our tent is." Khazak calls my attention back to him, walking us around the campfire to one of the smaller tents—though it still looks slightly larger than the others.

"Is this tent bigger?" I ask as Khazak undoes the ties holding the opening flap down.

"Yes, by ten whole square meters!" He says it like I've won a prize.

"What did I do to earn such incredible accommodations?" I deadpan.

"Sleeping with the captain comes with perks," he jokes, stepping inside and dropping his bag to the tent floor before stepping back out. "I am going to go speak with the rest of this week's patrol unit. Please put our things away and then come find me there, pup."

"Yes, Sir." I can do that. The fact that it wasn't a request isn't lost on me. He's gotten more confident with his orders in the last couple of weeks, and I don't mind it. I like following orders, when they aren't being given by a dickhead.

I put our weapons to one side and drop my bag in one corner. The tent isn't very big, maybe ten-by-eight feet. The walls and floor are made of a thick leather attached to a sturdy wooden frame, the corners of which are buried to firmly anchor it to the ground. The poles go straight up for about five feet before bending at a point to meet in the middle. I can stand up alright towards the center, but the orcs probably need to crouch some.

First thing to take care of is the bedroll. I pick what I decide feels like the softest patch of earth under the tent floor and unfurl it, smoothing out the corners with my hands. I find a small pillow in the center, realizing now that we forgot to pack a second one. *Dammit.* I grab some of our clothes out of the smaller bag, making sure to keep them all neatly folded and stacked. I don't think we need anything else, so I straighten up the bags and weapons, nodding to myself when I'm finished before stepping back outside.

I make my way over to the open tent where Khazak and Arik are standing with the other orcs. I don't recognize two of them, but the third I've gotten to know pretty well—Glasha Silentfang. She smiles when she sees me, her short brown hair falling over the right side of her face. The left side of her hair is shaved, exposing the silver rings pierced into her right ear. Most orcs around here seem to have brown eyes, but she's one of the few I've seen with green. I first met her when she helped me kick Khazak's ass in a rug'bal game (*it's basically football*) during my first week here. Since then, I've seen her at the station, where we've had lunch together, worked out together, even sparred a little. I like her a lot.

Khazak notices my approach and smiles, pulling me over to him. "For those of you who have not yet met my *avakesh*, this is David." Khazak uses the title for me in his language that means something between slave, servant, and pet. You get used to it. "David, these are Officers Stonearm and Proudblade."

"Hi." I say much more meekly than I intend. "Nice to meet you."

"Hello."

"Hi."

Men of few words. *Works for me.*

"Over the next week, Rangers Silentfang, Deepfist, and I will periodically walk a patrol route through this section of the forest while the officers remain here and keep guard at the campsite," Khazak instructs. Mostly me. Okay *exclusively* me, since everyone else obviously knows what they're doing. "We will walk one more patrol today before it gets dark and we have dinner. Then we each take a two-hour shift, keeping watch overnight until morning."

"Well, *we* do all that alone while *you* get a nice warm body to keep you company," Deepfist half-jokes, half-gripes to my right.

"If you are so jealous, get one of your own, Arik." Glasha rolls her eyes.

Noises behind me have me turning around, facing the other large tent across the campfire. When it opens, a small amount of smoke billows out as a sixth orc steps out to join our band. He looks different from the rest with no uniform to speak of, instead wearing brown robes that reach the forest floor. His long grey hair is matted, the individual locks adorned with jewelry that look to be made of bone and metal. His equally grey beard reaches his chest, and when he gets close, I can *smell* him. He doesn't smell bad exactly, but well... Dude's been out here a while. He speaks to the group, and not in Common, so I just nod politely.

"David, this is Wu'dag Bonespirit, the camp's resident shaman." *That's* what that smell is. "He is responsible for creating and maintaining the wards and illusions in this part of the forest."

A shaman is a natural spellcaster, like a druid or a witch. They get their spellcasting powers from a connection to the world around them—the whole "magic is everywhere" deal. All natural casters can see and communicate with nature spirits, but shamans' abilities allow them to connect to them directly, able to channel and amplify the spirits' powers with their own. I know all this because Mike used to go on and on about random magical info.

"So, *this* is one of the little shits I felt a few weeks back." Wu'dag gives me a once over. "Scrawnier than I expected."

"I'm working on it." *I'll show him a little shit...wait.*

"Huh." The older orc steps closer, squinting his eyes as he peers at me. "Anyone ever tell you that you have a weird aura, kid?"

"...Not exactly." They didn't use the word *weird*. "My twin is a wizard. I've got um..." *Shit, what did that woman from the elven institute call it?* "Latent magical potential. All my siblings do, but me a little more. It rubbed off on me, or we share enough of the same genes or something?"

I'm not doing a very good job of explaining it, but it basically means that while I can't use magic to cast spells, I still have some flicker of it inside me. It's like having the flint but no fuel for a fire. There's no way to "turn on" the magic because there's nothing *to* turn on; it just is what it is. Nowadays, it doesn't mean much since most magical items are configured to work for anyone, but it used to be that they'd have to be powered, or at least activated, by the magic of the person wielding them. A spark to light the flame.

"Huh." He squints again. "Yeah, I guess that could do it. Looks like we need an extra compass stone." He stands up straight and turns to the rest of the group. "Alright, stones out. Time to sync up."

All of the orcs around me, including the shaman, reach into their pockets and pull out smooth red-colored stones, no more than an inch or two wide. They gather in a circle, hands outstretched, clutching the stones together. The shaman takes his free hand and holds it aloft over them, slowly chanting a spell. I see Wu'dag's eyes glow first followed by the stone in his hand, then I see the same glow coming from each of the others' enclosed palms.

"This is for him." Wu'dag drops the stone he held in Khazak's open palm. "I will be in my tent if you need me."

"Alright, David and I will take the first patrol, then Glasha, then Arik." Khazak speaks to his troops. "See you back here for dinner."

Everyone salutes and disperses, Khazak turning to me. "We will fill our waterskins and grab our equipment, then head out. We will be walking for at least a couple of hours."

My eyes go wide. Hours? Wow, okay. We go back to the tent and retrieve our weapons and a pair of waterskins from Khazak's supply bag. After filling them at a barrel under the big tent, we start to walk away from camp. I see the illusion warble as we pass through it, and a glance behind us reveals nothing but the forest. We walk for a while, not following any sort of path that I'm able to pick up on. I try to look for landmarks like before but don't see anything. We go straight for a while before turning in another direction. We do this for a while in silence before I finally need to ask.

"Are we following an actual route here?" My voice ringing out in the quiet forest almost sounds wrong.

"Hmmm." Khazak smiles, considering me for a moment. "Yes and no. There is a general path we are following, but we have a lot of leeway. We need to cover a certain amount of ground, and sticking too much to the same path might make it easy for someone to slip by."

"Is that something you have to worry about a lot?" It seems like they've been doing this for years.

"Not really, but we do not want to get complacent." He turns to me and smirks. "Cannot have someone raiding our ancient temples."

I roll my eyes at the obvious dig. *That was one time!* We continue walking in relative silence. It's nice though. After spending these past weeks together, the two of us have gotten pretty comfortable around each other. Plus, seeing as this is a patrol, spending the whole time talking would be distracting and kind of defeat the point.

"I was curious..." The sun is starting to set when Khazak breaks the silence between us. "Does it still bother you when people bring up the arena and ritual? Our match?"

"I wouldn't say it bothers me, exactly." I've gotten over that part of it, at least. "It can just be a little embarrassing when I think I'm meeting someone new, and it turns out they were a witness to me very publicly losing my virginity."

"Would you like me to say something?" It's a genuine request. Despite what he says, I know there are some aspects of the way we "met" that he still feels guilty over.

"No, I know they don't mean anything by it." I can handle the teasing. I know it's not malicious.

"Alright, another question. Was that truly your first time?" It's not an accusation; there's a measure of concern in his voice betraying why he's asking. "Not that I have any reason to doubt you. I just know by the time I was your age I had already experimented quite a bit with both men and women."

"I mean, you know I had girlfriends. I did a *lot* of kissing back in the day, and I've touched more than my fair share of tits over dresses. But no," I shake my head, "you've been my first for everything else."

"I see." He's trying not to, but I can hear a little disappointment. "I feel I need to apologize. Your first time should have been more—"

"Hey, come on. We've been through this already." I turn to face him, walking backward. "Not only were we both tricked, I ended up liking it anyway. Plus, as screwed up as it was, you can't say it wasn't memorable, right?"

"I suppose you are correct," Khazak huffs, begrudgingly agreeing with me. This has been a minor sticking point for us. He continues to relive his guilt over what happened—him basically ravishing me in an arena full of strangers—while I would just prefer to move on.

"What was *your* first time like?" I jump at the chance to change the subject. I've never actually heard him talk about anyone in his past like that before.

"Awkward and hurried. And a little painful." Khazak shakes his head as he recalls. "I think we were fifteen? Me and another boy from school. We were in my bedroom, and somehow the house was empty. We had no idea what we were doing."

"Painful, huh?" *I know that feeling.*

"Yes, but not for the reason you are thinking," he gripes. "He was very...enthusiastic about oral sex. *Too* enthusiastic. He sucked me so hard, he gave me... I think you call them 'hickeys' on the head of my cock."

I can't hold in the guffaw that flies out of my mouth and quickly clamp both my hands over it. "He left hickeys on your *dick*?!"

"Several," he deadpans. "He took the 'sucking' *very* literally—" Khazak cuts himself off, eyes going a little wide. "David, do not move."

I freeze in place. *What?!*

"Everything is okay. Just stay still." Khazak's hands are out toward me, but he doesn't look panicked. "Look down. Just behind you."

I slowly peer downward as requested, and right behind my left foot is a plant, a dark purple flower, maybe a foot high. Actually, there's a whole patch of them.

"What is it?"

"A very poisonous flower known as 'Ralor's crown,'" Khazak speaks calmly. "You have not touched it yet. Just step over to me carefully."

I nod slowly, moving away from the flower patch. I see now the way each of the petals bloom out then curl back in, each flower resembling a small purple crown.

"What does it do?" I ask when I'm safely away.

"In its current form, it would leave you with a very unpleasant rash before making you feel sluggish and causing your muscles stop responding correctly." He looks down at my legs to make sure there's nothing on them. "The real danger comes when it is processed into a poison. That increases its potency tenfold, enough to kill a person."

"Fuck, and it just grows out here?" Seems like a bad plant to keep around.

"It is native to the area, but we do not normally allow it to grow so near the city. It is too dangerous." He eyes the patch suspiciously. "This must have cropped up recently."

It is spring, time for plants to start growing. "What do we do about it?"

"You and I will do nothing, but once we get back to camp, we will let Shaman Bonespirit know so that he can take care of it." Makes sense. Plants are probably that guy's whole deal.

"Sounds good." We have been walking a while now. "Is it time to head back yet?"

"Yes, actually." Khazak doesn't move though, instead reaching into his pocket. "Here, this is yours."

He hands me one of the red rocks from earlier, the compass stone Wu'dag handed him for me. He then takes a few steps away from me. "Hold it in your fist and stretch your hand toward me."

I do as asked, and the stone in my hand begins pulsing in a steady rhythm. I drop my hand and the pulsing stops, only to return when I point my fist at Khazak again.

"The stones are all linked. When one is held and pointed in the direction of another, it pulses." He takes out his own stone to show me. "The stronger the pulse, the closer the target stone. Try and see if you can find camp."

"Okay." I turn to the direction I think camp is, holding the stone out in front of me. I slowly scan it across the horizon until I feel it vibrate in my hand, and I freeze. It starts to beat steadily, but much more slowly than it did with Khazak. "I think I found it."

"Glasha and Arik would have left for their own patrols by now, so it could easily be one of them. Keep looking, and see if you can tell the difference."

I nod, happy to prove that I know what I'm doing. I keep using the stone to scan the horizon line, finding two more pulsing beat patterns. One feels almost as slow as the first, but the second is a little stronger. It's also in between the other two, so that has to be it.

"Okay, got it this time." I turn to Khazak, confident in my answer.

"Lead the way, pup."

It's nearly dark by the time we get back to the campsite. I see the two officers and Wu'dag seated around the campfire, some meat cooking over the fire. My stomach growls at the smell, hungrier than I realized.

"Welcome back." Wu'dag greets us with the officers as we join them by the campfire. "Anything out of the ordinary?"

"Actually, yes." Khazak frowns. "We found a patch of Ralor's crown about five kilometers north."

"Huh. I just cleared out a patch of that last week." Wu'dag frowns. "I will take care of it first thing in the morning."

"Thank you, friend." Khazak nods, the two of us joining the group, and I groan happily when I take my seat on a log by the fire. I've done more walking today than I have in three weeks.

Glasha returns about half an hour later, then Arik another half hour after that, and the seven of us sit down for dinner—which ends up being some rabbits the two officers caught while we were patrolling, a signal of what future meals out here may be like. I've had rabbit before; it's not bad. Plus, by now I've learned to trust the orcs of Tah'lj and their cooking.

The rest of the night is quiet. After eating, the orcs hang around the fire and swap stories from their weeks. Glasha has her sword out, applying oil to it slowly as she listens to Arik talk about a barfight he broke up two nights ago. I join the two of them, happy to prove to Khazak I know how to take care of my equipment. I see Khazak disappear with Wu'dag into his tent for a minute at one point, but then he's back out and sitting next to me by the campfire. After a couple of hours of this, everyone heads into the tents to sleep except Khazak and me, ready for the first round of watch.

"It's kinda nice being able to do this with someone else," I speak low, not wanting to disturb anyone sleeping. The only noises are the crackling of the wood in the campfire and the chirping of the crickets in the forest. We can relax a little more now than when we were on patrol. Me and my friends would do the same thing when on the road, but with five of us, we always had to do it alone. We also didn't have any magical illusions to help hide us.

"It is." Khazak smiles as he adds another log to the first to keep it going. "Having you here all week with me will be nice."

"And will make Arik jealous," I joke.

"Can you blame him?" Khazak walks over to where I'm sitting, standing in front of me. He gently takes a hold of my chin, stroking his thumb over my lip. "I certainly do not plan to keep my hands off of you."

My breath hitches a little as the words pass through me, heating something familiar in my stomach. I'm nearly eye level with his crotch, and I can already see a familiar lump starting to form. I look up at his eyes, heavy with lust.

Then a cough rings out from one of the tents, and I remember we're not actually alone. I stumble back from his hold, falling off the back of the log with a thud. When I look up, I see Khazak with one hand over his mouth, struggling to hold in his laughter. He reaches out with the other to help me up, clearing his throat when he's finished and mumbling an apology.

After that a display of nerves, he doesn't try to make another move, and two hours later, we wake up Arik for his watch shift. The orc bids us goodnight as we crawl into our own tent, Khazak first. We undress, though not fully nude like we would at home—never know when you might have to get up at a moment's notice—and Khazak slides into the bedroll, holding it open for me to follow. I curl into his side, resting my head on his shoulder. Since we didn't pack a second pillow, he can be my pillow.

"Sleep well, David." Khazak turns his head to kiss the top of mine. "We have a busy day tomorrow."

I nuzzle against him, too tired to reply, the sounds of the crickets in the night air already putting me to sleep.

Chapter 2

I dream again about flying over the ocean. This time is *different, though. The storm in the sky is raging, the wind howling as lighting cracks around me. The waters below are anything but calm, waves reaching high into the air before they come crashing down. Between the surge and the storm, it's taking all I have to stay in the air, looking in every direction for signs of clearer skies.*

I wake to the sounds of birds chirping, the remnants of my dream slipping away. *Haven't had one of those in over a week.* The morning air is cool, and it makes me pull one of my legs back under the bedroll. Khazak is spooned up behind me, his arm under the pillow we're sharing. No matter how we fall asleep, we always seem to end up in some other position by morning.

I stretch myself out, making sure to press back against his warm body. I feel a familiar lump against my lower back, one that I'm matching in front. And if we weren't only a few feet away from a bunch of *other* sleeping orcs, I might be tempted to do something about it. As it is, I shimmy my way out of the bedroll, reaching for my pants so I can step outside and pee. I hear a slight grumble from Khazak as I close the tent flap behind me.

There's a light layer of fog blanketing the forest, the sun still low on the horizon. Glasha is sitting by the campfire, the last one to take watch, which means she's also the first one up. She waves a hand at me as she tosses another log on the fire, which has gotten low over the course of the night. I wave back as I sleepily stumble beyond the camp's boundary, looking for a nice tree to stand behind. By the time I'm finished and stepping back into the tent, I'm greeted by the sight of a bleary-eyed Khazak stretching his own limbs.

"Good morning." He smiles up at me sleepily.

"Morning." I crawl back into the warm bedroll. "Ready for our first full day on patrol?"

"Someone is eager." He sits up, stretching once more.

He climbs out, pulling on a clean set of clothes, though not his full uniform. I also finish getting dressed, pulling on a clean shirt and my shoes before we leave the tent together. Glasha is still the only one up, and I'm not sure what time it is or how long she's been at it. When Khazak finishes his own morning stuff and the two of us join her by the fire, I notice Wu'dag reentering the camp from the north, a covered basket hanging from one hand. Poking out from underneath the cloth covering is a familiar purple flower, and I'm only just realizing the orc is wearing gloves as he heads over to us.

"Good morning, Captain. Just finished clearing the flower patch." He lifts the basket slightly.

"Good morning and thank you, Shaman Bonespirit." Khazak gives a small bow of his head from his seat.

"You brought it back to the camp?" I figured he was just gonna use his magic to wither the plant or even burn it.

"Given that it's springing up a lot this year, I thought it would be smart to keep the antidote on hand in case of any accidents," he tells us before pointing over at his tent. "I'll be brewing that this morning, so please do not enter my tent until I give the all clear."

"Understood, shaman." Khazak turns to Glasha. "How long until the others are due up?"

"Forty minutes or so," the orc woman answers.

"Perfect." Then he turns to me. "Are you any good with a bow?"

"I'm alright." I shrug. I was a decent shot on the archery range.

"Have you ever been hunting?" he asks as he stands.

"No, not really. Why?" I stand as well, following him back to our tent.

"Because we are on breakfast duty." He grins and grabs his bow.

"Does the shaman actually live in the camp?" I ask after we've been walking for about fifteen minutes.

"He does." Khazak nods to my right. "Each of the patrol camps has a resident spellcaster, typically nature-based, two shamans, a witch, and a druid at the moment."

"Seems like it would get lonely." I don't think I could handle not living in a city when I'm not traveling.

"I cannot imagine it does, considering there are always at least five other people around at any given time," Khazak reasons.

"Didn't think about that." Now I wonder if he ever wishes he could be alone.

"I have seen him in town, gathering supplies or for the occasional celebration, but he once told me he did not enjoy living in the city." Khazak pauses by a tree for a moment. "He feels that he fits better into the forest. I think most of the camp spellcasters feel that way."

I guess if you're connected to nature the way they are, living in it full time probably isn't that bad. Still not sure I'd want to do it. I'm not even sure I'll be happy by the end of this week. I was just getting used to not sleeping on the ground anymore.

What? I've accepted that I'm a little spoiled now.

We keep walking until we come across a clearing.

"This spot will do." Khazak examines the perimeter. "Over here."

He leads us behind some bushes, crouching down low. I copy him, seeing that at this height I can peer through and into the clearing ahead of us. Satisfied, Khazak drops the bag from his shoulder and reaches for the bow and quiver on his back—handing them to me.

"You want me to do it?" *Isn't he the hunter?*

"Worried you are incapable?" His eyebrow quirks up.

"No." I glare, taking the bow. "What are we hunting?"

"That will depend on what comes along." Khazak bends down on one knee, beckoning me to follow.

He has me move ahead of him to watch the clearing while he moves behind me. Khazak's left hand comes up to cover mine as I hold the bow, helping me to position it correctly. I feel his other hand move down my arm to take my other hand, bringing them both up to grab the string.

"Good," he rumbles low in my ear. "You want to make sure you are steady but still able to maneuver your upper body for your target."

This is all very unnecessary—the bow might be a little big, and I'm not an *expert*, but I've handled a bow before. Plenty of times. But when I feel his hot breath ghosting across my neck, I find myself not caring. He has me practice drawing the string back, testing its strength. The bow is a little heavier than I'm used to, but I get the hang of it.

"Very good, pup." He sits back in a more comfortable position. "Now, we wait."

I'm not sure how long we're hiding in that bush for, but it's a while. I start to get bored, knowing there's not much to be done about it; we can't talk because we have to listen for our prey and not risk scaring it off. We don't really hunt for our food in Lutheria, at least not most of us. *Maybe this is why.*

"David, get the bow," Khazak whispers, seconds before I hear the sounds of something in the forest ahead of us.

Grabbing an arrow from the quiver, I kneel up into position, notching it onto the bowstring. I can feel Khazak behind me, not as close as before, trying to watch for the target along with me. There are a few moments of silence, and for a second, I think that whatever we heard may have turned around and left, but then I see the bushes on the other side of the clearing move.

It sounds big. *Maybe a deer?* The leaves rustle again, and I see a flash of brown fur. That's it. I pull back the arrow, aiming for the spot where I expect the creature to emerge. Then I feel a hand on my shoulder.

"Wait!" Khazak whispers hurriedly.

What? I turn to look behind me, annoyed, but slowly release the tension on the bowstring, no longer aiming. I look to see what this creature I am no longer supposed to be hunting is. Then I hear a sharp intake of breath—my own.

What emerges into the clearing is a deer alright, but unlike any I've ever seen before. It's a male, and everything you see about it appears normal—brown and white fur, black nose and yellow-brown eyes—until you get to its head, where it is sporting a set of large crystalline antlers. The sunlight streams through them, fracturing like a prism and scattering small rainbows across the forest floor.

As it stands there, two more deer emerge from behind it, a female and what I can only assume is their fawn. It moves forward on unsteady legs, its mother watching every step. The two of us wait in silence as the happy little family passes through, never noticing the two men watching them from the bushes.

"Wow." My voice is still barely above a whisper, even though the deer are long gone. "Sorry, but I don't think I could have killed that thing even if you wanted me to. What was it?"

"It is alright." Khazak smiles. "*Dhur'ovuk*. A crystal hart. They are very rare. Seeing one is a good omen. And killing one is the opposite."

"I think I get why." I'm still kind of in awe. "Those antlers were incredible."

"They grow them at the start of spring, and they keep growing until the end of autumn," Khazak explains. "Once they enter their rut, they will use them to compete with other males for a mate, and normally shed them by the end of winter."

"I've never seen an animal like that before." I think that was my first encounter with an *actual* magical creature.

"Their antlers are a powerful magical regent, used to amplify spell effects," Khazak continues. "It is not uncommon to see people out in the forests in late winter gathering them. In the past, we have had issues with poachers, which is one of the reasons we patrol the area."

"Aww, so we're out here to protect them." I pick up the bow and dust off my knees as we stand and exit the foliage. "So, what do we do about food?"

"Come. We will find another place to hunt, and if we still turn up empty, we can try our hands at some fishing." Khazak grins.

"Ooo, fishing I *have* done before." I hand the bow back to Khazak, so he can strap it to his back.

"We have poles and bait back at camp. We can search east of here first before we—" Khazak stops himself, his head turning to look at some bushes. "David, climb up the tree."

"What?" I look in the same direction he is. I don't see— Then I hear it. Something stomping in our direction, fast.

"David, tree, *now!*" Khazak shouts, shoving me toward the nearest tree before starting to climb himself.

I barely have time to grab ahold of a branch before a *massive* boar bursts into the clearing. I mean it's huge—even on all fours it might be taller than Khazak. Its dark brown fur is heavily matted, and one of its tusks is broken, though it doesn't look any less deadly. It stomps one of its hooves into the ground with a grunt as it looks around, its dark eyes stopping on me and the tree I'm dangling from. With a snort and a roar, the boar charges the trunk of the tree, slamming into it with enough force that I lose my grip and hit the ground with a thud.

"*David!*" Khazak calls from above as I quickly try to get to my feet, a sharp pain shooting through my right ankle when I make to stand. *Fuck.* I must have twisted it when I landed. I hear another bellow from the beast behind me, and I scramble to get away. It knocks into my back, sending me forward and flat on my face. I can feel where one of its tusks hit me, though it thankfully didn't break the skin. Yet. I have my sword strapped to my back, but it's so small that I flounder, unsure whether I should try and get up again or just curl into a ball.

Khazak makes the decision for me, whistling loudly as he drops to the ground to draw the boar's attention. Bow in hand, Khazak fires an arrow that lands right in its flank, making the creature squeal in anger. Turn to face its new challenger, it runs at the orc as he notches another arrow. Khazak leaps out of the way as the boar passes him, firing as it turns around and landing another arrow directly in its side. It's still moving, and now it looks angrier. Standing, Khazak notches two more arrows—at the same time—aiming steadily at his target. With a rage-filled bellow, the boar charges once more. Khazak lets the arrows fly, each landing with a wet and heavy thud, one in its snout and the other directly in its eye. With a final screech, the beast collapses mid-charge, corpse sliding along the ground toward Khazak.

Carefully, Khazak makes his way over to the boar, pulling his longsword from the scabbard on his back and driving it into the body, ensuring its demise. Then after laying the blade on the ground, Khazak moves over to me.

"Are you alright?" He kneels over my prone form, checking for my injuries.

"I think I twisted my ankle when I fell." I hiss at the twinge of pain that comes when I try to move it.

"Let me see." Khazak helps to lay me flat on the forest floor, rolling up one of my pant legs to inspect my ankle. "This may hurt, but I need to check if anything is broken or needs to be set."

I nod, whimpering when I feel his fingers pressing against the injury. *Fuck, that hurts.* Leg injuries are the worst. How am I going to get around? How am I going to get back to camp? Hell, how am I gonna get back to the city?

"Definitely twisted, but I think that is all." Khazak nods confidently. "Alright, hold still."

He places both hands over my injury, eyes closing as he mumbles...an incantation? I feel his hands start to get warm, and then my injured ankle begins to tingle. *Is he casting a spell?!*

"What the hell?" I whisper as I watch Khazak heal my ankle. "You're a spellcaster?!"

Khazak looks at me puzzled. "I can use a small amount of nature magic. I thought you knew."

"No. How would I know that?" I move my ankle around carefully. Feels a lot better.

"I mean, I *am* a 'ranger.'"

"Okay, but I didn't know you meant *that* kind of ranger." Rangers are typically known for things like scouting, hunting, and protecting forests, and some of those rangers can cast small amounts of magic. Sorta like a druid-lite. Look, magic is very confusing. "Does that mean all the other rangers are spellcasters, too?"

"Fair enough. A few are, but most are not." He frowns when I scowl at that reply. "David, I promise this is not something I was keeping from you."

"Feels like it." I can't help but feel a little prickly. I thought we were past all the secrets and not telling each other things. "How come I've never seen you using it before now?"

"I did not have a reason to use it before now." I scowl more at the lack of explanation. "David, what I just did to your ankle is about the extent of what I am capable of. I am not that powerful, and also do not generally like using magic for things I am capable of doing myself. Frankly, given the source of my magic, I have even *less* of a reason to use it in the city. Other than a small amount of healing, everything I can do is related to animals and the outdoors."

I guess he has a point. We haven't exactly been outside much before this week, and it's not like he has any pets. Though he probably could have made finding that old lady's dog a lot easier. Or healed my scraped-up knees after that first time I ran away. When I really think about it, it's just...not really a big deal when I consider everything else that's happened between us. "Okay. I believe you. Sorry for overreacting."

Khazak smiles. "Can you walk?" He stands and offers me a hand up.

"I think so." I tentatively try putting weight on my injured ankle. "Feels maybe a little uncomfortable, but it doesn't hurt."

"Good. When we get back to camp, Shaman Bonespirit will be able to heal you better than I can." Khazak turns to look at the dead boar. "We can get the rest of the patrol to help carry that back. I would say we found more than just breakfast."

"I didn't think you guys had wild boars around here." I've never seen one before.

"We do not." Khazak kicks the body lightly with his foot. "This is not wild; it is feral. It likely escaped from one of the human settlements on the coast and has been surviving out here for some time. Possibly years, given its size."

After dusting myself off, we start the walk back to camp. As always, I have a million questions about the new bit of info I just learned. "So...what else can you do?"

"What do you mean?" Khazak tilts his head.

"Your magic. What else can you do with it?" I really haven't met that many spellcasters, and the ones I have are all wizards or some kind of priest.

"Ah, well..." He pauses to think. "I can use it to tell what the weather will be like, usually through the next day. I can manipulate a small amount of earth and water and affect the growth of certain flora. I am able to search for specific animals and plants, especially of the magical variety. And in addition to what I did to your leg, I can detect and heal certain poisons. I can also communicate with animals to some degree."

"You can talk to animals?" That piques my interest.

"*Communicate,*" he clarifies. "Animals do not talk. They use body language and sometimes sounds and noises—most that we cannot even perceive. My magic makes it easier to understand one another, even pass along a message to another person. Oh, here is a useful trick." Khazak pauses, holding his hands out to the sides and inhaling deeply.

"Shhhhhhh..." Khazak breathes out, as if shushing the woods themselves. All around us, the sounds of the forest go silent, sounds I didn't even realize were there. The wind blowing through the trees, a bird chirping, squirrels jumping from branch to branch. Everything is quiet.

"Wow," I try to say, but it barely comes out a whisper. Smirking, Khazak moves forward, motioning for me to follow. Once we're a few feet away, I can hear the sounds of nature return as well as our voices.

"How did you do that?" I'm hoping for an answer that isn't just "magic."

"The spell controls the movement of the wind in the area, stifling any sound traveling within it." I can tell he's proud of that, even if I didn't fully understand that explanation.

"Why didn't you do that when we were hunting the deer?" Seems like it would have been useful.

Khazak chuckles. "As I said, I do not see the purpose in using magic for something relatively trivial. Besides, if I had, I might not have heard the boar as it approached."

"How *did* you hear that?" If he hadn't, we might have ended up the boar's meal instead. "More magic?"

Khazak taps one of his large pointed green ears. "These are not just for show."

Everyone is awake and milling about when we make it back to camp. Khazak sits me by the fire while he talks to Wu'dag, who then comes over to take a look at my foot. While he does that, Khazak gathers three of the other orcs, as well as what looks like a pallet you'd use to carry an injured person, to bring back breakfast. Wu'dag kneels in front of me, inspecting my ankle.

"Always getting in trouble, huh?" I roll my eyes as he places both hands on my ankle, and I can feel the warm tingle of his magic flowing into me. "There we go. Should be good as new."

I flex and rotate my ankle, pleased to find that it doesn't hurt at all. "Thanks."

"That is why I am here." The shaman stands, brushing off his robes. "Cannot wait to see what caused all the trouble."

Twenty minutes later, the four orcs march back into camp, the body of the boar carried between them. They stop just after reaching the camp's border, moving the body off the pallet and onto the ground near the edge.

"Damn boys." Wu'dag whistles as he steps over, walking around the body. "This will feed us all week. Hold on."

The shaman steps into his tent while Glasha heads for the supply tent. Wu'dag returns with a small pouch, but Glasha comes back with a bunch of knives. *Right, we have to actually butcher this thing.* She hands one of the knives to Arik, setting the rest to the side. Both orcs stand back while Wu'dag reaches into his pouch and sprinkles a white powder over the corpse as he walks around it, casting a spell. I see the powder start to glow, but then it's gone, absorbed by the body.

"What was that?" I ask Khazak.

"Preservation spell," Wu'dag answers for himself. "Just needs a pinch of salt. A lot of priests and healers use it to preserve bodies after death, to wait for a funeral or in case the body needs to be transported. However, it can *also* be used to stop meat from spoiling."

"How long does it last?" *Learning all kinds of things about magic today.*

"About a week." Wu'dag eyes the corpse as the two orcs wielding knives roll the corpse onto its side and start making their cuts. "Ugh, I cannot usually stomach this part. I will be in my tent."

I quickly realize my stomach shares Wu'dag's sentiments. I know we have to drain and clean the meat first but...there's a lot of blood. Like, *a lot.* Turns out I am more than happy to leave that part of where my food comes from a mystery. I hope the tent walls block out the hacking noises. "I think I'm gonna go, too."

"I have a better idea." Khazak smiles, a twinkle in his eye. "How is your ankle feeling?"

"Never better." I kick out the foot in question.

"Excellent." He turns to the other orcs. "David and I are going to go and get cleaned up." The orcs wave us off, Khazak stopping to grab his bag from our tent on our way out. We leave camp and head southwest.

"So, I noticed you didn't jump on the pig-slicing bandwagon back there. Not a fan?" *Not that I blame him.*

"Not when I can help it," he admits. "There is a reason I use a butcher in the city. I am lucky. Not everyone can afford that. We have only kept livestock in V'rok'sh Tah'lj the last fifty years or so. Many orcs still supplement their diets by hunting. We will likely see a few in the forest over the course of the week." It is a big city, and orcs need more meat in their diets than most.

We walk for another fifteen minutes when I hear running water in the distance. I remember the small stream we crossed on the way here and figure it's that. There are some hills ahead of us that Khazak seems to be headed for or at least leading us around. The sound of water only gets stronger as we climb up, and when we reach the top, I am amazed by the sight that greets us.

"Welcome to Shad'rok Springs," Khazak announces. I look over the springs ahead of us, the focal point being the large pool in the center. The water is so clear that I can see turtles swimming underneath. There are other smaller ponds around the center pool, and a few places where the springs split off into rivers and streams. There's even a small waterfall feeding into the whole thing.

"It's beautiful." So beautiful it almost feels wrong to be here.

"Very." Khazak takes my hand, leading me down to the shore where he drops his bag. He reaches for his shirt, pulling it over his head and smirking. "Feels good too."

I take the hint, pulling off my own shirt before reaching for my belt. Khazak's naked a split second before I am, wading into the shallow waters with a hand outstretched for me. The water is cool as it hits my legs, though not in an unpleasant way. We walk a few more steps before reaching the edge of a drop, the small lake going deeper than it appears. I can still see all the way to the floor, though.

I'm the first to jump in, Khazak right behind me. The temperature is a small shock to the system, but I warm up quickly, especially with another body so close. There's some touching, even flirting as we swim together. At one point, I dive down to see if I can touch the bottom (*I can*), and on the way back up, I goose him on the ass, which devolves into a short-lived splash fight, which then morphs into a little making out. Which it turns out is *not* that easy to do when you're swimming. After a while, we're both just floating there together, enjoying the peace around us.

Eventually we have to get out—we are out here to work after all—and we wade our way up the shore to our clothes. Sucks that we have to air dry now, but that was worth it. I see Khazak bent over and reaching into his bag and have to fight the urge to pinch him again. He's got a nice ass.

He pulls out a big green and white blanket, shaking it out and spreading it flat over a patch of grass. Tossing the bag to one side, he lays down, patting a spot at his side for me to join him.

"What's all this?" I ask as I lower myself to the blanket.

Before he answers, Khazak pulls me to him. I shiver as he kisses me, our wet bodies cooling in the spring air.

"It was recently brought to my attention that you lost your virginity to a brute." He tucks a lock of wet hair behind my ear. "As your *kavan*, it only seemed appropriate that I remedy that." He calls himself the corresponding title to my avakesh, meaning guardian and protector as well as owner. I ignore the fact that *he* is the brute in question because I wanna see where this is going.

He leans in to kiss me again before moving his lips to my ears and then neck. He sucks a wet trail of kisses down my shoulders and chest, running his hands across my stomach light enough to tickle. He lathes his tongue over each of my nipples, reaching over to his bag with one arm when he moves to my stomach. After rummaging around, his hand emerges clutching my trusty cleansing charm. I'm glad one of us remembered to pack that.

He kisses my stomach before placing the small stone in the same spot, where it warms as it activates. This handy little thing is enchanted with a spell that cleans me out and even lubes me up a little, which makes prepping for sex a lot easier. I gotta admit—I find it kinda hot when he does it to me, getting me ready for him to use—though I'm getting the feeling that it's not going to be *that* kind of a session. He puts the charm away while he moves down to my thighs, licking and then biting the insides gently before turning his face directly into my crotch. He nuzzles against my sack before moving up to my rapidly growing cock, engulfing me fully.

I moan, reaching down by reflex to grab his hair, and I realize this is maybe the first time he hasn't bound my hands during sex or ordered me to keep them in place. It's...different. I run my fingers through his damp hair as he bobs up and down, catching his eye when he looks up at me. With a final lick, he releases my length, motioning for me to flip onto my stomach.

He spreads my legs, hiking one up slightly as he lowers his mouth to my body again, this time running his tongue across my hole. I shudder and bite my lip. *I love when he does this.* He slowly licks over my hole again and again until he decides he wants more and pushes it inside of me. I can't help but press back when he spears me on his tongue, steadily driving it in and out of me. He squeezes my backside with both hands, gently kneading the flesh as he feasts.

It almost feels like it's over too soon, or it would if I wasn't so eager to move onto the next part. He flips me back over, climbing up my front as he reaches into his bag once again. He slots our bodies together as he kisses me again, and it is certainly an interesting thing to taste yourself, your own (clean) ass, on someone else's mouth. It's not bad, just different, and I've certainly gotten used to it the past few weeks. When he pulls back, I see he's grabbed the oil. I love that he's always so prepared.

He moves to lay beside me, keeping me flat on my back and pulling one of my legs over his. Uncorking the bottle, he pours some onto his fingers and reaches them between my spread legs. I feel his slippery fingers slide between my cheeks until they find their target, slowly circling my rim. The first finger enters me slowly, the feeling of being breached making me close my eyes and moan. Khazak leans down as he presses in deeper, stroking his finger over that little nub inside me he's informed me is called my prostate, and I jump at the jolt of pleasure it sends through my body.

He keeps pushing inside, not stopping until he reaches the last knuckle, before kissing me again, stroking my tongue with his own as he pumps his finger in and out of my body.

Soon a second finger joins the first, and I whimper once I start feeling the burn of being stretched. Khazak doesn't stop until both fingers are easily gliding in and out of my hole, which doesn't take very long thanks to all the practice I've been getting lately. Once he's satisfied, he moves between my spread legs, slicking his cock up as he lifts them to his shoulders.

He rubs the head of his cock against my hole briefly before pushing in. The position is a little awkward, the angle not great for leverage and the ground less than comfortable, but that kind of adds to the charm of the whole thing. I mean, I'm supposed to be losing my virginity again, right? Awkwardness is expected.

Of course, once he gets the rest of his cock in me, my thoughts aren't on things being awkward. They're a little too focused on "oh gods, I have his huge dick inside of me." He stops once he's all the way in, running his hands up and down my thighs and chest while I adjust. When I'm ready, I give him a squeeze, smiling to myself when I feel his dick twitch in response. He kisses my calf as he starts to move, pulling out only an inch or two before pushing back in.

His hips find a steady rhythm as he pumps himself in and out of my body. He's pulling out at least halfway on each stroke, and I'm really starting to feel it. My hole is relaxed, no longer feeling any burn, just the pleasant feeling that comes as he slides over my prostate and the familiar pressure that starts building in my groin. My cock is half-hard, as it usually is when I'm getting fucked, leaking a steady stream of pre-cum onto my stomach.

My hole trembles as his speed increases, the pressure nearing its peak. The more we've done this, the easier it's gotten for me to cum this way. A dry, prostate, or anal orgasm: I've heard them referred to as all three by now. I reach both hands down to squeeze behind his thighs, encouraging him to keep fucking me through it. I bite my lip as it washes over me, exhaling with a moan when I feel my hole futilely pushing out. *Yeah, that's the good stuff.*

He keeps up this rhythm for the next few minutes, fucking me through one more orgasm before I feel him start to lose control. Which works for me because as I said, the ground isn't exactly comfortable. I move my legs from his shoulders, reaching up for him with my arms. He lowers himself, bending me in half while keeping his dick buried to the hilt. I'm essentially being held down on my shoulders, and I am really glad we lucked out on a patch of grass without any rocks.

At this angle and with more leverage, the speed he's fucking me increases. A lot. He's got both his hands under my arms, gripping my shoulders to hold me in place. He kisses me, fast, hard, and sloppy, all tongue and teeth. The strength of his thrusts threatens to slide me off the blanket. He growls into my mouth as he slams his hips into me, and boy, I didn't think I was gonna cum a third time, but I am *there.*

Apparently, setting me off is enough to set him off, and he growls again as his dick pulses inside of me. I can feel his cum, hot and thick as it shoots into me, his body pressing forward with every shot. His hands are still squeezing my shoulders, holding me to him tightly as he unloads. By the time he's finished, I just know I'm gonna leave a mess on this blanket when he pulls out, no matter how hard I try to hold it in.

We pull our faces apart and catch our breaths, our bodies covered in sweat that we traded for the water covering us earlier. *May as well take another dip.* He leans up, releasing my legs so they can fall around his hips, and they are definitely going to be sore later. I reach a hand up and run it down his chest.

Worth it.

Carefully, he pulls back, allowing his softening length to slip out of me gently, a familiar sticky, wet feeling following. I try to tighten up by reflex and am reminded how useless that is when I feel a familiar twinge of pain and no less of a mess. *Oh well, not my blanket.* Khazak falls beside me, pulling me into him and throwing his arm over my waist.

"Wow," I say again.

"Wow indeed." He strokes a hand down my cheek. "Did you enjoy that?"

"Yeah, a lot." I nod, kissing his palm. "Though I'd still take a rough roll in the hay with the brute any day."

"I do not think he has plans to go anywhere." He leans in to kiss me. "What did you think of the springs?"

"They're amazing." They really are. Kinda sad we have to leave now. "Thank you for bringing me."

"I hope I can bring you back." He leans in to nuzzle my neck. "And now you can tell my sister I finally brought you."

"I'll be sure to do that." I roll my eyes, pulling my head back so I can kiss him softly on the lips. Then my stomach growls. *Right*, we haven't eaten yet, and other than Khazak's load, I'm emptier than usual right now.

"I suppose we should get back to camp." Khazak sighs, standing and holding out a hand for me.

"Do you think they've finished carving up that pig yet?" I ask, stretching my sore limbs and following Khazak to the water to rinse off once more.

"Only one way to find out." We both dunk ourselves in the water quickly, and I take the opportunity to clean the cum that's leaked onto my thighs.

Khazak rolls up the blanket after using some of the cleaner and dryer portions to dry us off. When I'm finished lacing up my boots and we turn to leave, I give the Shad'rok Springs one final look. I really hope we come back here before I leave in a couple of months.

"I think next time I want to figure out how you can fuck me under the waterfall." *Priorities!*

Chapter 3

"Is that everything?" Khazak looks up after reattaching the bedroll to his backpack.

"Yep, just double checked the tent." I drop our other bag at my feet, so I can set our weapons down more gently.

It's Solisday and the end of our week on patrol in the forest. Compared to the excitement of the feral boar on the first day, the rest of the week was quiet and boring. And filled with pork. *So much pork.* Grilled pork, pork chops, pork ribs—one day Arik even ran back to town to get bread so we could have pulled pork sandwiches. It was all delicious, and I was impressed with the amount of cooking the orcs were able to do over a campfire, but I think I'm good on eating anything pig-related for a while.

Outside of meals, we did three patrols a day, though the only things we saw were birds, deer, and the occasional hunter. When we weren't walking around the forest, I was either reading in the tent or getting my ass kicked sparring with one of the rangers. There were also a few times Khazak and I were able to either sneak off alone or come back a little late from our patrol and have some fun. He never tried anything in the tent thankfully, but by the end of the week, I was almost ready to. I missed being able to roll over and just...get the day started right, you know?

Overall, not a terrible camping trip, just a long week. I am eager to get home and take a nice hot a shower after spending the week bathing in cold river water. It'll be great to sleep in a real bed again too. The replacements for Arik and the two officers have already showed up, so now it's just me, Khazak, and Glasha waiting to be relieved.

"Good. Having to make a return trip because you forgot something is...not pleasant," Khazak remarks while taking a seat by the campfire.

"Do you speak from personal experience?" He seems way too prepared to let something like that happen.

"Not me, but would you find it hard to believe that Deputy Rockfang has had to do it more than once?" Khazak smirks, happy to sell out his friend.

"I would not find that hard to believe at all." That totally seems like something Ragnar would do.

"I think he has taken to leaving an extra set of supplies at camp to avoid the issue altogether," Glasha adds, chuckling. "Ah, I think our replacements have arrived."

I look in the direction Glasha is facing and see two figures walking toward the camp, an orc and a dwarf, both wearing the leather armor of a ranger. I don't think I know the orc, but I've seen the dwarf at the station, though his name escapes me. He's one of the few non-orcs on the force. Between rangers and officers, there are a few dwarfs and halflings, a couple of elves, and a gnome on the forensic team (according to Khazak). A very diverse group. I've actually interacted with dwarfs before back home, though they looked a little different. Like the other non-orcs I've seen around here, he has naturally tan skin and black hair, including a thick beard which has been woven into very intricate braids.

The two rangers cross the threshold into the camp, scanning the area with their eyes now that they can actually see it. Both make a beeline for us when they spot us. The orc moves to speak with Glasha, but the dwarf stops in front of Khazak.

"Captain Ironstorm." He salutes.

"Ranger Hazatin." Khazak returns the salute.

"Deputy Rockfang asked me to pass along a message." The dwarf's accent is a new one to me, his voice dipping lower when he pronounces some of his vowels. "There has been a robbery that Chief Grandtooth has asked you to look into."

"Another one?" Khazak sounds worried, remembering the last time the chief assigned him a case personally: a missing shipment meant for the city's militia that left us with more questions than answers.

"Yes, but this is from a different requester." Hazatin's tone lacks any real seriousness. "The break-in was at the Temple of the Three."

"Oh no," Khazak groans unhappily, and I notice Glasha holding in a laugh.

"Why 'oh no'?' I can't help but ask.

Khazak and Hazatin look at each other, but neither answers me, so I turn to Glasha.

"The temple's head priest can be rather...*intense*." Glasha grimaces. "He is...how did Deputy Rockfang describe Nylan after forgetting their lunch plans one day? A 'drama queen?'"

I can't help but snort a laugh at that. Nylan is Ragnar's avakesh: half-elf, half-human, and definitely a full drama queen. "Why does he want the captain, specifically?"

"I volunteered at the temple while growing up. I was something of a favorite of High Priest Bhok's. As a result, he has made a habit of personally requesting me when our assistance is required," Khazak grumbles. "Being the head of the main religious institution in the city, the chief has a hard time telling him no." Khazak turns to Hazatin. "Thank you for the information."

"Of course, sir." He nods. "Deputy Keenguard has already started putting the case file together for you at the east station."

"Understood." Khazak salutes him. "May your patrol week be slow and uneventful. *Rumk'r Avon.*"

After the dwarf repeats back the same phrase, which means "many blessings," the two of us grab our bags—as does Glasha—and we begin the journey back to V'rok'sh Tah'lj. I think about waiting until we're home to start with my pestering questions, but Glasha's cool.

"I thought your family wasn't religious?" At least that's what he said when he first told me about religion within the city.

"They are not, but when I was younger my father— Orlun—thought it would be a good way for my sister and I to be involved in the community." He specifies which of his dads he's talking about because I've explained to him how confusing it is when he has *three.*

"What did you do, exactly?" I know "getting involved" can mean a lot of things.

"Mostly assisted during worshipping services," Khazak explains. "Preparing altars, lighting incense, reciting prayers."

"Wow, so were you like a devout believer then?" The few times I went to church as a kid I wasn't involved in a thing.

"No more than any child is, I think." Khazak shrugs. "I liked the sense of duty it gave me. I continued doing it long after my sister had stopped. High Priest Bhok was more than capable of leading a room and would often sway me into taking on more responsibilities. I liked what I was doing until it became apparent that he was hoping to train me to be his replacement. I dropped the position shortly thereafter."

"He tried the same thing with a friend of mine," Glasha adds from my right. "My parents had the same thoughts about it being good for me. I did not mind it, but the high priest was clearly interested in training my friend further, which he did not want. When he dropped out, I was worried his interest might fall on me and used that as an excuse with my parents to quit."

"Did you also like the responsibility you got from it?" Maybe it's like tradition for rangers to do that.

"No. I liked sleeping in," she deadpans.

"Hell yeah." I bump my shoulder into hers, even though it is several inches higher.

It's late afternoon by the time we get home, having split with Glasha once we were back inside the gates. The first thing we do is strip down and get in the shower, and the third thing we do is eat an early dinner. I'll let you imagine what the second thing was, but let's just say we almost needed another shower by the time we were done. Mentally and physically exhausted after spending a week in the woods, I pass out on the couch at some point in the evening. I wake up to Khazak's hand gently shaking my shoulder, and he moves us to the bed for the night.

The next day we're up a little earlier than usual since our walk to the other station is longer than our normal route. A fact which my feet aren't crazy about, but at least they are a lot less sore in these new boots I got a couple of weeks back. We walk east, past our normal workplace and then the arena in the center of town. I can't help but make a joke about "the place where we first met" as we pass, which draws a small smile outta Sir.

We arrive at the other station about twenty minutes later. It looks remarkably similar to ours, right down to the layout. I recognize a few of the people here, but it's mostly fresh faces to me. Khazak makes some introductions as we pass, but we head straight for the back where Deputy Keenguard's office is. Only one door is open, and we walk straight in.

"Captain Ironstorm." The deputy captain stands at our entrance and salutes.

"Good morning, Deputy Keenguard." He returns the salute.

"Have you already been informed of the situation at the temple, sir?" The deputy returns to her seat. She looks a little tired. I don't mean that in a rude way, just that she's probably been working since last night. She and Ragnar both work a lot of night and weekend shifts, so that between the two of them and Khazak, at least one "captain" is usually on duty. It happens, but it's actually pretty rare for them to work a full shift together.

"I was given some information, but please catch me up." Khazak takes one of the seats in front of her desk, and I take the other.

"Two nights ago, there was a break in at the House of the Three." She passes some papers across her desk. "There was no vandalism and only some supplies were taken. Specifically, the sanctuary's store of brimstone."

"Brimstone?" Khazak sounds incredulous. "I'm being asked to investigate stolen *brimstone*?"

"I know, sir, but you know how the chief gets when the temple is involved." Keenguard sounds very apologetic.

"He never says no to his cousin," Khazak mumbles. He didn't mention *that* wrinkle before. "Do we have any more information?"

"Afraid not," she sighs. "High Priest Bhok was insistent that it be you he speaks to."

"Of course," Khazak sighs in return.

"Officer Silentfang in the forensics laboratory is prepared to go down with you whenever you are ready." She offers a small smile. *Wait, Silentfang? Glasha works in the forensics lab?*

"Thank you, Deputy. Excellent work." Khazak stands, taking the papers with him. "We will head down there shortly. I do not like that we are already a day behind."

"Yes, sir. Please let me know if you need any assistance." She salutes on our way out.

We cross the hall to what *should* be Khazak's office, which is confirmed when he opens the door and sets down his bag. It's much sparser than his other office, nothing hanging on the walls or sitting on the desk. In fact, the whole thing might be a little smaller.

"Is her office bigger than yours?" I point my thumb across the hall.

"I saw no reason to take the larger room when I would use it so infrequently." *He's a good boss.*

"I bet Ragnar was jealous." Or at least pretended to be.

"He has been actively plotting my demise ever since," Khazak jokes after setting his bag down on the desk. "Come, let us get our mage and then begin the investigation."

We walk to the forensic lab, which like the other station is a large room located toward the back of the building on the opposite side from the captain's offices. It's split in two, one half filled with desks for the officers working there, and the other half with lab equipment. There are potion beakers with different colored liquids, desks set up with crystals and mirrors on them, and all manner of magical items in glass cases that I couldn't begin to imagine what to do with. All the officers salute Khazak when we enter, including the gnome I've heard about.

"Good morning." Khazak returns the salute, and they all relax. "I am looking for Officer Silentfang?"

"Right here, sir!" A female voice speaks up, attached to the body of an orc raising her hand. One that is definitely not Glasha. She a little shorter than me with shoulder-length black hair pulled into twin braided ponytails. She's wearing a pair of round silver-rimmed glasses over her brown eyes and a less elaborate uniform than Khazak's. She smiles as she walks up to us.

"Pleasure to be working with you, Officer Silentfang." Khazak salutes at her approach.

"Please. Call me Nikka, sir." She salutes again smiling, then she turns to me. "You must be David. Nice to meet you. My sister has told me a lot about you."

"Nice to meet you too, Nikka." She seems bubbly. "Glasha is your sister?"

"That is her." She nods. Cool.

"Do you need to prepare anything before we leave?" Khazak really wants to get this over with.

"No, sir, Captain. All ready to go." She holds up a small journal and tugs on the strap of the bag she's got around her shoulder.

It's a short walk to the House of the Three, only a few more blocks east past the station. It sits behind a large courtyard, the stones arranged into patterns of circles and spirals. The building itself is bigger than most of the others I've seen in the city, though not nearly as big as the arena or tribal hall. It easily takes up a quarter of the block. The walls are made of wood and stone, like most of the other buildings, with a rounded domed roof adorned with flowers and leaves. Above the entrance is a symbol of a triangle, which is made up of three four-sided diamonds: one red, one green, and one blue.

The courtyard isn't packed, but there are some people, mostly orcs, milling about. Along the outskirts on either side are smaller structures that look like altars and statues.

They're the areas where the most people are congregated, some bent over in prayer. *Shrines to other religions?* I think I remember Khazak mentioning something like that to me.

We head straight for the building's doors and walk into a large open room. There are lined rows of benches (*pews?*) with a few orcs seated, worshipping in silence or maybe just thinking. In the front of the room is a large statue. Well, three statues. Three figures are set against the wall, laid out in a triangle. On the bottom right is a burly looking orc with short, spiky hair. Seriously, he's all muscle. To his left is a more feminine looking orc, though I wouldn't say for sure that they're necessarily female. Above them both is a third orc who *is* a woman, at least judging from the large breasts on her chest. She's upside down, suspended as if she's floating, or even swimming down toward the others. All three orcs look at peace, and all have one arm extended to each other, hands touching at the center of the statue.

Two orcs in large red robes are speaking in front of the statue. One of the two notices our entrance and begins making his way down the aisle to us after waving off his companion. He's tall and thin, his robes flowing in the air behind him. His long white hair has been braided, and his left tusk has a slight crack in it.

"Khazak!" The orc calls out before speaking in Atasi.

"High Priest Bhok," Khazak says in Common for my benefit. Usually that gets everyone else to respond in the same language.

"It has been too long." He reaches out and clasps one of Khazak's hands in his own. "I do not think I have seen you in here in years."

"Yes, sorry... Work takes up much of my free time these days." *Well, that's definitely a lie.*

"Of course. I am sure you are very busy." It doesn't sound like he doubts Khazak's sincerity. "Are you still reciting your nightly prayers?"

"Yes, sir. Of course." *That* lie sounded believable at least. "High Priest, this is Officer Silentfang and my avakesh David. They will both be assisting me in the investigation."

"I had heard about that." The priest eyes me up and down before offering a small bow. "It is nice to meet the both of you."

"If you could direct us to the location of the break-in, we can get started." Khazak tries to gently move things along.

"Right this way." The priest turns on his heel and leads us toward the statue, then enters a side door on the right. He takes us into a hallway, one side lined with windows and the other with doors. At the end of the hall is another door—or what's left of one. It looks like it's been hacked to death, chunks of wood all over the floor. I can make out shards of glass mixed with the wood, the sunlight reflecting off them onto the ceiling above.

"Here we are." The priest comes to a stop in front of the destruction, a broken window on our right. "This is the closet we keep the ceremonial supplies in."

"You were the one who found it this way yesterday morning, correct?" Khazak steps up to look over the damage with the priest.

"That is correct." He nods. "It must have been around six when I came to gather my materials for the day."

"Thank you." Khazak squats down to inspect some of the damage closer. "And we are sure this happened overnight? Who was the last person here?"

"That would also be me." Bhok sighs. "We have had the odd vagrant hiding in the building overnight, so I always walk through each of the rooms once before I retire in the evening."

"The only thing stolen was brimstone?" Khazak sounds skeptical.

"Yes, all of it." Bhok nods. "Enough to last us the rest of the year. Now I must order more and hope it is here in time for the festival this weekend. I just cannot fathom who would do something like this."

"I promise we will do everything we can to locate the person responsible, sir." Khazak stands and does his best to reassure the older orc.

"Thank you, Khazak." At that moment, the door we walked in through opens again, another orc in robes calling out. "Sorry. I must prepare for my next sermon. You remember where my office is?"

"Yes, sir. I will let you know when we have some information for you." Khazak nods.

"Thank you. Please give my love to your fathers and siblings." He turns and leaves.

"Well, I think it is safe to say they did not use magic, officer." Khazak looks over the destruction.

"I agree, sir. I will still see if I can pick up traces of anything." Nikka closes her eyes and brings her hands together, chanting softly to herself.

"Thank you." Khazak steps carefully over some of the larger pieces of wood and glass to get into the closet doorway. "By the look of these grooves, I would say they used an axe. No finesse at all."

"Looks like they knew exactly what they were doing, too." Khazak looks to me for more of an explanation. "The only broken window is right in front of the supply closet, and if they brought an axe, they probably knew the door would be locked. You wouldn't bring an axe just to break a window."

"Which means our suspect is likely a parishioner," Nikka comes to an even better conclusion than I did. "I was not able to detect any residual magic, sir."

"As I thought." Khazak takes another step into the closet. "Let us see if our friend left us anything more tangible."

"What would someone steal brimstone for anyway?" I ask both of them. I've heard of brimstone, but I'm not sure I've actually seen it before. "What is it used for?"

"It produces a lot of smoke when you burn it," Nikka responds as she takes notes on her pad. "The smell is… interesting. It is used in ceremonial pyres, or added to incense, or used to bless rooms. Outside of the church, if you know your chemistry, you can actually do some pretty interesting things with brimstone and fire." A sudden look of realization crosses Nikka's face. "Sir, the high priest mentioned the *Shatu Uzu'gor* this weekend. There are always a lot of fire dancers and street performers. It might be worth being on the lookout for anyone using an excessive amount of brimstone."

"Good thinking, officer. Please make a note of that in your report," Khazak tells her as he emerges from the closet, where his eyes catch something on the door frame. Smiling, he carefully plucks what looks like a torn piece of black cloth from the splintered wood. "Seeing as the priest's robes do not come in black, I think we can assume this belonged to our assailant."

"Here you are, sir!" Nikka steps forward, holding a small jar from her bag.

"Thank you, officer." Khazak drops the cloth into the jar. "As we are already a day behind, please take that back to the lab immediately and attempt to scry on its owner. David, go with her. I am just going to quickly update the high priest and then will be right behind you."

"Yessir," we respond in unison.

The two of us exit the temple as Khazak goes to update the priest alone, which I suspect might have something to do with wanting to avoid me learning of any embarrassing stories from his youth. *That's fine. I'll just ask his sister.* It's a quick walk back to the station, and Nikka takes us right to the forensics lab.

The room is emptier than it was this morning, most officers off working their own cases. Nikka sets up at one of the desks with scrying equipment—at least I'm pretty sure that's what it is. At the center of the table is a *very* detailed map of the city. I think I can make out each individual building. Next to the map is a large mirror laying flat on the surface of the desk.

"How does this work, exactly?" I've never actually seen someone "scry" before, but I know it's a way for some spell-casters to locate a person or thing from a distance.

"Well, if this *is* from the thief's clothing, I should be able to channel my magic through it and pinpoint his location on this map, assuming they are still in the city." Nikka sets her bag down and removes the jar with the cloth scrap. "I can also try to bring up a visual image of them and their surroundings, but that can be a little trickier."

"So, what's to stop someone from scrying on one of us and discovering the city's location?" I ask, suddenly worried people back home might already know exactly where I am.

"Anti-scrying enchantments around the city's perimeter," she explains. "Strong ones, too. They make it impossible for anyone outside of the city to scry in, but as long as you are inside the enchantments, the magic should work just fine."

I nod. I'm not exactly sure if anyone back home is looking for me, but at least I know my location is secure for now.

Nikka reaches up to remove her necklace, a simple gold chain attached to a small animal fang, no longer than an inch. She wraps some of the chain around the fingers on her other hand before opening the jar and placing the cloth scrap in her palm. Closing her fist, she holds it palm-down over the map, letting the necklace dangle freely from her fingers.

We both look up at the sound of the door opening and see Khazak entering the lab.

"Just about to get started, sir," Nikka calls him over.

As Khazak moves to join us, Nikka begins to chant to herself as she moves her hand slowly over the map. The fang on the necklace glows as the spell activates, swaying in the air over the city. A second later, the chain goes taut, and with a gentle *thunk*, the fang plants itself onto the map, standing straight up.

"Got them!" Nikka declares excitedly. "It looks like they are in a warehouse… Lot 549. Let me see if I can bring up a visual."

Nikka moves her focus over to the mirror, placing her hands on either side of it. I see the surface of the mirror start to look cloudy, like smoke is swirling around on the reflective side, but nothing else happens.

"Damn, they are blocking me," she gripes.

"Why didn't it work?" I watch the mirror go back to normal.

"Magic is not foolproof," Nikka explains. "There are still ways to hide from it."

"It may also mean the thief is aware we are looking for them." Khazak inspects the spot on the map where the fang still stands. "Officer Silentfang, please pull all records we have for that lot and bring them to Deputy Keenguard's office. David, you and I are going to the warehouse, now."

After splitting from Nikka, the two of us leave the station and head south, walking at a quick pace. Judging from the map, it'll take us ten minutes if we hurry.

"So, did everything go alright with the priest?" I can't help but ask, I'm still *really* curious about a young temple-going Khazak.

"Hmm? Oh, yes, everything was fine." Khazak turns to answer me. "After I updated him, he asked me about volunteering at the temple again. Thankfully, my job and all its duties are more than enough of a valid excuse. However, I *did* let him know that my sister was back in town, and that she has nothing but free time on her hands."

"Oh, I'm sure she's going to *love* that." The twin in me understands: when you're given an opportunity to pull one over on your sibling, you *gotta* take it.

"Should at least make for interesting conversation next time we see her at dinner." He sounds pleased with himself.

"And what's this I hear about a festival happening next weekend?" I ask about the other thing on my mind. The high priest and Nikka both mentioned something.

"Yes, that." Khazak smiles coyly. "I *was* going to let that be a surprise, but I suppose it is a little late now."

"Yeah, cat's outta the bag," I add.

"Who puts cats in bags?" Khazak asks, puzzled.

"It's just a saying." *Who does put cats in bags, though?* "What is the festival?"

"The *Shatu Uzu'gor.* It begins Aquaday evening and continues through Solisday," he informs me as we walk. *The name sounds familiar.* "Translated, it means the Festival of Steel & Thunder. It is a celebration of relationships like ours."

"What happens?" Celebrate how, exactly?

"A lot of outdoor parties. Drinking, eating, more drinking. There will be street vendors and demonstrations." Now I'm curious: what *kind* of demonstrations? "I still want to leave some things a surprise, but let us say that we will finally get some use out of that harness I had made for you. It is one of the few times the city actually gets any kind of tourism."

"People really come here for all that?" Would people from home come if they knew what it was about?

"There are more people like us in the world than you think, David," he responds.

"You mean people who are twins?" I joke, giving Khazak a cheesy smile when he looks over to correct me. Then he looks concerned and quickly pulls me over to him, the sounds of horses galloping on my left. I turn just in time to see a blur of black as a horse-drawn carriage flies past us. *Why does this feel familiar?*

"Slow down!" Khazak shouts after them as he lets me go, then nods toward his right. "We are almost there."

We stop before we enter the next lot. Most of the buildings in this section of town are workshops or warehouses of some kind. This next building is no different, but it looks much more run down. The color on the walls has faded and some of the windows are broken. I think the roof might even have a hole in it.

"Yeah, this place gives off big evil villain lair vibes," I comment quietly. "How do you wanna do this?"

"Let us try and look inside first." Crouching, Sir leads us to one of the warehouse's windows.

We wait on either side, carefully turning our heads to peer inside the building. It's dark, the only light coming in through the windows, but I don't see anything. I look over, silently asking if he sees something I don't, but he shakes his head then nods at the front door. He tests the knob, finding it unlocked.

"Weapon at the ready," he whispers to me, and we both draw our swords as he opens the door.

We walk inside slowly, Khazak in the lead as we carefully eye our surroundings for any movement. It's easier once my eyes adjust to the dark, but I still don't see anything. It's so eerily quiet in here that I can hear my own heartbeat.

The first part of the building is mostly desks, all covered in dust and old papers. Just beyond that through an open doorway is the rest of the warehouse. Huge ovens line the walls, a smelter and an anvil next to each one, all of them long since rusted over. Along another wall are a series of crafting tables, a pile of old bows lying atop one. *They made weapons here.*

"David." Khazak whispering my name snaps my head to attention. He's standing near one of the desks. "Look."

He's pointing down at the desk, and at first, I don't realize why. It's just another empty desk. Then I realize this one isn't dusty like the others. *Someone's been here.* I look around quickly to see if our assailant is nearby.

"We need to search the rest of the building, but I think whoever was here is already gone," Khazak says at a normal volume.

We come across a black robe in one of the building's side rooms, likely ditched after they learned we were tracking them, but the rest are all empty. We walk around the perimeter outside once before heading back to the station to report our findings. When we enter Deputy Keenguard's office, we find not just Officer Silentfang and the requested files, but also Khazak's best friend and other deputy, Ragnar Rockfang, waiting for us. *His shift today isn't until way later.*

"Captain." Keenguard is the first to notice us, and all three orcs in the room stand and salute. "Were you able to find them?"

"Other than this, afraid not." Khazak drops the robe on the desk and returns the salute, letting everyone relax. Khazak then turns to Ragnar. "What brings you in, Deputy?"

"I forgot my bag in my office yesterday, and when I came in to grab it, I found Officer Silentfang looking for records. They weren't actually in our office, but I offered to come and help look back here." He gestures to some files on the desk. "You won't believe what we found."

"What is it?" The five of us crowd around the desk.

"The original owner of that warehouse is Thrax Grimrock, father to one *Thog* Grimrock." Ragnar points to words on the paper I can't read.

"No way." Thog Grimrock is currently sitting in a jail cell, accused of stealing a shipment of supplies meant for the city's militia. We arrested him three weeks ago after a foot chase through the city's outdoor market, and he's been awaiting his trial ever since. Khazak and Ragnar have both tried to get more information out of him, but Thog has stubbornly stuck to his story, claiming he worked alone and destroyed everything.

"That is very...*interesting*." Khazak eyes the paper suspiciously.

"Interesting? It's more than interesting; it's motive." Ragnar spread out the other files. "Twenty years ago, Thrax Grimrock ran a weapon-smithing business out of that warehouse with a contract to produce supplies for the militia—until it was discovered he was *also* making weapons for the Warhunter Rebellion."

"*Shit.*" Khazak is actually taken aback by that info. *He almost never curses.*

"After that, he was arrested, tried, and put away. The factory was seized, and his family lost everything." Ragnar's voice gets a little quieter. "He died in prison two years ago."

"That is unfortunate," Khazak says somberly. "I can see how this gives us more motive for Thog's actions, but I am not sure I see the connection to the robbery at the House of the Three."

"What do you mean? Obviously, the person hiding in the factory was the same person who helped him steal the militia shipment," Ragnar scoffs.

"We do not know that for certain. This evidence is purely circumstantial." Khazak sounds much more levelheaded.

"This is *too* much of a coincidence, sir." *At least he remembered the "sir" that time.* "I want to talk to him again. I think we can use this new information to get more out of him."

Khazak considers this for a moment. "Alright, one more interrogation, but that will be the last. His trial is in two days."

"Thank you, sir. I will prepare things back at the station." With a salute, he's gone.

"Deputy Keenguard, I want to run a full search of the warehouse as well as get interviews from all the neighboring businesses." Khazak is back in full Captain-mode. "I want any information on anyone who may have come in or out of that building."

"I will get officers started on that immediately, sir." She salutes.

"Thank you." Khazak turns to Nikka. "Officer Silentfang, though I doubt anything worthwhile will come of it, please analyze the robe our assailant was wearing." He sighs before smiling. "And good work today."

"Yes, sir. Thank you!" she replies with a salute and a smile. "I will have my report and notes submitted by the end of the day." She turns to me. "It was nice to meet you, David."

"It was nice to meet you too, Nikka." *She's sweet.* With a salute from Khazak and an awkward wave from me, we make our exit.

"What happened twenty years ago?" I ask as we make our way back to the other station. "What's the Warhunter Rebellion?"

"A dark time for the city." He sighs. "There was a member of the Tribal Council, Zanik Warhunter, who held some...*extreme* views. He felt that as a people, we had 'gone soft,' and advocated for a return to a more brutal time in our history. That the strong should rule over the weak.

Unfortunately, he had a large number of supporters who felt the same. When the time came for his term to expire, he refused to step down and attempted to overthrow the entire Tribal Council and seize power for himself. He even managed to kill one of the other council members."

"Shit." A fucking *coup*? Those actually happen?

"It was more than just citizens. He had supporters in the government, in the militia. A small civil war broke out." Khazak doesn't sound happy to be reliving this. "My father was ranger captain at the time, and my other father insisted on volunteering as well, so they left me at home to look after Ayla and Yogik while they fought. That was when they met Jarek, and also when Ruda lost his foot." The second part of the sentence is said much sadder than the first.

"I'm sorry." Khazak told me he'd had a hard time when he first met his stepdad Jarek, but I didn't realize why.

"It is alright." He gives me a half smile. "My family came out of things much stronger than many others. But still, I find myself hoping that this connection between that time and Thog is nothing more than a coincidence."

We head toward the jail cells when we arrive at the station, which is also where the interrogation room is. Ragnar is already waiting for us outside and gives me a funny look when we approach.

"You want him to sit in this time?" The question isn't accusatory, but it still makes me bristle.

"Right. David, I suppose you should—"

"Oh, come on. Let me in this time, please?" Last time they did this, I had to sit in the breakroom and wait. "I swear I'll just sit in the back quietly and listen."

The two orcs share a look, and Ragnar shrugs.

"Alright." Khazak nods his assent. "Pay attention but... make sure you remain silent. Even if he tries to provoke one of us."

"Yes, Sir." I nod and mime locking my lips with a key.

After sharing a look, the two rangers open the door and walk in, me right behind them. Thog is seated with his hands cuffed, a chain attaching them to the table in front of him. Khazak and Ragnar take seats in chairs opposite him, and as there are no other chairs to be found, I just lean against the back wall of the room silently, arms crossed.

"Brought your pet this time?" Thog sneers at me.

"Mr. Grimrock," Khazak starts, ignoring the man's words, "I trust your stay has been comfortable?"

Thog narrows his eyes at Khazak but doesn't answer.

Khazak presses forward. "Another robbery has occurred, and we were hoping you would be able to answer some questions about it for us."

"It is a little hard to rob someone from a jail cell, Captain." Thog rolls his eyes.

"No, Thog, it's not the robbery we have questions about," Ragnar cuts in, voice and attitude more biting than his casual words would let on. "It's where we found the thief hiding: your father's old factory."

Thog snaps to attention at Ragnar's words, his face a mix of confusion and surprise.

"Yes, we were hoping you could explain that odd connection for us." Khazak's tone has remained steady since he first sat down.

"I... I do not know anything about this." Thog sounds a little nervous when he answers, but I'm not positive it's out of guilt.

"Please," Ragnar sharply draws the attention back to himself. "We all know you weren't acting alone. Was this the guy you were working with?"

Thog says nothing, but glares at Ragnar.

"Were you hiding the stolen supplies in the factory?" I'm not sure if Ragnar expects an answer. "What do you need that much brimstone for anyway?"

Again, no reaction from Thog, but Ragnar continues. "Just seems like a really interesting choice, don't you think? Especially after everything that happened with your dad."

I can see Thog's already clenched fists tighten at Ragnar's taunt, and Khazak turns his head slightly to eye his deputy carefully.

"You told us you hated the militia, but that's not completely accurate, is it?" Ragnar's voice starts to get heated. "Your *entire family* must hate them after your father's arrest."

Thog doesn't move, but his face darkens, and it feels like we're walking a tightrope here.

"Probably even more so after his death, right?" Ragnar starts getting louder. "He was only a year away from release, wasn't he? I bet that *really* pissed you off."

Thog looks like he's currently trying to murder Ragnar with his eyes but still remains silent.

"Is that it? Revenge? Were you mad your daddy died in prison, so you decided to get back at the people who put him there?" Ragnar suddenly stands, leaning over the table. "Why did you do it, and *who the hell are you working with?!*"

"*Deputy*," Khazak does his best to reel Ragnar in without Thog noticing he's gone rogue.

"I told you," Thog grits out, "I do not know anything about this robbery or your stolen brimstone."

"I *know* you're lying!" Ragnar shouts.

"That is *enough*, Deputy Rockfang." Khazak stands, crowding Ragnar's space. With a final glare to Thog, Ragnar exits the room. Khazak turns to Thog. "Thank you for your time, Mr. Grimrock. An officer will be in to return you to your cell. I believe your advocate will be visiting tomorrow to discuss your upcoming hearing."

Ignoring Thog's rolling eyes, Khazak gives me a look to follow as he turns and exits the room. Ragnar is waiting for us right outside, and as a group, we move down the hall and away from the cells into Khazak's office. Khazak moves behind his desk while Ragnar drops in one of the chairs in front dramatically, and I take a seat on the couch.

"I'm sorry. I know I let myself get too heated in there." Ragnar crosses his arms, looking at his lap.

"Yes, that could have gone better." Khazak shakes his head. "I would have liked to keep the information about what was stolen a secret while the thief is still at large, but in the end, I do not think he actually knows anything."

"He's lying! He has to be." Ragnar turns in his seat to face me. "David?"

"I dunno." I scratch the back of my head. "He seemed genuinely surprised when you brought up his dad's factory. I think he might be telling the truth."

Ragnar makes a frustrated grumble. "I really thought I had something."

"We will solve this, Deputy," Khazak consoles his friend. "Try to cheer up. In two days, that man will no longer be sitting in one of our cells, and then you will have the entire festival this weekend to focus on other things."

That goes for me, too. Things like eating, drinking, and whatever other surprises Sir has in store for me.

Chapter 4

Thog's trial takes place two days after the robbery, and it's a fairly boring affair. He has the same "advocate" (their word for lawyer) that I did, Naruk Redwish. I still don't trust the guy after he lied to me and Khazak, manipulating us into fighting each other, but I have to admit, he's good at what he does. There was a lot more talking than at my friend's trial, not that I could understand a word of it.

Even though we know he was working with someone else, we can't prove anything, and since Thog confessed to everything, there's not really anything to argue against. He's sentenced to five years in the city's prison (which is different than where my friends are) for stealing from the city's militia. I can tell Khazak and Ragnar aren't exactly happy about it, but Ragnar seems more upset.

The rest of the week drags on, and the knowledge that something fun awaits us after work on Aquaday only makes it feel longer, especially the last couple of days when I can see the booths and stages being set up. By the end of the week, there's this weird energy in the air, and I can barely concentrate on anything. I'm practically bouncing in my chair waiting for Khazak to tell us we can go home. I want to find out what's gonna happen already!

"Should we eat before we go out?" I ask as we pass the kitchen.

"Definitely not." Khazak shakes his head as he marches confidently toward the bedroom. "There will be more than enough food tonight."

"Yay, I love food." I sit on the bed while he rummages through chests.

"Really? I had not noticed," he snarks, and I throw a pillow at his bent over form. "That is ten," he tells me as he stands back up, some clothes in hand, moving to the other chest.

"Worth it, Sir." We're both referring to the new system we have regarding my "behavior" and correcting it. I now earn demerits. Spanking demerits—to be doled out at the end of the day before bed. I've actually been pretty good lately; I made it the entire week in the woods without earning a single one. Being around the other rangers helped I think, but once we got back to the city, well... Ragnar and Nylan are bad influences.

"I wonder if you will feel that way by the end of the night," he threatens ominously, arms full and headed to the bed.

The first thing I notice is the black leather harness, something his friend Brull crafted for me weeks ago. I haven't worn it since I tried it on. Next to that is a pair of black pants, pants that frankly have gotten a little tight since I've put some weight back on. On top of the pants is a green jockstrap, which seems to be a favorite of his...and that's it.

"No shirt?" I look over to verify.

"You will not need one," he tells me with confidence, still gathering his own outfit.

I almost have to squeeze myself into my pants when we get changed. Gonna be time for new clothes soon, I think. Though judging from the way Khazak is looking at my ass, it might be worth hanging onto these a little longer. I need help getting the harness on. I'm not even sure which way is up, but Khazak gets it over my head, adjusting my collar to lay on top.

Khazak is dressed similarly, though his pants are less tight. His harness is also bigger. Where mine stops above my nipples, his is angled down farther, the straps crossing under his pecs entirely. Over that is a tight dark brown leather vest, which wouldn't be a color you'd think would work, but it fits in with his skin tone perfectly. Calling it a vest is also a stretch; it's basically two strips of leather down both of his sides. His shoulders are completely exposed, and it seems like it serves only to emphasize...all the good stuff. His arms are just as beefy as ever, accentuated more by the dark tattoos around his bicep, while the muscles of his chest are framed perfectly, coarse black hair covering his torso like a small forest.

"Like what you see?" He smirks when he catches me staring.

"Maybe." It *is* a nice package.

We throw on our boots, which go really well with the rest of our clothes, and Khazak grabs his trusty satchel. We stop at the front door on the way out, Khazak running back to the bedroom for what is apparently the final thing we need to complete our look, and something I'm still not crazy about: a leash. This one is more intricate than the others he's used on me. It matches my collar, all metal and made of up thousands of tiny rings like chainmail. On one end is a leather strap to act as a handle, and the other has a clasp that attaches to my collar. Given the entire outfit, I'm less annoyed about it than usual.

"Remember our training on protocol?" Khazak asks as he clips on the leash.

"Is tonight going to be one of those times?" I ask, adjusting my collar.

"In some ways, but less formal and more fun. Does that make sense?" He looks me over as he asks.

"I think so, Sir." *And if not, I'll figure it out.*

It's still light out when we step outside, the sun still has a couple of hours before it goes down for the night. We walk south, which is where most of the city's bars are located. There are more people out than normal at this hour, and that number only grows as we get closer. Coming up on a cross street, I see two guards posted on either side of the road ahead of us, watching the crowd as they pass through.

"Are they looking for the brimstone thief?" I ask Khazak.

"Yes, but they are primarily there to ensure no one underage wanders in." Khazak sounds amused. "As the nights progress during the festival, things tend to get more than just clothing optional."

My face heats up as I consider the implications of that statement.

Now that we're walking around it, the entire red-light district seems more like a well-lit district. There are even more people here, men and women dressed like Khazak and me, including some in collars and leashes. I can hear the sounds of music being played coming from multiple directions and smell all kinds of food. My stomach growls, and Khazak's orc hearing must be good enough to pick it up over the crowd because he gives me a look before leading us to one of the food carts.

He holds up two fingers to the orc working the cart and reaches for his pouch. The guy reaches back, grabbing two kabobs of something that smells very much like chicken, before pausing to look at us. His eyes are drawn to the leash connecting us, then to Khazak's face. He waves off Khazak's attempt to pay with a smile, saying something cheerful as he hands over the food. I manage to catch the word "*kritar,*" which I have learned means "captain," so this guy knows who Khazak is, and me by extension.

"Expect a lot of that this weekend," he tells me, his voice a little excited as we walk away.

"Being the captain's avakesh has its perks," I declare happily before digging in.

"That helped, but that is not why he gave it to us." Khazak smiles, taking a small bite of his and swallowing before continuing. "Have you noticed all the couples around us?"

"Yeah, I didn't realize there were so many avakesh-kavan pairings in the city." So far, I've seen a few out in public and only met one personally.

"There are not." Another bite. "These people probably all enjoy our...style of doing things, but do not, or cannot, take things further. The festival is an opportunity for them to play a little more publicly, while those of us in a real *uzu'gor* pairing tend to reap a few extra benefits from their admirers."

"So, how'd he know we were really together like that?" We certainly look the part, but so do most of the other people here.

"*That* is where my public persona came in handy." He winks.

We walk around the district, taking in the sights together. A few outdoor bars have been set up, complete with impromptu dance floors. There are a *lot* of people here, the most I've seen in one place since fighting in the arena. It's not just orcs either; I see elves, humans, dwarves, gnomes, halflings...

"You weren't kidding about the tourism thing." The crowd is still like 80% orc, but this is the most non-orcs I've seen since my arrival.

"Yes, and the number grows every year. It seems we are starting to become more and more of an open secret," Khazak adds wryly.

"Isn't that kinda dangerous with the whole 'hidden city' thing?" Seems like something you'd try to minimize at least.

"Honestly, I am not sure how much longer keeping the city hidden will be sustainable. Given our size and population, it is rather impressive we have been able to do it for this long," he says bluntly. "It will only be a few more years before the city will be forced to expand."

"Really?" *Expand* how, exactly?

"There is only so much room left inside the walls," he states, "and our population continues to grow. That is one of the reasons we started keeping livestock—there is not enough room for everyone to hunt."

We pass (and stop at) even more food and drink carts. Some are selling *dar-buk*, which are these fluffy little pastries stuffed with a sweet red jam. Khazak showed me some of the berries used to make it when we were on patrol. They were unripe, squishy-looking green orbs, almost like a raspberry but with the outside covered in tiny seeds. He said they turn red as they grow, which also indicates how sweet they are.

I see some of the fire dancers Nikka mentioned, and I'm mesmerized by what they are able to do. Rings and batons, lit on fire and thrown into the air, juggled back and forth between dancers without ever flinching or stumbling through their *incredibly* complicated dance routine. *How are they not covered in burns?* The whole thing is pretty amazing.

As we walk together, I feel the leash occasionally brushing against my bare skin. Given how close we've stayed tonight, wearing it seems almost pointless, like it's just for show. Which I guess it is. Soon I notice that we're in a familiar part of the city, and sure enough, I see the shop of Khazak's friend Brull coming up on our left. If it's possible, the streets are even busier here with lots of people coming in and out of Brull's specifically. Makes sense, given the kind of stuff Brull crafts and sells here.

"This weekend is one of the busiest times of the year for Brull." Khazak reaches over to unclip my leash. "Because of the crowd, I do not want to risk you getting hurt." I actually feel a little sad when he removes it, though I hide my frown. Don't need him knowing that.

We walk inside, and the shop is wall-to-wall people. The shelves are all half-empty, and the same goes for the wall racks, which normally are hung with all sorts of costumes and harnesses. There's even a couple of orcs squeezed into one corner trying things on. Brull is behind the counter dealing with customers, two other orcs back there helping him. I see him occasionally stepping into the back room and returning with what I'm assuming is a specially ordered item. We move toward the counter to try to catch his eye.

"Khazak! Great to see you!" he calls when he finally has a chance to notice us, stepping to the side. "David, looking good in that harness."

"Thank you, sir." *See? I remember my protocol.*

"The festival bringing in the business as always?" Khazak asks.

"You know it. Glad I spent the last two weeks making extra stock." He turns to look over the crowd. "Might have to stay up tonight making more if I wanna make it through the weekend."

"We will let you get back to it. Just wanted to stop in and wish you a happy festival. *Rumk'r Avon*." Khazak ends his sentence with the familiar Atasi saying.

"Rumcar Avon," I repeat as best I can.

"Getting better." Brull smirks at me then turns to Khazak. "Can I still count on the two of you for the demonstration tomorrow?"

"Of course. We would not miss it for the world." I give both orcs a funny look but say nothing until we exit.

"So, you wanna tell me about this demonstration?" *That sounded a little brazen.* "Sir." *Better.*

"Another surprise." He chuckles when I roll my eyes. "Every year during the festival, Brull likes to do something to attract customers. A show, of sorts. Do you remember the first time we were there, and what happened?"

"You mean the 'funishment?'" I assume he's talking about the time he tied me down and paddled me in the middle of Brull's shop while also giving me a handjob in front of some customers. That was an interesting day.

"I *refuse* to call it that, but yes." I stick my tongue out at his denial of my new word. "It will be a bit like that, though not at all a punishment."

"So you say." *Sounds suspicious.*

"So I say," he challenges with a smirk.

"What are we doing now?" I don't think I'll be getting any more answers on the previous subject.

"Meeting Ragnar and Nylan to get the rest of our evening started."

We walk away from Brull's, eventually coming upon one of the outdoor bars set up for the festival. There is a band playing on a stage next to the dancefloor, complete with drums, flutes, and guitars—or at least that's what the instruments resemble. They sound different from what I'm used to, but there's a steady bass line the people are dancing to. We spot Ragnar and Nylan standing at a table off to the side.

Ragnar is dressed similarly to Khazak, though his outfit is all black. I think it's his elf half that makes him look a little slimmer and younger than my orc, but he's still plenty muscular, and his leathers frame him no less impressively. Nylan is as tall and skinny as ever, dressed in a harness similar to mine, along with a pair of *very* short shorts. If he's cold, he's not showing it, smiling brightly with his dark hair perfectly coifed as always. The couple waves us over when they see us.

"Have you been waiting long?" Khazak asks Ragnar after grabbing each other's wrists and exchanging an orc-hug.

"Nah, still on our first drinks." He picks up a mostly empty mug. Nylan has a glass too, but the liquid inside is pink. "Got out here as soon as we could. I traded patrol shifts with Tuskrunner two weeks ago, so I wouldn't miss anything. Boy, why don't you go get us another round?"

"Yes Sir!" Nylan chirps happily right before finishing the last of his drink and grabbing the empty mug.

"Pup, go with him and get some drinks of our own." Khazak unclips my leash again. He reaches for his pouch, but Ragnar stops him.

"Hey, it's your first *Shatu Uzu'gor* with your own avakesh. Drinks are on me tonight." Ragnar flashes his best friend a grin.

"If you insist." He turns to me. "A beer for me, David, and whatever you would like."

"Yes, Sir. Thank you." I walk with Nylan over to the busy outdoor bar where we wait for our turn with the bartender.

"So, what do you think?" Nylan gestures to everything.

"It's...a lot, but so far it's been fun." Orcs sure know how to party.

"This is one of my favorite times of the year." Nylan looks over the crowd happily. "So much dancing. So much drinking. So much public sex."

"How many of these festivals have you been to?" They've been together a while now, I think.

"This is our sixth. I can still remember our first." Nylan smiles, reminiscing. "Did I ever tell you how I became Ragnar's avakesh?"

I shake my head no. He told me some of the story when I first met him, but I was a little preoccupied with my own shit to press him for more details.

"We had already been together for two years," he starts. "Traditionally, when a couple wants to go through with the Ritual of Steel & Thunder, the avakesh-to-be will commit some sort of "crime" against their would-be owner. Theft is the most popular choice, though I've heard of some real brats that decided to go with vandalism instead. In any case, they're 'arrested' in a big, over-the-top display, usually by a ranger or officer the couple is friends with. Then the arrestee issues the ritual challenge, their lover accepts it, and the two are taken to the arena where…you know the rest."

"That sounds kinda fun, at least hearing the way it's *supposed* to go." I try not to grumble the last part too much. I'm not upset about being in this situation with Khazak anymore, but sometimes I can't help but feel a little raw thinking about how Redwish tricked us.

"I hope you know how terrible Khazak feels. I mean, we all do, but him…" Nylan leans his shoulder into me. "It really sucks that someone would take something that's supposed to be fun and romantic like that and twist it."

"It's okay, it worked out in the end. It's not like it's your fault. It's not even Khazak's." Still, the city should really consider doing something to ensure this doesn't happen to anyone else. "Alright, what did you do to Ragnar to get arrested then?"

"Alright, so like I said, we had been together for two years at that point," Nylan continues his story. "We'd been talking about moving in together for a while, but we kept getting into fights about where we were going to live. He had this crappy little apartment over on the west side of the city, while I was living in a place that was bigger *and* closer to both of our jobs. So, one day while he was at work, I went over to his apartment and took his stuff."

"You stole some of his things?" Seems simple enough.

"No, David. I took *everything*." He opens his eyes wide for emphasis. "I hired some people to clean the place out and cram all of it into my apartment. It was a mess, but I got it done all in one day. After Ragnar came home to empty rooms, he stormed right over to my place and arrested me himself. *Then* he made me wait almost a full day in a jail cell before he accepted my ritual challenge. I thought it was because he was busy moving all of his stuff back to his place, but when we got home after the match, I saw that he had spent the day organizing everything in mine, combining our things. I loved it…after some arguing over his furniture choices."

"That sounds really sweet." I'm almost kinda bummed I didn't get to do something like that. "What about the match?" I noticed he completely skipped over that part.

"…He chased me screaming around the arena for fifteen minutes until he finally caught me." It's Ny's turn to grumble. "Then he tickled me until I gave in and he fucked me in front of the crowd."

"I would have loved to see that," I tease.

After finishing our story, the bartender finally comes over to serve us, and Nylan starts to tell her our order. "Wait, do you want a beer, or one of what I'm having?"

"What are you having?" I gesture to his empty glass.

"Ooooo, you won't be able to pronounce it, but you'll love it. It's sweet and *very* strong," Nylan informs me happily.

"Alright, sure." I've had a few beers since I've been here, but never in a situation where I could actually relax and enjoy them.

He finishes talking to the bartender, who leaves and returns a moment later with our drinks. Dropping some coins on the counter and thanking her, the two of us gather our glasses and return to our owners.

"Good boy." I get a hand stroking down my back as Sir takes his beer from me.

I take a sip of my drink, and *woah* is that strong. Sweet too, just like Nylan said. The flavor is actually a little familiar, but I can't put my finger on it. It's similar to the dar-buk filling.

"What do you think?" I must have made a face cause Nylan is laughing a little.

"Strong. But good." I smile and take another sip.

The four of us stand around talking and nursing our drinks. There is thankfully no work talk, except for Nylan telling us the story of some customer he had this week arguing with him over a book title. I'm the first one done with my drink, and when Nylan notices, he immediately offers to get me another. I eye him suspiciously but say yes because even though I'm pretty sure he's trying to get me drunk, I think I'll be okay around these three.

By the time I finish drink #2, I'm starting to feel warm and fuzzy, and I can feel myself swaying a little to the beat.

"Yessss." Nylan watches me and grins before turning to Ragnar. "Can we go dance now? Pleaaaseeee, Sir?"

"Uh-uh, you know I'm gonna need at least one more of these before I'm ready for that." He holds up his mostly finished beer, making his half-elf pout.

Maybe it's the alcohol (*it's definitely the alcohol*), but from across the table, I tell Nylan, "I'll dance with you."

His face brightens at my offer. "You will?"

"Yes, you will?" Khazak asks from my left, amused.

"Did you wanna dance with him?" Am I'm cutting in?

"No, that is alright." He chuckles. "I do not dance."

"Aww. Why not?" I poke him in the side. "'s fun."

"I'm glad you think so. Come on!" Nylan grabs me by the wrist and pulls me onto the dance floor.

Nylan weaves us through the throngs of people dancing, stopping when we find an open spot on the floor. His hips are already moving to the beat of the music, and I start to do the same but hesitate. I manage to shake it off, but I'm still moving a little awkwardly.

"You okay?" Nylan gives me a funny look.

"Yeah, sorry." It seems silly to say out loud. "I just realized I've never actually danced with a guy before."

"I thought that might be the case." He smirks. "Figured I might be a little easier for your first time than either of those big lugs." He jerks his head in the direction of our owners.

"Thanks." I laugh, moving a little more confidently.

"I promise it's not that different from dancing with a girl." Nylan steps a little more into my space.

I start to match my rhythm to his, and before long, Nylan reaches out to take my hands, placing them on his hips while his go on my shoulders. Soon enough, the two of us are dancing with ease, the alcohol more than enough to make me forget about feeling self-conscious. The only things I'm paying attention to are the music playing and the half-elf in front of me.

I like dancing. I used to do it all the time back home. Just, you know, with girls. This really doesn't feel that different. Nylan is a little feminine I guess, but that's not what I mean. Looking around, I can see that we're not even the only two men dancing together right now. Most of the couple around us are mixed-gender, but there's more than one pairing of two men or women on the floor. No one is batting an eye.

"So, how have you two been doing?" Nylan asks, breaking my trance.

"What do you mean?" Me and Khazak?

"No more fights or...attempted jail breaks?" His eyebrow quirks up at the second part of his question.

"No, nothing like that." I roll my eyes. "We've been getting along pretty great."

"That's good to hear." He smiles as he shimmies. "We were always hoping Khazak would meet someone like you."

His words give me pause. "Ny...you know that we're not really a couple, right? I'm still leaving in two...a month and a half." *Wow, time really flies.*

"Yeah, I know... It's still nice though." His smile turns sad for just a second.

The tempo of the next song slows down, and the drums start to beat a little louder. Nylan takes the opportunity to pull me in even closer, our crotches all but grinding against each other. Shit, I think he's even half-hard. *Maybe I am too.*

"Are you sure we should be dancing like this?" Not that I try to stop him.

"Why? Worried we'll get in trouble?" he taunts.

"Just wondering what our owners would think if they were watching." Might not necessarily be thinking anything bad.

"Oh, I'm counting on them watching." He peers over my shoulder in the direction of their table. "Look."

He turns us so that I'm able to look, and I can see both Khazak and Ragnar, eyes locked on us. Their faces are mostly amused, but there's something else there too, something darker. Nylan spins around, drawing my attention back to him.

"I do *not* like to be kept waiting," Nylan growls as he pushes his ass back onto my now *definitely* half-hard cock.

I look down at Nylan grinding back against me. He's got a cute lil' bubble butt back here. I stare at it, somewhat mesmerized, my hands still on his hips. I'm so distracted that I don't notice anyone else walking up to us until I feel a tap on my shoulder.

"Mind if I cut in?" Ragnar asks with a smirk, not bothering to wait for an answer as he whisks Nylan away from me with a squeaked out "Yay!"

I smile as I watch the two of them start dancing, Nylan's arms wrapped Ragnar's neck, looking up at him with so much adoration. It's really sweet, and not even in a cheesy way. I turn, figuring I'll head back to the table to join Khazak, only to come face-to-face with the man himself.

"Oh, hi. We can go back to the—" My words are cut off when Sir grabs my harness and pulls me to him, a look of determination on his face. "I thought you didn't dance?"

"Well, it is apparent that will have to change, lest you run off with some pretty thing you meet on the dancefloor without me." His words say "I had no choice," but his face says "I have something to prove."

"Wait, are you *jealous*?" I tease gleefully.

"Not jealous." A hand snakes down my back to grab my ass. "*Possessive*."

I don't respond to that, just grin as we start to move together. Both our movements are a little stilted—his from lack of experience and mine because I've never danced with someone where I wasn't leading. His hands are on me the same way mine were on Nylan earlier. It's a little strange at first, but then I feel them tighten possessively and I shiver.

With all the alcohol in our systems, it doesn't take long to relax. No clue if our dancing is any better, but at least I'm not thinking about anyone else. We move together to the rhythm of the bass, and I watch a bead of sweat roll down his bare chest. I'm practically dripping myself. When we grind against each other, I can feel his cock growing, and it puts Nylan's to shame.

Feeling adventurous thanks to the drinks (*I might need another of those in a bit...*), I try copying Nylan's moves from earlier, flipping around to press my back against Khazak's front. Immediately, two arms wrap around my chest and stomach, holding me against him. Because of our height difference, his dick is half against my ass and half against my lower back, but that's more than enough to work with.

I close my eyes and sway to the beat, feeling Khazak's length continue to grow against my back. My own dick is a solid lump in my jockstrap, which I can only imagine clearly visible to anyone looking thanks to how tight my pants are. Khazak's arms tighten around me, and I feel his hot breath against my neck. The hand on my stomach slowly snakes down, following the trail of fur on my stomach into the top of my pants. His fingertips ghost through the top of my pubic hair and make me shiver again.

I could really get used to this.

Several hours, drinks, and dances later, the four of us finally leave the outdoor bar together. The first stop is to get some food, which ends up being a bowl full of these *incredible* tasting pieces of chicken that have been breaded and fried in oil. Those get washed down with a full glass of water from a tavern, which both orcs get into Nylan and me in the interest of not waking up with a hangover.

After we are sufficiently hydrated, the four of us remain in the tavern to talk. Well, Khazak and Ragnar talk because Nylan and I are both pushed to the floor a few minutes in to kneel between our respective orcs' legs. Feeling my ears and face pinken as my face is drawn toward Khazak's crotch, any thoughts of embarrassment are shoved away when a thick green cock is shoved into my mouth.

To my left, out of the corner of my eye, I can see Nylan getting similar treatment, a green hand in his hair guiding him up and down. The two orcs above us continue to talk as if we aren't here, aren't currently sucking them down in the middle of a tavern. They aren't even speaking Common anymore, having switched at some point without me noticing. Being ignored like that, combined with the casual use of my mouth, is doing something to me, and I can feel myself growing hard in my pants again.

The cock is hot and heavy in my mouth, the familiar taste of Sir's precum hitting my tongue each time I slide over the head. After all the dancing and working up a sweat, the smell of his musk is so strong, and it hits my nostrils every time I sink down on him. It's intoxicating, and the longer it goes on, the further I sink into a headspace where the only things that exist are him and me and what we're doing. How I'm serving him.

I tense up briefly when I feel someone behind me. The hand in my hair continues to guide me, like one of the barmaids isn't swapping out the empty water glasses above me. But then they're gone, as if coming across a customer getting his dick sucked in the middle of the establishment is perfectly normal. Which it probably is right now.

"Good boy." The praise is whispered above me, sending a wave of warmth through my body and guiding me down into that headspace.

It happens again, of course, and not just from a tavern worker, but other customers who want to stop and watch the proceedings. Each time I notice someone, I get brought out of things a little, though the more it happens, the less it affects me, the murmured words of praise helping me to sink back down.

When I look up, the look I get back is full of lust, pride, and a big dose of cockiness. *He's showing off on purpose.* He wants people to see this, to see me on my knees for him. After a while, I'm not sure he's even trying to cum, or if I'm even trying to make him cum. I'm just enjoying what

I'm doing and thinking about the fact that he wants to show me off like this only sends more of that familiar warmth to my belly.

All good things must come to an end though, and after both men have had enough oral attention, Nylan and me are pulled up from our knees and saliva-slick dicks are tucked back into pants. After leaving a generous tip on the table (especially considering I think we only had water), the four of us exit the tavern and say our goodbyes. Nylan has to work a morning shift tomorrow, but we have plans to meet up again in the evening, or so we are informed by our owners.

By the time we get home, I'm starting to get a little sleepy. I've sobered up a bit, but I'm still kinda buzzed and feeling good, despite the drowsiness. I walk up behind Khazak as he opens the door, snaking my hands around his waist to cop a feel.

"Are you sure you can even stay awake for that, pup?" He jokes as he walks us inside, me still awkwardly hugging him from behind. "Besides, I believe you earned a few demerits today."

"Did I? Are you sure you're remembering that right, Sir?" *Uh oh. Time to backpedal.* I release his waist. "You had a lot to drink tonight."

"Not *nearly* as much as you, puppy." He turns to face me, sounding suspiciously sober. "Do you have any idea how strong those drinks Nylan kept feeding you were? And you had *five.*"

"That many?" My voice goes higher than I meant it to.

"Mhmm. And let us not forget you little performance on the dance floor." He takes a step toward me, an evil smirk on his face. "A *very* blatant attempt to provoke myself and Ragnar."

"Hey, that was all Nylan." I half-smile with a half-nervous laugh, pointing at the orc as I take a step backward.

"I am sure it was." Another step, same smirk. "Yet you made *no* attempts to stop him."

"I didn't want to be rude?" He's not buying it, and I take another step backward, this time hitting the back of the couch.

"Yes, and I am so proud of how polite you have become." His words drip with sarcasm as he crowds me against the couch. "Which is why you have only earned yourself another ten. I believe that brings the total to twenty. Correct?"

"Correct, Sir." I bite my lip, still half-smiling. Lying isn't gonna do me any favors, and I know Khazak is only teasing me anyway. I mean, he really is going to spank me, but I've come to look forward to these kinds of "punishments" in their own way.

"Pants off," he tells me as he pulls off his vest. "Then turn around and brace yourself against the couch."

"Yes, Sir." I nod, bending down to take off my boots before starting on my pants. When I finish, I'm only in my harness and jockstrap, bent over and holding on to the back of the couch.

"Good boy," he tells me, standing at my side and running a warm hand across my ass. "You are to count them for me. Ready?"

"Ready, Sir." I squeeze the edge of the couch and wait for the first blow.

smack *Left cheek.* "One, Sir." See, it's not that these spankings hurt less.

smack *Right cheek.* "Two, Sir." I mean, they do in the long run because I'm not left feeling them through next day.

smack *Left.* "Three, Sir." It's that these types of spankings—the counting kind, rather than the "until you cry" kind—usually lead to *other* fun activities.

smack *Right.* "Four, Sir." Which is why I'm not worried. Khazak enjoys this game as much as I do.

smack *Both, oww.* "Five, Sir." But *fuck* if they don't still sting.

Sir spanks me fourteen more times, alternating between sides and keeping me guessing. Pain grows with each strike, but so does a familiar warmth, starting in my ass and spreading to the rest of my body. It also gets my blood pumping, particularly in the area around my crotch. By the time we almost finish, my whole body is flushed, and I can feel the front of my jockstrap tenting.

smack *Both.* I hiss in pain. "Twenty, Sir." I stand up and stretch as a hand rubs across my freshly-pinkened ass, unable to hold in a yawn. As much as that turned me on, I'm feeling pretty relaxed too. Spankings are weird.

"You took that beautifully, puppy." He turns me around and gives me a kiss on the forehead. "We have a busy day tomorrow, so now it is time for bed."

"You sure there's nothing else you want with me, Sir?" I try to give him my best bedroom eyes before he turns me to face the hallway.

"There are plenty of things I want to do with you, pup," he admits as he walks us into the bedroom. "But tonight, I have something far more fun in mind."

"What's that?" I ask with a yawn, lifting my arms so he can pull my harness off.

"Not allowing you to cum until tomorrow," he states, completely serious as he pulls off his own.

"Aww, what?" I pout, followed by another yawn. "Who's that fun for?"

"Me," he jokes, pulling me over to him. "But somehow, I think you will survive. I promise I will make it up to you tomorrow."

"Promise?" I half-ask, half-mumble as we climb onto the bed together.

"Promise, pup." He pulls the covers up over us and settles us onto the pillows.

"M'kay, Sir," I mumble against his chest, and a light kiss to the top of my head is the last thing I feel as my consciousness fades away.

Chapter 5

"**You look like shit, David,**" Liss grouses from across the table.

"Elisabeth!" Corrine manages to look offended on my behalf.

"What? He does." She shrugs.

"Good to see you too, Liss." It's Astraday morning, and I am back at the labor camp for visiting day. I almost didn't make it. After our late night out with Ragnar and Nylan, Khazak and I nearly overslept and forgot about it. He was the one who remembered while we were still groggy and lying in bed, leading to us very quickly throwing our clothes on and rushing down here so I wasn't late. Which is why I look like shit.

"You alright?" she asks, actual concern in her voice.

"Yeah, just worked late. That's all," I lie.

"You working this festival thing, too?" Aaaand now I feel bad for lying. "They've had me and Adam setting things up the last few days. Mostly stuff like booths and stages, but yesterday? We set up a bunch of bed pallets in a park. Big ones." She pauses, leaning closer to me over the table. "You hear what this festival is supposed to be celebrating?"

"Yeah, it's pretty crazy stuff." *Of which I am an active participant.* "That's uh, why I was working so late."

"You know, when I left home with you guys two months ago, it was to prove I was more capable than my brothers, not to be the first to end up in jail." Liss sighs. "At least they have no idea what's happening."

"Trust me, you aren't the only one happy their family is clueless right now." Liss and I share a knowing look, but out of the corner of my eye, I see Corrine looking down a little awkwardly, and I realize I've never actually heard her talk about her family before. "Sorry, Cor, what about your family? Do you want to write them a letter or something? It might take a while to get there, but I can make sure it's sent out." I checked with Khazak about how sending out mail from here might work, mostly out of morbid curiosity. While there's no spell-o-gram office in the city for obvious reasons, they've got a system for sending both regular mail and messenger pigeons from here.

"Actually, I'm an orphan." Liss's and my eyes go wide. "No, no! It's okay. I was raised by the church. I'm not even sure if I really *am* an orphan or not." She tries to give us both a cheerful smile.

"I am so sorry, Corrine. I had no idea." I feel like such an asshole right now. "Is there anyone else you wanna contact? Someone from the church?"

"Oh gosh, no. I can only imagine what Father Mitchell would say about this." She shakes her head quickly. "Thank you, though."

"How else are you doing?" Out of everyone in here, Corrine is probably who I'm most worried about. "Nate said they have you transcribing books?"

"Yes! It can be a little monotonous, but some of the books they have us working on are very informative. A lot about the history of the city or local customs. It's really interesting! Not that Nate thinks so." *I recall his complaints.* "I also joined this really nice Bible-study group with some of the other...prisoners." She hesitates on the last word.

"There's people who follow the same religion as you in there?" Khazak did mention that before.

"A couple! It's not a 'Bible-study' exactly—it's open to everyone," she starts recounting happily. "We all get together and recount stories and fables from our faiths, and then we compare to similar tales in others. There are so many parallels in scriptures from all over the world. It's fascinating!"

"That's great, Cor." I smile as I listen to my friend tell me about one of the few bright spots in her life, wishing I could somehow make it brighter.

"I'm a horrible friend," I croak as I leave the labor camp with Khazak.

"Why do you say that?" He follows after me, sounding concerned.

"Because I'm out here partying while they sit in jail." I almost wish I *had* woken up hungover, then I'd at least feel as bad physically as I do mentally. "I almost missed seeing them today because I was up all night drinking and dancing at a bar and on a dancefloor my friends set up!"

Things are silent for a moment. "I understand why you feel guilty, David, but this is beyond your control." The logical side of me knows that's true, but the rest of me wants to yell at that side to shut up. "Even though I know it does not feel this way, their predicament is not your fault, nor can you help the way your own has worked out. Even as misguided your attempts have been, you have done your best to help them."

"It just feels wrong to be having fun while they toil away in there," I grumble, stuffing my hands in my pockets.

A hand rubbing my back tries to offer me some comfort as we return home. It's still pretty early, and we don't have anywhere to be just yet, so after a small breakfast, Khazak coaxes me back into bed for a nap. I'm still tired from the morning, so it doesn't take much before I'm drifting off next to him.

"Feeling any better?" Khazak asks when he feels me wake a few hours later.

"A little." There's still some guilt, but I guess it's settled. "Still wish there was something I could do to help them."

"You have done and tried to do a lot for them, David. Including several *illegal* things you were nearly rearrested for yourself." *Oh hey, there's some more guilt.* "You have done all you can. The rest is out of your hands."

"Yes, Sir." I sigh.

"Come. We have a busy day ahead of us." He leads the way to the bathroom. "I am going to show you a few cleaning techniques to prepare for our 'demonstration' at Brull's."

"Can't I just use the charm?" That thing is unbelievably handy.

"Normally yes, but we will be getting dinner right after, and we will want to save it for our plans in the evening." That sounds a little ominous but also like it will probably be fun.

"Yes, Sir." I'm not supposed to use the charm more than once a day, but my butt also doesn't usually get this much attention in a single day.

After showing me what to do, I take a shower that is *far* more thorough than any shower I have ever taken before. *Never had to flush myself out before.* Definitely prefer using the charm for that sort of thing. After taking a shower himself, Khazak dresses us in outfits similar to yesterday's, though this time with a shirt to wear over my harness, at least temporarily.

After reattaching my leash, we leave for Brull's. Things seem even busier than they did yesterday, and the afternoon is just getting started. There's less dancing and partying given the hour, but just as much drinking as none of the bars look empty. When we reach the shop, there's a crowd gathered outside, milling around a small wooden stage that's been set up in front of the building.

Brull is on the stage, adjusting equipment. There's a small table with some items on it, a familiar looking padded bench, and a frame made of thick wooden beams, larger than a doorway, with a set of small metal hooks along the inside. Brull himself is decked out in his own gear, wearing a harness similar to Sir's, the bottom resting against his big green belly. He's got a pair of black leather pants on, but the only other things he's wearing on his upper body are a thick black armband on his left arm and a pair of gloves. I don't think there's a single thing on him that *isn't* leather. Not a bad look, honestly.

"Khazak!" Brull calls when he notices us. "Glad you could make it."

"Would not miss this for the world, friend." Sir steps up to the side of the stage.

"All done setting up out here. Let's go in the back so we can go over everything." Brull turns to the crowd. "Show starts in five minutes, everyone!"

The crowd shouts happily in response as the three of us move into the shop. There are a few customers, but most people are outside waiting for the show to start. The people I saw working behind the counter yesterday are still here, and we step past them into the back of the shop where we are alone.

"So, you decide on a game plan?" Brull turns to ask Khazak.

"Yeah, and were you going to let me in on it at any point?" Both orcs look at me, eyebrows quirked up. "Sir."

"I thought we would start with stripping him and putting in the new tail," Sir responds to Brull but makes eye contact with me as he talks. "Then we could tie and edge him in a few different positions and try a little flogging before the finale."

"Sounds good to me." Brull replies, both orcs eyeing me like a piece of meat.

"What do you think, David?" Khazak turns to me.

"I... I don't even know half of what you just said." Despite that, I'm still turned on.

"Do you trust me?" He walks forward into my space.

"...Yes?" Brull bellows a laugh at my response.

"Are you sure?" Khazak jokingly asks. "I promise you will enjoy this, pup. None of this is a punishment. It is meant to be a fun and enjoyable experience, one I trust Brull to be a part of. But if at any point it feels like it is becoming too much, I want you to say the word 'jailbreak,' and everything will stop."

"I trust you, Sir." I nod before pondering his word choice. "...Jailbreak, really?"

"I wanted something I would be sure you would not forget." He grins cheekily. "Shall we greet our audience?"

The three of us walk back outside to a burst of applause that grows as we climb onto the stage. Brull moves forward to address the crowd, and I look over at Khazak as he unbuttons his shirt, pulling it off dramatically when he's finished. I get why we overdressed now.

"Thank you all for coming to Flamemaul's!" Brull begins. *I don't think I knew that was his last name.* "As many of you know, Captain Khazak Ironstorm is a close personal friend, and today he has agreed to give a public demonstration on proper avakesh use and aftercare. I have of course provided all the equipment you see here myself, so please enjoy the show, and make sure you buy something! Remember, for all your leather and bondage needs, come see Flamemaul!"

"Strip," comes the order from Sir once Brull has finished advertising himself, and I move to obey. "Pants as well."

That part of the order has me blushing, and once I have my shirt off, Khazak takes it from me so I can kneel down to take care of my shoes. By the time those are both off, Khazak, Brull, and the entire audience are now staring at me. I stand, hesitating slightly before taking a deep breath and going for my belt. I hear a few shouts and whistles as I pull off my pants, exposing the blue jockstrap Sir put me in, but I ignore them and dutifully hand them off to my owner. After setting our clothes to the side, Sir grabs my harness, pulling me into him for a deep kiss.

"Inspection," comes the next order when we break apart.

I move into position, legs sliding apart slightly as my hands come up to cup the back of my neck. I face the audience, since I assume that's kind of the point, doing my best not to focus on any one face as they stare at me standing here in nothing but a collar, harness, and jockstrap. At least until I see Nylan in the crowd, standing next to Ragnar. *Wait, what?* I tilt my head when we lock eyes. I thought he worked today.

"I took a late lunch just for this," he shouts at me through cupped hands because of course he did. I roll my eyes.

The sound of a throat clearing to my right draws my attention back to an amused looking Khazak. I bow my head sheepishly, drawing some chuckles from the crowd. Brull moves to stand next to us, joining in with Sir to look over my body.

"Cute looking puppy you got here, Captain, but I think he's missing something," Brull states cheerily.

"I think you are correct. Turn around and grab the end of the bench, pup." He nods at the wooden contraption behind us.

"...Yes, Sir." I hesitate only a little, turning around and exposing my naked ass to the crowd, drawing even more cheers when I bend over to grab the end of the bench. Immediately, I feel not one but two sets of hands stroking along my back and butt, and I shiver at the contact. Brull hasn't been hands on with me before, really. Their touches feel different, and I can tell them apart right away. Khazak's hands are familiar and soft, aside from some small calluses on fingers from years of archery. Brull's are rougher, likely from all the years of working with metal, wood, and leather.

The hands leave me, and I hear rustling to my right, then the familiar sound of a bottle being opened: lube. I jump when I feel slick fingers prodding at my ass. Sir's form stepping up to my left side lets me know it's his. With his free hand, he strokes my chin, drawing my attention.

"Doing alright?" he asks me in a low voice.

I nod in the affirmative. I'm a little nervous...okay *a lot* nervous, but I can handle it. I mean, I was doing more than this in the tavern last night. Though I was at least kinda drunk then. The fingers probing me shake the thought from my head, but they're gone after a minute...only to be replaced with something bigger, blunter, and colder at my entrance by Brull, who comes up on my other side grinning. My breath hitches as it's pressed farther in, the object growing wide fast, but tapering off almost just as quickly. What I now know is a plug finishes sliding into place, making me shudder to more cheers from the audience.

"Much better. Why don't you give us wag, pup?" I turn my head to look back at the plug, trying to figure out what Brull is talking about, and am greeted with the sight of a short, furry, black dog tail protruding from my butt. The plug he's inserted has a tail attached. I see it shake slightly with the movement of my body, and I wiggle my ass intentionally to watch it wag back and forth, not unrealistically. The crowd eats it up.

"Good boy." Brull pats my butt and grins.

Khazak helps me stand up, which causes the plug to move, which feels *weird*, and I stutter in my movements. I'm turned back around to face the crowd, and I realize I'm also being positioned under the frame. I can see Brull already rigging rope through some of the hooks as I'm centered underneath it. Khazak helps hold me in place as Brull wraps the rope around my arms and wrists in an intricate pattern. When he finishes with each arm, he has me pull, testing the strength. He's good. I could probably break out if I really tried, but it would be a struggle and not very pretty.

My legs are kicked apart, and my arms are spread up and out along the beams, my chest exposed. Two sets of hands return to my body, gently stroking over my chest, stomach, and back. I shudder when a finger moves over an exposed nipple, earning me a chuckle from the larger orc on my left.

"Sensitive. You think about getting him pierced?" He teases my nipple again.

My eyes open wide and shoot to Khazak, who looks amused by my response. "We have not discussed it, no."

"Something to consider." I have to fight the urge to shake my head no. "Maybe I'll bring some clamps next time." *Clamps?!*

The hands continue to tease me, moving downward to my ass and groin. My dick is already tenting the front of my blue jock, and I hump forward at the first contact I feel on it. Khazak is the first one to reach my groin, hand ghosting over the fabric covering my cock before grabbing me more firmly. At the same time, I can feel Brull's hand grab my ass from behind, squeezing it appreciatively.

After a little more teasing, Sir pulls the pouch of my jock to the side, freeing my length from its entrapment. I can feel my hardness throb in the warm air. His hand returns, grasping me gently as he slides his thumb over my head, already slick with pre-cum. Behind me, fingers on the hand squeezing my ass delve toward my hole, pressing on the plug lodged within me and drawing a moan when I feel it push against my prostate.

The two sets of hands continue to tease me, roaming up and down both sides of my body, tweaking my nipples, tickling at my stomach and thighs, stroking my cock, and teasing my plug. At one point, Sir pushes two fingers into my mouth with the order to "suck." My arms are tied tightly to the frame above me, and I have no option but to accept everything being done to me. All while the audience watches, enraptured. I'm pretty sure a few of them are jerking off, but I'm not really paying attention.

The hands on my cock—they keep switching—keep bringing me close to the edge, only to pull away and leave me throbbing angrily in the air, seeking any sort of contact or friction. This goes on for I don't know how long, but by the end of it, I'm whimpering with need, pulling at my bonds and all but begging to cum.

"Ssshh, good boy," Sir soothes me, leaning in to stroke my face. "I think he has had enough; we can move on to what is next." The crowd cheers at Khazak's declaration.

"Aye aye, captain." Brull enjoys hamming it up.

Khazak gentles me as Brull moves around, untying and unwrapping the rope from my arms. By the time both arms are free, I'm no longer a leaking, horny mess. It's only temporary, as I am moved and turned around, my arms drawn behind me as I'm laid face down over the padded bench.

After aligning my arms how they want them, I can feel the rope returning to wrap around them.

This feels familiar, especially when my dick, which is still hard, is aimed down, its length on display along with my tail-plugged ass. The rope around my arms is tightened until they are immobile, settled into place on the small of my back. A quick spank delivers a jolt that has the tail wagging whether I mean it to or not. As the hand soothes my ass, Sir steps around to my front.

"How are you doing, puppy?" he asks low enough for only me again, searching my eyes.

"Good, Sir," I breathe out. I'm horny, maybe a little frustrated and starting to get that warm sink-y feeling, but I'm good.

"Good boy." Khazak leaves my side and returns to his spot behind me. "We are going to start with a paddle."

"*Start?*" My indignity is cut short by the first *whack*, making me yelp and the audience laugh.

The strikes with the paddle sting at first, though not as much as I would expect. That's partially because Sir isn't trying to hit me very hard but also because I think the paddle is made of leather and not wood. Not that I can see behind me to confirm. The smacks come in steadily, and after every few, they pause, a hand reaching forward to tease my cock and keep me at full hardness. I whimper, both at the contact to my dick and the paddle strikes once they start to build.

The sinking feeling only gets stronger the longer paddling goes on, and it almost feels like I'm floating on this bench, even with my arms behind my back. At some point, the paddling stops, and I hear movement behind me. I see Sir walk back around to my front, and I look up at him a little dopily. He smiles down at me, stroking a hand down my cheek softly, before raising his head and nodding.

The first strike of whatever Brull hits my ass with next is a surprise again, though I don't jump this time. I'm not sure what he's using; it feels like a single strike at first, but then a dozen tiny little pin pricks follow it. I don't have much time to contemplate, my eyes drawn to Khazak unbuttoning his pants and fishing out his cock, which he quickly feeds into my mouth.

Brull continues as my mouth is filled, hitting my skin almost rhythmically. A hand on the back of my head, Sir slowly fucks his cock in and out of my mouth. With my arms bound, I have little choice but to accept the assaults at either end, but I really don't mind. I've completely lost track of time. Hell, I barely remember there's an audience behind me; they've been watching silently since the paddling.

"Do you like your new tail, puppy?" The question has me tilting my head up, mouth still full. *It does feel good.* I nod my head slowly. "Do you want to thank Brull?"

I nod my head again as Khazak pulls himself out of my mouth and tucks himself away. Even with my mouth free, I don't feel like being verbal, watching quietly as he leaves my side again only to be replaced with Brull. The larger orc smiles down at me before making eye contact with Sir behind me, double checking something before he...unbuttons his own pants. *Oh. That's* how I'm thanking him.

His other hand goes behind my head as I come face to face with his dick. He's big, maybe as big as Khazak, but as it heads toward my mouth, I barely have time to register the size difference when I feel a big green hand spank my ass. I yelp, my mouth now full of Brull, as I feel another spank on the opposite cheek. Then a hand ghosts over my mostly hard cock, bringing it back to life once again.

The twin assaults continue unabated. Brull is rougher about fucking my face than Khazak was, while Sir is making sure to pay as much attention to my dick as he is to my ass.

Before long I find myself rocking back to meet his strikes, my cock so hard I'm certain I'm leaking. I know Brull is, the salty taste filling my mouth when he pulls back far enough for the hooded-head to pass over my tongue.

The warm feeling permeates every inch of my body. The spanks on my ass no longer sting, feeling more like a dull thudding against my skin. Each strike fades into more of that warmth that spreads through my body. The hand wrapped around me is stroking steadily, but Brull seems to be setting a rhythm all his own in my mouth.

"Shit, mind if I feed him?" Brull asks Sir above me.

"Go ahead" is the response. "Pup, swallow."

I don't really have much of a choice—Brull pulls back enough to leave the head of his cock in my mouth, hand coming up to wrap around his exposed shaft. He strokes himself quickly as his face screws up in concentration, and a minute later, I can feel his cockhead expand just before he explodes. With a low growl, Brull fills my mouth to the breaking point. I do my best to swallow but inevitably something spills out. The taste is similar to Sir's, but I can still notice a difference, and if I may, it's not as good. Not that cum tastes *great* to begin with. *You know what I mean!*

Brull lingers in my mouth, hand still on my head while my tongue seeks out any seed still hiding around the head and hood of his cock. Once he's satisfied with my cleaning job, he pulls out with a sigh. With nothing occupying my mouth, all my attention is focused on the things Sir is doing to my dick and ass, the steady spanks of his hand never ceasing. My dick feels impossibly hard, and if I had the leverage, I'd be fucking into his fist now. I don't, so I mostly just lay there and try to follow his hands as best I can. I can feel the tail moving left and right as I wriggle, and I can only imagine how silly I look.

"Do you want to cum too, puppy?" I try in vain to turn my head at the question, but I can't, so in response I just grunt in the affirmative as I nod and try harder to fuck his hand. "Just a little longer..."

I whine at the answer, desperate for more friction as the hand around my dick slows its strokes. My protests are ignored, the hands on my ass and dick continuing at their new pace. A minute later, the hands begin to speed up again, pushing me toward the brink once more. Then, once I'm getting close, they slow down again, drawing out another whine. This continues over and over, each time bringing me to the edge and each time backing off. My whines turn into growls, and I can hear Khazak laugh at my frustration.

"Careful there, pup." He spanks me twice in quick succession, and I whimper an apology. "Good boy. Now *cum*."

My cock explodes at the order, given at the same time as his hand connects with my sore cheek a final time. I moan, or groan, or maybe even yell as I shoot my load, no doubt coating the hand stroking me through my orgasm. At the same time, the crowd explodes with cheers, which is only partially a new experience.

Sir strokes me through each shot, releasing me only when he's sure I am empty. I lay there in a daze on the bench, drained both physically and mentally. That warm sinking feeling hasn't gone away, but I am becoming more aware of my surroundings, and I think I feel a chill coming on. Two sets of hands are on me again, stroking and gentling my body as my arms are untied and released. Once I can feel the blood circulating through them again, I'm helped to my feet and turned around slowly to face my audience. Their renewed applause makes me think about everything they just witnessed, and I bury my face against Sir's chest as it turns red.

"Alright, I hope you all enjoyed the show!" Brull steps forward to address everyone. "If you are interested in owning any of the implements you saw us use today on this cute pup, we can help you find everything you need inside the store as well as answer any of your questions. I hope you all enjoy the rest of your weekend!"

"Great job, David." I turn my head to see Nylan standing at the side of the stage with Ragnar. I smile at the compliment. "I gotta get back to work, but that was totally worth using my lunch break."

"We'll see you both later," Ragnar says from behind his elf, ushering him away so he's not late for the rest of his shift.

"Yes, I must say that was quite impressive, Captain." This new voice comes from the other side of the stage, and I turn to see an older, familiar looking orc watching us. His head is shaved, but he's got a big bushy beard, which is brown with flecks of grey. To his left, wearing a collar and attached to a leash, is another orc around the same age, though of a slightly larger build, shirtless with his nipples pierced. His head is also shaved, but his beard is black and trimmed short, right below the silver bullring hanging from his nose. The guy talking looks familiar, but where do I... *Oh.* He's the judge who oversaw my friends' trial after we were arrested. Which ended up being a very good thing in the end because sentencing them to the labor camp for two months is a relatively light punishment around here.

"Thank you, sir." Khazak straightens up at the praise. "I cannot take all the credit. He has taken to his training wonderfully."

The older orc looks at me then, and I do my best to straighten my posture, despite how out of it I feel. "Yes, I can see that you are a good match for each other. I hope you both enjoy the rest of the festival."

"You as well, Councilman." Sir gives a small bow as the two older men make their exit. When he turns to me, I can see how happy the compliment made him. I smile back as best I can, my eyes feeling droopy, but I can't suppress the shiver that follows. Khazak looks at me with a small amount of concern. "Brull, do you mind if we——"

"Go ahead, brother. You know where the bed is."

Khazak helps me walk inside the shop, which is filled with people now that the show is over. Even in my stupor, I can feel their eyes on us. Ignoring them aside from a friendly wave, Khazak walks us to the back room, then through another door just off to the side. It opens to a small room with a bed, a bathroom in one corner through an open doorway. This must be where Brull sleeps.

Pushing me onto the bed first, Sir climbs on behind me, pulling me into his chest once he's on the mattress. Stroking a hand down my back, I feel him reaching for the plug still lodged inside of me. Gripping the tail by the base, he gently tugs it out. My body expels it once it passes the widest point, and I whimper at the empty feeling it leaves behind.

"You did very good today, David." The praise is whispered into my hair. "I am very proud of you."

Still unable to bring myself to be verbal, I whine low, curling farther into his chest. I'm not sure why I'm feeling this way. Raw, tired, my body's temperature somehow both hot and clammy at the same time. I close my eyes, the dim light of the room helping me to relax and drift. The hand continues to stroke my back, and as the words of praise are whispered, I fall into a light sleep, Sir wrapped around me to keep me safe.

Chapter 6

Ⅰ wake to the feeling of a hand brushing along my back. *Khazak*. How long have I been out? The hand stills when my body stirs, allowing me to pull away.

"Welcome back." His voice is soft but teasing. "How are you feeling?"

"Okay, I think." I cuddle forward into him. "What *was* that?"

"It is called 'dropping.'" He keeps petting my back. "Sometimes, when things get intense as they did on stage, the body's hormones become elevated. Did you notice yourself feeling any different?"

"Yeah. It kinda felt like I was falling into a trance." I remember the warm floaty feeling from earlier. "It was almost like I was floating outside of my body."

"That is called subspace." *Good to know.* "Afterward, as you come down and your body's chemistry returns to normal, it can leave you feeling fatigued, or cold, or even depressed. It is something that can happen to either person involved, dominant or submissive. When I noticed the signs, I took you in here to rest."

"Will I be okay?" I'm not feeling exhausted anymore, but still a little sluggish and sorta just...down.

"Yes, some feelings may linger, but you are already sounding much better." His hand moves to my neck, and he thumbs my ear. "I would give it a few more hours."

"Do we have to go anywhere?" We're in Brull's bedroom right now I'm pretty sure.

"No." He chuckles. "We can stay here a bit longer."

Which is what we do, though not before Khazak beckons me to sit up and makes sure I drink a glass of water. There's a pitcher on the bedside table I'm not sure was there before. Then we just lay there together, cuddling, and slowly the melancholy feelings begin to fade. When I'm ready, I sit up, wanting to stretch my legs.

"Feeling better?" Khazak asks, sitting up to join me.

"Yeah, I think so." I look around the small room, spotting his bag and our clothing in a neat pile on the floor.

"Brull brought them in while you were napping," he tells me, seeing where my eyes fall. "Same as the water."

Aww. "I should thank him."

"You already have." He lightly thumbs my lip. "Remember?"

That certainly jogs my memory, and I get a flash of Brull feeding me his dick earlier and blush.

"Are you okay? Was it...alright?" He sounds nervous when he asks, watching my face carefully.

"Yeah, I wasn't expecting it but...it wasn't hard to get into." Despite some of his bristles, I like Brull. "But... I thought I remember you saying something about not sharing me?"

"I said I would not share you with my brother. *That* would be strange for what I hope are very obvious reasons." Glad to hear they aren't big fans of incest around here. "Brull is someone I trust, especially in *that* area. I had a feeling, should something happen, that you would feel comfortable with him."

"How did you know it would happen?" That was a gamble if you ask me. *Yeah, I still lie to myself sometimes.*

"I did not, for certain." Khazak stands and stretches his arms. "I knew he would be helping with the bondage, and that he would be flogging you, but for the rest, I waited. I wanted to see what would happen in the moment, what developed naturally. Had I sensed things going the other way, or had you said something, things would have proceeded differently." He runs his hand through my hair. "I would say it worked out."

"Yeah." I'm feeling bashful for some reason. "What did he...*flog* me with, anyway?" I'm only familiar with that term when it means like, getting lashed as punishment. Something that thankfully hasn't been done for years back home in Northlake.

"This." Khazak bends down to pick up an object lying next to his bag. "A cat-of-nine tails. He gifted us this one as a thank you for the demonstration."

In Khazak's hand is something that looks like a short whip. Well, several whips, all attached to the same black wooden handle. Each of the lashes are short and flat, strips of leather maybe a foot and a half long. The end of each strip is tied into a tight knot, which explains the thud I felt followed by pin pricks.

"Did you enjoy it?" He's gauging my reaction again.

I pause and think before nodding my head. "I'm not sure what I expected, but it wasn't that. It was different than being spanked, and it definitely helped with the whole... subspace thing."

"You looked amazing as you took it, and the marks it left on you were lovely." Khazak smiles as he places the flogging device into his bag before stepping over and putting his hand on my shoulder to turn me and look at my backside. "Pity they are already fading." Right then, my stomach growls. "Hungry?"

"I guess so." I put my hand on my belly. *Haven't eaten since breakfast.*

"Good." Khazak reaches out to help me up from the bed. "Because we have dinner plans."

We make a quick trip to the bathroom to freshen up, and I can't help but use the mirror to check out the marks he's talking about. The skin of my ass is pink, a few lines visible along the tops and bottom. I gotta admit, they look pretty nice. I trace my finger over one, biting my lip at the slight twinge of pain, which I oddly don't dislike feeling.

After that, the two of us get dressed. *Actually* dressed—the harnesses go in the bag, and our regular shirts are pulled on. It helps me feel a little more like a human again. A *person* again. We exit into the front of the store to say a quick goodbye to Brull, who is busy handling the evening rush. Looks like the night's festivities are just getting started.

We make our way out onto the streets, already packed with other festival goers. We wander around for a bit; I assume because we're still a little early for dinner. We watch another intense and dangerous looking fire-dancing performance where they seem to only barely miss burning their partner to a crisp. Khazak swears they aren't using any magic.

Eventually, my stomach's growling gets loud enough that we head to the restaurant. I can't read the sign on the place, of course, but Khazak tells me the name of the place is *Bauzi'kro*, which translates to "The Iron Pan.". It's no less busy inside, though it doesn't seem like we need to worry about getting a table when Khazak walks right in. I don't know what I was expecting, but it's just like any other restaurant. A large room filled with tables. Most of them are full, but I spot Ragnar and Nylan at the same time as Khazak.

"You guys having a good night?" Ragnar asks, retaking his seat after we've all hugged our hellos.

"For the last half hour this one has been awake." Khazak rubs my neck as he teases.

"Good nap?" Nylan asks me from across the table.

I nod, the weird nonverbal feeling returning now that we're around people again.

"Really great performance, guys," Ragnar tells us both. "I've been trying to get Ny to do something like that for years, but he's too shy."

"See, when David whines and moans, he sounds hot. When I do it, I sound high pitched and nasally." Nylan shakes his head. "Nobody wants to hear that."

"...Scared you can't take as much as me, huh?" I can't help but taunt the half-elf.

Nylan doesn't say anything—that might mean committing to something he's not sure he wants to do—but he narrows his eyes at my challenge. Our orcs both laugh, and the three slip into small talk with me occasionally adding something. A few minutes later, another familiar looking orc makes his way over to our table.

"Evening, boys. Enjoying the festival?" Rurig, one of Khazak's fathers, steps up to our table wearing a slightly stained apron. Khazak told me he owned part of a restaurant, but I didn't realize that's where we're eating.

"Yes, Ruda. Very much," Khazak answers with a smile. "Has it been busy?"

"Just look around." Rurig gestures to the full room. "I only even came in because they needed the extra hands." He looks over to Nylan and Ragnar slyly. "Good thing they did not need extra feet, eh?"

I laugh along with the two of them—Nylan even snorts—while Khazak groans. "You make that joke every time."

"Because it's funny every time," Nylan sucks up from his seat, a smart thing to do when food is involved.

"Flattery will get you everywhere, sweetheart." The stout orc ruffles Ny's hair with a warm grin. "What about you, David? Having fun?"

Even though I'm sure he has no idea what I've *actually* been up to, I still try and fail to not have my whole body turn red at the question. Then I remember I need to answer. "Yes, sir. It's been very, uh, interesting."

"I bet." My turn to get my hair ruffled. Then he picks up one of my arms, inspecting its size. "Still too scrawny. Good thing you are here to eat."

"Are the chefs the ones to come out and take the orders now?" Khazak tries to draw the attention off me.

"My own son, trying to get rid of me." Rurig puts his hand over his heart in mock pain. "Alright, what can I get you boys?"

Rurig takes Ragnar and Nylan's orders first before turning to Khazak and me.

"I will have the—"

"I know your order," Rurig cuts off his son with a wave of his hand, making Khazak roll his eyes. "What about you, kid?"

"I, uh." I haven't even looked at a menu. *Did we even get menus?* "I'm not sure what you—"

"You know what, I remember what you ate at dinner the other week. I am going to surprise you," Rurig cuts me off as well, and Khazak and I share a look. "Food will be out in a bit. First round of drinks is on the house!" With a smile and a slap to his son's back, Rurig leaves us, a female orc bringing over four mugs of beer a minute later.

Once the beer and conversation start flowing, I feel a little more relaxed and like my old self. I still don't have much to say, but I'm happy to sit and listen while Ragnar and Nylan talk about their day.

"So, the *same* customer who argued with me about that book title came back in today with a friend to back him up. No matter what I do, he won't believe me when I—food!"

Nylan spots our meal being carried toward our table on a large metal tray. I can see the steam rising from some of the plates—all except Nylan's salad. Ragnar got a steak, and Khazak a large meat-filled sandwich. It looks like I also got a steak, except mine is already cut up. Rurig knows I can use a knife, right?

I don't get much time to contemplate before an arm is around my waist, pulling me into its owner's lap. Who also happens to be *my* owner. I'm caught off guard by the sudden movement (and the fact that he's able to lift me so easily), and I look back at Khazak, wondering what's bringing this on. He hasn't fed me like this since...shit my first week with him, I think. A quick glance across the table reveals Nylan doing the same thing, Ragnar already bringing a forkful of salad to his elf's mouth.

In fact, a look around the restaurant shows plenty of couples doing this, men and women alike. That must be why my steak came pre-cut: to make it easier for Khazak. A few are even kneeling on pillows, including the man at the table right next to us. In fact... I think that's Councilman Bloodfield and his avakesh from earlier. They're seated with a woman who is as well-dressed as the councilman, and all three seem to be having a nice evening.

A forkful of steak tapping my lips reminds me that it's rude to stare, and I sheepishly take the bite while Khazak chuckles. After that, I forget about any awkwardness over my seat, leaning back against his broad chest and relaxing.

The more Khazak feeds me, the more I feel like my old self. I debate trying to eat the next few bites of steak sexily, but I'm not actually sure that's possible.

"You have something on your..." Khazak swipes a thumb against my lower lip after feeding me. Before he can pull it away, I dart my tongue out to lick it off, drawing the whole thing into my mouth. His eyes darken with heat when I nip it lightly before pulling back. Okay, I was wrong.

Later, when we're nearly done eating, I can't help but notice when the woman at the table next to us stands. She kisses the councilman on the lips, and his avakesh on the forehead before making her exit. The two male orcs look ready to leave themselves, and the councilman drops some coins on the table to pay as they both stand—noticing us when they turn around.

"Captain Ironstorm." He's surprised to see us again.

"Councilman Bloodfield." Khazak actually tries to stand with me still on his lap, only stopping when I flail, trying to keep my balance.

"No need for that, Captain." Bloodfield takes the seat Nylan was in previously, nodding for his avakesh to do the same in mine. "Are you all enjoying the festival? I suppose I do not need to ask you that." He winks at me, reminding me that he was in the audience for my earlier "performance."

"It has been a very enjoyable weekend so far," Khazak answers for the two of us.

"I actually had a question for you..." Bloodfield then starts speaking *very* fast in Atasi, and I am completely lost. I frown, the only one unable to understand the conversation. Still, it seems rude to ask a man of his age and rank to speak in another language just for my benefit, so I mostly just try to look like I know what's going on, to mixed effect.

"Your name is David, correct?" Bloodfield's avakesh asks me quietly, seeing through my ruse.

"Yeah, it's nice to meet you..." I hope I'm not supposed to already know this.

"Xugar." He flashes me a smile. "It is nice to meet you as well."

"Now you know what I sound like when I'm not whimpering and moaning." I wiggle my eyebrows.

"My master and I thought that was quite an impressive display, especially for someone so new to this." He sounds really formal but also genuine.

"Yeah, there have been a lot of 'firsts' in the last few weeks." *Most of them good.* "Like eating in someone's lap in public."

"My master and I dine here together every year." He smiles warmly at the thought.

"Can I ask who you were having dinner with earlier?" Seemed pretty intimate.

"My master's wife?" Yeah, okay, a wife is *definitely* intimate.

"I didn't realize." So, the councilman has a wife *and* an avakesh? Wow. Now I'm even more curious. "Do you..." I'm not sure how to word my question. "...Serve them both?"

"I serve my mistress in many of the same ways I do my master." He nods his head knowingly. "However, sexually is not one of them. She has retired for the evening to allow us to enjoy the festivities with one another."

"That's nice." They've got an interesting dynamic for sure. Though I'm just now realizing that I basically just asked about the councilman's sex life. "Sorry, I probably shouldn't be asking you about that stuff."

"It is alright. Learning too much about the sexual proclivities of a stranger is almost a festival tradition at this point." He looks over at the rest of the group. "For example, right now your kavan is telling mine the details of your first encounter. It sounds like you put up quite the fight."

I swivel my head around at Khazak who seems quite pleased to be telling this story. "What are you—" I'm cut off with a piece of steak, and I scowl at the orc as I chew. *He's lucky this is good.*

The conversion wraps up not long after that, Councilman Bloodfield standing with Xugar. "Well, I hope you men enjoy the rest of your evening, and I hope the two of you behave." He looks at Nylan and me before turning to Xugar. "Come, boy. We have *many* stops to make before we make it home tonight."

"Yes, master." Xugar bows to us before following his owner out of the restaurant.

The four of us wrap up our own dinner not long after that. Khazak leaves money on the table, despite the server telling us our meal has been covered. Benefit of being the owner's son, but Sir seems like the type to refuse that sort of perk when he can. Bellies full, the four of us head off for the rest of our night.

After some more walking around and letting our food settle, we end up at an outdoor tavern. We have a few drinks but take it much easier than we did the night before. Nylan and I actually manage to get the two orcs dancing without having to get them drunk first. I think we're only there for only an hour or two when Khazak tells us it's time to wrap up.

"Where are we going now?" I ask as we leave the tavern.

"The park, for the final part of our night." He turns to Ragnar on his right. "You have the ticket?"

"Right here." He pats his left pocket.

"What's happening in the park?" *Besides more surprises, apparently.*

"You will see." Khazak smiles knowingly.

What I see when we approach the park is dozens of tents spread across the grass and among the trees. There are light stones set up on poles at various points, each softly glowing in a different color. I hear music being played from somewhere, the low thrum of a drum beat in the background. The fabric the tents are made of is near-translucent, the shadows of the people already inside visible from a distance. When we get closer, I can see that each one is just a large bed pallet with a canopy. I feel a stab of guilt. *This is what Liss and Adam were setting up.*

Ragnar hands a slip of paper to an orc on the outskirts of the park, who looks at it before leading us to one of the tents. Ragnar and Nylan climb in first with Khazak and me right behind. The base of the tent is essentially a large mattress with a short wall of pillows along the edge, and each couple settles on opposite ends of the "floor."

"So, what happens now?" I'm asking all the dumb questions tonight.

"We enjoy a night under the stars together." Khazak pulls me down to lay with him.

That sounds kinda nice, if not cheesy. Then I hear a moan coming from somewhere else in the park, and I remember what this festival is really all about. *Also, we're literally on a giant bed right now.*

"I got us something *else* for tonight, too." Ragnar reaches into his pocket to produce a small round tin.

"Really? You do not think we are getting a little too old for that?" Khazak looks at the tin unimpressed.

"Oh what, grandpa? Not cool enough anymore?" Ragnar mocks as he removes the lid, dipping a finger in. His fingertip emerges covered in a dark liquid that he proceeds to suck into his mouth while Nylan does the same. "Besides, David's still young." He closes and hands the tin over to Khazak.

"What is it?" Besides some kind of drug, obviously.

"*Ruhax*. A narcotic, and technically a poison." Khazak uncaps the tin. "In large amounts, it can make you sick and cause you to hallucinate, but in small doses, it stimulates and enhances your senses. It lasts several hours."

"Is it...safe?" I am admittedly curious. I've smoked weed a few times, back at the Academy, but never so much as tried anything else.

"Safer than many other drugs." He shows me the contents of the tin. "As it is a poison, should something go wrong, I would be able to help you, or we could take you to the healer's clinic. Please do not feel obligated to take any just because these two did."

"...I'll try it." He's not exactly talking it up, but he's not saying that he doesn't want to do it either, and he's right that his magic should be able to help if it gets to be too much. *Right?*

With a small smile, he dips his index finger into the liquid, coating it more than Nylan or Ragnar. He swipes the finger along his tongue as he snaps the lid shut before grabbing me by the back of the neck and kissing me deeply. I can feel the liquid on his tongue as it pushes against mine, but it doesn't taste like anything. The kiss goes on longer than I'm expecting, and by the time he pulls away, I almost don't remember why he kissed me in the first place.

"It will take at least a half an hour, possibly a little longer, before we start to feel anything," Khazak tells me, pulling me to rest alongside him. "Plenty to do until then."

He's not wrong, though most of those things seem to be kissing. A lot of kissing. *Not a complaint*. It starts slowly at first, the two of us on our sides, Khazak bringing his lips to mine as we lay against the pillows. His kisses are soft, his beard scratching gently against mine as his tongue gently maps my mouth. One of his hands is on my side, rubbing up and down my hip. The sound of lips smacking coming from the other side of the tent says that Ragnar and Ny are doing the same.

Of course, all the kissing and touching gets me worked up in no time. It's made worse when I feel a hand come up and unbutton my shirt, dipping in to run over my chest. I shiver when he passes over a nipple, suddenly needing more contact. First, I try grinding against him, then when that doesn't move things along, I try to climb on top of him, all without ever removing my lips from his.

"Easy, pup." Khazak laughs as he pulls back. "We have all night."

I whine in frustration. *Just because we have all night doesn't mean I don't want more now.* Still, I let Khazak continue to kiss me at the pace he sets while he very slowly undresses the both of us. I make a noise of protest when his hand reaches for my belt, but a quick glance over reveals Nylan in nothing but a black thong, straddling Ragnar's lap, so I relax while I'm stripped to my blue jockstrap.

"Alright, there's something I've been wanting to see," Ragnar tells us over Nylan's shoulder before leaning down to whisper in his ear.

Nylan looks over at me, a strange smile on his face. Then I notice Ragnar reaching into his pocket again—this time pulling out a cleansing charm that he places on Nylan's belly. I look back at Khazak, who is already holding our own charm and does the same to me.

"Why do you not go and see if there is something Nylan wants?" Khazak whispers in my ear before sending me to the center of the tent.

It takes me a second to register the implication in Khazak's question, but the knowing look Ny gives me when I turn to face him clues me in. *Oh.* I kneel up, shuffling over to him.

"Hi," I say, nervous as a teenager.

"Hi." He smirks before leaning in to kiss me.

Kissing Nylan is different from when I kiss Khazak. Softer, less intense. It actually reminds me a little of kissing girls, though thankfully my dick seems able to tell the difference. It's more at attention now than it ever was then. I reach my hands out for his waist, pulling him closer, and I can feel his erection brush against my own.

We fall onto our sides together, inching closer as we keep kissing. I feel Nylan's hand moving from my chest around to my back, and then down to grab my exposed ass. I do the same to him, feeling his mostly smooth butt under my fingers and squeezing. Our bodies flush, the kissing gets more intense, when I am overcome by the sudden urge to pin Nylan to the bed. I flip him onto his back, quickly settling between his spread legs and resume our kissing frenzy.

"Seems your pup fancies himself a top," Ragnar comments on my right.

"To be fair, he has not yet had the opportunity to be anything other than my bottom," Khazak adds on my left.

A bottom? I'll show them a bottom. With a growl, I grab Nylan's wrists, pinning them above his head. This unfortunately has the opposite effect from what I intended—everyone laughs, including Nylan. *Jerks.*

"Alright, boys. Let's lose the underwear," Ragnar orders.

"Yes, please do," Khazak agrees.

Releasing Nylan's limbs, I sit up, moving slightly to the side so that both of us can slide off our underwear. Ny throws his toward Ragnar, and I do the same with Khazak, and there's a brief beat of awkwardness before he pulls me back on top of him, continuing our make out session. There's a little moaning as our two dicks grind against each other before Nylan pushes back on my chest.

Flipping to lay on his other side, Ny inches his face to my crotch. He wastes no time in swallowing my cock down to the hilt, no indication he's going to gag whatsoever. I groan in surprise at the wet heat that surrounds me, then notice I'm face to face with his own cock. Not to be outdone, I grab the half-elf by the ass and haul him forward, sucking him down in return.

"Fuck, that's something else I've been waiting to see." I hear Ragnar's voice coming from behind me.

"It is a rather nice sight." And that's Khazak from the other side. "Perhaps we should have set something up sooner."

Nylan and I ignore them for the most part, both slowly bobbing up and down the other's length. He's got a decent sized cock, not that I have that many to compare to. He's smaller than Khazak, Brull, or even myself, but I don't know that he's actually *small*. I have to shake the thoughts from my head; this isn't what I should be focusing on right now.

I know I've sucked a dick before, but this is still different than what I'm used to. For one, it's not green, as the only other two dicks that have been in my mouth have been. The position is also different: when I open my eyes now, I'm face to face with Nylan's ballsack. Since his length is easier to handle, my nose brushes against it every time I sink down. Soon though, I stop examining our differences and fall into a steady rhythm of swallowing him.

Nylan's hands roam up and down my ass and thighs. He grabs me, squeezing and kneading my ass as he pulls me closer to his mouth. I copy his movements, gripping his smooth cheeks in my hand, and soon enough we are humping each other's mouths in the center of the tent. I don't even notice at first, but at some point, it seems like the rhythm we settle into matches the beat of the music outside.

Nylan is the first one to change things up again, flipping us so that I'm on my back while he straddles me. After a little more sucking, he hooks his arms behind my legs and pulls them back, exposing my ass to the air. Then, after letting my cock fall from his mouth, he licks his way down, past my balls and *right* over my hole. *Fuck.* He starts eating my ass immediately. *Two can play at that game.* I pull my mouth off his own dick, maneuvering his ass so it's directly over my face. This close I can see that he's not as hairless as I thought, a fine dusting of peach fuzz covering his rump, which I dive right into. *It's a good thing we're both so flexible.*

"Fuck," I hear Khazak mutter.

"You said it," Ragnar adds.

The two are content to let us go on like that for a while, but eventually I notice the weight shifting around us, and a shadow looming over me. Releasing Nylan's ass and letting my head fall back, I see Ragnar standing over my face, cock jutting out with a bead of pre-cum gathered at the tip. I don't have to wonder what he wants, as a second later my own legs are dropped, the sounds of Nylan's mouth being stuffed letting me in on what Khazak is doing. Tapping his cock against my lips, Ragnar enters my mouth.

He moves in and out slowly at first but picks up speed until he's shallowly fucking my face. All I can see from this angle is the bottom of his cock, his balls, and his legs, and if it weren't for Nylan's weight on top of me, I might forget there was someone else here at all. At least until I feel a cool, slippery finger snaking its way toward my hole. Judging from Nylan's moans, I bet Ragnar is doing the same. *How long have they been planning this?*

The feeling of my ass getting filled, even with fingers, is not an unpleasant one; my moans join Ny's. I'd love to imagine the picture the four of us make right now, but all I can focus on is the feeling of being filled at both ends, the smell and taste of Ragnar's cock, and the low thrum of the music in the background. I'm feeling warm and maybe a little tingly, and I'm not sure when that started, but *something's* happening.

Above me, I hear and feel Ragnar give Nylan a tap on the ass before shuffling back from my head. The elf rolls off me to the side, releasing his own hold on my owner's dick. Before I have a chance to move, I'm gathered up until I'm straddling my Sir's lap, his wet cock slapping up against me.

"How are you feeling?" he asks, searching my face closely.

"Good, I think." I'm sweating, but not in a bad way. Everything feels just a little heightened. Even Khazak's hands stroking my skin have a spark to them. "Warm, kinda tingly."

"Hmm, your pupils are dilated, so I would say the ruhax has taken effect." He smiles, drawing me in for a kiss before pushing me to lay back.

My legs are lifted to his shoulders as he shuffles closer on his knees. Turning my head, I can see Nylan having the same done to him, giving me a grin when he looks over. I can see what Khazak means about pupils—Nylan's are blown wide. Above us, the sheer white of the tent canopy is bathed in blues and purples as the light stones outside glow. I feel the slick head of Khazak's cock pressing against my hole only moments before he breaches it.

I moan as my owner stretches me open once again, looking up at his furry muscled chest and stomach. He keeps pressing forward until he's fully inside of me, only pausing for a moment before he pulls back and begins to fuck. I don't know if it's the drug or maybe our warm-up earlier in the day, but it only takes a few strokes before I can feel the pressure of my first orgasm starting to build.

"Shit, already?" Ragnar asks as I fall over the edge a couple of minutes later.

"I told you," Sir hums appreciatively, rubbing his hand along my stomach. "He has only gotten more responsive the longer I have known him."

As if to prove his point, Khazak takes his time fucking me through four more. At first his hands are tight on the backs of my legs, pressing them to my chest as he pumps himself in and out of me. Between orgasms #2 and #3, he flips me onto all fours, hands gripping my waist tightly as he pulls me back onto his dick. I can barely form a coherent thought with all the sensations running through my body.

Not sure how long we've been at it now, but I earn a break of sorts after that. I'm pulled backward onto Khazak's lap, his length still lodged firmly inside of me. I whimper as the thick trunk of his meat is jostled, pressing harshly against my prostate, but then a hand on my chest is stroking gently, a water flask held to my lips. Open mouthed kisses are pressed to my neck and shoulders, Sir's tusks butting gently against my skin.

Once things are calmer, he starts to rock himself into me gently. It's much less intense and much less likely to have me cumming uncontrollably, which is exactly what I need right now. I relax, resting against Sir's shoulder and almost dozing.

"You know, all these years it's been me sharing my avakesh with you." Ragnar's voice has me lifting my head sometime later, looking across at the couple seated similarly to us. "Seeing as you already let that old perv Flamemaul go first, it seems only fair that I get a turn."

"I'd like to see that," Nylan adds with a horny smile.

There's something about Ragnar's words, the way he casually asks Sir to use me, that has a familiar heat pooling in my stomach. The fact that his own slave and lover is on board certainly doesn't dissuade me. I turn my head to look at Khazak to see he's already looking back at me, contemplating an answer.

"That 'old perv' is the same age as your boy there, but I suppose that is fair." With just the *hint* of a sadistic glint in his eye, Sir lifts me from his lap, his length slipping out of me as he pushes me over to Ragnar.

His lap now elf-free as Nylan crawls over to Khazak, I climb onto Ragnar, straddling his waist, his cock grinding against mine. I'm not exactly sure how he wants me, but this seems like a good place to start. *He's not telling me no.* A hand on the back of my neck draws me closer, his mouth meeting mine. His other goes to my ass, squeezing as he grinds our crotches together, making me moan into his open mouth.

The hand on my neck joins his other on my butt to lift me higher, letting his cock slip behind me. One arm around his neck, I take the initiative and reach back to guide him toward my hole. *What? I wanna know how he measures up.*

I've been in this position before with Khazak, but it's still a little awkward finding the right angle. There's a brief moment where I'm grumbling into Ragnar's mouth, but once I find it, I sink right down. He's not as thick as Khazak, I already knew that, but *wow*, he has this slight curve up that strokes *right* over that one spot. I shudder as I make my way to the base. Then the hands on my ass are grabbing and lifting me before dropping me *right* back down.

"Fuck," I curse, breaking our kiss.

"Don't mind if I do." *Ugh, he's worse than me.*

His hands still on my ass, he uses them to hold me up slightly, and with the extra space, he snaps his hips up to meet mine. I yelp, bracing myself against his shoulders as he fucks up into me. I feel my dick between us, half-hard and occasionally slapping against his skin. He doesn't tire of his position or pace, pausing occasionally only to take a quick breather. It doesn't take long before I can feel myself building to another climax—the first one not brought on by Khazak.

"Gonna...cum," I feel the need to announce.

"*Fuck yeah*," Ragnar growls, unable to stop himself from fucking me a little faster.

Still gripping his shoulders tightly, I look past him and outside the tent. For the first time, I notice there are figures walking around. I wouldn't exactly call it a crowd, but there are definitely people gathering, walking around, and peering into tents like very public peeping toms. It seems that is the intention, in fact. And of course, just as I finally feel myself cresting over the edge, just as Ragnar slams me down onto his lap to really feel my hole spasming on his length, I lock eyes with someone looking into ours.

I think that might have made me cum even harder than usual.

The people don't go away as Ragnar pounds into me, but I stop looking at them, worried I'll feel too self-conscious to continue. I close my eyes, pulling back to kiss Ragnar more as my hips begin moving of their own accord. I manage to wring one more out of myself while riding his pole before he takes back control, which I remember is something I really, really like.

I'm a little fuzzy as to how long Ragnar has me to himself, but at some point, we move. Nylan is now in the center of the tent, lying on his stomach. I am also in the center of the tent, right on top of *and* inside of Nylan. *Another first!* Ragnar kneels in front of us, his thick and angry looking cock being passed back and forth between our mouths. Behind us, Khazak is bent over, face to my ass as he laps at my hole, his hands on my hips driving me in and out of Nylan.

I nuzzle down against Nylan's neck, gently nipping at his pointed ear as my hips pump up and down above his ass. I'm starting to get overwhelmed by the sensations: the warm thick tongue prodding at my hole, the tightness around my cock, the sounds from Nylan's mouth (when it isn't stuffed with orc dick).

Soon I can add the feeling of my own ass being filled as Khazak climbs over the both of us, his still-slick cock prodding against my hole for only a second before sliding all the way in. I groan, overcome by the feeling of stuffing and being stuffed at the same time. Each time he snaps his hips down, he fucks me farther into Nylan, pulling more moans from the half-elf's mouth. Ragnar soon takes his turn in my mouth, Nylan licking against the base of his owner's shaft and balls while I'm filled at both ends.

Deciding he needs more leverage, Khazak pushes himself up on his hands. I whimper as he slips out of me, then he's pulling me back with him, positioning me on my hands and knees. Not hard to figure out what happens next, and he re-enters me as I look across to see Ragnar has turned Nylan around to do the same.

We're both of us on all fours, only inches from each other's faces as our owners resume their fucking. Each time they press in, we are pushed forward a little more, until we are finally close enough for our mouths to meet. Moaning eagerly, the two of us kiss as we are thoroughly fucked face to face.

"Oh fuck," Nylan whispers pulling away, face screwed up as he lets out a high-pitched *squeak* of a whimper as he's fucked though his own anal orgasm.

I quickly recapture his mouth, especially since I feel my own rapidly approaching, and I'd rather muffle my own sounds. If things continue—and I have no reason to doubt that they will—they are going to start getting very, very intense. As the orgasm crashes over me, one of my hands reaches blindly for Ny's, squeezing tightly as I'm fucked through...fuck, is it seven or eight now?

I'm not actually trying to keep track. *I bet someone watching outside the tent is.* Doesn't matter. Our two men seem to have found their position and tempo of choice, and two sets of hands continue to almost bruise our hips as they fuck us in the night air. Nylan and I can barely keep ourselves up, both our chests collapsing to the mattress at some point during the fuck fest.

Our hands still grip each other tightly and our faces are turned together, though neither of us is actually able to focus on the other. I can feel myself drooling, and my eyes roll back as I start to ride another prostate-gasm, the muscles in my hole fluttering weakly against the bulky invader. I have no idea when either of the orcs are going to cum; I'm not sure they're even *trying* to cum. I'm not sure of anything right now. *I didn't think having your brains fucked out was a real thing.* Maybe they'll get so fucked out I won't remember enough of this in the morning to feel shame.

I doubt my ass is gonna let me forget.

Chapter 7

"**And every time he would cut off one of its heads, two** *more would grow in its place!*"

Mikey whimpers on my left. He never did like stories about fighting monsters all that much.

Meanwhile, I'm practically bouncing in my seat. "How did he finally kill it, Yaya?"

"He had help." *Our grandmother smiles down at us warmly.* "His nephew, Iolaus, waited nearby with a torch. Each time the Hydra lost one of its heads, Iolaus would use the torch to seal the neck closed and stop any more heads from growing back."

"Wow." *I am in awe.*

"Sounds scary." *I look over at Mike, who is curled into himself.*

"Hey, 's not scary," *I scooch closer to him and put my arm around his shoulder,* "'cause if we ever have to fight a monster, we have each other. Right?"

"Right." *He nods, smiling at me a little more confidently.* "What happened next, Yaya?"

The sun is shining in my eyes, and it makes me roll over and bury my face into my pillow. Wait, why is the sun in my eyes? Did we forget to close the curtains? It's never this bright in the morning in our bedr—

Memories of last night begin filtering back into my head: meeting up with Ragnar and Nylan for dinner, walking to the park, the tin of ruhax... I can see that I'm still on the bed pallet. We all are; Khazak is spooned up behind me while Ragnar and Ny are on the other side in a similar position. I'm the only one awake.

We're covered by a sheet, but a quick look underneath confirms that *yep*, still naked. I look around and see our clothes piled in one corner next to Khazak and Ragnar's bags. I think for a minute about how I can get from here to there and dressed without anyone noticing.

Then I pause.

You took part in what was essentially an outdoor orgy last night, David. You didn't just have sex with Khazak, you also had sex with his best friend and his best friend's boy/partner/slave. You were practically performing for an audience at certain points. Maybe... Maybe you can just chill out. Maybe, since you're definitely not the only naked person in the park right now, you can just go back to sleep and enjoy the morning.

I roll over, burying my face in Khazak's chest—might as well use all that bulk to block out the pesky sun. My movements make him shift, pulling me in closer and throwing a leg over mine. I smile and relax, not quite dozing off but resting. My body could certainly use it, all sorts of soreness making itself known the longer I'm awake.

It's at least an hour before the others stir. I've heard a few of the other park patrons stumble their way home by now, and I guess it's our turn. I shift over when Khazak sits up to stretch his limbs before he falls back onto the pillows and turns to look at me, sleep still in his eyes.

"Good morning." His voice is rough from the night.

"Morning." *So is mine.* I move back into his space. The morning air isn't cold, but the body heat is still nice.

"Did you sleep well?" He leans his weight against mine.

"Think so." I nod against his chest.

"Mornin' guys," Ragnar greets us, while Nylan grumbles and pulls the sheet over his head next to him. "He says 'good morning' too."

"Good morning," Khazak answers for me.

"We're still meeting up later, yeah?" Ragnar stretches as he asks.

"That is still the plan, yes," Khazak agrees before yawning.

"Good. Because after last night, I need a shower and at least three more hours of sleep." Ragnar pauses as his stomach growls. *For once, it's not mine.* "And a really big breakfast."

"Me too." Nylan's head finally pops up.

"Oh, you gonna join us now that you're hungry, boy?" Ragnar smirks down at the elf.

"Sorry, Sir." The elf stretches himself over his owner's lap, face down. "I guess all that meat you fed me last night just wasn't very filling."

smack Ragnar spanks the on-display rump in front of him. "Smart-ass."

The four of us get ready to leave after that. After getting dressed (and Khazak leaving a *very* generous tip for the people who presumably have to clean all this up), we climb out of the tent and exit the park. There's a little talk about getting breakfast together somewhere, but I think everyone really just wants to go home and clean up, so we split up there.

Once we're home, we head straight for the shower together. We spend the first fifteen minutes or so just standing under the hot water, letting the water running over our sore muscles. I can't even remember half the positions

I was bent into last night, but there's plenty of stickiness in my butt to let me know none of it was imagined.

We don't go back to sleep, but we do spend the rest of the morning on the couch, not really doing much of anything. I know Khazak and Ragnar mentioned meeting up again later in the day, but I'm not sure what for. It's only when we're eating lunch that I get any real information about our plans for the night.

"So, what are we doing tonight, exactly?" I hope it's nothing crazy. I can't believe I'm saying this, but partying three nights in a row might be too much.

"We are seeing a play." Oh, that doesn't sound bad at all.

"A play?" I saw a few of those in school, but that was years ago. "What's it about?"

"I think you will like it," Khazak tells me as he cleans our plates. "It is about the honorees of the festival, one of whom was a founder of the city."

That does sound interesting, especially when you consider everything going on at this festival. *Must have been a pretty cool guy.* I'm surprised that the clothes Khazak pulls out are a little on the boring side. I know it's the last day; it's just been kinda fun getting to wear things that are less-than-normal out in public. Though around here, they're not *that* out of the ordinary.

When we leave the house, I realize I still don't know where we're going. *Have I even seen a playhouse in town?* When I notice that we're heading in the same direction as most of the other people out right now, I figure out that we are going to the arena. They must use it for more than just fights. That brings up some weird feelings. We haven't been there since...

Since I challenged Khazak to a fight, lost, and got fucked in front of a crowd of people.

After that, he owned me. Technically forever, if that's what he wants, but thankfully, he only wants to own me for the amount of time my friends will be in jail. There have been a few hiccups since then, but I think we've managed to reach an agreement and establish a nice friendship. A friendship-with-benefits. *Really fun benefits.*

We walk around to the north side of the building, where we're supposed to meet Ragnar and Nylan. As we approach the doors, the crowd slows down, everyone congregating into lines. We join one briefly but step to the side once we're in the lobby, looking around for our friends. We spot them looking at one of the wooden panels along the walls. The bottom floor of the arena is covered in them, each one depicting a different scene.

"*Zratza*, Ragnar," Khazak calls as we approach them. *That's the Atasi word for hello.*

"There you are!" Ragnar turns to face us before throwing his thumb behind him. "Have you guys seen this yet?"

"Seen what?" Khazak asks as we both step around him to look at the panel.

It's...*us.* The scene on the panel—it's the two of us. At least I think it is. I can only see half my face. It shows Khazak on the right, his sword drawn back as he charges toward me on the left. I have my own sword drawn, and it looks as though I'm about to leap out of the way. I think this might be the final moments of the fight, right before my false win, when I had *him* on the ground.

"Is that...?" I need confirmation that I'm not seeing things.

"You and me?" Khazak is looking at the panel in awe. "Yes, I believe so."

"Why?" It doesn't look like he expected this either.

"All the panels adorning the Hall of Honor depict great battles or performances that took place here." He looks over at me, proud. "It would seem ours made the cut."

Something about the way he's looking at me makes me blush, and I'm glad when Ragnar cuts in a second later.

"Alright, quit staring at yourselves so we can find a place to sit before all the good seats are taken." I can hear the people filling the stands above us.

We rejoin the crowd as they file their way up the stairs and into the stands. The front rows are all taken, but we manage to find something in the middle. Once we sit down, I get a look at how the arena is set up. At the center is what looks like a small camp: a number of tents set up around a fire. There are even a few trees spread out, setting the opening scene. There's no backdrop, which means the stadium's full audience can view the proceedings.

People around us continue to fill the stands, and I can see from across that the place is pretty packed. Everyone is talking but not about anything important, just waiting for the show to start. When one of the gates on the arena floor opens, the audience breaks into applause.

Two older women walk through the open gates, both orcs with black hair pulled back into a bun. They're the same two women I talked to before my fight, who offered to help me "prepare." *They must be in charge around here.* The two of them step onto the stage, the crowd going silent as they address everyone in unison.

"They are making a small introduction. This is the sixty-fifth year of the festival, and this play has been performed at each one." Khazak leans over to translate for me. "It is about to begin."

With a flourish, the two women cast a spell that blankets the arena floor in a thick fog. I can see the silhouettes of people as they move through it but can't make out how many or who, not until a minute later when the fog dissipates to reveal a now populated stage. As soon as the fog is gone, the action begins.

A group of orcs now populates the camp. I count six in total, all wearing very heavy looking brown leather armor.

I say heavy-looking because as thick as it seems, the actors seem able to move in it very easily. It's also very exaggerated, the shoulder pads flourishing in ways that make no sense for battle. *Stage armor.* The focus seems to be on three orcs in the center who are talking. I have no problem hearing them, thanks to whatever magic is being used to amplify their voices, but that doesn't mean I can understand them.

"The one on the left with the longer black hair? That is the 'hero' of the story, the head of the Steelrun clan, and the leader of the entire Proudhunter tribe," Khazak whispers, pointing at the tall orc with very broad shoulders on the left. "Their scouts have reported an impending attack from an opposing tribe, the Ragebloods, with whom they have an intense rivalry."

Well, I guess as long as I have Sir here to translate for me, it won't be so bad. "What's his name?"

"Khazak." *Wait, what?*

I don't get any clarification because at that exact moment six *more* orcs appear, all clad in black-colored armor. Like literally from out of nowhere—I assume through more magic. A fight breaks out with each orc conveniently having their own sparring partner. Funny how that works out.

All six pairings break into their own skirmishes, spreading out into the arena. The weapons of choice seem to be swords, but I spot a couple of axes in the mix as well. One by one, each fight resolves, mostly with the interlopers being defeated, sometimes in death. One of them manages to escape, running back through the open arena gate after taking out his attacker.

There are only two orcs still standing. One is our main character, "Khazak," and his opponent is a smaller orc with short brown hair, wearing the same black armor as the rest of his compatriots. While the larger orc is clearly stronger, this guy is a lot faster, moving with much more finesse—dodging, rolling, even flipping out of the way. It's impressive, even knowing they probably had weeks to practice.

The smaller orc manages to trip stage-Khazak, sending him tumbling to the ground. Sword in hand, he rears back, ready to end things...when at the last second Khazak rolls out of the way and trips him in return. He is quickly disarmed on his way down, Khazak standing with his sword posed at his enemy's neck in victory. *Yeah, okay, maybe I'm seeing a few similarities here.*

In the aftermath of the battle, the remaining orcs gather together once again. It looks like the "good guys" lost two men, but so did the invaders with the third running away. The three remaining black-armored orcs are pushed to their knees in the center, where "Khazak" grips his opponent roughly by the hair and speaks down to him before the stage is filled with fog again.

"He was declaring his tribe's victory and speculating that they would make good use of their new prisoners." Khazak quickly fills me in on what his stage counterpart was saying.

"Wait, can we go back to the part where he has the same name as you?" *Are we not going to talk about that?*

"Yes, he does, and the orc he just defeated is the play's other hero." Khazak points to the action resuming on stage. "His name is Vakesh of the Gorecrash clan."

The fog dissipates to reveal a new scene. The tents have been moved to the sides and in the center is what looks like a fighting ring. Standing around it are at least a dozen orcs, all wearing the same brown colors as the orcs in the first scene. Inside of the ring are two orcs in the middle of a fight, both stripped down to only loincloths.

It's over pretty fast—a few punches are swung before it turns into a wrestling match with one orc quickly pinning the other to the ground. Outside the ring, a more official-looking orc (*I dunno, it's his clothes or something*) says something that causes the orc winning the grapple to drop his opponent, a triumphant smirk on his face. As the other orcs cheer, he drags the defeated orc off to one of the tents, his captive barely putting up a struggle. *Not hard to figure out what's gonna happen there.*

The orc says something else and gestures for two new opponents to enter the ring: Vakesh and Khazak. They are dressed the same as the last duo, both clad in a pair of loincloths. The two move to opposite sides of the ring, Khazak looking cocky while Vakesh is considerably more nervous. The orc overseeing the match shouts, and the two leap into action.

Another fight starts, one which sees Vakesh on the defensive, dodging wherever he can. He's got a lot less room to work with here, and things end the same as the last fight with the new prisoner pinned to the floor by his opponent. I'm expecting the rest of the scene to play out the same way, the two of them going back to a tent, but it doesn't. Khazak rears up and declares something loudly to the gathered orcs around him. Expecting a translation, I'm instead hauled into the lap of *my* Khazak. I look back at him questioningly.

"I thought it would be easier to translate this way." He shrugs, but the playful look on his face says otherwise. "Khazak just declared his intent to personally own Vakesh."

The last orc didn't do that when he won, but whatever. *Drama!* I figure that's where the scene will end and am once again surprised when the Khazak on stage keeps one of Vakesh's arms pinned to his back, reaching down with his free hand to tug the smaller orc's loincloth down past his ass. Then he reaches into his own and pulls out his dick. His very erect dick that I somehow didn't notice until just now. *What?!*

I want to turn around and ask, but I'm too mesmerized by the action in front of me. Stage-Khazak spits into his hand, slicking it over his cock before angling his hips down and slamming into Vakesh, straight to the hilt. He *really* starts to fuck him too, and as much as Khazak seems to be enjoying it, Vakesh is clearly struggling. His face is contorted, if not pain then at least discomfort, as he is pounded into. If Khazak—my Khazak—had fucked me like that the first time, I'm not sure I would have taken to it the way I have. No kissing, no prep work, just right to business.

That doesn't mean it's not still hot to watch—and knowing they're acting certainly helps me not feel guilty. I'm not the only one who thinks so either, judging from the growing lump I'm sitting on. Even a few of the men and women on stage are groping themselves. Still, I jump when I feel Sir's hand snaking into my crotch to grab at my dick.

"Sssshh," he whispers before I can protest. "People are trying to watch."

I roll my eyes, though a glance around reveals that he's not wrong. But the fact that everyone is *also* groping themselves makes me feel a lot less bad. The guy on our right has just straight up pulled out his dick, whole hog. *Not bad looking.* There's a much better show on stage, though.

Things come to an end a few minutes later when stage-Khazak cums with a very loud growl. I'm not sure he actually came, especially considering we have a lot more play to go. He pulls out with and stands triumphantly over his prey, still-hard cock hanging between his legs. The magical fog once again rolls in to change the scene.

The hand in my crotch moves to rest around my waist, though I can still feel Sir half-hard underneath me himself. The next few scenes play out in quick succession, all carrying the same theme: the two orcs grow closer, even though it is apparent they should not. Khazak shows Vakesh how to clean his weapons, the two standing just a little too close for a little too long. Vakesh helps tend to Khazak's injuries after he returns from a hunting trip. Khazak begins taking more of his meals with Vakesh—and tries to shield him from some of the abuse of the other orcs.

Throughout all of this, it is made clear that this is not a relationship of equals—namely by the thick leather collar locked around Vakesh's neck. There's also the way Khazak ends every interaction by loudly and roughly establishing his authority, usually by somehow physically dominating Vakesh. Knocking him to the side, shoving him to the ground—anytime there's a tender moment between them, Khazak has to react.

Still, the moments of tenderness do not go unnoticed. The other orc slaves can see the difference in how they are treated, and they begin to resent Vakesh for it, even bullying him. The free orcs of the tribe see the favoritism as well and do what they can to make life harder for the slave when they think their leader isn't watching. Khazak himself is torn between wanting to protect his slave and the pressure from his tribe to be a more ruthless master. One orc in particular seems to take pleasure out of relentlessly taunting Vakesh.

"That is Riktal, the tribe's second in command," Sir informs me as the scene changes again. "He is also *supposed* to be Khazak's best friend."

I can't tell if that's the actual plot or just Sir inferring something, but after witnessing the way the dude spent the last few scenes insulting, intimidating, and otherwise attacking poor Vakesh, I'm not sure I'd believer this guy is *anyone's* friend. The last scene ended with him tripping the guy right in front Khazak, to which he did nothing but pretend to laugh. It's clear Khazak's inability to stand up for Vakesh is starting to affect things between the two of them.

The fog rolls in and fades once more, showing the two orcs walking together through the forest. I assume it's a forest. The few trees I see are all spread fairly far apart, probably so none of the action gets blocked. From the bows on their backs, it is apparent they are on a hunting trip. I think the fact that they are hunting together is significant in itself because before Khazak was going out on his own. Maybe he did it to get them both away from the others?

But Vakesh is having none of it. All his responses to Khazak are short and stilted, and his face betrays no emotion to the other orc. Khazak continues to try to get the smaller orc to open up, growing more and more frustrated, until he finally explodes with anger, drawing Vakesh into a shouting match. One that I can't follow at all, but that is also short-lived because a *giant fucking bear* appears behind them. *Is it getting bigger!?*

The priorities for the two orcs change for obvious reasons, both dodging in separate directions as the bear charges them. It rears around to come at them again, further separating the two and making them draw their bows. Arrows are fired with a few connecting but even more missing. I actually feel myself getting anxious each time they come dangerously close to hitting each other.

Finally, as the orcs weave between the trees, it happens—just as Vakesh lands an arrow in the bear's side that has it facing him and roaring in anger, one of Khazak's arrows pierces him in the leg. Both orcs shout—one in pain and one in regret. The bear charges at the prone Vakesh, and without even thinking, Khazak calls out to it, firing arrows and doing whatever else he can to draw its attention.

It works, but that's where Khazak's plan ends. As the bear turns on him, he reaches blindly for the sword on his back. The bear stomps forward, a little sluggish from blood loss but no less deadly. Khazak trips as he stumbles backward, landing flat on his ass with his back against a tree. Just as the bear draws close, Vakesh pushes himself up, and with a cry that is half anger, half pain, he *leaps* onto the back of the bear, driving his own sword down into the beast. With a final roar, the bear collapses in a heap, Vakesh rolling from its back to the ground.

Khazak rushes to Vakesh's side, pulling him away from the slain bear. His voice is full of concern as he inspects his slave's injuries, a broken arrow sticking out of his thigh. After a few more words, Khazak grips the arrow shaft in his hand and quickly pulls it from Vakesh's body. *Gods, I hope that was fake.* As Vakesh cries out in pain, Khazak covers the wound with his hand, applying pressure until the injured orc is able to take over. He then wraps his arm around Vakesh's shoulder, helping him to sit up before reaching into his bag again, this time pulling out a roll of bandages.

Vakesh watches thoughtfully as Khazak wraps the bandage around his injured leg. Immediate danger taken care of, the two orcs begin to talk, the tone of their voices giving way to worry and warmth. I still can't understand what they're saying, but with the way they're looking at each other and the dead bear, it's not hard to piece together. Khazak finishes, but his touches grow no less tender, the larger man leaning in closer, until their lips touch for the first time...

Wait, did it just get darker? The sun was already low in the sky, but the lighting is somehow *different.* As the kiss on stage deepens and Khazak moves to lay over Vakesh, I see the dead bear in the background shrinking away into nothingness. Which is good because I don't know how many people really want to watch a sex scene next to a dead animal. Though the mood lighting almost puts things over the top.

Not that I mind when I feel a tusk-framed mouth kissing my neck or when the hands around my waist move down to my thighs. A glance to my left shows Nylan in a similar position, sitting on Ragnar's lap while the orc molests him. Both Ragnar's hands are up the front of his boy's shirt, and I can see from the outside that they are latched onto both of his nipples, something that makes Nylan squirm in his seat.

On stage, the action progresses, Khazak removing both of their shirts. He runs his hands over Vakesh's chest, the prone orc shuddering at contact. Then, without warning, the larger orc grips the smaller's pants by the waist, ripping them from his body. Those pants were probably made to rip like that, but it's still hot. Vakesh seems too caught off guard by the action to move, or maybe he's just decided he doesn't want to run. Either way, I'm into it.

Sir—my *own* Khazak—dips his hands into my clothing, one scratching his blunt nails down my thigh while the other moves across my stomach. I can feel him growing hard again, and I grind down on instinct just as his hand reaches my crotch. He bypasses my cock entirely, going straight for my sack, cupping it gently. He rolls my balls between his fingers, just as his other hand leaves me.

The onstage-Khazak is working on preparing his boy, hiking Vakesh's non-injured leg up and burying the first of his fingers in the other orc's hole. *We really got lucky with these seats.* Not that the other end of the small stadium minds, I can see just as much action going on over there. Sir's missing hand returns, this time with something cold in his palm. When he presses it to my stomach, I feel the workings of a familiar spell; it's my cleansing charm.

The hand on my balls releases me and moves farther downward, Sir spreading his own thighs to further spread mine. His fingers prod at my hole, and I'm thankful as they stretch me open because onstage, Khazak already has Vakesh on his side and is kneeling up over one of his legs, preparing to mount him. As stage-Khazak pushes himself forward, my Khazak's fingers leave my hole, and after a little maneuvering and a hand across my waist holding me steady, I'm lowered onto his cock.

I'm glad the charm adds some lube because I'm not sure Khazak used much more than spit on himself. I can see stage-Khazak's ass flexing as he bottoms out inside Vakesh at the same time that I am fully seated on my Khazak's lap. Just as stage-Khazak's hips begin to pump into his boy, mine snaps his hips up, drawing a groan from both bottoms. I blindly reach an arm behind me, grabbing for Sir's neck to steady myself as he uses his strength to lift and lower me on his cock.

Fuck. At this angle, he's rubbing against my prostate on each stroke, and gravity is making sure I take *every* inch. I look left, sure that Nylan is going through something similar, and *yep*, he's straddling Ragnar, the two in a heavy lip-lock. *Can't see the show that way, Ny.* I feel Khazak biting into my neck, and I whimper.

I can't help but look around the stadium at the rest of the audience, some of them like the two of us, and others in all sorts of positions. I catch a few people bent over the seat in front of them, some with their heads in someone else's lap, and more than a few masturbating. The guy on our right is going to *town* on himself. All while Sir sucks marks onto my neck—I can feel them, and they are *definitely* going to be visible tomorrow.

I feel the cock inside of me flex, and I wonder if he's getting close already. After everything we did last night, that's pretty impressive. Fuck, I think *I'm* already getting close. Judging by the groans and growls coming from the stage, so are the two actors. If Vakesh hasn't already; his moans are nearly continuous. *I don't think they're acting anymore.* Stage-Khazak's cock is slamming in and out of Vakesh's ass, and I can see the poor orc's knuckles tensing as he struggles to hold himself steady against the fake-forest floor. Can't be good for his leg.

Stage-Khazak's thrusts are getting volatile, and I think the real one's are too. I watch as the orc on the arena floor slams into his partner, doubling over to capture the smaller orc's mouth as he growls out his orgasm. That, plus the relentless pounding of the *real* Khazak's thick shaft, is enough to send me over my own edge. I cry out weakly as my anal muscles push against the intruder with no hope of moving him.

I barely have the mind to keep a grip on the back of Sir's neck as he drives himself into me, or me down onto him, I'm really not sure anymore. Not really thinking anything beyond, "oh fuck, more dick." All around me, I can hear the sounds of people reaching their own climaxes. I can also smell it—cum has a very distinct scent. There's also the matter of the teeth on my neck, each bite sending another spark of electricity down my spine. I truly don't know how much more I can take and am ready to thank the gods when I feel Sir's cock finally growing inside me, right before he brings me down to his lap one final time. He holds me there, his body quaking with a groan as he breeds me deeply.

I barely register the lights returning to normal, but then I hear the voices on stage return, and I lift my head. Khazak is holding Vakesh in the afterglow, speaking to him in hushed whispers.

"He is apologizing, telling him that he regrets the way they met, the way things have been," Khazak rumbles against my back. "Calling himself a coward and saying that he wants things to be different."

I can hear a familiar twinge of regret in my Khazak's voice as the two orcs on stage continue to hold one another, the fog rolling in once more with a single bell chime.

"Intermission," Khazak tells me as I feel his softening cock slip from my hole. On my left, Nylan climbs off Ragnar with more of an audible *pop* than I would have expected.

Before I can stand, I feel something cold and blunt pressing against my entrance—a plug. I turn as Sir helps me to stand, my legs a little wobbly with an indignant look on my face. My pants, which were halfway down my thighs, are pulled all the way up. At least I won't leave a wet spot on the seat of my pants. Though I can't say the same for the front of my underwear. I take comfort in the knowledge that I'm probably not the only one.

The four of us file down the stairs to the lobby. It's crowded, most people lining up for the bathrooms for obvious reasons. Thankfully our hygiene needs are not as bad as a few others (*thank you, cleansing charm*), so we are happy to wait in a corner for things to die down first.

"What do you think so far?" Khazak asks when we're in the corner.

"Of the play or of the fact that you share a name with one of the characters?" I give the orc a questioning look.

"They share more than just a name," Ragnar muses.

"What does he mean?" This should be a fun story.

"Well, according to my father, Khazak Uzilag is our ancestor." *Wait, does he look embarrassed?* "He is who I was named after."

"He is? Why didn't you tell me?" I'm asking about the play, but I'm also curious about who this other Khazak is in general.

"That was part of the surprise." *Mission accomplished?* "But also, what would I have said? 'By the way, the play we are seeing is about my great-by-many-times-over-grandfather.'" That *does* sound a little too braggy for him.

"He was also worried that if you knew beforehand you might lie about what you thought of the play," Ragnar adds, earning a glare from Khazak. "He cares about this stuff more than he's letting on."

"I did not want my connection to the story to color your impression," Khazak defends. "I wanted your honest opinion."

"Well, so far? I like it. Honestly." That gets him to smile. I can tell he's feeling defensive, and for what it's worth, I believe him; this is *exactly* the level of control freak I have come to expect from him.

"Well, I hope you enjoy the second half just as much." He reaches down to squeeze my hand.

"Oh yeah, David? You might wanna be careful about looking through the crowd too much," Nylan adds from Ragnar's side. "A few years back, I did the same thing and locked eyes with an old teacher of mine... Things got really awkward the next time I saw him in the book shop."

"I'll keep it in mind." *Oh god, Khazak's parents aren't here, are they?*

The lines for the bathroom eventually thin out, and the four of us finish cleaning up (though Nylan and I remain plugged) before returning to our seats. Well, Khazak and Ragnar return to their seats, and Nylan and I return to our seats on their laps. Easier for translating, right? Sir also seems to take some pleasure in jostling the plug inside me, making me shudder. *Damn, it smells like sex up here.*

A few moments later, a familiar sounding bell chimes, and the action on stage resumes. The scene has shifted back to the camp. Things are similar to before with Vakesh performing menial tasks for Khazak. The difference now is that Khazak is no longer holding back his affections. He stands up for Vakesh, both to the other slaves and free orcs. Of course, this still does not earn Vakesh many friends, but at least now he can count on the protection of his owner.

The other slave's behavior I understand, if only out of some form of jealousy; they may not want to fall in love with their captors, but they would certainly appreciate being handled with a little more care. But the free orcs I don't get. Most seem to back down when their leader makes his intentions known, but Riktal, the second in command and his "best friend," doesn't seem to care. He's already decided he doesn't like Vakesh.

Things seem to come to a head one night (or day—I really have no way of telling the time in most of these scenes) when Vakesh is tending to Khazak's weapons. Riktal starts trying to provoke him, even knocking the sword from his hands as he works. Vakesh fumes quietly but takes it all, knowing he can do nothing from his position.

"He is taunting him about his relationship," Khazak tells me. "He is saying that no matter how he may feel, he will never be anything more than a slave. He also is insulting his honor, laughing at him for what he has allowed himself to become, happily turned into another orc's bitch."

I can see Vakesh's rage building, and I think for a second he might actually snap, and that this play is gonna take a wild revenge turn. But no, Riktal keeps talking to him and things seem to...calm down, though the look on Riktal's face is no less sinister. But whatever he's saying, he's got Vakesh's attention.

"Riktal has concocted a plan," Khazak translates. "Under the cover of night, he and his men will sneak into the Rageblood tribe's camp where they will take out the enemy while they sleep. He needs Vakesh to lead them there." The orcs on stage look very intense.

"Wow. That is a...*really* stupid plan." Sure, if everything works out perfectly, you've ended a battle before it starts, but if even one thing gets screwed up? You're trapped and *vastly* outnumbered in enemy territory.

"I agree. That is why Riktal is going behind Khazak's back. He would not approve of this," Khazak explains. "It is also a plan with little honor, something the tribes held in high regard at the time. Riktal is using that to his advantage, telling Vakesh that this is his opportunity to prove his loyalty to Khazak and the tribe. And Vakesh is desperate to prove himself."

I can see the orc on stage wrestling with his decision before he gives a curt nod, and I guess that's that. Riktal looks pleased, though just as menacing, and the scene changes again. The orcs, Riktal's group, are walking through the forest at night, a darkened campsite off to one side of the arena. Vakesh looks a million kinds of nervous. There's a little talking as they walk—mostly more taunts thrown at Vakesh—but he signals for them to go silent when he sees they are approaching his tribe's camp.

Things are quiet, a few orcs standing guard around tents, but even more asleep. Our group of infiltrators sneaks in, silently taking out the guards before they can alert the others. The plan seems to go off without a hitch, and the group converges on a large tent at the center of the camp. Vakesh steels himself as he reaches for the flap—*that must be the tent of the tribe's leader*—but just as he goes to pull it back, an orc appears from the other side of the tent, holding a sword. Then all the "sleeping" orcs wake up, outnumbering our invaders are two to one. This new orc smiles evilly at Riktal and then Vakesh, saying something that has multiple orcs turning their heads.

"That is Tark'han, the leader of the Rageblood tribe," Khazak explains. "And he just greeted Vakesh with 'Hello, brother.'" *Brother? More drama!* "He is thanking him for leading the enemy into their trap."

"Vakesh was planning this the whole time?!" I *really* must have missed something in the translation.

"No. But Riktal and the others do not know that." Oh shit, he's fucked. "Watch."

The scene shifts again (*dammit*) back to the Proudhunter camp. Khazak emerges from his tent looking worried, no doubt because Vakesh is missing. He begins searching the camp, noticing quickly that even more people are missing. Finally, he decides to wake one of the other orcs up to find out what's going on.

As this new orc responds, I watch the rage on Khazak's face grow. No doubt having now learned of Riktal's plan, he begins shouting at the orc who stands there dumbly at first before snapping to action after having what I assume are orders barked at him.

"He has just ordered all available men to prepare to join him," Khazak translates. "He worries he may be too late to catch up and fears it will be more of a rescue mission than anything else."

Stage-Khazak turns to one of the other orc slaves, one who was disdainful of Vakesh earlier. He speaks quickly and harshly, practically interrogating him, probably for the location of the camp. Khazak's voice gets louder, angrier, until he's almost shouting, but still the slave remains defiant, even rolling his eyes. Finally, his tone shifts, the anger dropping into something much softer. Something that sounds worried. *That* gets the slave to open up and start talking. Sir makes to translate it for me, but I wave him off. I figured it out.

The scene shifts *back* to the Bloodrage tribe's camp, now in the midst of battle. One that is going very poorly for Riktal and his group. As his tribe fights for their lives, he barely manages to defend himself against Tark'han. Vakesh stands at the center of it all looking on, unable and unsure of what to do or which side to help.

Tark'han's men maintain their upper hand, and one by one, the invading Proudhunters fall to the blades of the

Bloodrage orcs until only two are left, one of whom is Riktal. He's giving it everything he has, but it's useless, and from the look on his face, he knows it. He doesn't look surprised when Tark'han's sword is finally driven through his chest, but he manages to give Vakesh a final sneer as he crumples to the ground. After receiving a nod from Tark'han, the only other Bloodrage orc still in battle withdraws, allowing the surviving Proudhunter to escape. *What?* Vakesh begins speaking to Tark'han, likely asking the same thing I want to. As Tark'han turns to his brother, his face can only be described as full of disgust.

"He wants Khazak to think that Vakesh has betrayed him. See the orc on the right?" Sir points to an orc now standing next to Tark'han as the orc monologues at his brother. "That is the orc who escaped in the first scene. After reporting back, Tark'han sent spies to look for his brother. He has learned about Vakesh's enslavement and is disgusted by his willing submission to an enemy tribe's leader. Those same spies then informed him of Riktal's plan, allowing the Bloodrage tribe to set a trap."

That sounds awfully convenient, but I'm not a writer. And speaking of convenient, Khazak and his men have just shown up, the escaped orc among them. The two tribe leaders stare each other down. Tark'han is the first to break eye contact, looking down at Riktal's corpse with a smirk and forcing Khazak to look down too. The sight of his best friend and second-in-command's body fills Khazak with so much rage that you'd think he belonged to the other tribe. He turns his stare to Vakesh as he draws his sword, and with a shout, another battle begins.

With Khazak's troops, things seem more evenly matched, which I'm not sure makes sense, but I'm too invested in the story at this point to care. While they battle on the outskirts, Khazak charges toward Vakesh and Tark'han in the center, grabbing Riktal's discarded sword with his free hand on the way. Now dual-wielding, he crosses swords with Vakesh first, the smaller orc reluctantly forced to defend himself. Lucky for him, his brother comes up on Khazak's back. The Proudhunter leader uses his second sword to deflect the attack but is forced to move unless he wants to be trapped between the two.

The three of them dance like this for a while, Khazak and Tark'han on the attack while Vakesh stays largely defensive. All the while, the two orcs are yelling, shouting at Vakesh, who continues to look torn between the two. I swear I think I saw the guy's heart break after a particularly vicious sounding line from his brother. So far, Khazak has been holding his own against the two pretty well, but I can see it starting to wear on him.

With a well-timed swipe, Tark'han manages to knock the sword from Khazak's off hand. Seeing an opportunity, Vakesh strikes at Khazak's other hand, disarming him completely. In the confusion, Tark'han rushes in with a well-placed kick to Khazak's stomach, sending the orc tumbling to the ground at Vakesh's feet. Sure of his defeat, Khazak can only look up at his former lover's face in disgust, waiting for his death.

Vakesh stands over the prone Khazak, sword arm pulled back. The pose is one of a practiced warrior, ready to strike, but his face... His face is just *broken*. Tark'han comes up behind his brother, hand on his shoulder as he speaks into his ear. I already know what he's saying. *Do it. Kill him and prove yourself.* He's so smug, so sure of himself.

Which is why he looks so shocked when he finds his brother's sword driven through his stomach.

"Oh shit," I actually say out loud.

Tark'han falls to the ground, blood already pouring from his mouth. He looks up, cursing his brother's betrayal with his final words. Vakesh drops to his knees as the life drains from his brother's face, looking even more broken than he did before. Khazak stands, unsure if he should approach or run. The battling around them draws to a close with many of the Ragebloods retreating in the face of their leader's sudden demise (even though this is their camp). Though they are the victors, the Proudhunter tribe looks unsure of whether or not to celebrate, all eyes drawn to their leader and his (former?) slave.

Vakesh finally stands, though is unable to lift his head to look Khazak in the face. The two speak, stiffly at first, though slowly they begin to warm to each other.

"Vakesh is explaining the truth of what transpired, about both Riktal's and Tark'han's plans," Sir translates. "Khazak is mournful of his friend's passing but also angry with him for putting himself, Vakesh, and the rest of the tribe in danger."

Then stage-Khazak says something that has Vakesh meeting his eyes in an instant, anger flashing across his features for a second before he says anything in return.

"He wants to release Vakesh," Khazak whispers. "But in response, Vakesh is questioning if he really wants to give up after *everything* they have been through together."

I don't need a translator for what happens next. Vakesh closes the distance between them and pulls Khazak in for a kiss. As the fog rolls in one final time, the audience breaks into applause. Once it dissipates, the full cast of the play can be seen on the arena floor, including the bear who I watch morph back into the shape of an orc. *I forgot druids can do that.* The group take a bow as the crowd gives them a standing ovation, one I have no choice but to join as my former chair stands himself. *Honestly? Great show. Would see again.*

With the play done, people start to make their way out of the arena. Following right behind Ragnar and Nylan, we re-enter the arena's lobby beneath the stands. Khazak again pulls us to the side once we can get free of the crowd.

"There is someone I wish to speak to before we head home," Khazak explains.

"Well, this has been a *really* fun weekend, but we have work tomorrow," Ragnar tells us as we split up for the evening.

"I miss sleeping in a real bed," Nylan complains as he hugs me goodbye. "See ya, David. Goodbye, sir."

As the two of them make their exit, Khazak leads me down a hall to a wooden door, knocking twice. A familiar orc woman opens the door, one of the two who seem to run this place. I spot her counterpart standing in the room behind her.

"Khazak!" She looks happy to see us and steps to the side, waving us in.

"Curator Brightdrum, I wanted to congratulate you and your sister on another successful festival." Khazak smiles at them both warmly.

"Please, Khazak, we have known you your entire life." The second orc crosses the room to meet us. "We are just Agra and Ti'gat."

"And you know we cannot take all the credit," the first orc continues. "The whole city works very hard to make this festival happen every year." *Everyone around here is so humble.* "Tell me, did you happen to see the new panel we added to the Hall's walls?"

"Yes, we did. It is truly an honor." He puts his fist across his chest and bows. "Do you not agree, David?"

"Yes, it's an honor," I try not to say too stiffly.

I get a small laugh at my response. "You know, we were not sure you were gonna make it after you lost your match. Glad to see we were wrong."

"He is nothing if not resilient," Khazak clasps my shoulder, and I try not to roll my eyes.

"That certainly—" Agra pauses at the sound of a cat meowing, all four of us turning our heads up to the rafters to see the cat in question poking out from a hole in the wall above the rafters. *The hell?*

"Spirits be damned," Agra mutters before turning to her sister. "Some of the actors are having issues removing their makeup glamours."

"We better get over there," Ti'gat says with a sigh before standing. "I hope you both had a wonderful festival." She looks at me thoughtfully, clearly wanting a response.

"It's been a lot of fun. *Really* interesting." It wasn't anything like I could have expected, that's for sure. "Is it a lot of work cleaning up after all this?"

Ti'gat waves off my concern. "Oh sweetie, once everyone has gone, we are just gonna hose this whole place down."

Khazak and I make our exit after that, the sun setting behind us as we walk home.

"I forget what a big deal you are around here sometimes." Like *really* big. "Also, what was that thing with the cat?"

"I am not a 'big deal.'" *Yes he is.* "And that cat was Agra's familiar. She and Ti'gat are both witches. I believe Ti'gat's is a crow." That explains it.

"They're the ones in charge of the festival? What was it that you called them?" Besides witches.

"Yes, much of it." Khazak nods. "Their official title is 'curator.' They are responsible for recording important events in the city's history, not just like we saw on the panels but actual written documentation." His voice drops low as he continues. "Underneath the Hall of Honor is a vault that not many in the city are even aware of. It contains a number of important records and artifacts, things too important or dangerous to be left out in the open. The two of them are the guardians of its contents. I meet with them regularly to discuss security concerns."

"See? You *are* a big deal." *He should just own it.*

He rolls his eyes (*I'm rubbing off on him*) and presses forward. "So, what did you think? Of the play and of the festival."

"I liked it a lot. Both of them." Some of it for obvious reasons. "Even aside from the fun stuff, it was nice to get to know a little more about your friends, and the city, and I guess your great great great grandfathers or whatever."

"'Or whatever' indeed." He smirks down at me. "I am glad you had fun, David. It was nice to have someone to celebrate with this year."

I return his smile, though I can hear the sad unspoken message in his words clear as day. He won't have someone to celebrate with next year.

Maybe... Maybe I can come visit next year. Just for this... *Just for him.*

Chapter 8

"And after we finished breaking down everything from the festival, Liss and I went back to helping to build houses," Adam finishes recapping his week. "It is *exhausting*, man."

"Sounds like it." I want to commiserate with my jailed friend, but I know I'm gonna come up short.

It's Astraday, which means visiting day and the start of a new week. After the insanely fun festival last weekend, the rest of the week at work was slow and uneventful. Even with the ranger's scouting, there's been no new leads on the brimstone robbery. Between that and the mess with Thog, morale has felt kinda low around the station.

"What about you? How's the work stuff going?" Only Adam would be in jail and still be interested in hearing about my work week.

"It's been good, pretty busy," I lie, desperate to change the subject. "Have you guys made any friends here? Corrine said she joined a bible study group."

"The people Adam hangs out with in here are considerably less educated than that," Nate snarks and rubs his neck. "Honestly, everyone is."

"Don't be a jerk, Nate." Adam gives him an elbow nudge. "It's not easy. Most of them don't speak Common, but there's a few guys I'm friendly with. And hey, we're almost halfway through our sentence."

"Shit, you're right." Just a little over a month until they're released. "By the next time I see you, it'll be *over* halfway."

"Thanks for the calendar update." *God, do I fucking hate Nate.*

"And how are you doing?" *Why am I even asking?*

"Fine." He's rubbing the back of his neck again. "Just... ready to get out of here already."

"We all are, Nate," Adam points out. "Even David."

"Yeah." Even me. *Right?*

After visiting hour ends, it's a quiet walk home. The reminder that my stay here is nearly halfway over brings up some weird feelings. If Khazak notices anything, he doesn't say it. I ignore them, pressing forward with the rest of our plans for the day, which include sitting on the couch, reading, and taking a nap. After all the craziness of last weekend, I'm happy for it.

Solisday is a different story because it's time for another family dinner at Khazak's parents. We still get to wake up late since it's the only thing we're doing today. As the hour draws closer, I start feeling a little anxious as I remember some of the hiccups of last time. *It'll be fine, David. Just don't act weird if you find out he's got four grandmothers or something.*

We leave earlier than we did last time, Khazak clearly hoping to avoid any extra guilt or clean-up duty for not having helped with the cooking. Familial guilt can be a powerful motivator, and one I am well acquainted with. It's Jarek who opens the door for us when we arrive, hugging us once we are inside. Jarek is Khazak's stepfather. He has a slim build with short black hair and a neatly trimmed mustache-goatee combo. He looks about fifteen years older than Khazak, and I would guess he's probably that much younger than his other two husbands as well. I don't know the full story of how they met, just that it happened after Khazak was born.

"Boys, we were not expecting you this early," Jarek locks the door behind us. "Your father only just got started in the kitchen."

"We wanted to see if we could be of any help." *Who is this "we" he speaks of?*

"Rurig will love that." Jarek smiles, knowing his husband.

"Actually, where is Yogik?" Khazak asks after his brother, the family's middle child.

"I believe he is in the kitchen as well," Jarek replies, nodding.

"Perfect. Would you mind taking David to say hello to Ayla and the others?" *Huh?* "Yogik and I need to have a discussion, and then we will join you." *Uh oh.*

"...Sure thing." Jarek looks at his stepson questioningly before leading me from the hall.

Jarek walks me into the living room, or the den, or whatever they call the room with the couches and fireplaces around here. Ayla, Khazak's twin sister is here, as are his younger siblings Urzsa and Ignatz. They look different, their hair color now a matching red. They're playing some sort of board game at a table in the corner, barely lifting their eyes at our entrance.

"David!" Ayla gets up from her seat to greet me. "It is good to see you again."

"You too, Ayla." I happily return her hug. Khazak's sister just returned from a year-long globe-spanning trip, and frankly, I think she's awesome.

"Ignatz? Ursza, do you want to say—?" The two young orcs grunt and half-wave in my direction, making their father sigh. "Sorry about them."

"It's okay, I have a younger sister." *At least there's only one of her.*

"Were we like that when we were younger?" Ayla asks, nodding her head in their direction.

"Antisocial? No. Quiet? Yes, you and Khazak were, at least." Jarek sounds more amused by his children's behavior than anything else. "Yogik never shut up."

"So, David, did you enjoy the festival last week?" Ayla asks me. I hesitantly open my mouth to answer before she holds her hand up. "We don't need any of the details, just a general question."

"It was...a lot of fun." I think carefully about how to word my responses here. "It was also kind of crazy? I don't think I've ever heard of anything like that anywhere else in the world." *If there are, I'd like to know about them.*

"Imagine how popular it would be if people actually knew about our city," Jarek adds. "What about Khazak? Did he have a good time?"

"Yeah, he was practically giddy." I remember how excited he was at times. "All the food, the drinking, the dancing..."

"Wait, you actually got *Khazak* to *dance*?" Ayla looks shocked at my news. "*My* brother?"

"I mean, beer was involved, so I don't think I can take all the credit." I'll keep the story of how he got jealous to myself for his sake.

"He has been waiting for years to have someone he could take." I remember Ragnar saying something similar. Both Ayla and Jarek look genuinely happy to hear about Khazak and the festival.

"I didn't even find out he was named after your great-great-great—" I circle my finger in the air a few times since I'm not sure how many times I need to say that. "—great grandfather until we saw the play on the last day."

"Really?" Ayla looks curious. "I'm surprised he was able to keep that to himself considering how obsessed he was with that story when we were teenagers."

"'Obsessed' is a strong word," Jarek counters. "It is also an accurate word." *Maybe not.* "Khazak had always taken a small amount of pride in being named after one of V'rok'sh Tah'lj's founders, but once he was old enough to learn more about the rest of Khazak Steelrun's life, he really connected with it."

"'Connected?' David, he bought his first boyfriend a collar," Ayla deadpans. "It was weird."

"It was *adorable*," Jarek defends his stepson from his stepdaughter. "Poor thing was heartbroken when the boy rejected it. Barely came out of his room for weeks."

Aww, I can just picture a sad little Khazak (okay, not *that* little) crying into his pillow over a boy he liked. It is both one of the cutest and saddest things I can imagine. It also makes me realize even more how important me wearing Khazak's collar is to him. He had it specially made, his family's crest engraved into the lock.

Ayla and Jarek are both chuckling when we see Khazak entering the room with Yogik in tow, and all three of us quickly straighten our posture. *That was obvious.*

Khazak gives us a weird look but doesn't say anything before pushing his brother forward. "Yogik has something he would like to tell you, David."

"Yes." Yogik looks back at his brother, annoyed, but continues somewhat stiffly. "I am very sorry if anything I said last time you were here made you uncomfortable. I was only joking, but it was still inappropriate."

"Thanks." *Okay, this is pretty funny.* "I, uh, accept your apology."

Yogik smiles and nods his head. "I believe I am still needed in the kitchen." He turns to his brother as he leaves the room, his annoyed look meeting Khazak's smirk.

"Yog hit on David after the last dinner?" Ayla questions at their brother's hasty exit.

"Something like that," Khazak grumbles, probably remembering what I told him about Yogik asking to share me. "Now, what was it you were all talking about when I came in the room?"

"Just some old things about when you were in school, you know," Jarek tries his best to play it off.

"Mhmm," Khazak hums his agreement but narrows his eyes at both orcs suspiciously.

"Oh, I forgot to tell you Ayla! He took me to Shad'rok Springs a couple of weeks back." I shoot for a subject change that I think will make both twins happy.

"Really?" Ayla smiles, looking pleasantly surprised at her brother. "What did you think?"

"It was beautiful. The water was so clear." I reach over to tug on Khazak's wrist. "I'm kind of hoping we can go back before I leave."

"I think that can be arranged." Khazak smiles and reaches for my hand, giving it a squeeze.

"You only have about five weeks to go now, right?" Jarek's question makes Khazak's smile falter.

"Uh, yeah, just about." I try not to let any of the melancholy I feel show. "Just talked to my friends this morning actually. They are pretty eager to get on the road again."

"I know it was an unplanned detour on your journey, but I do hope you still enjoyed the time you spent here," Jarek continues.

"Yeah, you managed to get here in time for not just the festival, but to meet me!" Ayla adds cockily. "Actually, that reminds me. Khazak, do you know who *else* was happy to hear about my return? High Priest Bhok. He stopped by a couple of weeks ago after he learned I was back in town. Ended up staying for dinner and mentioned that someone told him I had a lot of free time. You wouldn't know where he might have gotten that idea, would you?"

"You know, David, I think I hear my father calling for us." Khazak steps backward, hand on my shoulder to pull me with him.

I snort a laugh because no, he didn't, but go along with him anyway. I'll see Jarek and Ayla at the dinner table, and the info I learned about Khazak as a teen will keep me entertained for quite a while. We enter the home's large kitchen together. I see one of Khazak's fathers, Orlun (who he and Ayla seem to "take after"), standing over a large grill near an open window. Yogik is next to him, helping to move things from a plate to the grill while his father watches. Khazak's *other* father, Rurig, is going back and forth between two stoves, each covered in pots and pans, as well as grabbing whatever spices or other additions he needs from one of the many shelves and counters in the room. It's very warm, but it smells *amazing* in here.

"Oh good, you are back." Rurig looks over after noticing our entrance. He points at me. "You, over here." Stepping over to the round orc, he stands me in front of one of the stoves, pushing the wooden spoon from one of the pots into my hand. "Stir." He then turns and starts talking to his son quickly in Atasi, putting him to work as well.

The whole scene in here reminds me so much of home. Me and Mikey helping mom with dinner or being on kitchen duty at the academy. Everyone talking and laughing while the head chef (or mom) gives the orders. Even though

I can't understand what they're saying, I can still hear the love in their voices, even when they're grumbling at each other. *Shit, is this actually making me homesick?*

Whatever it is I'm stirring smells pretty good. It's some sort of sauce, red in color and smelling vaguely of tomatoes. Rurig occasionally comes by to add something else to the pot, dipping a pinky in to sample afterward. Over on a counter to the left, Khazak is carving into some sort of roast he pulled from the oven a few minutes ago, and it looks like Yogik is now taking things *off* the grill. Dinner should be ready soon.

When things are finished, Rurig starts handing the completed dishes to Khazak, Yogik, and me to bring out to the dinner table. Jarek and the others are already seated, and fifteen minutes later, Rurig's said his form of a blessing and all of us are eating our fill. That sauce I was stirring ended up going over some really well-cooked chicken. *I'm gonna miss this food when I'm gone.*

"David, how has working with the rangers been?" Orlun's question catches me off guard. Since Ayla's been home for a few weeks now, there's less of a conversation buffer to protect me.

"It's been...good." *I feel like I said that weird. I mean, it has been, right?*

"David has been quite the asset." Khazak takes over for me as he reaches over to squeeze my leg. *Phew.* "The other week he actually chased down a fleeing suspect all on his own, and he's been learning Atasi in his free time," he brags. I'm *also* the reason that all four walls surrounding the station have had permanent alarm runes etched into them, but he doesn't mention that.

"You know, when I was just starting my position as captain, we had a kavan/avakesh pair working together on the force." Orlun looks between the two of us. "They were quite

skilled at undercover investigations. They had this system..."
He pauses, trying to think of something. "Khazak, what was
it that Ragnar called it when he heard the story?"

"A 'honeypot,' I believe." Khazak's response sounds
wary for some reason.

Orlun claps his hands together. "That was it—a honeypot. The avakesh, she would act as 'bait' for their targets, making friends or flirting to gather information. She
was quite beautiful and could immediately disarm someone
with her charm. Once they had what they needed, her
kavan would walk out of the shadows, and they would take
the suspects down together. The two of them once managed to infiltrate and arrest an entire smuggling ring on
their own with zero casualties. I was always very impressed
with their work."

"Yes, Orda, we have all heard the stories." *Aww, I haven't.*
Then Khazak turns to me. "Do not get any ideas," Khazak
warns me with a laugh. *Too late.*

Later, when we're walking home (with a full stack of leftovers), I recall some of what Ayla and Jarek were saying
about Khazak "connecting" with the other Khazak's story.
It's obviously important to him.

"How come you never told me the story of Khazak and
Vakesh before?" Unless he's been planning the surprise for
that long?

"Actually... I did try to, once." He looks over at me with
a grimace. "It was the night of your last escape attempt.
There was a book I started to read..."

I wince as the memory of the night comes flooding back.
I remember Khazak reading a book about an orc warrior,

right before I drugged him with some hypnograss and tried to break my friends out of jail.

"I'm sorry," I apologize almost without thinking. *Not that it isn't deserved.*

"It is alright, David. I think we are passed all that now, right?" He looks over for confirmation.

"Maybe we can try reading it again some time?" I would actually like to know more about them. *I wonder how much detail it goes into regarding the sexy parts.*

"I would like that." He smiles, nodding his head once.

"It must have been kinda cool to find out who you were named after as a kid." I'm pretty sure he's one of the statues we've passed in front of the tribal hall.

"I have a question." Khazak raises one hand slightly. "Was 'Khazak' the only shared name you heard last weekend?"

"...Yes?" *This feels like a trap.*

"Do you remember the name of the festival? In Atasi." It doesn't *sound* like he's mocking me.

"Uh, it's..." *Shit,* I know this, we just talked about it a week ago. It's... "Chad Uzugir?"

"Close. '*Shatu Uzu'gor,*'" Khazak corrects me. "Now, do you remember what my last name is, also in Atasi?"

"I..." I know this one too. It's on the tip of my tongue. I think it might be... *No, that can't be right.* "Is... Is it the same word?"

"Also close. *Very* close." He looks pleased. "It is 'Uzi'gor.'" *Wait, what?*

"You know it sounds like you're saying the same thing, right?" I hope I'm not hearing things again.

"That is because I essentially am." *I am so confused.*

"So, your family has the same name as the festival?" It kind of makes sense—his grandfathers are at the center of it. "I can't believe I missed something like that."

"Actually..." *Uh oh.* "That is *also* the name of the battle that tied us together. The *Nagul Uzu'gor.*" *What.*

"I'm not dumb!" I blurt out, an old reflex of mine I thought died years ago.

"I did not think you were," he tries to assure me. "They are foreign words you have only heard a handful of times. I understand why you would not make the connection."

"Does that mean this whole thing, the ritual, the festival, is important to your family?" *It is named after them, after all.*

"No, not particularly." Khazak shrugs. "For one, the names are *not* actually identical. 'Uzu'gor' literally translates to 'steel and thunder,' while 'Uzi'gor' is a stylized surname meaning 'Ironstorm.' We are more than proud of our lineage—my father could boast about being related to Khazak Steelrun all day—but as far as I am aware, I am the only living relative with any actual interest in owning an avakesh. Which is probably a good thing as once I learned about the more *intimate* aspects of their relationship, I am not sure I would have wanted to ask a family member any of my questions."

"That's a good point." *I wonder if finding out about Khazak and Vakesh's relationship was weird for anyone else in the family.* "So, how *did* you learn about it?"

"Books." *That seems like him. Nerd.* "Though my family figured out my interests easily enough as I got older."

"Yeah, your sister and Jarek mentioned something like that." *I'll spare him the reminder about his first collar.* "Even they seemed surprised that you hadn't told me about any of it. Why didn't you?"

"Because it is *embarrassing*, David," he scoffs and rolls his eyes. "I was a moody and hormonal teenager who became childishly fixated on a four-hundred-year-old story. It affected *all* of my early relationships and still brings up a lot of memories that make me wince when I think on them. Not to mention how overly romanticized the story is. That play is not even close to accurate."

"How do you mean?" I figured some of the play was made up, but the basic story must be the same.

"They were practically mortal enemies when they first met. That is not something two people just get over." Good point—near-death experience notwithstanding. "The things Khazak put Vakesh through would make anything I could possibly do to you look like a walk in the park."

"What *did* the play get right?" I know they ended up together, at least.

"Well, though it is *very* condensed, the first half of the play is not wholly inaccurate. It took the two of them many months before they actually began to warm up to one another, and there are actual written accounts of the bear attack," he starts explaining. "The second half though is where a lot of things are invented or changed for the sake of drama. Vakesh's brother Tark'han had no idea he had survived the strike on the Proudhunter's camp. There was no ambush waiting for Riktal's men, nor any plan to get Khazak to turn on Vakesh. It was wholly a surprise when they showed up in the camp that night."

"It was simply such a bad plan that Riktal's group really was almost wiped out," he continues. "By the time Khazak showed up, there were almost no survivors. He really did fight Vakesh and his brother, and Vakesh did end up stabbing his brother, but he was not killed, only maimed. In the confusion, the two of them and the rest of the Proudhunters escaped."

"Wow." I can see the appeal of adding all the betrayal to the play. "What really happened after that?"

"Vakesh and Khazak's relationship continued to grow. They combined their surnames, Uzilag and Lo'gar, into

Uzi'gar, to show that even though Vakesh wore Khazak's collar, they were still partners." *I wonder how many people had trouble believing that.* "Their names are where the terms *kavan* and *avakesh* come from. Years later, the two brothers reconciled, which was one of the events that lead to the signing of the peace treaty between the six tribes and the founding of the city."

"Yeah, I was kind of expecting that to be how the play ended." Seemed like a pretty big moment in their lives, at least.

"I believe there is a version the writer created with a third act that covers that. It is just not very good," Khazak reasons. "Honestly, I am not even sure I can say the version we saw is 'good.' Contrived plot aside, there are only six speaking parts, all of them men, and the sex scenes have only gotten more graphic as time has gone on."

"That's a bad thing?" I joke. "You said Khazak's original last name was 'Steelrun,' right?" I don't know how much more room I have left in my brain for names. "How did that turn into 'Ironstorm?'"

"Vakesh's surname was 'Gorecrash.' They didn't translate things into Common then, but combined you would expect something like 'Steelcrash,' and in the four hundred years since, that has evolved into 'Ironstorm.'" *Languages are confusing.*

"So uh, I hope this isn't rude to ask, but how does that work, exactly? Male orcs can't get pregnant, so you can only actually be related to one of them, right?" I bite my lip 'cause I really hope I'm not offending him. "Like... Orlun is your father by blood, right? There's just such a strong resemblance."

He huffs a laugh. "Yes, Orlun is my 'biological' father. And though I do not have proof beyond what is written in a few history books, he has said we are descended from

Khazak Steelrun." I guess that would be kind of hard to prove. "I am told there is still a family resemblance, but all we have to go on are statues and drawings from centuries in the past, so I am not sure how much I believe that."

"So, what about your mother?" He hasn't actually told me much about her, but I don't think it's because of any mystery or drama. He once told me about his fathers having some sort of arrangement with his "aunts" regarding children.

"What would you like to know?" He turns and offers me an honest smile. "Her name is Murza, she is alive and well, and still lives in the city with her wife and my youngest cousin. When my fathers Orlun and Rurig were young and newly married, they wanted to start a family. While two men cannot have a child themselves, they had some friends in a similar situation, two women who also wanted a family. So, an agreement was struck: the couples would assist each other in getting pregnant, with each couple claiming the children from one of the pregnancies as their own."

"They did this four times, including twice more after they met Jarek, resulting in me and my four siblings," he continues. "I have four 'cousins,' some of whom are technically my half-siblings. We see them on larger holidays like the solstices and equinoxes; I think you can understand why they did not make an appearance during this last festival. Despite our ancestry, my family does not place an abundance of importance on bloodlines. I was raised to believe that family is more about who you choose to be with than a shared lineage. Nurture over nature. Which is why some orc families can have three fathers and not have anyone 'freak out.'"

"You know, I get why you were so into it." I ignore his reminder of my reaction to learning about his *three dads* at the last family dinner. "Being named after one of your hometown's heroes *and* finding out he was into the same uh, kinky stuff that you are... I might get a little obsessed, too."

"I am still glad I grew out of it before I finished school," Khazak muses. "I learned I had even better role models to look up to, like my father."

"Orlun was a ranger too, right?" I figure that's who he's talking about.

"He was Captain, one of the most decorated in V'rok'sh Tah'lj's history." He sounds so proud. "Between the militia and the rangers, he has dedicated his entire life to helping and protecting other people. His tenure was very popular both with the citizens and troops, but what really inspired me was how happy his life was. The family he was able to create. We have had our fair share of problems, but overall, the spirits and the Three have truly blessed my family. Even when we fight, we are happy together. I watch my father sometimes and can just see the contentment he feels when he looks at all of us. I only hope that one day I am able to have that same sort of family myself."

"Wow, that's...kinda beautiful." And deep. *Very* deep. "I wish I was able to look up to my dad the same way."

"There are many people in the world to look up to, David." He smiles as we near the house. "All that really matters is the kind of person you want to be."

Chapter 9

The week after our second family dinner starts off with a celebration when my friend, Orim Broadedge, is promoted to a full ranger! I'm really happy for him. Orim is actually the first person I met after waking up in a jail cell following me and my friends' arrest, and I wasn't exactly polite. Despite that, the two of us got close after I started working with Khazak, and have spent the last month or so helping each other learn the other's language, one of many things he's been doing to prepare for the promotion. Safe to say he's a lot farther along than I am.

Then two days later on Aersday, things get interesting again. The morning starts off normal: a little morning sex, a quick shower, and off to work. I'm lying on the couch in Khazak's office, nose deep in my *Learning Atasi* book, when a commotion in the room outside grabs both our attention.

When we walk out into the station's main room, we see an older looking orc being helped inside, his arm thrown over the shoulder of the woman on his left. He's tall with white hair that I think I can see has some dried blood in it. He's also walking with a limp. The orc helping him inside is much younger, wearing the loose clothing of someone who spends a lot of time on a boat.

The officers in the station give the man space as he's helped to a chair. Everyone is staring, unable to draw their attention to anything else as they wonder just what is going on. They do manage to part to make way for Khazak as he walks toward the man with me right behind him.

"Mister Stouthand, are you alright?" Khazak asks before turning to his left. "Contact a healer and get him some water."

"Yes, sir." Two officers scurry to take care of the orders.

"Please, can you tell me what happened?" Khazak asks after kneeling down in front of the man.

"I was... I was on the road home from Yasurdi, bringing back some supplies for the farm," the older man starts. "It was just me and my horse, Bist. I saw the river up ahead when a black carriage pulled up alongside me." *Black carriage?*

"You only made it home this morning?" Khazak sounds surprised. "You must have been traveling all night."

"I make the trip every month. It has always been safe," the farmer counters, shaking his head. "Before I even knew what was happening, someone from their carriage jumped onto the back of my cart! They grabbed me and threw me off, and then everything went black."

"*What?*" Khazak's eyes go wide as Mr. Stouthand recounts his attack.

"My partner and I were just coming down the river when we saw him unconscious on the bank," the orc who brought Stouthand in tells us. "We managed to revive him and brought him here as quickly as we could."

"When did you find him?" Khazak asks the boat captain.

"About forty-five minutes ago. We came in through the shipyard," is her answer. She's stout and looks older, her medium length hair just starting to grey. Her outfit says that she has been outside for a while.

"Do you know how long ago you were attacked?" This question is aimed at the farmer.

"I... I am not sure." Stouthand shakes his head.

"It is alright. Did they identify themselves, or were you able to get a look at them?" Khazak is doing his best not to press the man, but he needs the info.

"No." He shakes his head again. "The driver and the one who jumped onto my cart were both in black robes. Other than that, I could not see a thing."

"What color were their horses?" I hear myself asking. Khazak turns to give me a questioning look.

"They were black as well," he responds. *That can't be a coincidence, right?*

"They might have gotten far by now. We will need to move quickly." Khazak stands. "Ranger Deepfist, David, come with me."

"Where are we going?" I ask as we march out the front doors to the station.

"I am going to show you where we keep the horses."

I follow Khazak and Deepfist—Arik—west of the station to a part of the city I haven't actually been yet. It doesn't look like anything special, but I don't get a chance to really look around as we head straight for a stable. A small one, but it still takes up most of the block. *How did I miss this?*

After walking inside the main building, the two orcs inside tending to the horses stop what they're doing and salute Khazak. By their uniforms, I can tell they work for or are part of the ranger force. Khazak returns the salute quickly, then begins speaking fast, holding up three fingers. Then he looks back at me with a question on his face. "Can you ride?"

I open my mouth to answer because yeah, horseback riding *was* actually something they taught at the knight academy, but then I see one of the creatures behind him he claims is a horse. Sure, it's horse-shaped, but it is *massive*. I mean big, bigger than any horse I've seen in my life. I know that given the size of your average orc, they'd have to be that big, but holy shit.

"Normal, non-monster sized horses." My eyes are wide as I stare at the behemoths in their stalls.

My answer makes Khazak laugh, and he turns back to the stable attendants, this time with only two fingers up. Two horses are brought out, one black and one brown, and they are just...huge, muscled beasts. Arik climbs on the brown one and Khazak the black, then holds his hand out to help me up. *I know how to climb a horse!* The saddle stirrups are just higher than usual.

"This feels embarrassing," I grumble from my seat behind Khazak.

"How will you ever survive?" Khazak teases before sending the horse into a small gallop.

We take off from the stable toward the west gate. We're moving fast, the city's buildings whizzing by in a blur, but we slow down as we approach the gate so they can open it.

"Why haven't we used these before?" I ask while I have a chance.

"We primarily use them for travel and business outside of the city." That's all I get because as soon as the gate is open, we're off.

We're moving so much faster than we did in the city. I'm a little scared at first since all we can see ahead of us is miles of trees, but I don't need to be. Khazak and Arik, or maybe it's their horses, have no problems weaving through the forest. They probably train for this all the time.

We ride for maybe twenty minutes before the forest starts to thin out, and I see a river on our left off in the distance. A little farther and there's a dirt path running along the base of the mountains on our right. We follow the path, and as we approach the river, I see a wooden bridge set up for crossing. It's high enough for a decent sized boat to slip under, and (I hope) sturdy enough to support two very large horses and three men.

"Keep your eyes open for any tracks," Khazak tells me after we cross, the path turning west with the river. "We are close."

"Captain," Arik draws our attention, indicating we should slow down. I see why as we approach the river—tracks on the dirt path. I can make out horse hooves and the smooth groove of wheels, but there's only one set, mostly along the left side of the road.

We keep following the path west, guiding the horses through the grass alongside it so as not to disturb the tracks. A little farther up and we get to a place where it looks like the tracks have moved on the path toward the center. We stop and dismount, and I stand back as I watch the two orcs inspect the tracks.

"This must be where the carriage came in," Arik concludes.

"How do you know that?" I look down to see if I'm missing something. "There's only one set of tracks, right?"

"With the right spells and enchantments, it is not impossible to hide the tracks of horses or a carriage. Though not easily. When it appeared, it forced the farmer to the left." Khazak sighs before scanning our surroundings. "Over there."

Arik and I follow Khazak a short walk back up the way we came. Just over a small hill, he bends over and picks up a straw hat.

"I believe this belongs to Farmer Stouthand," he comments, dusting it off. "Alright, we will follow the tracks we do have and see what we find."

We remount the horses, walking a slow trot next to the dirt path to the city. We get close to the bridge and see where the cart's tracks go off the path, continuing to follow along the river. I can't see anything after that, but Khazak and Arik are still staring at the ground intently. The forest gets thicker, and soon I know we're back in orc territory.

"Captain—" Arik starts, and I look around Khazak's torso to see what he found.

"I see it," Khazak is already headed toward the cart in the distance.

We dismount once we're closer. It's just a simple wooden cart, plain as can be. A horse is even still attached. The animal seems alright, if not a little spooked. The cart is also *not* empty, like you would expect after a cart-jacking. Both orcs look just as puzzled as I do.

"Is it just me, or does this seem kinda..." I wave my hand in the cart's general direction. "Full?"

"No, we will need Farmer Stouthand to confirm, but this is very odd." He looks up from the cart and off into the distance. "I am also disturbed by how close we are to the city. Keep a distance from the cart until we can be sure no traps have been set, magical or otherwise."

I peer off into the same direction he is, and faaaaar off in the distance, I can *just* barely make out the city's wall. *We are close.*

"Ranger Deepfist, David, please search the area but remain nearby." Khazak moves to mount his horse again. "I will return with reinforcements."

"Yes, sir." Arik salutes.

"Yes, Sir." I try to salute.

The two of us split up, each slowly searching one half of the forest, making sure to keep the cart in sight. It's completely silent out here, and no matter how hard the two of us look, we both come up empty. About twenty minutes later, Khazak returns along with another horse and three officers.

"The immediate area is clear, sir," Arik reports as he approaches.

"Thank you, Ranger Deepfist." Khazak nods as they all dismount. "A search party is on the way to help comb the area. Officer Frostsong, please check the cart for any potential traps before you assist the others."

"Yes, sir." The forensic mage steps forward, already scanning the cart with his magic.

After he gives us the all clear, the rangers conduct a very careful physical inspection before deeming it safe. It's decided that the best thing to do is to bring it back into the city so that the farmer can check the contents. I volunteer to drive the cart back with Khazak riding his horse alongside me. Steering one of these is a lot less intimidating than riding them.

I take note of the horse pulling the cart. Bist, I think the farmer called him. He's older but not unhealthy. The same breed as Khazak's, just a little smaller. Definitely a workhorse, probably not used to doing more than pulling this cart around. Poor guy got more of a workout today than he has in a while.

"I didn't realize you had horses here in Nova." I know plenty of people brought horses with them, but I didn't think any were native.

"There are a few species of wild horses on the plains in the west, but *these* horses were actually a gift, or at least the original herd was." Khazak pats the mane of the black horse he's riding. "They were originally from Northern

Albion, gifted by a visiting delegation of elves almost a century ago. Farmer Stouthand's family has been responsible for raising them." Then he pauses, turning to me. "'Nova...' Is that what you call this part of the world?"

"Yeah, 'Nova Mundus.'" I nod my head.

"You know those words literally just mean 'New World' in Ancient Elutian, right?" He looks over, one eyebrow cocked.

"No, I did not." I shake my head. *Why would I know that?* "Why, what do *you* call it?"

"It goes by many different names." I groan at his answer. "Most of them hold the same meaning. We call it 'Avural Ug'dol.' It means 'turtle island.'"

"Why is it called that?" I have seen *some* turtles but not like a ton.

"Its shape resembles a turtle. Or so I am told." He shrugs.

We return the horse to the stable and take the cart back to the station. The farmer comes in a little later to inspect it, but he'll need time to do a full inventory. He agrees that it looks like most of his items are still inside, and he's just as confused as we are. It's the afternoon by the time the search party returns, and unfortunately, it's empty handed.

"No luck, sir. We could not find a sign of anyone or thing out there," Arik reports to Khazak in his office.

"Damn." Khazak wipes his hand down his face in frustration, fingers combing through his beard. "Spirits help me, what is happening in this city?"

It's late in the evening and almost time to go home when the officer helping the farmer returns with a list of what is actually missing. Only one thing.

"*Flauk?* All the stole was some dammed flauk?" Khazak asks in frustration.

"That is what he said, sir," the officer confirms from across the desk.

"What is 'flauk'?" I ask after the officer leaves Khazak's office.

"Fertilizer. You would know it as…" Khazak pauses as he tries to think of the word. "Saltpeter. It is mined by dwarves in the west, who then send it to a group of halflings who process it into fertilizer."

"Eww, fertilizer?" As I scrunch up my nose, there's a knock on the open door as Ragnar enters the office, ready to start the night shift. *Damn, is it that late already?*

"I heard there was another robbery?" He comes in looking both worried and excited.

"Yes," Khazak sighs. "This one took place just outside of the city."

"Do you think it's related to the last one?" Ragnar takes a seat across from Khazak.

"Unfortunately, yes. Once again stole a single item was stolen: flauk. Saltpeter," Khazak repeats the information we just learned. "Additionally, we were told they wore the same black robes as the one we found at the factory."

"Wait, the carriage!" The mention of the robes jogs my memory. "I've seen it before."

"You have?" Khazak asks me.

"Yes, and so have you. Twice." If I'm remembering right, at least. "The first time was on my first day here when I saved that little girl. The carriage that almost hit her was black with black horses. Then it happened again a few weeks ago when we were on our way to the factory. *You* pulled *me* out of the way that time."

"I remember that." Khazak's eyes go slightly wide.

"That can't be a coincidence." They passed *right* by us. "They must have fled the warehouse once they knew we were tracking them."

"If that is true, then it means they are taking the cart in and out of the city." Khazak turns to look at Ragnar.

"We need to speak with the guards working each of the gates, and then we need to tell the entire force to be on the lookout for that carriage." He pauses and looks at the clock on his wall. "Perhaps we should stay and continue working a little longer."

"Are you sure? They probably won't try anything again so soon. I'll talk to Keenguard and make sure we get the info to everyone." *Wow, is he actually asking to do more work?* "I can talk to the guards tonight, too. That way you two can attack everything with fresh eyes in the morning."

"That sounds like a good plan, Deputy." Khazak smiles at his friend.

"Who the hell steals sulfur and saltpeter anyway?" Ragnar asks no one in particular.

Sulfur? "Did someone steal sulfur?"

"Yeah, the brimstone." Ragnar turns to answer me. "That's just sulfur."

I don't think I knew that. *Sulfur and saltpeter.* Why does that sound familiar?

The words continue to nag at me as we pack up our things and head home for the night. I stop thinking about them sometime during dinner, and it's not until the next morning when I see a tired looking Ragnar leaving for home that they return. *Sulfur and saltpeter.* I spend the rest of the morning in the breakroom, trying to figure out why those words are stuck in my head.

"*Drepa lat*, David." I look up from my cup of coffee to see Nikka walking in. *Must be working at this station today.*

"Drepa lat, Nikka." I repeat back her 'good morning.' Turns out reading about a language doesn't mean much until you actually start using it.

"You are getting better." She smiles as she pours her own mug of coffee and sits to join me. "What is on your mind?"

"Just something that Deputy Rockfang said yesterday." I chew my lip as I continue to think on it. "'Sulfur and saltpeter.' Those words mean...something, but I can't remember what."

"Sulfur and saltpeter?" Nikka frowns. "Those are two of the ingredients in—"

"Black powder," we both say in unison, Nikka's words finally making things click.

"The only thing missing is—"

"Charcoal." "Carbo—I mean charcoal." *Less in unison.*

"Where did you hear those words?" She sits up straight, as one does when talking about explosives.

"Yesterday, there was another robbery—this time the only thing they took was saltpeter," I inform her.

Her eyes go wide. "Do you think we can expect another robbery for charcoal?"

Nikka's words jog something else from my memory. "Actually, I'm worried it might have already happened." I stand and motion for her to follow.

I find Khazak in the front of the station talking with some officers and tap him on the shoulder.

"What is it?" He can see that I look hurried.

"Can I see the list from the first robbery? The missing militia shipment?" I need to see *exactly* what was on there.

"The book is locked up in the evidence room." He turns and dismisses the officers he was speaking to. "Let me help you find it."

We follow Khazak to the evidence room, which only he and a few others have access to. It's filled with all sorts of shelves and boxes, each item belonging to a currently open case. Khazak heads straight for a bookshelf against the far wall, moving his hand along the spines as he searches.

"Here we are." He pulls the red book from the shelf, flipping through its singed pages. "You said you wanted to know what was in the missing shipment?"

"Yes, please." *I hope I'm wrong.*

"Alright, we have two-dozen steel longswords, ten set of full-plate armor, five chainmail tunics, 80 kilograms of fuel—"

"What kind of fuel?" Nikka pipes up.

"Hmm, it does not specify, but given where it was coming from, I would assume charcoal," Khazak says nonchalantly.

"Fuck." Exactly what I didn't want to hear.

"What is it?" Khazak looks confused.

"Well, that, plus the sulfur from the church, and the saltpeter from the farmer equals..." I count off with my fingers in the air.

"Oh no." Khazak connects the dots the same as we did, standing up straight. "I need to contact Chief Grandtooth and Deputy Keenguard. Officer Silentfang, please gather the files we have on all three cases. David, I need you to go to Deputy Rockfang's home and ask him to come in. Meet back in my office as soon as possible." He pauses. "And for now, please keep this to yourselves."

"Yes, sir!" Nikka nods and salutes.

"You got it, Sir." I am less formal.

We split up to take care of our respective assignments. Ragnar and Nylan live in the northwest from the station, kind of between our place and the park. A bleary-eyed Ragnar answers the door after a few knocks, and I apologize for waking him early before his shift tonight, explaining as much as I can in hushed tones. *That* wakes him up, and he throws on his uniform and comes back to the station with me. Khazak, Nikka, and Deputy Keenguard are all gathered and waiting for us when we arrive, but there's no sign of Chief Grandtooth.

"The chief is unfortunately busy and unable to join us." Khazak sighs, answering my question before I can ask.

"Bureaucrat," Ragnar mumbles under his breath.

"I will be meeting with him later to discuss what we talk about here." Khazak pretends like he didn't hear that. "This is too important to wait."

"What is going on, Captain?" Keenguard crosses her arms, looking concerned.

"David said you found something important related to the robberies?" Ragnar repeats the words I used to get him down here.

"If we are to believe that all three are connected, then as David and Officer Silentfang have discovered, it is possible our assailants have been gathering the ingredients to manufacture black powder." Ragnar and Keenguard's eyes both go wide. "Obviously, we need to take care of this immediately, but given our lack of information, I do not wish to cause an unnecessary panic. As it is, we will need to double patrols inside *and* outside of the city. Everyone is working overtime for the foreseeable future."

"Yes, sir," Keenguard responds. Neither deputy looks happy about the news, but there aren't many other options. "I will ask the officers to keep their ears to the ground for any rumors."

"Thank you." Khazak looks at Ragnar. "Deputy Rockfang, were you able to speak with the gate guards and find out if they had seen the black carriage?"

"I talked to them, but no one had seen anything. They didn't even have anything in the visitor's logs for the hours around when the farmer was attacked. They will report to us first thing if they see the carriage or learn something. Same goes for the rest of the squad." Ragnar sits up straight, looking serious. "Sir, I know it's not exactly protocol, but I think we should speak with Thog Grimrock again."

"Given the seriousness of the situation, I was considering that myself, Deputy." Khazak sighs. "Please contact the prison and arrange for Mr. Grimrock to be brought in for additional questioning."

"Yes, sir." He nods.

The rest of the day is spent running around the city, passing along information or gathering people for meetings. Even Ragnar, who I figured would go back home to finish sleeping before his shift sticks around to help. By the time Khazak and I finally leave that night, he's still hard at work. I'm actually impressed.

"So, is it just me or does it seem like Ragnar's been working harder than usual?" I ask after starting the walk home.

"No, I have noticed it as well. It is a nice change of pace." Khazak grimaces at his own words. "That sounded bad. Ragnar is a wonderful deputy—he would not hold the position otherwise—but he has not always taken the job very seriously. I am happy to see him growing into the ranger I know he can be."

"He just needed a kick in the ass to get him moving. Probably helps that we figured out our enemy might be cooking up something explosive." *Nothing like a little danger to get people acting serious.*

"There is something I was curious about," Khazak starts. "I hope this does not offend you but... how did you figure that out?"

"Why? Doesn't seem like something a dummy like me would know?" I look over to my right to catch the wince Khazak makes when I ask.

"I apologize. I should know by now not to underestimate you," he admits. "Was it something your brother taught you?"

"Actually, you can thank the academy for that one." I remember the lesson well. "Lutheria is on a really big island, but it's still an island. Using canons is something they actually still teach."

"I had not considered that." Khazak tilts his head.

"It wasn't like we were making the black powder ourselves, but the instructors still wanted us to know how it worked." Just one of many things they drilled into our heads. "CSS: charcoal, sulfur, and saltpeter."

"Thankfully, given our location, I do not think we will have to worry about canons much." He's got a point.

"No, but they could still make some nasty bombs." *That's not what I'm really thinking about though.* "But what I'm more worried about is rifles. Guns. Do you guys use those around here for hunting?" I haven't noticed any, at least.

"Not generally, no." Khazak frowns. "Aside from the fact that they are loud and scare off everything you aren't aiming at, bullets have a tendency to fragment, which can leave meat inedible or damage something else. We try not to waste any part of our kills here."

"Then hopefully our thieves haven't taken a sudden interest in firearms." I have no idea how difficult it would be to get your hands on one around here.

"Yes, hopefully." I can tell I just gave Khazak a whole new set of worries. "Do you have any experience with them yourselves?"

"Not really." Nothing more than what I've seen at least. "About halfway through last year the academy started to train a rifle contingent but... I don't really know how well it was going. It was dangerous. One guy died when his own gun backfired on him. I avoided the whole thing."

"Not the wrong idea, I think." Glad that makes two of us.

We go in bright and early the next morning to find Ragnar waiting for us. He looks tired, probably on his fifth or sixth cup of coffee, but he seems oddly collected. He stands when we enter.

"Captain." Ragnar salutes, his turn to be in full business mode. "Mr. Grimrock is in the interrogation room. We are ready to start when you are, sir."

"Lead the way, Deputy." Khazak returns the salute, sharing a small look of surprise with me at Ragnar's continued hard work.

The two of us follow him to the interrogation room where a guard has been posted outside. He's wearing a uniform that is different from the others I've seen. *Must be from the prison.* Entering the room reveals Thog seated and cuffed to the table, another guard in a similar uniform standing next to him.

"Are we finally getting started?" Thog grouses from his side of the table.

"Sorry to keep you waiting, Mr. Grimrock." Ragnar sits at the table while Khazak and I stand in the back.

"Let me guess: I am here because of something I could not have possibly had anything to do with?" Thog asks from his seat.

"Not a bad guess." *Yeah, a 'guess.'* "There has indeed been another robbery."

"Well, I have been locked in a cell since I last saw you, so I am not sure what you need from me." The imprisoned orc rolls his eyes.

"What's interesting about this robbery is that, just like the last one, only a single thing was stolen. Want to take a guess at what?" Thog only cocks an eyebrow and shakes his head no. "Flauk. Saltpeter. Fertilizer. And the time before that, the only thing taken was brimstone. Something about that just seems really odd to me. For the last two nights, all I could think about was why would someone steal saltpeter and brimstone?"

"Now, when we include the robbery you *claim* to have committed, some of my colleagues were able to make a pretty troubling connection," Ragnar continues, sounding incredibly put together for someone who's been up all night. "One of the things in the militia shipment you said you 'destroyed' was charcoal. Do you know what you get when you combine charcoal, saltpeter, and brimstone?" Thog shakes his head no again. "Black powder. Do you know what that is?" Another headshake. "It's a powder that explodes when it's ignited. People use it to fire cannons, or rifles, or to build bombs."

Thog's posture goes still, but he remains silent.

"I'm going to be honest with you, Thog. If that's what this person or these people are doing, then I'm worried. I believe you when you say that you don't know anything about these robberies. Really. But I know you know *something*, and I need you to tell me what that is."

Thog looks at Ragnar, then down at the tabletop.

"Please," Ragnar pleads. "Thog, people are going to get hurt."

For a split second, I see a look of hesitation on Thog's face, like he wants to say something, but it's gone in an instant, and he's stonily staring down again. "I told you. I do not have any idea what you are talking about."

Ragnar watches Thog's face closely for a moment, looking for any sign that he might change his mind, but no. He's done. "Alright, take him back to his cell," Ragnar says with a sigh as he stands. The three of us exit the room, moving to Khazak's office where Ragnar takes a seat on the couch.

"I really thought he was going to tell me something." He sounds dejected, and so much more tired than he did fifteen minutes ago.

"I did too," I speak up. I don't want Ragnar thinking he did a bad job. That was almost inspiring. "There was a second there, right at the end, where it looked like he wanted to say something, but then it was gone."

"You did some good today, Deputy. I am honestly impressed with how you ran that interrogation, and all of your hard work from the last two days." Khazak puts his hand on his friend's shoulder. "If Mr. Grimrock does not want to talk, there is not much we can do to make him. Which means I need *you* to go home and get some rest because unfortunately for the rest of us, this is going to mean a lot of extra work."

I groan inwardly. *Yaaaay. More work.*

Chapter 10

It's dark in the forest, the trees blocking out most of the *stars and moonlight. Pretty spooky. Good thing I'm only here to—Wait, why am I in the forest at night? Before I can think about that too much, I hear some rustling ahead of me, and I'm frozen in place as a large, black, wolf slinks out from behind the brush. Its fur is like an empty void, and its eyes are red as blood, almost glowing. As it comes toward me, two more wolves appear, each just as large as the first one with the same red eyes and pitch-black fur. I start move away, and when the first wolf growls, baring its bright white teeth at me, I trip, falling backward over some dammed tree roots. Seeing an opportunity, the wolf leaps at me, jaws snapping—!*

"...and then I woke up," I finish recounting my nightmare.

"That *is* a really weird dream," Liss agrees with me.

"And they've only been getting weirder." *This is the second one about wolves, too.*

"Do you normally have dreams like that?" Corrine asks from her seat on Liss's right.

"Not before coming here." I shake my head. "They didn't start until...shit, maybe when I hit my head in the temple ruins?"

"Is that why you look so tired?" Liss doesn't beat around the bush.

"...Partially." I narrow my eyes. "Work has been...rough."

"Oh? Has work been rough for you?" I wince at Liss's sarcastic tone.

"I know, I know. Sorry." I sigh, wondering how much I should tell them. "There's been these robberies over the last few weeks. We haven't had much luck in tracking down the people behind them, and it's starting to look like they might be planning something really dangerous. Everyone's been working extra shifts." *Longer ones, too.*

"I'm sorry, David." Corrine frowns. "I wish there was something we could do to help."

"...Yeah, sorry." *Aww, Liss actually means it.*

"It's fine. I think you guys have more than enough to worry about in here. And in a few more weeks, it won't be any of our problems!" I try to sound positive, but something about that statement makes me feel a twinge of sadness. "Actually, that reminds me: Can you let Adam know I'm gonna miss visiting day next week? We're on patrol duty in the forest again."

"Maybe a week in the woods will do you some good." Corrine tries to cheer me up. "You can relax."

"Trust me—with everything going on, it's going to be anything but relaxing."

We leave for the patrol camp after lunch the next day, this time through the north gate. I'm so mentally worn-out from all the long shifts lately that I don't even think to ask about or pay attention to our path there. I just trail after Sir like a mindless drone. I'm not even sure *he's* paying that much attention.

The north camp looks pretty similar to the east camp we were at four weeks ago. It's also more crowded, thanks to Khazak deciding to double all the patrol shifts. I'm not really complaining, or at least I'm trying not to. If these assholes are somehow getting in and out of the city without using the gates, then we have to do whatever we can to catch them, hopefully in the act. At this point, that's all we can hope for.

After dropping our stuff off in our tent, we join the other *nine* orcs crowded under the large open tent. Everyone salutes as we approach, but as soon as Sir returns it, several of them *immediately* start to talk at the same time. I wouldn't be able to understand them even if we spoke the same language.

"I know, I know." Khazak holds his hands out in front of him in surrender. "I need to speak with Druid Darkwolf first, then I will answer all of your questions."

He leaves us and heads for the tent on the other side of the fire, the orcs going back to talking amongst themselves while we wait. I notice now that everyone else still has their bags or packs on them. I see Glasha and Arik as well as some familiar looking officers, but everyone else is a new-ish face. All except one: Orim!

"Hello, David," he says with a smile as I approach. "It is good to see you."

"*Zratza*, Orim." He sounds so much better than I do. *Shit, how does this next part go?* "*Kip'ra sol'tu vu.*"

"Close. It is '*sil'ta*,'" he corrects me with a grin. "You have improved much."

"Still not as good as you." *Can't even say 'I am happy to see you,' correctly.*

"I have been practicing much longer than you have." He squeezes my shoulder to console me.

"I know, I know." I smile to let him know it's alright. I'm not actually bothered or anything; it's just that learning stuff from books has never been my strong suit. I'm glad Khazak likes to read out loud because I tend to get bored with a book a few pages in.

Khazak makes his way back over to us with another orc in tow, I assume the druid. She's younger than Shaman Wu'dag was, but still old enough to have plenty of grey streaks in her long black hair. She's dressed more athletically, a set of light leather armor adorning her body and a set of boots on her feet.

"Ranger Broadedge, David, this is Druid Drasta Darkwolf, the spellcaster for the north patrol camp." She stands at Khazak's side while he makes introductions.

"It is good to meet the both of you." She gives each of us a small bow of the head. *She might be the first orc I've met who isn't a hugger*. "The captain has informed me you have a busy night ahead, so let us get things started."

She hands Orim his own compass stone before instructing the ten of us to gather up so that she can sync them. We form a circle—a very squished circle—but manage to get everyone's hands in the center. Once she's done charging them, and I feel the stone give a familiar pulse in my palm, I slip it back into my pocket. The only reason I didn't forget it was because I never took it out of Sir's bag.

"As you have all noticed, things are a bit crowded in camp at the moment," Khazak starts speaking to the group. "Unfortunately, until we manage to deal with our potential assailants, this is how things are going to be. Everyone will need to bunk up with someone else for the week." There are a few groans. "That includes me. Additionally, our patrol schedule been doubled, and two officers are now responsible for walking a perimeter around the camp. So, figure out what your sleeping arrangements are going to be and quickly. The first round of patrols starts in ten minutes."

The group breaks apart after that, rangers and officers talking to each other to figure out who's going to sleep with who. Which we will apparently *also* be doing. I turn to Sir for some clarification.

"You know, I could point out that there are *already* two people sharing your tent." *Okay, maybe I want to complain a little first.*

"You could, but somehow I think you will refrain." He cocks an eyebrow. He has perhaps been *slightly* less tolerable of my 'smart-ass mouth' this past week as Ragnar put it.

"Okay, well, I was thinking we could maybe ask Orim since it's his first time out here and all?" I know he's older than me, but I want to look out for my buddy.

"That is very thoughtful of you, David." He gives me a warm smile. "Please go ask him. I need to speak with Druid Darkwolf again about changes to the warding spells in the area."

He leaves us again, and I look over to see Orim looking a little like the awkward new kid at school. It kinda reminds me of when me and Mikey started taking different classes, and I got nervous he wasn't going to have an easy time making friends. He was fine, of course, and also Orim's a 6'2" bald orc with a full beard, but still.

"Orim," he looks over as I approach, "would you like to share a tent with Captain Ironstorm and me for the week?"

"Yes, thank you." He nods his head, looking relieved.

"Great! Let's get your stuff inside." It'll be just like camping with my friends.

"How many more of these do we have to do tonight?" I ask Khazak wearily. We are headed back to camp after our *third* patrol of the night, the sun having set about twenty minutes ago. It's dark. *Really* dark.

"This is the last one," he responds, just as tired as I am. "You *do* know I am not enjoying this any more than you are, right?"

"I know. I'm sorry." It's been a *long* week. "Do you think this is going to work?"

"I certainly hope so because I am at a loss for what to do next." He sounds frustrated. "We spent the entire week searching every corner of the city and *still* turned up nothing. It feels like all we are doing is waiting for their next move."

"Hey, we'll catch them," I try to reassure him. I understand how he feels, having a problem but the only thing you can do for it is to wait. I hate wait—***THUD***

"*Oww, fuck!*" I stumble backward after walking face-first into a tree.

"Are you alright?" the dark, Khazak-shaped shadow asks me.

"No, I just walked into a fucking tree." *I hate trees.* "How do you even see where you're going right now?"

"Fairly decent night-vision. Something most orcs have." The shadow moves closer, and I feel a pair of hands grip my shoulders to adjust me. "I should have thought about that before we left camp. Druid Darkwolf would have been able to improve yours."

"She can?" One of the hands moves up to cup my chin, inspecting the damage.

"Enough to ensure you will not attempt to get friendly with any more trees." He takes my hand as he steps back. "About as good as an orc or a dwarf but less than an elf or gnome."

"What about you? Can you heal me?" I gesture in the dark at my face. "We're talking about the moneymaker."

"No, but I will clean you up when we get back to camp." He chuckles, leading me away by hand.

Food is already on the fire by the time we get back to camp, which is even harder for me to find thanks to the illusion hiding the campfire. From the inside, you can actually see where the camp perimeter ends, a ring of darkness surrounding the light of the fire. Dinner is rabbits and birds, and frankly less than an ideal amount for eleven people. We make do though, and everyone starts eating once the last of the rangers has returned. Khazak assigns one of the officers to spend the following morning fishing, something Druid Darkwolf offers to assist with.

After our earlier talk about eyes, I can't help but look around at the others while we sit around the fire, noticing for the first time just how wide all of the orcs' pupils are in the darkness. *Must be useful for hunting.* We aren't up for too much later after that, everyone exhausted from all their patrols. The watch shift is decided, and everyone turns in for the night.

When I wake up next, it's dark, almost pitch black, the only light coming from the faint glow of the campfire barely penetrating the stretched leather walls of the tent. *What time is it?* Khazak is asleep behind me, arm around my waist with a leg thrown over mine, while Orim is in his own bedroll in front of me. We've probably only been asleep a few hours since we haven't been woken up for our watch shift yet.

Ugh, why am I awake? Especially if I'm going to have to wake up again in like an hour anyway. I silently grumble to myself and try to find a comfortable position to fall back to sleep in. As I shift, so does the body behind me, and I can feel Khazak hard against me, only noticing now how hard my own dick is. We haven't had sex all week, too busy or tired from work. I know I was a virgin a couple of months ago, but we've been having sex at least every other day up until now. I have needs!

I reach down and give myself a squeeze. I haven't jerked off in all this time either. Like, over a month. That's gotta be some kind of record for me. I wonder if I could...*pull* one off right now (*heh*). I mean, I know I'm capable—you don't grow up sharing a bedroom with a twin brother and not learn how to rub one out in secret—but what do I do with the uh, aftermath?

...*I guess I could eat it?* The thought makes my stomach roll. I've swallowed the cum of a *few* men at this point, but something about the thought of tasting my own just seems different and weird.

...I mean, I'm still gonna do it. *What?* I'm fuckin' horny!

With a hand still holding on to myself, I shift my top leg downward *very* slowly, trying not to wake the orc I'm sharing a bedroll with. I've done this before but never with someone *directly* behind me. Or touching me, either. But I'm less worried about waking up Sir than I am Orim. *Hell, Sir might join in.*

I grip myself firmly, sliding my hand down and pulling the skin back from my head. I think for a second about spitting to get things slick, but I'm not sure how silently I can do that. Plus, it's the middle of the night, and my mouth is pretty dry. 'S alright, I can make it work.

I start to stroke myself slowly, just small movements of my wrist. It feels good, but it's not enough. There's no way I'll cum like this. Feeling a little bolder, I start to use my whole arm, making the top of our bedroll moving slightly with each pump of my hand. It's *still* not quite enough, but maybe if I just mo—

"What do you think you are doing?" Khazak's voice whispering in my ear almost makes me yelp in surprise.

"Jerking off?" I answer in a whisper once my heart stops pounding.

"Right now? You could not wait for a more opportune moment?" His mouth is right next to my ear, and it makes me shiver. "Did I give you permission to do that?"

"What? We haven't had sex in like five—" I pause when I process the second thing he said. "Since when do I need permission to jerk off?!" I try to aim my voice behind me, my eyes watching Orim's form, paranoid we're going to wake him.

"I am not sure why you were ever under the impression that you did not. I own that part of you the same as everything else." The way he's whispering in my ear is hot, even when he says something ridiculous like that.

"You can't—"

"Can and have, David." His tone is full of finality.

"But—"

Orim's sudden mumbling cuts me off, making me freeze. I can't make out what he's saying, but Sir does and responds. Orim says something that sounds vaguely like a question, and when Khazak answers him, he chuckles, saying something else before rolling over and facing away from us.

"What just happened?" I am a little too freaked out to pay attention after getting surprised by both orcs in the last five minutes.

"After I informed him of our busy schedule and your apparent *dire* need for attention, he wanted to give us some privacy." I can *hear* the smirk on his face.

"I do not have a 'dire need'!" I whisper-yell.

"And yet you have spent the last two minutes complaining about not being allowed to masturbate." If it wouldn't get my ass tanned, I'd elbow him in the stomach right now. "You have not even tried asking me for permission yet."

"Fine. Can I jerk off?" I'm not even sure I want to anymore at this point. My dick is only at half-mast after all that. Also, *everyone is awake now.*

"No," he responds smugly. *I don't know why I thought that would work.* "But now that I am awake, I suppose it is my responsibility to make sure you are taken care of."

"What? He's *right* next to us." I immediately get Khazak's words. I know Orim said he was giving us 'privacy,' but come on. "I get that you guys are open with this stuff, but that still seems pretty rude."

"Ruder than continuing to loudly whisper next to him while he is trying to sleep?" Okay, I am seriously starting to weigh the pros and cons of nut-tapping a smart-ass orc in a tent in the middle of the forest. "You know, there is one option that would not be rude at all."

I don't get what Khazak is implying until he nudges me in Orim's direction. The fact that I'm still considering doing anything right now, and that my dick isn't completely soft, tells me I'm not against the idea. I've certainly gotten more comfortable with checking out a man's body lately, and I'd be lying if I hadn't done that to Orim at least once or twice. I'm just a little worried it might make things weird between us. Not that things got weird with Ragnar or Nylan...and it *would* be less rude than just fucking next to him...which I've apparently decided is happening now.

I tap Orim gently on the shoulder, getting him to turn around and face me. When he does, the lack of light means I can't tell how he's looking at me right now. I'm not sure how much of that conversation he was paying attention to or even understood. When I lean forward and slowly press my lips to his, there's a small sound of surprise before he begins kissing me back gently.

I feel the rumble from Sir's chuckle behind me, his own cock not having lost an inch of its hardness. After running his hand down my chest and stomach, he flips down the top of our bedroll, turning away from me so that he can rummage through his bag. As I continue to slowly kiss Orim, I feel a familiar magical charm being pressed to my stomach followed by the sound of a vial of oil being opened.

I place one hand on Orim's side as Khazak turns me slightly, so he can better access my ass. In turn, he rubs his hand along my back, finally daring to slip his tongue into my mouth. I eagerly deepen the kiss while a slick finger prods at my hole. Orim's tusks are larger than Khazak's, and I'm still impressed by how easy it is to kiss with them. I groan low into Orim's mouth as the finger inside me pushes deeper.

One finger becomes two, and then three, Sir wanting to make sure I'm really opened up. I appreciate it because after not taking anything up my ass for the last week, I really seem to have tightened back up. *That's not something I've ever thought before.* Orim's cock is pressing into my thigh, and I am thankful for his mouth swallowing down my whimpers since I still don't want to wake up anyone else in the camp.

Khazak shifts behind me, lining up his groin with my ass and prodding me with his hard length. I reach back with the hand I had on Orim's shoulder, holding myself open as Sir guides his cock home. I gasp when the head breaches me, grabbing Orim in front of me to hold myself steady as Khazak enters and stretches me.

I reach my hand down to the new ranger's cock, squeezing it and pulling a few moans from its owner. Khazak's grip on my hip tightens as he bottoms out, tearing me from Orim's mouth as I adjust to him. After giving me a moment to recover, Orim reaches for my head, this time guiding me toward his chest.

Swiping my tongue out against his green skin, I find my mouth placed right over his nipple. Feeling him shudder as I slide over it, I latch on with my mouth, sucking lightly and getting another shudder. Behind me, Sir pulls his hips back before pressing himself back into my hole. He pumps himself into me at a steady pace, the faint sound of our skin slapping together filling the tent.

I continue to nurse on the nipple in my mouth, occasional biting down gently. I'm grateful as it helps muffle all my moaning and groaning. Orim's hand is still on the back of my head, holding me to his chest as he trembles above me, the occasional moan falling from his lips. I reach my hand up to squeeze his other pec, moving my fingers across the broad hairy muscle and teasing his other nipple with my fingertips. All while Sir continues to fuck into me.

Like he always does, Khazak knows exactly how to fuck me, and it's not long before I feel the tension in my body starting to build. The closer I get to cumming, the harder it becomes to focus, and I end up letting go of Orim's chest to grip his arm tightly trying to anchor myself. I'm not even playing with his chest anymore, just using it to muffle my noises as I start to fall over the edge for the first time in days.

"*Oh fuck,*" I whimper into Orim's skin as I feel my hole spasming against Khazak weakly.

He fucks me through it, never stuttering or slowing. Orim's thumb strokes the back of my neck, and after I come down a little, I manage to gather my wits enough to go back to sucking on the tit in my mouth, even though I'm pretty sure I've drooled all over him at this point. I need the distraction because I know it's only a matter of time before it happens again.

Or maybe not since I can already feel Sir behind me start speeding up. He probably needed this as much as I did. The hand holding my hip in place gets tighter, and if I wasn't the one getting fucked right now, I might have the sense to worry about any extra noise we might be making. But I don't, so I just keep nursing on the orc in front of me while the one behind me fucks me as deeply as he can, growling low through (I think) gritted teeth.

Inside me, it feels like his cock is growing larger as he unloads. It pulses with every shot, the familiar warmth that follows spreading deep within me. Orim releases my head, and Khazak and I both breathe deeply as we bask in the afterglow. The inside of the tent is warm, smelling like sweat and musk, and honestly, it's pretty nice. Sir bends forward to nuzzle at my neck.

I feel his softening cock slip from me, and I do my best to tighten my hole, so I don't leave a mess on our bed-roll. Although it's not really *my* mess. I reach forward for Orim blindly, wanting to make sure he knows I haven't forgotten he's there. I just...need a minute. Which is exactly how much time I get before Khazak flips me around to face him, giving me brief kisses to my forehead and lips before lifting his head to look over me.

"Your turn, ranger," he tells his subordinate, reaching behind me to hand over the vial of lube, then grabbing my ass and spreading me open.

"Thank you, Captain, for granting me the use of your avakesh," Orim responds as he shifts himself closer to me.

Something inside me shivers at the way they're talking about me, not *to* me. The way Sir flipped me over and offered me without even asking, the way he's holding me open right now. *I am so fucked up.* I can feel the messy state my ass is in, trying in vain to not to let any of Sir slip out of me. Orim slides his slick cock up and down across my hole before he tentatively presses in.

Khazak's mouth finds mine as his ranger enters me. I haven't gotten a good look at Orim's dick, but he felt thick in my hand, maybe even thicker than Khazak. After the first inch or so, it starts to feel thick in my ass as well, and I whimper pitifully into Sir's mouth as I'm stretched even wider. I'm actually glad Sir went first; it feels like I might have needed the extra stretching and lube for Orim to fully sheath himself within me.

Khazak kisses me lazily as he watches, or mostly listens, as I'm fucked right in front of him. He strokes his hands down my sides and chest lightly, making me shiver when he tweaks one of my nipples. Behind me, Orim pulls himself back a few inches before smoothly gliding back into me, aided I'm sure by the load already inside. His technique is different from Khazak and Ragnar, much gentler and more unhurried. Maybe it's because I'm his friend? Or maybe he's worried about damaging the captain's property.

Either way, it feels great, especially combined with the slow sleepy kisses Khazak is pressing against my mouth. His hands continue to rub and tweak my chest, and I can feel myself getting close again. I reach for Sir to hold myself steady. Sensing what is about to happen, he kisses me hard before tearing his lips from mine.

"He is getting close, ranger," Khazak informs Orim. "You almost have him there. *Fuck him.*"

Oh fuck, that's all I needed to hear, and a second later, I cum again, this time on Orim's cock. I bite my lip, struggling to hold in my moans and keep the tent's noise level down. I feel Khazak's hand on my chin, lifting it up before he recaptures my mouth, swallowing the sounds of my pleasure.

Apparently, that was all Orim needed to hear too because he finally cums as well, growling loudly as he drives his cock into me one, two, three times, and holding himself there. I cry out weakly when he pulls me backward, using his strength to hold me in place as he explodes within my hole. Each shot of his thick member leaves me feeling even fuller than the last. *Fuck, is there even any room left?*

The three of us lay there together in heap, limbs thrown over one another, all of us covered in a sheen of sweat.

Orim's softening cock is still inside of me, his arm over my waist, while I rest my forehead against Khazak's chest and catch my breath. One of Khazak's legs is in between mine, and his hand traces patterns in the sweat on my shoulder. It's nice, the three of us resting together as we slowly return to the land of the living.

Which is why the sudden rapping against our tent makes me squawk and jump. *What is with people scaring me tonight!?* Both orcs laugh, and I bury my face in Khazak's chest to hide my embarrassment. Before I or anyone else has a chance to cover ourselves, Orim is slipping himself out of me and turning over to open the tent flap. When I realize what he's doing, I try to dig myself into Khazak even farther.

"Sorry, we uh, did not want to interrupt." It's Arik, who must be on watch right now. "But it is time for your watch shift."

"Thank you, Ranger Deepfist. We will be right out." I can hear Khazak's amused tone above me.

Things are only slightly awkward when we stumble out of the tent half-dressed. I can't bring myself to make eye contact with anyone, but I do notice that the other officer on watch is sporting a pretty prominent hard on. Something I am going to choose to take as a compliment. Once the awkward feelings have passed and everyone else has returned to sleep, it is just the three of us sitting around the fire together.

"Thank you for that, Captain, and you, David." Orim is smiling kinda shyly for someone who just fucked and bred me. "I have not...done that with more than one person before."

I open my mouth to say 'you're welcome' but realize how weird that sounds in regard to sex. It's not like I was doing him a favor.

"I should be thanking *you*, Ranger Broadedge," Khazak answers before I have a chance, sitting next to me and running his fingers through my hair. "As you can see, if my pup goes too long without being serviced, he can get rather cranky."

I turn and narrow my eyes at my owner. "I never should have taught you how to be funny."

"Who said I was joking?" he replies with a smirk. I can only grumble in response.

Chapter 11

"Can your magic heal sore feet?" *All these hills are killing me.*

"I suppose that is one potential application," Khazak chuckles. "Tell you what: if you manage to continue behaving today, I will do that before bed tonight."

"I *always* behave," I lie.

It's Ignisday, our third day in the forest and second full day on patrol. It's late afternoon and the sky is grey, covered in a thick layer of clouds that hides the sun's position, but we shouldn't have a problem making it back to camp before it's dark. Just like yesterday, all of today's patrols have turned up absolutely nothing. I know we have four more days out here, but I was really hoping we'd have found something by now. We're heading northwest, which explains all the fucking hills. I can see the mountainside off in the distance ahead of us.

Other than all the extra bodies and walking, this patrol week hasn't been that different from the last one. Just with a *lot* less free time. Which has been fine, because after me, Khazak, and Orim had our bout of fun in the tent, it's been hard to make eye contact with Arik and the officer who overheard us. We haven't had a repeat, mostly because I haven't gotten as desperately horny again yet, but I guess the possibility is always there.

After our play time, I was feeling a little worried that things might change between me and Orim. It's not like he's the only friend I've had sex with since being here (Hello, Brull, Nylan, and Ragnar), but he's the first one I made on my own instead of someone I met through Khazak. I'm happy to say Orim's been acting like his regular old self, which makes me feel like I can do the same.

"Have you noticed where we are yet?" Khazak asks casually.

"What do you mean?" I look around. *Am I supposed to know this place?*

"Look closer." He smirks. "You and your friends were here six weeks ago."

"What? This isn't..." I look around us again as we continue to walk. Those mountains *do* look kind of familiar. "Are we close to the ruins?"

"Yes, very." Khazak nods. "Follow me."

We climb down the other side of the hill we are on and finally find some solid flat land. The mountainside is just ahead of us, a small dirt path along its base going east to west. Wait, *now* this place is starting to look familiar. Sure enough, as we move around the mountain and another comes into view, I realize this is the path my group took to get to the ruins. Coming up, I see where the mountains give away a little and reveal a small alcove with the entrance. When we finish turning the corner, there's just one problem: I don't see a cave.

"Wait, where's the entrance?" I halt in my tracks, staring at the solid rock ahead of me.

Khazak ignores my words, only gesturing with his hand for me to keep following.

"Your group actually managed to avoid tripping any of our alarms right until you strayed from the trail and moved north to get to the entrance." He almost sounds impressed. "Of course, the only way to avoid them completely would have been to not to break in to ransack the place like thieves in the first place."

"Hey, we're not 'thieves,' and we didn't know we were 'breaking in' anywhere!" I maintain that we're at least innocent of that.

"What *would* you call yourselves then?" We come to a stop in front of the mountainside.

I pause to think. "...Treasure hunters?"

He looks very unimpressed with my answer.

"We're all very sorry," I tell him flatly. I know he's not asking me to apologize again, but it still feels like I'm supposed to. "Are you sure we're in the right place?" The mountain looks...mountainy? I still don't see a cave anywhere. I am very confused.

Wordlessly, Khazak takes two steps forward—and disappears into the mountainside. *Goddammit, it's another illusion.* I walk forward myself, coming face to face with a smirking Khazak and the cave in question, the entrance blocked by several boulders. Boulders that I seem to remember being around the cave the last time we were here, not inside of it.

"It does look very different with the illusion," he reasons while looking at the cave.

"Yeah, especially if you haven't seen the illusion before." *Of course*, it looks different. "I guess the boulders are a good way to keep people out if they get past it."

"Yes, we replaced them after your group removed them from the entrance," he tells me, looking at me funny. "What do you mean you have not seen the illusion before?"

"Exactly what I said. I've never seen this. This wasn't here before." *What is he talking about?* "What do *you* mean about my group moving the rocks? Those weren't there either."

"Yes, they were." He looks between me and the cave. "Or at least they were supposed to be. What exactly did this area look like when you first arrived here that day?"

"Like I said, there was no illusion, and I guess the boulders had already been pulled out." I mime pulling one with a rope. "They were already where you found them when your group followed us in. We just walked right into the cave when we got here."

"That is...concerning." Khazak looks at the cave again uneasily. "We should to get back to camp, so I can discuss this with the others."

"How would we have moved those boulders anyway?" I ask as we start the walk back. Adam and Liss are strong, but not that strong.

"We assumed one of your mages had a hand in that." Khazak shrugs. *Could Nate or Corrine do something like that?* "Did you notice anything else strange about the temple once you were inside?"

"Other than the huge murals and magical torches?" I remember the way everyone jumped when I lit the two braziers. "There was one thing. Whatever is under that lead box, it was making some kind of a ringing or buzzing noise in my head that no one else seemed to be able to hear."

"That is odd, especially considering what is under the box." He looks confused.

"What's under it?" And will it make my head explode?

"A basin that has been carved into the altar." His brow furrows. "It is made from unknown metals and is certainly magical, but tests revealed no obvious purpose. The lead box is there to prevent the magic from being detected by anyone passing by and deter looters."

"That's...weird." All that headache for nothing? "What is that temple doing all the way out here anyway? I don't think you guys built it."

"Correct. That distinction belongs to a group of elves that lived in these mountains thousands of years ago." *Makes sense. It was full of elf stuff.* "However, its existence was a mystery to the current elves in the area."

"It was uncovered by an earthquake?" That's what the people in Holbrooke told us.

"A thunderstorm, actually. A very powerful one." *A storm did that?* "It caused a small rockslide above the temple. When rangers went out to scout the next day and make sure the mountainside was stable, they noticed that behind some of the rock was an area that seemed hollow. After that, the city excavated and uncovered the temple entrance. My father, Orlun, was captain at the time and one of the two rangers sent in to scout the temple."

"Was it booby trapped?" I ask a little excitedly as we climb a hill together.

"No, it was not," he laughs his answer. "They determined that the temple had been constructed by elves. Additionally, next to the altar, they found a sword."

"A sword?" That sounds *way* cooler than booby traps.

"That is what father said." He nods. *I wonder if he's seen it himself.* "After that, a decision was made to contact the leaders in Pákannon."

"Where's that?" *I can barely remember the name of this place.*

"Not too far in the north, a city with a fairly large elven and human population. It is where Nylan is originally from." *That's right. Nylan moved here when they were all still kids.* "Given their current location, we felt it likely that they might share a connection with the elves responsible for constructing the temple."

"Did they?" That's what he said at least.

"Not one they could find." Khazak shakes his head. "The temple is at least 4000 years old, and from what I understand, even the elves do not have many surviving records from that era. There was nothing to indicate the temple ever being constructed or utilized. But that is not the most interesting part of the story to me."

"What is?" I have to admit I am pretty drawn in. Rockslides, ancient ruins, a cool sword.

"What is a 4000-year-old temple dedicated to Zeus doing halfway across the globe?" I never thought about that, but I also don't know that much about religion in general. "There is not *one* recorded instance of even a single Olympian worshipper anywhere *near* this part of the world before a few hundred years ago. The elves in Pákannon themselves thought that if their ancestors *were* Olympian worshippers then there should be some proof that would have survived until today, and they could find none. So, who built the temple, and why?"

"...I don't know." I realize he isn't actually waiting for an answer.

"Nor does anyone else." He looks over at me and shrugs, smiling.

"What did the sword look like?" Always asking the important questions.

"Long and curved, made from the same magical metal as the basin." It's a *magic* sword? "Since the two were obviously connected, the group investigating the temple ran all sorts of tests and attempted many different Olympian rituals. Though the temple is obviously focused on Zeus, there are actually numerous references to the rest of the Olympian pantheon. From what I understand, that is not out of the ordinary. In Olympian dogma, Zeus has a tendency to pull focus away from the other gods."

"Bit of a drama queen?" I remember hearing about Ragnar's nickname for Nylan.

"You could certainly say that," he agrees. "The group expanded their attempts to include the other gods, and in the end, I believe they even tried sacrificing a few animals— to no avail." *That sounds gruesome.*

"Where's the sword now?" I wonder who gets to keep something like that. Probably the elves.

"It is kept in the vault under the Hall of Honor." Good place to keep it, I guess.

"The elves let you keep it?" It's pretty obvious they were the ones who forged it.

"I think the city was surprised as well. There was hesitation in contacting them in the first place, concerns they might try to make a claim of ownership to a part of our lands." Which would be extra unwanted for a city that enjoys its secrecy. "Now that I am older, I have found that elves I've interacted with are far more interested in things like diplomacy and trade than reclaiming some ancient piece of their past glory. Because they were found on our land, they said the temple and sword belonged to the city."

I can see that. Elves are known for being *super* diplomatic. Their cities are a lot more connected to each other across the globe than most other species, and they're responsible for the signing of a number of peace treaties, a lot they aren't even a party in. They are the reason the Lutherian founders were able to cut ties with Albion without fear of reprisal or the future threat of war. Though we'll see how much longer that lasts. A low rumble of thunder from above cuts my personal history lesson short. Shit, if it starts raining now, then the rest of the night on patrol is *really* gonna suck. Especially if we have to take this path again—these hills suuuuuuck. I take a second to lean against a tree and catch my breath before we start the climb up one of the bigger ones.

"No time to rest. We need to get back to camp before it rains." *Or not.* "Druid Darkwolf may be able to do something to make our trek easier, in addition to improving your eyesight. You will certainly need it tonight."

She's done that the last two nights, and it's pretty cool being able to see the forest at night. Not a lot of color, though. I push myself off the tree trunk and begin to climb the hill, keeping any complaints to myself. I have been spank-free for the last *eight* days, thank you! That's a record, I'm pretty sure.

"What was..." Khazak pauses, his eyes darting to the left. "That."

I look where his orc-hearing has drawn his eyes, and off in the distance, I see three black wolves climbing up the hill after us. My mind immediately flashes to the dream I had a few nights ago. *Three black wolves.* I turn back to Khazak and see him already drawing his bow.

"Keep climbing," he tells me as he begins to carefully walk backward up the hill, keeping his bow trained in the creatures' direction.

I do as ordered but still draw my sword from its scabbard. They might outnumber us, but the two of us are more than capable of dealing with a few wolves. We'll be fine. Still, where did they come from, and why are they after us? I keep looking back, but having them in our sights isn't doing anything to deter them. If anything, they start chasing us faster, which makes us climb faster.

Have you ever seen someone about to lose their balance? Like, you catch them right as they trip before they realize they're going down, and there's nothing they, or you, can do to stop it? That's exactly what happens when we get to the top of that hill. Maybe it was a tree root, or a loose patch of dirt, but one second, I'm watching the wolves, and the next I hear a shout from Khazak and turn just in time to watch one of his legs fly up as the rest of his body tumbles to the ground.

And then right down the other side of the hill.

"KHAZAK!" I shout as I watch his body roll, arms too tangled in his bow to stop himself.

I chase him down the hill as fast as I can without joining him and rolling myself, but once he picks up speed, I can barely keep up. The faster he goes, the more worried I get about where he's going to stop. *How* he's going to stop. He's gotten dangerously close to hitting a few trees already.

Sure enough, as soon as he reaches the bottom of the hill, his body slams right into the base of a large tree with a loud *thud*.

"Khazak! Sir! Are you alright?" I call out as I approach. He's still breathing at least.

"Yes, in pain but I think—" He pauses in the middle of rubbing his hand down his face, trying to stand up quickly despite the obvious pain. "Oh no."

"Don't move so fast. You cou—"

"Do not come any closer, David," he says sharply.

"What? Why not—" But then I see it. Where he landed at the base of the tree, and now covering his uniform, is a large patch of familiar looking purple flowers: Ralor's crown. Petals are even still on his hand—the hand he just wiped down his face. *Fuck.* "What do we do?"

"I do not... David, look." He nods behind me, and I turn to see the trio of wolves at the top of the hill, watching us intently before scurrying down the hillside. They're moving fast, like they took our retreat as a challenge. We don't have much time.

"You can heal poisons, right?" If there was ever a time to use his magic, it's now.

"Yes, but with this amount I am afraid it will take every-thing I have just to keep my lungs from seizing." He's still picking flowers out of his armor. "There is no time. You need to run."

"What?!" *What?!*

"I will hold them off...while you return to camp...for help." He tries to hold his bow up, but his limbs are sluggish.

"You *just* told me you're barely going to be able to keep yourself breathing!" He's already wheezing even! "How the hell are you supposed to defend yourself if I leave?!"

"We do not have...time to argue... Will you just...follow my orders, please?" he growls through gritted teeth.

"No! They're stupid orders!" *I don't follow stupid orders!*

"David...will you do...what I say...for *once*!" The usual impact of his glare is lessened by all the huffing and puffing.

"*Make me.*" I pull my sword out and slide into a fighter's stance. That is officially the most childish thing I have said during a life-or-death situation.

"David—"

"***Goddammit Khazak***, would you just shut the fuck up and get behind me already!? If you're still so *fucking* mad about it later, you can punish me when we're *both* back at camp, **alive**!" I turn to face our furry pursuers, sword in hand. They're almost to us. "Now will you get your ass out of the fucking flowers and against a tree, so I can protect you while you keep your fucking lungs working!"

"But—"

"***MOVE SIR, NOW!***" *Why is he still arguing with me!?*

I hear him shuffling behind me, and I do my best to follow with my ears, making sure I stay between him and the wolves. They've slowed down, stalking their prey. Can they tell one of us is injured? When I hear the noise behind me stop, I look back for a second to find Khazak settled against a tree, kneeling down with a hand on his chest. *Better be casting that damn healing spell.* He doesn't look happy, but I'm not sure if it's because of the poison, the wolves, or me.

You don't normally want to go into a fight with your back against the wall, but in this case, it would actually help to keep the wolves off Khazak. The tree will have to do. The wolves must know something is up because they start to spread out as they circle us, and soon my head is twisting in three different directions to keep track of them.

The one farthest on my left makes the first move, lunging toward Khazak with a bark. I rush to cut it off, lashing out with my sword in a wide arc to push it back. That leaves my back exposed for one of the other two to come in and nip at my heels, and they dodge the kick I try to give in retaliation. My actions win me no new friends, and all three begin to growl, shiny teeth on display. I can't help but bare my teeth right back. *Bring it on you furry four-legged fucks.*

The wolf on the right goes for Khazak next, and when I move to cut it off, the wolf in the center chases after me, forcing me to avoid it while I try to attack his buddy. I manage to shake both of them off of me, but then the *third* goes for Khazak. I watch as he clumsily pulls his long-sword from his scabbard, swinging it once, but as soon as the wolf is scared off, the sword sinks to the ground right next to the snapped bow, his limbs barely able to hold either weapon up.

The three surrounding us continue to make attacks we are barely able to fend off. It's like they're toying with us. We can't keep this up much longer. I need to figure out a way to drop one of them *now*. As I track one of the wolves stalking around us, my eyes are drawn to the slightly squashed flower patch behind it, and I get an idea.

Time to change tactics. I start acting more aggressively, striking out at each of the wolves with my sword and making them jump back with a growl in turn. I need them to see that *I'm* the threat. *I'm* who they need to be paying attention to. I swear I even bark at them as I do it, *anything* I can think of to get them to focus on me instead of Khazak.

It works because the next thing I know, I've got three very pissed off looking wolves crouched down and ready to pounce on me. I can't let up, not yet, so I keep lashing out with my weapon to keep them off balance while trying to get us closer to the flower patch. I don't need to go far, just enough to get one of them between me and the base of that tree.

As soon as one is in position, I rush it, surprising it enough to make it try to bite me in return. The second it rears its head, I give it a quick kick in the snout, stunning it for just a moment. Enough time for me to plant my left foot firmly in the ground and hammer the bottom of my right boot into its side. I kick it harder than I kicked the back of Khazak's leg in the arena all those weeks ago. I kick it harder than I kicked that *rugbal* goal. I kick it harder than I've ever kicked *anything* and send the wolf flying back into the tree trunk with a thud, landing in the flower patch below. *Yes!*

"But what about the other wolves, David?" you may be asking yourself. Not to worry because at the exact moment I see one landing in the patch of paralytic flowers, a pair of fangs sinks into my left wrist.

"Aaahhh, fuck!" I scream, bringing my sword around to knock the hilt against the fur-covered skull, forcing the wolf to release me with a yelp. I can see wolf #1 barely able to stumble out of the flower patch, but shit, where's #3?! I turn to see the wolf in question has already lost interest in me and has returned to stalking Khazak.

"No!" I cry out as the wolf lunges forward.

Somehow, Khazak manages to pull his bow up just in time to trap the beast's jaws on its broken grip. I rush toward the two, sword held high in both hands. I bring my weapon down as hard I can on the wolf's back, hearing a loud yelp and sickening crunch. The wolf's body crumples to the ground, and for a second, I feel a twinge of regret at ending its life.

Then I feel another set of teeth wrapping around my right leg.

"Motherfucker!" I yell in pain and anger, swiping out at the final wolf with my sword blindly as it retreats, just catching the tip of it on its face. A thin red line bleeds across his snout and lips, and with a final snap of its jaws and an angry bark, it turns and runs east, deeper into the forest until it disappears behind the hills. After checking to make sure the wolf near the flower patch still isn't moving, I allow myself to collapse against the same tree as Khazak.

"Are you alright?" I ask when I'm steady enough.

"Yes, but... you are...hurt..." He's still breathing heavily, which doesn't seem like a good sign.

"I'll be fine." My wrist and my leg are killing me. I'm bleeding, but not too deeply. "We need to get back to camp before that wolf comes back. Or something worse."

"I think...they were just...hungry..." Khazak is looking down at the wolf I felled in front of him.

I step around and see what he means. The wolf's body looks very thin, almost skeletal. Up close, I can even see patches of its hair are missing. I walk over to the flower patch to inspect the other wolf, and even from a distance, I can tell it looks similar. It's also not breathing, which means... *Not the time to feel guilty, David. It was trying to eat you. Now get moving because that could easily be Sir lying there next.*

"Can you walk?" I turn back to Khazak still leaning against the tree.

He manages to get both feet under him, but he stumbles when he tries letting go.

"Not without…assistance…" He sighs, or I think he does; it's hard to tell right now. "You will need…to go back… to camp by—"

"Do you seriously think that after all that I'm just going to leave you here to get eaten by something else while I'm gone?" If I wasn't so tired and bleeding, that would have sounded funnier. "I'm going to have to help you back."

"You cannot…touch me…or you will…be poisoned… as well…" He's got a point. He's still covered in petals and pollen.

"Can you toss me your bag?" It's still slung over his shoulder, also covered in flowers.

He shrugs off the bag, trying to swing it in my direction as it falls. Stepping toward it, I crouch down, opening the top with the tip of my sword and revealing the dark black interior. Sticking my hand in, I whisper a silent thank you when I manage to retrieve the large blanket we used a month ago at Shad'rok Springs. Ugh, the one I'm pretty sure we never washed. *Oh gods, why is it still wet?*

Shaking off my squeamishness, I drape the damp blanket over my head and shoulders. Then stepping over to Khazak with only a *slight* limp, I have him throw his right arm around me. After a couple of false starts, we manage to get him off the tree and onto me. Then we begin the slow walk back to camp.

"Very…clever," he tells me as we take the long way around another steep hill.

"Not that clever," I grumble. "There's a good chance either my back or your arm is covered in jizz."

He laughs kind of goofily at that. Which is concerning. Then he laughs again.

"My puppy…barked at…the other puppies," he giggles.

"Are you sure you're okay?" This would be cute if I wasn't worried about the poison. "Does this stuff usually make people act weird?"

"I think that...may be the...lack of...oxygen," he finishes wheezing out.

"Oh gods." I try to move us faster.

"You should have...listened to...me earlier." Sir decides *now* is the appropriate time for a lecture. "Why must you... always put...yourself in...danger?"

"Excuse me, *I* put myself in danger? Mister 'leave-me-here-to-fight-three-angry-wolves-while-I-am-barely-able-to-breathe'? Are you fucking kidding me?" I spit out with a lot more venom than I intend.

Khazak stops moving, forcing me to stop as well. A pair of green fingers carefully pulls away part of the blanket so that he can look at me. "You are...angry...with me."

"You tried to order me to leave you for dead!" *Of course,* I'm angry!

"I only...wanted to...protect you." He looks confused at my outburst.

"I wasn't the one who needed protecting!" I kind of want to drop him now.

"I... I am...sorry…" The sad way he looks at me is the only reason I don't.

"We can talk more when we're back at camp." When I know he can breathe again.

We walk the rest of the way in silence. It takes at least forty minutes, and it's almost completely dark by the time we reach the campsite. Before we even cross the threshold, the officers and Druid Darkwolf appear. We barely have a chance to warn them not to touch Khazak.

Once we are both cleaned off and healed up, the two of us sit around the campfire to rest, the two of us forgoing any further patrolling tonight. The other rangers are still off on theirs, and Druid Darkwolf took off to take care of the flowers and the dead wolves. She seemed just as surprised as Wu'dag was a month ago when we found the other patch.

"I only wanted to keep you safe." Khazak is the one to break the silence.

"Again, I wasn't the one who needed to be kept safe." I turn to look him in the eye. "We both know you didn't stand a chance. You act like I was supposed to be fine leaving you there to die."

"We got lucky tonight, David. You could not have known it would go the way it did." He looks at me, almost pleading. "Things could have just as easily ended with *neither* of us making it back here tonight."

"I'd rather die trying to protect someone than spend the rest of my life wondering whether or not I could have saved them." These are the kind of morbid thoughts you have late at night when you're preparing for your future as a knight, folks. "I get that you're looking out for me, and that I'm supposed to listen to you, but there isn't a single thing I would have done differently tonight. And I wish I could promise you that it won't happen again, but we both know that would be a lie."

"I suppose it would be." He looks down for a moment, smiling, before looking back up at me. "As happy as I am that we are both here tonight, I also cannot say I would have done anything differently."

"So... does that mean we call it even and skip the punishment?" I give my best cheesy grin, eager to drop the topic.

Khazak rolls his eyes, but before he can respond, Darkwolf re-enters the camp.

"Found the wolves and took care of them and the flowers." She's got no basket with her, so I assume she just destroyed them. "Wolves like that should not be anywhere near this area this time of year, especially not to look for food.

Something in the north must have disrupted their normal hunting grounds. You said there were three of them?"

"Yeah, three." I nod my head, and then remember my dream from last night again. *Three black wolves.* Was it some sort of warning?

"That is very strange," Khazak agrees with the druid. "Perhaps we should reach out to our contacts in Pákannon and—"

Khazak is cut off by the sounds of a loud explosion, powerful enough to shake the ground beneath us. Then there's another. And another. *They're all coming from the direction of the city.* As more explosions go off, I see pillars of smoke billowing into the sky, the clouds lit dimly by the fires burning below them.

Oh no.

Chapter 12

"We must return to the city, now," Khazak tells me and Druid Darkwolf before turning to the camp's officers. "Frostsong, Proudblade, remain here to relay this to any rangers returning from patrol: everyone is to return to V'rok'sh Tah'lj immediately. There is no time to waste."

All the officers jump to action, everyone running into their tents to grab their packs before taking off for the city. Khazak's bow is still broken and his armor unwearable, but he grabs his longsword and hands me my own weapon.

"Captain," Darkwolf calls for Khazak's attention, and I watch as she changes her form once more, this time into a large horse.

"Thank you, Druid," Khazak tells the horse as he mounts her.

He extends a hand to help me up next, and I'm grateful for it this time. Trying to mount a giant horse is even more difficult without a saddle. There's also a little bit of weirdness around the fact that I'm riding a person, but she's probably used to doing this given how fast she was to volunteer.

We take off, and I'm glad I'm not riding in front. Not being able to see where we're going this late would probably freak me out. I'm leaning against Khazak's back, my arms around his waist while he holds onto the horse's mane. The forest is dark, but as we approach the city, I can see smoke rising into the cloudy sky, illuminated from below by the orange glow of flames. If there was ever a time for that rain to start, it would be now.

There's only one guard at the gate when we approach, and he wastes no time in opening the way for us. Once we're inside, our druid-horse heads toward the nearest smokestack. We're in the northern part of the city, and I'm reminded that this is also the poorer section of town by the less-than-nice homes we pass along the way.

There a lot of people standing outside of their homes, and the closer we get to the fire, the more we see fleeing from that direction. We follow the smoke to the site of one of the explosions, an apartment building. *Oh gods, all those people.*

The scene here is even more chaotic, and soon there are too many people for the horse to move through safely, and we have to dismount. The druid immediately returns to her normal form and we all step up to the wreckage. From where we're standing, it looks like the explosion happened on the lower level of the building. Flames are pouring out of the unit on the lower left, and the walkway above it is all but destroyed.

"We need to evacuate this and the surrounding buildings," Khazak says, stepping forward to begin working.

"I am attempting to get the rain started," Darkwolf starts, hands already raised to the sky. "But I think someone may be doing the opposite, or is at least aiming to block my magic. I will continue trying while I work to control the flames, but it may take some time."

Khazak shares a look with me, no doubt suspecting the same person responsible as me: Councilman Murbank. He's planned all of this. With Darkwolf holding the flames at bay, the two of us begin pounding on the doors of the building, making sure each one is empty. We only make it through six before I can see the stress growing on Khazak's face as he calculates his plan for the night.

"I have to go to the station." He pulls me to the side after we clear another apartment. "I need to find out where the other explosions happened, and make sure the fire brigades are all coordi—"

"Go," I tell him. "I'll stay and finish helping here, then I'll come find you."

"Are you certain?" He's already stepping away from the building.

"Yes, go." He's got important things to do right now. Lives are at stake. "I'll be fine."

"Be careful, David," he orders me (*he uses a different tone, I can just tell*) before turning around and running in the direction of the ranger station.

I manage to clear out the rest of the bottom floor without any issues but hit a few roadblocks on the second. First, I find an elderly orc gentleman still in his apartment, hurriedly trying to gather together some papers. I startle him when I walk in the door, making him drop everything all over the floor. He looks so distraught when I try to get him to leave without them that I end up bending down to gather them together myself. He thanks me as I hand him the stack, looking fondly at the old drawing of a young orc woman on top before allowing me to escort him outside and down the stairs.

My next issue comes in the form of two orc women still in their own apartment. They aren't as old as the man I had to help down, but they certainly don't appreciate a young human banging on their door. They just sit there staring at me as I frantically explain why they need to leave, and I'm not even sure it's because they don't understand me. When nothing I say or do works, I go outside and get Darkwolf's attention, forcing her to stop working on the fire to come up and try help me.

While she deals with the two of them, I move on to the final apartment, or at least the final apartment I'm able to enter. The unit right above the explosion... even from here I can see that the inside is mostly destroyed. *Gods, I hope it was empty.* Not wanting to focus on what I can't do anything about, I bang on the door in front of me, the wood already starting to warm.

I hear something, not quite a response but enough to get me to open the door, a small amount of smoke escaping. I stay low to the ground as I force my way inside. I can see that the wall to the adjoining apartment has crumbled, and lying underneath the rubble is a woman. She's conscious and trying to console the two young orcs on the ground in front of her, each frantically pulling on her arms to get her out. Smoke is starting to fill the room, and it won't be long before it's impossible to breathe in here, and considering the entire building might collapse soon, I need to get them all out of here. Now.

I rush to her side to see what I can do. The woman and her sons both look at me relieved, though for very different reasons. Both boys start shouting at me, begging me to help their mother, oblivious to the danger around them. She speaks to me much more calmly, obviously wanting me to get her children out. I try to get both boys to understand what I need them to do, but the language barrier is an obvious problem. Still, I do manage to at least get them to move away from their mom and toward the door. They won't go any farther than that without me helping her though.

I inspect the wall that's lying atop her. It's heavy but doesn't look like it's crushing her. She's probably broken or sprained a few things but nothing she can't recover from,

I hope. The question is, can I get the wall off of her? It's heavy, solid stone, and I burn my fingers on it the first time I touch it. I have to pull down my sleeves and cover my hands awkwardly just to get a grip on anything. But it's still mostly in one piece, so maybe...

With no more time to waste, I crouch down and grab what feels like the sturdiest section of the wall. *One, two, three!* I stand, trying to lift as much of the wall up and off the woman as I can. As my arms and legs start to strain, I realize a flaw in my plan: what if she can't move on her own? As soon as I start to worry, two green blurs come in from my left, both kids rushing in to help. I can see that she's at least able to crawl, but time is *really* of the essence here. I'm not sure how much longer I can hold this up.

"Hurry," I grit out. Movemovemove*move!*

I drop the wall as soon as I see that she's out, jumping back so I don't crush my feet. When it hits the ground, the entire building rumbles, and with wide eyes, I quickly usher everyone out of the apartment. The boys are down first while I help their mother with her injuries. I can see Darkwolf at the bottom of the stairs, still arguing with the two women she "helped" out of the burning building. One of them is holding a small dog that won't stop yapping at the druid.

As soon as she sees me and I confirm that the building is empty, she goes back to trying to control the fire while I go to the surrounding homes to evacuate them next. The knights at the academy are part of Northlake's fire brigade, so I actually have a little training in this area. There's always a chance the fire could jump to another building, or that this one could collapse and knock one of the others over.

Thankfully, emptying out the rest of the homes goes much smoother. Most of them are already empty, the owners having enough sense to get out once they saw the fire. When I've finally finished, I can see a group of uniformed orcs have joined Darkwolf in taming the fire, while others are speaking with the building's tenants. Hopefully, that means Khazak was able to get back to the station alright. The apartment building gives another shake just before the left section of it crumbles. Looks like we were just in time. I know it's still bad, but *phew*.

With the situation here under control, I say goodbye to Darkwolf and begin my walk south to the station. I'm a little tired after all that, so I'm not exactly running, but I know I can't take my time or anything. Just as I finish catching my breath, another explosion rips through the air and makes everything around me tremble. I see the new smokestack rising into the air, and it's right in the direction I'm headed. *Oh fuck, the station!*

I break into a run, any feelings of exhaustion jolted out of me. All I feel is worry.

Please be okay. Please be okay. Please be okay.

I can't even describe the wave of relief that comes over me when the station comes into view unharmed. No, the smoke is coming from a few blocks behind it—the arena. I rush into the station only to be told that Khazak and Ragnar both went to the arena after that last explosion. I'm torn between relief that they're okay and worry that they headed straight into danger. I take off again, and as I come up on the large wooden doors of the arena, I find both men on this side of it, the two of them and a third ranger hacking away at them with large hatchets. *The hell?*

"Sir," I call out as I approach.

"David." He looks relieved to see me. He's also wearing a new set of armor.

"What's going on? Why can't you get inside?" I watch the other rangers continue to attack the door.

"All of the entrances have been sealed." He does *not* sound happy. "The doors are enchanted with defenses against magical attacks, so destroying them is our only way of getting inside."

"Captain," Ragnar draws both of our attention. "I think we're ready."

As the orcs step away from the door, I can see that they've hacked a smaller door-shaped outline into it. The third ranger with them is a very burly looking orc. Firedrum is her name; I remember because she's the other orc I fought along with Arik months ago in the temple, though I'm a little too preoccupied to worry about feeling bad about that again right now. When she steps the farthest away and takes a runner's stance, I understand their plan. She barrels toward the door, slamming into it with her armor-covered shoulder. There's a loud *crack* as part of the door splits, and she finishes the job with a few well-placed kicks.

As soon as our new entrance is clear, all four of us enter the building. It's dark, pitch black except for the very dim moonlight streaming down from the staircase leading to the audience seats as well as through the hole we just made. The first thing we do is climb the stairs, looking for the site of the last explosion. It's not hard to find, dead center on the arena floor. The ground looks collapsed in on itself, smoke rising from the hole. *Didn't Khazak say something about a vault under there?*

"Our first priority is locating the curators." Khazak leads us back downstairs. "Rockfang, Firedrum, you search that direction. David, you are with me."

We split up, each duo taking one of the dark hallways that circles the arena. It's dead quiet, which seems so strange knowing the absolute chaos that is going on outside. I can barely see a thing, but it's not as bad as the forest. I'm not even sure what we're looking for, but when I hear what sounds like a soft *meow*, I stop.

"Did you hear that?" Because if I did, there's no way he didn't.

"Yes, but where..." I see him scanning the dark hall. "There! One of the curators' familiars."

I look where Khazak points and start to follow but can't see anything until a pair of eyes flash as the light hits them. It's a black cat, the same one I saw here on the last night of the festival. Its fur makes the rest of it look invisible in the darkness, at least until we get closer, and the animal starts glowing. Undisturbed by the creature's sudden light-up fur, Khazak pursues it down the hall. It leads us through another of the arena's lobbies and down another hall before coming to a stop in front of a simple wooden door.

When we get close, I hear a knocking sound, and the soft glow emanating from the cat reveals the form of a small black bird sitting on the doorframe, pecking at the door below it. *The other familiar.* The witches must be inside. Khazak reaches for the door handle, grunting in frustration when it doesn't give. Still gripping the handle in one hand, he puts one of his feet up against the wall outside the door frame. Then, with a powerful yank, he rips the door off its frame, destroying the lock.

"Captain?" Ragnar and Firedrum come around the opposite end of the hallway just in time to witness.

With the door open, the cat and bird both make their way inside, the cat's light revealing the forms of the two curator witches on the ground, both bound and gagged. One of them stirs when we enter, muffled sounds coming from behind her gag. Khazak immediately kneels down, pulling a familiar-looking switchblade from his pocket to untie her while Firedrum does the same with her sister.

"What happened?" Khazak asks as the woman rubs feeling back into her wrists. She holds up a single finger as she slowly chants to herself, crossing her hands over her chest.

"I was not able to see much beyond their black robes." *That sounds familiar.* "They tried to poison us with darts, but they only managed to nick me. Ralor's poison, I think."

That would explain why her fellow curator still isn't moving, which is starting to worry me. She shuffles over and begins casting the same healing spell she did on herself. A second later, the other curator springs to life, unleashing a torrent of angry sounding words once she regains her ability to speak, including some *very* nasty curses I had Nylan teach me.

"I know, but we need to check on the vault first," the woman tells her sister as she stands.

With both witches mobile, they lead us from the room and down the hall. Their familiars in tow, they light the torches we pass with their magic, coming to a stop in front of a fairly nondescript wall. Both women move to a separate section, and using both hands, trace symbols onto the different stones making up the wall. Their fingers leave a trail of light that fades after a second or two, but I don't recognize any of the patterns.

When they're finished, the two witches step back, and a second later, the stones on the wall begin to shift and move, folding in on themselves to reveal a staircase and passageway behind it. The way down is dark, and there is a small amount of smoke rising up from the new entrance.

Covering our faces as best we can, the six of us quickly descend the stairs into a passageway that leads underneath the center of the arena. I can make out a set of double doors at the other end of the hall, illuminated from behind by what I'm guessing is the fire we saw from the arena's seats. Both women begin casting spells to control the blaze as we get closer.

There's no sign of the attackers once the fire is out, the vault in a complete state of disrepair. A number of objects have been burned and documents destroyed, but the witches tell us it's impossible to tell what without doing a more complete inventory of what remains. They start to immediately get to work cleaning up what they can and tell us that as soon as they can determine what may have been taken, they will let us know.

The four of us search the rest of the arena afterward but find nothing else out of place nor any sign of the black-robed thieves. As we exit the Hall of Honor, thunder crackles above us, and the rains finally begin to fall.

There are no more explosions after the Hall of Honor, but that doesn't mean the rest of the night is any easier. Counting the apartments and the arena, a total of six places were bombed: the eastern ranger station, the shipyard, the militia barracks, and the prison were all also hit. Khazak and I spend the rest of the night running all over the city.

Each bombing caused its own set of injuries and casualties, and it gets harder to stay composed the longer the night goes on. The story at each location is almost exactly the same. No one seems to have witnessed anyone actually causing the explosions. The best we get are people who *think* they may have seen someone in black robes in the area. We can't even figure out what common thread links all of the places attacked. It all just feels so random.

It's four in the morning by the time Khazak and I finally make it home for the night. Normally, we would have returned to our post at the patrol camp to finish out the week, but given the events of the night, Khazak is needed in the city. We're both exhausted, but neither of us can sleep, instead just sitting in the living room numbly, me on the couch and him in a chair in the kitchen.

We won't know the full numbers until tomorrow, but at least a dozen people were killed tonight and more than twice that injured. I keep thinking back to how the night started after the wolf attack. The explosions, the fire at the apartment building, all the other scenes of destruction. Why would someone do this?

A knock on the front door pulls me from my morbid thoughts. Not sure who would come by this late, but after all that, it can't be good. Khazak stands and opens the door, revealing a tired-looking Ragnar on the other side. He's holding some papers.

"Ragnar." Khazak is as surprised to see him as I am.

"Can I come in?" He looks even more stressed out than he did earlier. "It's important."

"Of course." Khazak steps to the side to allow him to enter. "What is going on? Did you learn something new about the attackers?"

"Not exactly." Ragnar walks into the living room but doesn't sit down. "Thog Grimrock was killed in the explosion at the prison tonight."

"What?" Khazak sounds taken aback.

"Holy shit, yeah, *what?*" I stand from the couch to join the two orcs.

"The bomb at the prison was placed on the outside wall of his cell." His face is deadly serious. "Since the first robbery, everything connected to this case has been difficult. No evidence, no leads, nothing except Thog."

"Yes, it has felt as if we have been playing on the defensive for some time now." Khazak nods his head toward me.

"It was not until David figured out they were manufacturing black powder that we learned anything new at all."

"Because that did us so much good." I figured it out *just* in time for them to still take us completely by surprise.

"No matter what we do, we're always two steps behind them," Ragnar gripes with me. "The only lead we had was Thog, and he didn't want to talk to us. Not until earlier today, at least."

"What do you mean?" Khazak's eyes go wide.

"Earlier tonight, I got a message from Thog, one he managed to get out through the prison guards," Ragnar explains. "He said he wanted to talk to me about something important. I was actually just leaving for the prison when the first bomb went off."

"His death... This cannot be a coincidence." Khazak is starting to make the same connections I am.

"Exactly what I kept thinking. Couldn't *stop* thinking." Ragnar looks between the two of us. "So much so, that before I went home tonight, I went to the prison to check the visitor's log and see if anyone *else* had spoken to Thog. Guess who he got a visit from yesterday?"

"Who?" I have a sinking feeling I already know the answer.

"Naruk Redwish." *Called it.* "He's made a *number* of visits to Thog in the last month. I know it's not out of the ordinary for a legal advocate to visit a client in prison even after conviction, but after what he did to the two of you, I thought the timing was just too strange. So, I did some *more* digging. Did you know Thog was in a *massive* amount of debt?" Ragnar hands some of the papers he is holding to Khazak.

"What? No." Khazak starts to read over the paper. "These filings show that *he* was the one who purchased his father's factory back from the city. Two years ago, not long after his father's death. Once he fell behind on payments, the factory was about to be reseized when a third party stepped in, purchased the building outright, and assumed Thog's debt. Why were we not given these files when he was first arrested?"

"I don't know, but it made me think back to the day of the second robbery. Officer Silentfang came into the central station looking for the building records, but *neither* of us could find them. When we both went to the eastern station to look, Deputy Keenguard already had them. So, why didn't she also give us these, too?" Ragnar hands over his remaining papers. "I did even *more* searching. That 'land management' company that owns the factory and Thog's debt? It belongs to Councilman Murbank. The same person who owns the shipyard where the *first* robbery took place and who has *also* made a number of visits to Thog in prison."

"What are you suggesting, Deputy?" Khazak asks with a hint of hesitation.

"We know Thog knew more than he was letting on but wouldn't say anything because he was protecting someone." Ragnar starts to pace a little as he talks. "But what if he wasn't protecting them because he wanted to. What if he was doing it because he *had* to?"

"You think the Councilman—"

"Just hear me out." He's talking with his hands now, too. "What if, in order to pay off his debt, Murbank made Thog take responsibility for the first robbery? And then what if he got nervous Thog would talk and decided to take him out while he had the chance?"

"Why kill him?" I ask. "It's not like Thog ever actually told us anything."

"Until whatever it was he was going to tell me tonight," Ragnar counters. "Remember the last time we spoke, and how it seemed like I was so close to getting him to say something? I think finding out that whoever he was covering for was going to hurt people got to him, and we probably weren't the only ones to notice. That might even be why Redwish was visiting."

"If the plan was for him to take the blame for the first robbery, why all the theatrics?" Khazak interjects next. "Why did he run when we arrested him? Why the strange unburnable book?"

"Maybe he didn't know exactly how it was going to happen?" Ragnar reasons. "He obviously didn't know anything about the last two robberies or what was happening tonight, probably by design. He couldn't tell us what he didn't know."

"So, Murbank told him that when he was arrested to make it look real?" I'm starting to join in on Khazak's skepticism.

"I think he knew what was expected of him, just not when or how it would be coming. In the moment, his panic was probably real." Ragnar sounds completely confident in his theory. "Just like the rest of it—the less he knew, the less he could tell us. Think about it: after his confession, he was all we could focus on, even with the other robberies, because he was the *only* source of information we had. The book was enchanted, so that it couldn't be destroyed, which he obviously didn't know about since he tried to do it anyway. Making sure we found it gave us no choice but to tie Thog to all the robberies and kept our focus on him instead of anywhere else."

"This is...quite the conspiracy you are painting, Ragnar." Khazak sounds exasperated. "Do you have any proof?"

"No, not exactly." Ragnar deflates a little. "I *know* it sounds crazy, but so many things make sense. All of Thog's motivations, the lack of evidence, the way these people are able to act right under our noses without us ever noticing."

"Let me make sure I am understanding this, Ragnar." Khazak leans back against the kitchen counter. "You believe that Councilman Murbank, Deputy Captain Keenguard, Advocate Redwish, as well as any number of rangers and officers have all been conspiring together to attack the city tonight?"

"I *know* what it sounds like Khazak, but please, I need you to trust me on this," Ragnar pleads with his friend and captain. "Why did Keenguard already have those files, and why didn't she give us the rest? Why is it that any evidence we find always leads directly to a dead end? How were these people able to set off multiple bombs *inside the city* tonight without a *single* eyewitness? The only thing that makes sense is that they already have people on our side doing their dirty work. Hell, they probably waited to attack this week specifically because they knew you'd be all the way out in the forest on patrol." Ragnar pauses, looking afraid that we both think he's nuts. "I know it seems crazy, but you have to believe—"

"It is not that I do not believe you," Khazak cuts Ragnar off, sounding tired. "It is that I do not *want* to. Since we learned these people were moving in and out of the city, I have struggled to think of an explanation that is not 'there are traitors among you.' The fact that they are able to traverse the forest without setting off any alarms... The only way they could do that would be if they were wearing one of our badges."

"What this about badges?" I look over in confusion.

"Our badges, the ones sewn into our uniforms." Ragnar points to the emblem on the front of his uniform, the Atasi equivalent of the letter "V" surrounded by trees. "They have an enchantment that hides the wearer from the alarm spells in the forest, so that our patrol groups aren't constantly setting them off."

"Anytime a citizen leaves the city, whether to go hunting or for travel, they receive a similar badge at one the gates," Khazak continues the explanation. "The gatekeepers log each time a badge is given out and returned, but none of the logs have matched up with the time tables we have for our crimes. I find it highly unlikely that a number of our officers would have suddenly misplaced theirs, so either someone is lying to us, or they are able to move between the city and forest some other way entirely. If not both."

"Shit, maybe the first robbery wasn't even a real robbery." Talking about alarms and people potentially lying makes me think back to some of the other weird things we've encountered. "Remember how the mages couldn't find traces of magic on the storage unit? Not even from the alarms that should have gone off? Murbank owns the whole place. What if they never set the alarms to begin with? How do we know they ever even stored the items there at all? They could have just taken them straight from the boat to wherever they're hiding everything now."

"Murbank, Keenguard, Redwish, and who knows who else? They're all working together to make...something happen." Ragnar's sentence started strong, at least. "We just need to figure out what."

"I have a feeling we may not learn that until we can determine what exactly was taken from the vault under the Hall of Honor," Khazak says with a sigh. "That was clearly their main target tonight. The rest were just distractions to keep us and the rest of the force busy."

"And to tie up any of their loose ends." I actually feel pretty bad for Thog if Ragnar's right. "Murbank is the most powerful person connected to all this. I mean, he's one of the most powerful people in the city. Not to sound too cynical, but he's a politician, right? Is he up for re-election or something sometime soon?"

"His term on the Tribal Council ends at the end of this year, but he's not eligible for re-election." Ragnar shakes his head at me. "No one is. Councilmembers can only serve a single term."

"*Shit.*" Khazak's curse gets both of our attention. "I have heard rumors, barely even rumblings really, that certain members of the Tribal Council have been floating the idea of amending the law to allow former councilmembers to serve again. But again, only rumors."

"That *has* to be his plan." That's damn good motivation if I've ever heard it. "Attack the city, send everyone into a state of fear, then pass a law and run for re-election on a platform of public safety or something. I dunno."

"Hmm." Khazak considers my theory. *Whatever. I thought it sounded good.* "Have you talked to anyone else about this yet, Deputy?"

"No, I came straight here after getting the files." Ragnar shakes his head. "I don't know who else to trust with any of this. The only reason I think I was even able to get them without someone noticing was because of how crazy tonight was."

"Good. I want to keep this between the three of us for now." Khazak nods to himself, arms crossed over his chest as he thinks. "Until we can determine what exactly their plan is, I am not sure who we may be able to confide any of this information with."

"So, what's the plan then, Sir?" I can tell he's working on something.

"We need to determine what exactly they were after in that vault, but that may take the curators a few days at least." He frowns before looking at the papers in his hand. "However, in the interim, we may be able to use these files to speak with Murbank."

"You think that's smart?" Ragnar asks, not doubting but just wanting to be sure.

"We will need to be very careful not to let on what we suspect, but we may be able to get more information out of him or at least catch a misstep in his explanation." Khazak puts the papers down on the counter. "Remember, none of us can speak about this to *anyone*, not even Nylan, not yet. I do not even want us discussing this at the station or anywhere else. The only place we talk about this is here."

"Understood. I haven't said a thing to Ny yet. He thinks I'm still working." Ragnar nods, already planning to keep this from his avakesh. "I actually need to get back home. He's probably waiting for me, worried."

"I will speak with the curators tomorrow and determine when to best confront Murbank." Khazak sighs to himself. "It is a bit strange to think that the three of us may be the only people in the city standing between it and a massive conspiracy."

It is weird, but I have faith that our little team can stop it.

Chapter 13

After we manage to grab maybe a couple hours of sleep in the early hours of the morning, Khazak and I are both back at the station the day following the bombing. The rest of our (or at least Khazak's) patrol week in the forest has been cancelled, another ranger taking our place. There's just too much to do, and so much of it requires the captain's oversight. There are six different sites to investigate, cleanup crews to organize, victim's families to contact...

I don't envy the people responsible for the last thing. I think not being able to speak their language is what saved me from having to do any of it, but it's also the reason I can't really do any of the other things Khazak needs. Instead, most of my day is spent acting as a courier, delivering papers and packages between the station, the bombing sites, and tribal hall. It's a lot of walking, but I don't mind. In the month and a half I've been here, I've gotten a pretty good idea of how to get around the city on my own.

By the end of the day, I've worked up a pretty good appetite. Which is a good thing because after work, we head home for a quick shower before we are off again to Khazak's parents for an impromptu dinner. From the way Khazak told me about it, plus his own reactions, it seems like the explosions have really shaken everyone. Myself included—I wouldn't mind some comfort food right now.

The mood when we get to the house is definitely more somber than the times I've been here before. His family is already pretty physically affectionate, but that's been cranked up even more tonight: so many long hugs, so many whispered words of reassurance that I don't understand. Even Ursza and Ignatz are nice to me, actually speaking to me without rolling their eyes or making fun of me for once. It's weird.

Eventually, things start to feel a little *too* weird, and I ask to excuse myself to the bathroom but actually go to Khazak's old bedroom. I just need a minute to myself. I hate to admit it, but all of this has me missing my own family. I almost wish I could see them, but even if that were possible, there's too much other shit we'd have to talk about. I'd like to see my friends, and I hope I will now that I'll be in the city on Astraday, but I still don't know how they're doing right now. The labor camp easily could have been one of the bombing targets.

At least I have Khazak—for now. I look around at his sparse childhood bedroom. Other than the old bows hanging from the walls, the only real thing of interest is his very full bookshelf. *Nerd*. I can't read most of the titles, of course, but I do spot a few books on how to speak Common. I also see what looks like a very well-worn copy of the story of Khazak Steelrun. Maybe I should try and find my own copy before I leave...

"There you are." Khazak—my Khazak—enters the room through the partially opened door.

"Sorry." I duck my head sheepishly. "Just needed to get away for a little."

"It is alright," he tells me as he moves to stand before me. "I am afraid that for my family, these attacks have brought back many unwanted memories of the Warhunter Rebellion."

"I didn't even think about that." I can only imagine what the events of yesterday might have dug up. "Was it a lot like last night?"

"There were fewer explosions, but yes. Only the rebellion lasted much longer than a single night." Khazak grimaces slightly as he remembers. "With all the connections we have discovered between the two, I can hardly blame them. I am more worried about what it may be doing to Nylan and Ragnar."

"Do you think that's why he's been so gung-ho about everything?" Showing up at 4 am to explain a massive government conspiracy theory is...a lot. "Do you not believe him?"

Khazak considers what I'm asking for a minute before moving to shut the door to his bedroom—after peeking out to make sure we've got no eavesdroppers.

"It is not that I do not believe him," Khazak starts to explain. "I just worry that because of his and Nylan's own connections to the rebellion, Ragnar may be driven to act recklessly in search of a solution."

"What are their connections to the rebellion?" Khazak never mentioned that before, but it would make some of Ragnar's behavior over the last month and a half make more sense.

"It is more Nylan than Ragnar, but it was the events of those nights that helped bring the two of them closer together." Khazak takes a seat on his bed, patting the spot beside him and I join him. "Nylan's parents were archaeologists with a particular interest in ancient elven ruins. They actually led the expedition to study the temple after it was uncovered in the rockslide."

"That's when they moved here?" Nylan said they met when they were kids.

"Correct." Khazak nods his head. "Though I am not sure they came with the intention of staying permanently, after the first few months, it became apparent they did not want to leave. I remember Nylan telling the two of us at school very excitedly that they would be staying. Except for Ragnar, he was the only half-elf in school at the time, something the two of them bonded over."

"Things were fairly normal that year, or at least that is the way I remember them until the fighting began in earnest," he continues. "It was one of the final nights of the rebellion when the battles were at their worst, and it was hardly safe to go out even during the day. Nylan's father insisted on joining the militia. He felt it was important to defend their new home. He left Nylan and his mother at home. He had no reason to believe they would not be safe..."

"Oh no." This is how Ny's mom died.

"Their home was attacked," Khazak confirms. "Nylan's mother was able to hide him inside a small chest. There were so many attackers, she had no choice. She went with them to protect her son, led them away from her home. Or at least that is what we believe."

"Why were they attacking to begin with?" She was just an innocent mother with a kid.

"I am not certain. It is believed that perhaps a faction within the rebellion was planning to ransom her." Khazak frowns, lacking a better answer. "Her and Nylan's family are somewhat well connected in Pákannon. However, it is a *much* smaller city than V'rok'sh Tah'lj, so I am not exactly certain what they were going to ransom her for. Not that it ended up mattering."

"Nylan's mother was a magician, though not an overly powerful one," Khazak continues his explanation.

Magicians are basically low-powered wizards who didn't really bother with training. That's what Mike used to call himself when we were in school. "They were outside the city, just beyond the north gate, when...something happened. I do not know if the attackers grew impatient or if she was just waiting until they were far enough from town but...there was an explosion. A magical one."

"Shit." Yeah, I can see why last night would bring up bad memories.

"The forensic mages said it was as though she had summoned all of her power at once, concentrated into a single spell she centered on herself." Khazak is looking at his hands as if trying to figure out her motives. "There were no survivors. The bodies were torn apart. My father said it took them days to sort out who they all were. And the people who came across the scene first? Councilman Murbank and his father, who was himself a councilman at that point."

"What! He was *there*, too?" Maybe it's because I don't like the guy, but that just seems way too convenient. "That can't be a coincidence."

"I am fairly certain Ragnar is thinking the same thing. I am telling you all of this for two reasons." Khazak holds up two fingers. "The first is to prevent Nylan from having to relive any of this by explaining it to you himself. I normally would not share something so personal, but I would rather you be prepared because of the second reason: I need you to help me keep an eye on Ragnar. Between his anger during the second interrogation, and the off-hours sleuthing last night, I am worried he may plan something without telling me."

"Of course, Sir." I can do that. Not just for Ragnar's sake but for Nylan's too.

"They did not find Nylan hidden in the chest until the following morning. He... He did not speak for a long time. He still gets claustrophobic." *Fuck, that had to be awful.* "Ragnar's father was one of the only elves living in V'rok'sh Tah'lj at that time, so the two families were already fairly close, and Nylan and his father stayed with them after that, temporarily. The man was inconsolable, but more than sad, he was angry. He wanted revenge. It was a long time ago, so my memories are not the best, but I actually felt scared of him, someone I had only ever known to be a gentle bookworm. I even remember my fathers arguing about whether or not it was safe to let him continue."

"Orlun wanted to let him fight, but Rurig felt he needed time, that he should stay home before he acted dangerously." Khazak pauses. "I wish he had taken his own advice. The following night was when he lost his foot, and then the night after that was when Jarek began looking after us."

"Wait, you were *still* being left home alone after that? You were like eight!" I thought it was for *maybe* a few nights at the beginning of the fighting.

"I know, and I was already not handling it well. I would spend most nights trying to console a crying Yogik while Ayla did everything she could to argue with me, hating that my parents put me in charge. Never mind my own feelings. I had to be the brave one." He's frowning as he speaks, but it doesn't sound like he's angry about it, not anymore at least. "Then, the night after one of my friends lost his mother, Orda came home in a panic, telling us only that Ruda had been hurt, and Jarek, whom we had *never* met before, would be looking after us. He was gone for the rest of the night, not wanting to leave the healer while Ruda had his leg amputated."

"That's...horrible." And it sort of taints the image I had of Khazak's perfect family.

"You were not the only person to think so. I am not even sure if Jarek knew my fathers *had* children at that point.

They had only met a few weeks prior. He was about your age, actually. We certainly seemed as much of a surprise to him as he was to us." Khazak's thumb strokes my thigh, as if to calm himself. "I would overhear him sometimes, either talking to himself or arguing with my parents. He sounded unhappy, angry. I thought he resented having to watch us, that he wanted to be out fighting. It was only later that I learned he was actually angry with my fathers for having left us alone at all. He saw how it affected me, not that I made it very difficult, arguing and fighting with him every step of the way. I think I made his job even harder than Ayla had for me. Nylan had just lost his mother, I was now terrified of losing my father, and this stranger was coming in and replacing me. That of course made me feel as if my father was saying I was doing a bad job, which *then* led to me questioning whether Ruda's injury was somehow my fault... I was a bit of a monster for a while."

"You were really young. Being forced to deal with all that at any age would be pretty tough." I'm not sure my dad would have been much better if he had to go out and fight like that, but at least mom would have been home. Not that that mattered for Nylan. "I'm trying to think of something nice to say, but Jarek was right. That was really, *really* messed up of your dads." I put my hand on top of his and squeeze.

"Thank you." He huffs a small laugh. "The fighting lasted another week. Warhunter refused to surrender even as he continued to lose ground. Commander Grandtooth was just a simple ranger then led the final charge against him and was the one to land the final blow. Something which helped with his promotion to ranger captain after my father's retirement a few years later."

"Is he someone we need to watch along with Murbank?" I don't trust anyone in a position of power aside from Khazak and Ragnar right now.

"Possibly, at least out of caution." He nods his head. "After that, things slowly went back to normal, as much as they could. Nylan and his father moved back into their home, though he was still frequently at either mine or Ragnar's. I remember Ruda preparing a lot of food to send Nylan home with when he visited. Jarek of course stayed around, and it was because of him that my family became involved with the Temple of the Three. He was not religious, but High Priest Bhok had counseled his parents, and he thought he might be able to do the same for my family. It helped me come to terms with how I felt about being left alone under all that pressure and seemingly gave my fathers a much needed 'kick in the ass,' as you like to say. It took time, but things improved after that."

"You all seem like a pretty happy family to me, now at least." Jarek sounds like a cool guy. "That's when you started to volunteer at the church?"

"It gave me an outlet for all my energy that was not dependent on my family." He gives my leg another squeeze. "Come. Dinner will be ready soon."

Dinner is quieter than usual. Current events have kind of pulled focus from anything else that might be going on. The room is filled with the sounds of chewing, cutlery, and a little awkward small talk. It's a very different vibe. I'm actually kinda glad when Orlun finally brings it up, asking about the apartment building and the people who lived there.

"All of the residents have been moved to temporary housing while the building is inspected. Not that it makes things much better for any of them," Khazak answers unhappily. "Between the explosion and the fire, we are unsure if the damage is extensive enough to require tearing the whole building down. "

"There was a woman who lived there with two kids." I'm only just now remembering the family. "She was hurt when a wall collapsed on her, and I had to help her out. Is she alright?"

"Yes, I believe her injuries were treated, and she and her children are together," he reassures me.

"I am sure you cannot wait to leave all this behind you, David," Rurig tells me from across the table. "You have, what, less than three weeks left at this point?"

"Uh, yeah." I nod. "Just about three weeks." Then my friends are out, and I guess I'm "free."

"Any idea where you'll be headed next?" Ayla asks me.

"I need to talk to my friends about that, I guess." I twiddle with my fork, only just realizing my complete lack of preparation.

"Better hurry," she tells me next. "You want to have enough time to plan before it is time to go."

I know I probably should have been thinking about what happens when I leave for a while now—I just haven't really wanted to. I've been putting it off because I guess I'm gonna miss this place. And maybe some of the people in it. It hasn't been nearly as bad as I would have thought. I've learned a lot of stuff here—about the world and myself. It's going to be hard to put all of it behind me in a few weeks.

There's a part of me that doesn't want to leave. I don't mean I want to move here—just that with everything going on, with the attacks and Murbank's murky dealings, I think I should stick around until we find the people responsible. It feels wrong to leave with that unfinished.

Ayla's right, though. I do need to plan for the next leg of our journey. I should probably start with figuring out where that journey is going to take us. I can ask Adam and Nate this weekend when I visit, but there's a few things I can do before then. Like getting some equipment together.

To do that, I need to talk to Khazak about a couple of things. The first is that I'm not actually sure where my old equipment is. I'm pretty sure the rangers, or maybe the guards at the labor camp, are holding onto my friend's stuff, but I don't know what happened to mine. I haven't exactly needed it. The weapon and armor provided by the rangers are even better than my own, but I don't imagine I'll be allowed to take them with me. I also don't know if my old armor is even going to fit me anymore, so if I have to buy a new set, I wanna know now. I just bought it a month before we arrived here when my previous set was too loose after getting off the boat.

Which brings us to the second reason I need to talk to Khazak: money. I know when we first settled on our "arrangement," we talked a little about me getting a job to earn some, but then I started working with him at the ranger station. I'm not actually sure if I've been getting paid or not. It's not like I've needed money for anything, which itself has been a little weird, but I'm kind of scared to find out. If I'm still broke, I might have to find something else to do these last three weeks. Something that hopefully pays a *lot*.

I don't work up the nerve to ask Khazak until we're walking home later that night, feeling too weird to ask about money around his family. Our arms are once again filled with leftovers from dinner, which has me wondering how long these would last out in the forest. The food is another thing I'm gonna miss from this place. And not having to pay for it.

"Can I ask you something?" I'm a bundle of nerves the second the words leave my mouth.

"Besides that question?"

I groan at his response. "Do you know where my stuff is?" I press forward. He's been hitting the dad jokes *hard* lately. "Like my bag and my equipment, the stuff I had before all of..." I trail off.

"I was wondering if you were ever going to ask about that," he answers with a smirk. "Your belongings are in one of the storage units in the old cell yard. We can retrieve them in the morning if you would like."

"Thanks. That would be great." That's one thing down. "I need to see if my old armor still fits."

"If it does not, we may be able to take it to an armorer and have it adjusted." For some reason, hearing him help plan my departure stings a little. "Unless of course you would prefer new armor. I am not sure your old set was particularly useful the last time you were wearing it."

"Or maybe I just need to start wearing a helmet, too." He's not wrong, but even better armor wouldn't have helped with a blow to the head. "But I'm glad you said that because I also needed to ask... Have I been getting paid? I know we talked about it, but then things sorta happened differently, and I didn't wanna make it seem like I was trying to be greedy since I know I've been eating your food and living in your house. I just need to get some new stuff for when me and my friends lea—"

"Yes, David, you have been getting paid," he cuts off my nervous rambling with a bump to the shoulder. "I was given a stipend once you started your position. I have been putting it to the side to give to you when you leave. I would have given it to you sooner had you asked about it."

"I didn't know I could," is the excuse I go with. It's not at all that I just didn't want to think about leaving. "Is it a lot?"

"It is a fairly tidy sum. You could afford to buy yourself an entirely new set of armor, a new weapon, and still have plenty left over." I'm not really used to having money like that.

"I probably need to get some new traveling clothes, too." The things I have, at least what still fits, isn't really suitable for a long time on the road. "Would you...help me pick some stuff out?"

"I would be happy to." Khazak's tusks shine in the moonlight as he grins, hopefully remembering the last time we went clothes shopping. Which is what I was going for. "We can go tomorrow after we retrieve your equipment if you would like. We can stop by the armorer, too."

"That would be great, Sir." *It's gonna be weird not calling someone "Sir" for a while after this. And maybe calling anyone else that at all.*

"So, tell me, now that we are away from my family's prying ears, what *are* some of the places you would like to travel to?" He sees my grimace at his question, the same one I didn't have a good answer to before. "I remember how much you loved Ayla's stories. Surely there must be some destination you have thought about. If you did not have to consider your friends, where would you want to go? Or what were your original plans before you came here?"

"We really didn't think that far ahead." I scratch my head, recalling our complete lack of planning. "We were kinda hoping that finding whatever we thought was in the ruins would lead us to the next thing."

We were pretty desperate at that point, so we took the info and ran with it. I try to think back to some of the stories I had heard about Nova before we settled on it as our destination and got on the boat. Traveling, seeing the world, that actually *was* something I wanted to do. Not counting V'rok'sh Tah'lj, I had hoped to see a lot more than just a few human settlements by now.

"Well, I read once that if you go far enough south, you can see a second moon in the sky." That one wouldn't require going to any place specific either. "I also heard that there is an island off the coast in the north that's ruled by werewolves. And that desert your sister told me about with the crystals sounded pretty cool, too. Maybe I'll go to one of those." *Except the werewolf island, probably.*

"It is true. If you were to travel south, eventually you would be able to see the second moon in the sky. Only during the day, however, as it is pitch black. The island you are talking about is called Beovin, and the entire ruling family *are* werewolves. I am told it is a very beautiful country." *Alright, maybe I will visit werewolf island.* "And I trust my sister's judgement when it comes to traveling. If she said that you would enjoy the desert, then I think you can expect just that."

"What about you? Do you ever want to travel?" I change the subject, not wanting to hear him talk about me leaving again.

"I did a long time ago, yes. When Ayla and I were still young, younger than you even, we traveled north together. It was a first for the both of us." I remember him telling me about how his sister's first trip quickly turned into a second, and third, and then she was never really home again. "The city we visited is called Manamequohi."

"It's called *what?*" That's even harder to pronounce than this place.

"Most people refer to it as Maname or simply Mana." He chuckles at my response. "It is an island that was originally settled by pukwudgies and then later humans."

"Pukwudgies?" *Oh no, more names.*

"Gnomes," he explains in words I already know. "I do not believe they were overly fond of the humans encroaching on their land at first, but after enough time and cooperation, it has become a very bustling port city. They specialize in magical and enchanted items. That is where I purchased my satchel."

"Wow, really? Do they still make them?" Maybe *that's* where we go first. I wouldn't mind getting one of those bags myself.

"I have to imagine so, given how useful they are. I am still using mine over ten years later." He shrugs. "However, they are *very* expensive. When Ayla and I both purchased one each, we had to tell ourselves it was an investment. After that, we did not have much money left, so we turned around and headed back home. I had already been considering applying to the rangers at that point, but Ayla wanted to keep traveling. Two weeks later, she was gone, and I was in training. I am sure she has gotten much more use out of hers than I have."

"So, do you ever want to go traveling again?" He didn't really answer that.

"I have thought about it at times," he admits. "Maybe one day, but between my career and my family, I simply do not have the time right now. Perhaps when I retire."

"You're gonna wait that long to go anywhere again?" Spending that much of my life in Northlake would have driven me insane. "You don't ever want to just take a vacation somewhere?"

"I have not really given it much thought." He shrugs again. "Truthfully, before your arrival, I had not thought about the outside world much at all."

"Well, you should. Turns out there's a whole lot of interesting people out there who can teach you a lot of things you never knew before." *Not that I'm talking about anyone in particular.* "Just, you know, try not to end up getting thrown in jail."

"Thank you for the advice, pup." He chuckles. "I hope that regardless of your next destination, the rest of your journey goes much smoother than your time here."

I want to correct him, tell him that my time here has been great, but I'm not sure how to do that without also telling him a bunch of other things I'm feeling that I frankly don't want to hear myself. So, I settle for a quiet walk home, and once we get the leftovers put away, I am more than happy to spend the rest of the night on the couch with Sir as he reads, the sound of his voice lulling me to sleep.

Chapter 14

I wake up early the following morning. Really early. The sun has only started to rise in the sky, dim grey light leaking in from behind the dark curtain. I sigh softly. It's been happening more and more often these days. I used to wake up early all the time at the knight academy, even before then when I was in school. I never really felt tired because of it, but it's annoying to just lay there for hours because you know you should be sleeping. It sucked when I had a roommate, but once I was senior enough for my own room, I started getting up and using the time to work out or try and finish my homework from the night before. Or jerk off.

At least there are far more interesting things to do with that time here. It's only been a few days since we've had sex, but that's kinda long for us. We haven't exactly had the free time or been in the mood much, but the fleshy swordfight currently taking place between our clashing crotches this morning tells different tale. Although... I really should let Khazak sleep a little more. The last few days have been so shitty and stressful, and I think he had problems sleeping even before the bombing. There's been a night or two where I've woken up to him tossing and turning. I wish I knew how to help.

So, I wait, I figure for at least another half-hour, but it's a little tough to tell time with no clock. I try to use the sunlight as a guide, my eyes peeking over the curve of Khazak's chest from my spot next to him. I just want to make sure I beat the alarm.

Once I'm satisfied with the time, I slowly and carefully wiggle my way out of my owner's grasp. It's not easy because while he's a fairly heavy sleeper, he's also very strong, and I almost have to fight to escape the hold he has on me. I manage it, slinking my way down his body until his arms are empty, pulling the bedsheet down with me.

He's on his side, one leg partially thrown up, putting me face to face with his cock. The angle is a little awkward, but I manage to find a position on my stomach that isn't too hard on my neck. I skip using my hands altogether, instead drawing my mouth closer to the free-hanging appendage. I know I have seen, felt, smelled, and tasted this thing so many times over the last couple of months, but I am still impressed by its size. This close, I can actually see it twitching in time with his heartbeat.

I lower my mouth over the hooded head, a small bead of pre-cum already gathered at the tip. The familiar taste hits me as I take more of him in, his hard green length quickly filling my mouth. I press my tongue flat against the bottom of his shaft, stroking lightly as I reach my oral limits before I begin to pull back.

Taking my time, I bob my head back and forth on his horizontal hardness, sucking in lightly to hollow out my cheeks each time I take him in. I hum softly to myself, pleased when I feel him give a slight twitch, a new bead of pre-cum bursting on my tongue the next time I pull back. *I'm getting good at this.* My own dick is rock hard, wedged up between my belly and the mattress, and I grind myself against the fabric as I suck.

As I work, Khazak's body gives more and more signs of life. First, it's more twitches, and then I'm fairly certain I can feel his hips humping forward in rhythm with my bobbing. I'm not sure if it's involuntary or he's waking up, and it's hard to look up at his face from down here, so I just keep at it anyway. He'll let me know when he wakes up, one way or another.

"Another" turns out to be a hand grabbing the back of my head a moment later after a brief pause in his thrusting. It's gentle, barely guiding me at all, but I know that could change at any second. His hips pick up speed, but still nothing I can't handle.

"Good morning, pup," a rough voice greets me from above, the hand on my head tugging lightly at my hair.

I try to mumble out a good morning with my mouth still occupied, but he taps his thumb against my cheek.

"It is rude to speak with your mouth full," he jokes gruffly, ending the statement with a strong thrust forward.

That signals a change of pace, and his grip on my hair becomes much stronger. Rather than trying to change the pace I've been working at, he decides to start pumping his hips forward in earnest, just holding me in place while he fucks my face.

I moan involuntarily. Him taking charge like that just flips a switch in me, and I just want to behave and keep doing what he wants me to. His strokes are still shallow enough to not make me gag, but drool is starting to pool in the corner of my mouth. I try to swallow, but when he picks up speed, I just don't have the chance.

Seeing as I'm not even taking half of him right now, I try to ready myself for what I know is coming next, him pushing all the way into my throat. He still manages to catch me off-guard, and I sputter around it, the hand behind my head preventing me from pulling away. I'm more prepared for the next thrust, and after a few more, I get used to the pattern he's pumping away at and can breathe.

He fucks his cock into my throat with relative ease, only the occasional gag when there's a particularly rough thrust. Khazak hasn't said anything since scolding me for talking with a full mouth, content to let his actions speak for themselves. The wet sounds of my mouth being plundered fill the room along with the occasional moan or grunt. I think I can feel him taking out some of the week's frustrations on me.

Suddenly, Sir drags my head forward, pushing as much of himself into my mouth as he can without choking me. As I mumble-shout in surprise, he swings his leg over my shoulder, turning both of our bodies until I am flat on my back with Khazak facing down above me. His cock still halfway into my gullet, he pulls his hips up before thrusting them back down, fucking at least another inch and a half into me at this angle.

It's a little harder to breathe, so I'm hoping this also means he's close. I've got both hands flat on the mattress, but I am fully prepared to use them to signal him for help if I think I'm starting to turn purple. I doubt it'll come to that though, even as his thrusting grows stronger, I can feel him start to tense up, which only means one thing.

With a loud growl, he presses himself down into my face as much as our two bodies will allow. I can feel the back of my head being ground into the bed as he fills my throat with the first shot, nearly making me gag and cough when he pulls back and repeats himself for shot #2. The rest of his cum fills my mouth, and I swallow as quickly as I can to avoid making even more of a mess than I'm sure my spit already has.

Falling back to his side and releasing my head, Khazak lets out a relaxed sigh as he settles on the bed. After swallowing down the remnants and wiping my mouth as best I can, I climb back up the bed to join him, happily allowing myself to be pulled against a muscular green chest. My own dick is still hard, but oddly enough, I'm kinda okay if I don't get off right now.

"Thank you." Khazak's still rough voice says from above. "I seem to have needed that."

"Me too," I reply, half against his skin. I feel one of his hands slide down my side, over my hip, and reach for my dick. I pull back to look him in the face. "Actually, I think I'm okay."

He looks he gives me is half curious, half turned on, but he leaves it at that, smiling as he sits up. "I suppose it is time for breakfast."

Breakfast is something he's made for me before, something that seems a lot like porridge, but more finely ground. think he called it hominy? He's made it a couple times; it's pretty simple and quick in the mornings before work. He said it's made from corn, which I haven't had a ton of, but I managed to convince him that it would taste even *better* with some cheese. They don't really do cheese a whole lot around here, but I got him to buy some last week, and I wasn't wrong. They go together perfectly.

When breakfast is served, I can't help but notice there's only one bowl before I am pulled into a lap. We haven't done this at home in a while, and not usually at all with things that involve a spoon, but Khazak wants to feed me. When I look over at his face, I get why. Just like why I wanted to give him the blowjob, he's just trying to offer me a little comfort after the last few days, which I am more than happy to accept.

With full bellies, the two of us get dressed and head into work for the day. It seems like it's mostly going to be more of the same, and I'm in Khazak's office looking over my language book when he walks in. Expecting to make another delivery, I put the book down and stand.

"Ready to retrieve your belongings from storage?" he asks.

I nod, though I had nearly forgotten about that. Khazak leads the way outside, back into the station's yard. I spot a couple of the officers using the training area off to one side, sparring with some quarterstaffs. Khazak and I go to the left toward the storage sheds. These are full of all sorts of equipment for the rangers, and I'm not sure which is the one with my stuff.

"Here we are." Khazak taps lightly against the big shed door before grasping the lock. He places it against the back of his wrist, the magical armband unlocking for us. I never got one of those, but after getting caught breaking into this place, he probably figured it would be best not to. Removing the chain wrapped around the door handles, he swings them open.

Inside is a *lot* of stuff, seemingly at random: a lot of bags, some boxes, some loose clothing. Maybe this is where they keep everyone's belongings while they're behind bars? Khazak steps inside, bending over to check the paper tags that have been tied to each bag, stopping when he finds mine. It's been so long I almost don't recognize it or the folded leather armor it's sitting on top of.

"We keep weapons elsewhere; we can get that next." Khazak closes and locks the storage unit after handing me my belongings.

After retrieving my old sword, Khazak leaves me to sort through my stuff while he gets back to work on the plan to investigate Councilman Murbank. Things are currently still in the "writing a polite letter" stage, but I have a feeling they're gonna escalate quickly. While he writes, I look through my bag, setting my sword and armor to the side. My too-thin bedroll is still attached to the bottom in the same condition as I remember it. Which is "not good." *Something to add to the shopping list.*

I open the flap on the top of the bag to inspect the contents, removing each one. I've got my compass as well as a very crude map of the coastline. There are a few small torches, plus some flint to light them with. Then we've got some rope, my nearly empty wallet pouch, and three empty waterskins.

"Aww, you guys took my food." All my trail rations and jerky are gone.

"It has been two months." Khazak looks up from his writing, shaking his head. "Of course we did not leave food in your bag."

"Shouldn't I get reimbursed or something?" *Or maybe I can just swap it for some of the much better tasting food they have here?*

"I will file an expense report." From the way he rolls his eyes, I don't think he will.

I look over my sword next. Just look because I don't think Khazak would appreciate me swinging it around in here. My trusty shortsword, no worse for wear than when I last used it. It's nothing fancy, but it could use a good polish and some sharpening. Maybe I can pick up a second one. I sold my last one in Holbrooke before we got here. Especially now that I've got some of my strength back, wielding a weapon in each hand should be even easier.

That just leaves my armor. It's a tunic and some leggings, both padded with leather. They're light, and I have to hold each one against my body just to be sure they'll still fit. Looks like they might be a little tight, but I could probably get them on with some squeezing. That means a lot of chaffing though, and that's not good for armor. It's a shame too because it's still in pretty good condition. Considering it was removed from me while I was unconscious, I'm surprised they didn't just cut it off of me.

"If you are worried about the fit, the armorer should be able to make any necessary adjustments." Khazak tells me when he sees me holding the tunic against my body. "And if not, they also sell new armor."

"Thanks." I know I supposedly have *some* money to my name, but I'm still gonna try to be as cheap as I can. "Who took it off me anyway? They were surprisingly gentle."

"That would be me," he responds, and then seemingly finishes his letter, putting down his pen. "I was also the one who carried you from the temple to the healer."

"You were?" Something about that makes me feel warm inside. "Well...thank you."

"It was the least I could do, seeing as I was the one to knock you out," he teases. "Actually, I was not even originally scheduled to be out there that week."

"You weren't?" I can't decide if that makes me lucky or not.

"I traded shifts with Ragnar the week before after he forgot about his mother's birthday." Khazak smirks to himself. "I suppose I should thank him."

"Damn, I was so close to ending up owned by him instead," I joke to cover for the warm fuzzy feelings I'd rather ignore. "So, since we are on the subject of me buying new armor... How much money do I have, exactly?"

"Let me see..." He leans over to open a drawer on his desk, pulling out a book I think is called a ledger. Almost looks kinda like the inventory lists in the burned book. "At the current moment you have... 4768 gral."

"Wow, that's a lot." Okay, so I'm not actually sure I know how much that is. "...Isn't it?"

"It is approximately 480 pieces of gold, so I would say so." My eyes go wide.

"Holy shit." I sit on the couch. "I don't think I've ever had this much money before."

"You have earned it, David." He puts the ledger away with a smile. "You can expect another hundred or so by your final day. I have been keeping your earnings with mine, but I am happy to hand them over starting now. I can take you to the armorer on our lunch break."

"We can go get some other clothes too, right?" Might as well get some other shopping done while we are out.

"Of course, we can make some other stops if you would like as well." He folds the letter on his desk while he answers. "But first, I need you to deliver this letter to Councilman Murbank's office in the tribal hall."

After putting my things away, I run out for my first couriering act of the day. This seems a little below my pay grade (seeing as I actually know what that is now), but at least this way, I can see if I notice anything odd. Once I'm at the hall, I have to ask for directions to his office, but I find it easy enough. Knocking on the big double doors, I am let into a very large waiting room. His secretary, a stout, shrewd looking orc woman, promptly informs me that the councilman is busy, takes the letter from me, and sends me on my way.

I inform Sir of this once I'm back at the station, and with a sigh, he contemplates his next move—which I think may be a more strongly worded letter. But before he sends it out, it's time for lunch. We eat quickly, scarfing down leftovers from the night before, and then it's time for some shopping.

The first stop is to the armorer. With all his leather-working skills, I think at first that we might be going to see Brull, but Khazak informs me that making armor isn't something Brull does. Instead, he takes me to the person responsible for crafting the armor for all of the rangers, both because he trusts the quality, and because it'll get me a nice discount.

She's an older looking woman, and one of few words as she inspects my old armor and then my body. She takes my measurements quickly and efficiently and tells Khazak she can have it ready by the end of the week for what works out to be about five gold. Considering a good set of armor can cost five times that, it's a steal.

With my armor taken care of, the next thing I want to grab is some new clothes. The stuff I have that still fits is nice but not really suited for extended traveling. We head to the same clothing shop we came to on my first day in the marketplace. I think about looking at weapons, but assuming we aren't immediately kicked out of the city after their release, my friends are probably gonna want to do a little shopping of their own.

"*Zratza, tik*— Oh, hello!" The shopkeeper swaps to Common once she sees us both, remembering me from my last visit. "How can I help you today?"

The question is directed at Sir, and though I am tempted to speak up for myself, I just roll with it. I won't get to enjoy having someone do the talking for me for much longer.

"My avakesh appears to already be outgrowing the last set of clothing we purchased here already." A green hand pulls me closer. "We are looking for items more suited to travel this time, that can be worn under armor."

"Going on a trip?" She looks at the both of us hopefully.

"He will be," he responds as I am gently pushed toward the shopkeeper.

With a nod, she pulls out her measuring tape and gets her own set of updated measurements. Once she's satisfied, she sets to work picking things off shelves for me. More things that are long sleeved to better protect from the elements. A lot of greens and browns, possibly to help me blend in with my surroundings better. There are also a few lighter shirts with shorter sleeves, probably for the days spent under the hot sun. *Summer is right around the corner.*

With a handful of new clothes, I look around for the changing area we used last time, a tall divider blocking out a corner of the room. I start to walk over, then notice I'm doing it on my own. I look over at Khazak, who instead of following me is aimlessly looking around at the clothes still on shelves. Huh?

"Are you not gonna help me try them on?" I ask with much more confidence than I would have two months ago.

"I did not think you needed my assistance this time." He looks surprised at my question.

"Someone's gotta tell me if they look good, right?" I try to give my best flirty smile.

"I suppose I am qualified for that." He smiles as he walks toward me and follows me the rest of the way to the changing area.

I put the pile of clothing down on the chair behind the divider, turning to face Khazak before I start stripping. And I do mean stripping. I start to very slowly unbutton my shirt, trying to look as sexy as possible as I reveal my lightly furred chest. From watching his face, it seems like it works, his eyes traveling down my chest to my stomach. Hanging my shirt over the back of the chair, I unbutton my pants next, pushing them down to slowly reveal the dark red jockstrap covering my crotch.

I wonder if I should get some new underwear, too? It probably wouldn't hurt, but if I'm being honest, these jockstraps are actually pretty damn handy. Not covering your ass aside, they do a great job of keeping all your bits in place, and the straps stay tight, which is more important than you'd think in a fight. Still not convinced of the combat applications of thongs, though.

Once the pants are off, it's time to start trying new things on, something else I make sure to take my time with. I turn to the chair, silently examining the pile like I need to decide what's first, making sure my ass remains on display. Of course, I just end up grabbing what's on the top, a dark brown shirt, but that just means I get to not wear pants a little longer.

I pull the shirt on by its sleeves, slowly buttoning it from bottom to top. I turn as I dress, Khazak's eyes torn between following my hands and staring at my butt. *Good.* When I finish with the shirt, I take a moment to stretch, gratuitously enough to make Khazak laugh before I reach for the pants.

It's not super easy to look sexy while putting on pants, but damned if I don't try, pulling them up to just under the curve of my ass, lifting it that much more before I finally let the waist slip over. What? I've had this entire flirting "asset" back here for years without knowing. I've got some time to make up for.

The outfit gets the approval I wanted, though not as much as the strip tease. I start to undress again, and as much as I'd love to take my time and draw all of this out, we do have to get back to work at some point. I still make sure I look damn good doing it, but I try on the next few outfits a little quicker.

Four gold pieces and one new wardrobe later, Khazak places my purchases into his bag, and the two of us bid the shopkeeper farewell.

"We still have some time before we are due back at the station," Khazak tells me as we exit the shop. "Was there anything else you wanted to purchase?"

There isn't a whole lot else I can think of supply-wise that I'd wanna get right now. Definitely not anything like food. But there is one thing in the last couple of months that I've realized is worth taking with me: books. Or at least, *a* book.

"Can we stop by the bookstore?" All the time we've spent reading by the fire has kinda grown on me.

"Of course," he answers with a nod. "Perhaps Nylan is working."

The bookstore is on the way back to the station, not far from the marketplace. I've been there a couple of times in the past with Khazak, just to pick up a book he's had the shop order for him. It's nice, if not a little small, and most of the books are in Atasi. But I know they carry some stuff in Common too, and if Ny's working, he'll help me out.

We walk in the open door to see that Ny *is* working, currently speaking with a customer. "Speaking" is generous. It looks more like he's being berated and is desperately trying to keep a smile on his face instead of yelling back. The person giving him a hard time is a short, older orc gentleman, and I of course don't understand a thing being said.

It takes a few minutes, but eventually the man is either satisfied with Nylan's responses to his questions, or he's just tired of yelling and decides to leave. He gives both Khazak and me a real stink eye as he walks out for no apparent reason. Real charmer.

"Hey guys!" Nylan greets us cheerfully once he notices us, then looks down behind the counter in front of him. "Are we supposed to have an order in for you, sir?"

"No, we are not here for me this time, Nylan." Khazak nods in my direction.

"Really?" He looks over to me, surprised. "You didn't strike me as much of a reader."

I could choose to take that as an insult to my intelligence, but I won't. "Yeah, just figured if I'm going to be on the road again in two weeks, it might be worth bringing a book or two with me."

"Aww, that's right. You're leaving soon." The elf frowns. "Not a bad idea, though. What kind of books are you looking for? Anything specific?"

"Uhh..." I probably should have thought about this more. "I don't know. When I was little, I used to love reading stories about heroes and dragons, but that's pretty childish, right?"

"What? No." He shakes his head. "There's tons of adventure novels for adults. People wouldn't write them if other people didn't want to read them."

"Oh. Well, I still don't know the names of any good ones." I scratch the back of my head, starting to feel like a dumb jock again.

"I can think of a few books you might like." Nylan taps his fingers against the counter as he thinks. "Give me a day or two, and I'll pull some and bring them by your place."

"That would be great." He's the one who works in a bookstore, so I'm happy to trust his judgement on what I should read. "Just tell me how much I owe you. I have money now!"

"Oh, I'm sure we'll work something out." Ny winks at me, and I learn that I am very okay with trading sex for books. "Is there anything else you might like?"

"Actually..." I look around the shop for a moment, spotting Khazak browsing the shelves against one wall. "There is one specific book I'd like to get my hands on. Can you get me a copy of the book about Khazak Steelrun? In Common if that exists?"

"Yes, I can." Ny's eyes go bright at the mention of that particular book. "I can *also* get you a copy of the steamy and very explicit romance novel loosely based on his and Vakesh's relationship."

"People actually write stuff like that?" It certainly sounds entertaining.

"You have *no* idea, David. There's a whole series, but only the first has been translated to Common so far." He looks very pleased right now. "I'll tell you what: if you *promise* to write to me and keep in touch after you leave, I'll figure out how to send you the second book when it's translated, wherever you are. Deal?" He holds out a hand for me to shake.

"Deal." I shake his hand, promise sealed. "So, how you been doing?"

I don't want to say anything that might come off as rude, but up close while we've been talking, I can see that Ny looks tired, which is not easy for an elf. He doesn't look terrible, but I can tell he's not getting enough sleep, and I have a good idea of why.

"I'm fine. A little rough the last few nights, I guess." He means since the bombings. "The attacks... They bring up some bad memories of my mom's death, which just makes me miss her a lot. I wish my dad still lived nearby."

"I'm sorry." I don't really know what else to say. I just wish I could help him feel better.

"It's okay. I wrote him a letter, but I probably won't hear back for a few more days. He lives pretty far up north now." Aww, I just want to give him a hug. "I think I understand why he wanted to move. At least I still have Ragnar here."

He says things are fine, but I can hear the sadness in his voice. Not even just sadness but fear. I want to tell him that he's safe, that we're going to catch who did this, but I don't know that for certain, and I don't wanna make Nylan relive all those memories. It strengthens my resolve about leaving before this is through. With my order placed, and after a strong hug goodbye, the two of us bid Nylan a good afternoon and let him get back to work.

When we get back to the station, the first thing Khazak does is check for a response from Councilman Murbank to his letter. There of course isn't one, and I can feel the displeasure coming off of him in waves as we walk back to his office. It does seem kind of weird that someone would ignore a message from the captain of the city's law enforcement, but maybe it's not. Councilman Murbank is one of the few people in town with more authority than Khazak, which is only gonna cause us more problems. *That settles it.*

"I don't think I'm going to be ready to leave in two weeks," I tell Khazak as he writes a second message to the councilman. "It doesn't feel right leaving in the middle of this, not without stopping whoever is responsible."

"That is very noble, David, but unnecessary." Khazak is still holding his pen. "You have more than earned your freedom as will your friends. I do not think they are likely going to want to extend their stays in the city after they are released."

"Then I'll catch up with them later." I shrug and cross my arms. "I'm not leaving when the city is *literally* under attack. I have friends here. If I left, all I'd ever do is wonder if you were all okay."

"I suppose there is nothing I can do to change your mind?" Glad he's gotten used to my stubborn nature by now.

"Nope." I shake my head. "You're stuck with me."

"Then we will just have to make sure to solve this mystery quickly." He smiles and nods to himself before going back to writing. "Starting with you making another delivery."

"Another request?" I ask, referring to the letter.

"Not anymore. Now it is a demand." *That's another one of those words that sounds hot when he says it.* "One I still fully expect to be ignored, which is why first thing in the morning I will be going down to his office myself to speak with him in person."

That's the kind of directness I can get behind. By the time I'm finished with the delivery, I'm already looking forward to the morning.

Chapter 15

"*This* is what we should have done in the first place," Ragnar says to Khazak as the three of us enter the tribal hall and head for Murbank's office. "Sending him those messages just gave him more time to hide whatever it is he's doing. We shouldn't even be here; we should be searching his home or the shipyard while he's not expecting us."

"I need to at least *appear* that I am trying to do this properly, Deputy," Khazak grumbles back.

I get what he's saying. Murbank is someone with enough power to strike back if he wants to. But Ragnar's also right—if Murbank knows we're onto him, we can't afford to waste time and risk him hiding whatever evidence we need to find. Plus, if he's not already aware of what we know, I have a bad feeling he's going to suspect something what with the captain *and* one of his deputies personally coming to interview him together.

I've been thinking about this almost non-stop since yesterday, especially after seeing Nylan. My eyes and ears are open, looking and listening for anything that might prove useful. Khazak takes the lead as we approach the office's double doors, Ragnar and I flanking him on either side.

"*Drepa lat*," Murbank's secretary announces when the doors open, then she notices who it is. "I am very sorry, sirs, but the councilman is unavailable at the moment. I will be happy to pass along a message for you."

"I am sure you will, ma'am, but I am afraid this cannot wait." Khazak starts to walk toward the door to Murbank's office proper.

"Sir, you cannot just walk in there!" Murbank's secretary stands when it becomes apparent that Khazak is going to ignore her.

"Given the gravity of the situation, I am sure he will understand." He prepares to push past her, Ragnar and me right behind him.

"The councilman is *very* busy and—"

Suddenly, the doors to the waiting room behind us swing open, and everyone turns to see Murbank entering. *Why didn't she just tell us he wasn't in?* If he's surprised to see us, he doesn't show it, which doesn't give me a good feeling.

"It is alright, Tholoma. I can make some time for the captain." The smile he gives us is innocent enough, but I don't trust it.

Satisfied with her boss's response, Tholoma returns to her seat behind the desk, still glowering. Murbank steps around us, pulling out a ring of keys to unlock his office door. I watch him slip them back into his right pocket before opening the door and holding it open, motioning for the three of us to enter.

Shit, this office is nice, *lavish* even (I bet Mikey would be proud of me for knowing that word). Huge paintings of landscapes line the walls, the largest hanging over a fireplace that is twice as big as the one at Khazak's house. On either side of it are huge bookcases, tall enough to reach the ceiling and filled with very expensive looking leather-bound books. At the center of the room is a massive wooden desk, the legs and sides carved into intricate patterns and polished brightly. A number of small stone orc busts sit atop the desk and on the bookcases, though I can't place any of their faces. *How loaded is this guy?*

"I am terribly sorry, gentlemen," Murbank apologizes as he walks around his desk to take a seat. "Between the council voting on recovery efforts and preparing for the charity gala, I have not had a moment to read your messages. Will you both be in attendance tonight?"

"I do not believe either of us were aware there was an event taking place tonight." The question catches Khazak off guard.

"This is the first I'm hearing of it," Ragnar confirms.

"Damn, I must have made a mistake when preparing the guest list with my secretary." He sighs. "I hope both you and your avakeshes will be able to make it. We are raising money to support the families affected by the bombings."

"Of course, sir. We would be happy to attend," Khazak answers. *We will? Sounds like a real stuffy shindig.* "Now, if I could get to—"

"Yes, please. To what do I owe the pleasure of the ranger captain and his trusty deputy coming to see me in person?" His eagerness to speak with us is throwing me off. He's up to something.

"It is regarding the recent attacks, I am afraid, as well as your former employee, Thog Grimrock." Khazak finally takes a seat in front of the man's desk, Ragnar sitting to his left while I continue to stand behind them.

"Such a tragedy." Murbank shakes his head. His feigned sincerity is starting to make me feel sick. "To think, if only he had not committed that robbery and been imprisoned, he might still be alive today."

"We actually have reason to believe he wasn't working alone," Ragnar spills, and I'm thankful that's all he says.

"Really? How interesting." He might be a good actor, but it's not hard to tell he knows something is up. He wants to know what else we know.

"Yes, and I am afraid we also learned of some new information regarding Mister Grimrock's situation." Khazak tries to take back control of the conversation. "Namely, that he seemed to be in a large amount of debt after attempting to purchase and reopen his father's old weapon factory. Debt that you now own along with the factory itself."

"Ah. You see, before the rebellion, his parents and mine were close friends." His tone is still calm, but it's changed. "Even afterward, my mother and father did their best to make sure Thog and his mother were taken care of. When he fell onto hard times, I could not help but offer assistance to my old friend."

"Would you mind explaining a little more about your relationship?" Khazak presses on this new bit of information. "He was your employee as well as an old friend?"

"Yes, when it became apparent that he risked losing it, I stepped in and purchased the factory myself." The councilman stands, walking to one of his bookcases as he speaks and adjusts one of the statues. I watch his movements carefully. "I gave him a job at my shipyard so that he could pay off his debt. When he was finished, I planned to sign over the factory. Pity we never made it to that step."

"That is very generous of you, sir," Khazak comments, turning in his chair to watch the councilman. "Seems rather odd then, that he would risk all of that by stealing from the very job you gave him."

"Yes, well, desperation can drive a person to do many things, especially the less fortunate." There's something about the way he says it, some undertone of smugness, that just rubs me the wrong way. What the hell does this guy know about what poor people go through?

"I understand you visited Mr. Grimrock a number of times in prison," Khazak comments as he stands, walking toward Murbank but still leaving plenty of distance between them.

"Despite his actions against me, I still considered the man a friend." He approaches Khazak, starting to lose his patience. "I also ensured his mother and younger siblings would be supported despite his imprisonment. Something that I continue to do now even *after* his death. Is that a crime, Captain?"

"No, sir. Merely trying to piece together the man's motive and see if there is a connection to his death in the other night's attacks." Khazak remains calm and collected despite the increase in hostility, though Ragnar is now standing as well.

"Seems like nothing more than a very unfortunate coincidence to me, Captain." Murbank faces Khazak, standing about an equal distance both to Khazak and me. "Even if he had not passed, he confessed and was sentenced months ago, and the case closed. I am not sure why you are still investigating this, *especially* when I know there are a number of open cases you and your rangers have yet to resolve."

"I apologize if I have caused any offense, sir." Khazak bows his head slightly, still sounding perfectly calm. "I merely want to ensure I am being as thorough as possible."

Alright, I don't really know why I do what I do next. Okay, that's not true: I know *why*. I just haven't fully figured out what the rest of my plan is yet. I can tell that this conversation is wrapping up, and we *still* don't know anything besides the fact that this guy is a fucking creep. So, with neither man's gaze actually on me, I take a step forward—and immediately trip over myself, falling right into Council Murbank.

"Oh gods! I am *so* sorry, sir," I apologize as I quickly try to right myself.

Murbank looks at me unhappily and maybe a little confused—and so does Khazak, actually—but it *doesn't* look like he felt my hand slipping into his pocket or that it's any lighter.

"Well, if there is nothing else you men need, I have a very busy day ahead." Murbank straightens himself and looks at the door. "Please let me know if there is anything *else* I can do for you; otherwise, I will see you all tonight."

"Of course, we would not miss it." Khazak gives his most professional smile. "Thank you for your time."

I can feel the councilman's glare on my back as we leave his office, same for his secretary. We don't say anything until we are far down the hallway and away from any prying ears.

"Well, he obviously does not want us to investigate this any further," Khazak comments. "Which is exactly why we are going to continue our investigation."

"Did we learn anything new from that?" I ask, conveniently ignoring the ring of keys in my pocket right now. "Other than that he's apparently a saint."

"I doubt his motives for providing Thog with employment were all that altruistic," Khazak responds. "You remember how small the house he was living in was. He was *not* paying that man well. It is likely he barely made a dent in his debt."

"I wouldn't be so sure about the family thing either." Ragnar shakes his head. "If anything, taking care of them just gave Murbank more ammunition for threats or blackmail."

"Do you think the family is worth talking to?" Maybe they can tell us something about Murbank if he's still involved with them like he says.

"Possibly, but if they *were* being used as pawns like that, I doubt they were ever aware of it. Which would have put even more pressure on Thog to hide the truth," Khazak points out. "I am far more interested in finding out why Mr. Grimrock ran into so many problems when trying to reopen his father's factory. Something about that seems odd."

"How do we do that?" I ask, turning toward the building's main exit.

"We spend some time in the archives." A hand tugs me away from the doorway, instead leading me down the hallway at the other end of the lobby.

"I hate the archives," Ragnar groans.

After some winding hallways and a few doors, we come to another office seemingly watched over by a much, *much* older woman. Like, there's something about her that makes me think of one of my old teachers or a librarian. She's happy to let us in, though Khazak waves off any further assistance. Best not to let too many people know what we're doing here.

Which is looking at a lot of papers. Seriously, the room is wall to wall shelves, each stuffed to the brim with books and files. Even if I knew what we were looking for, none of it is in Common, so there's not much I can do to help. Khazak asks Ragnar to search for the permits related to Thog's attempt at restarting his family's business while he looks into any changes to the city's laws that might have happened around that time that could have affected things. That leaves me to act as a lookout... I'm just trying to feel useful, alright?

"Ha! Got 'em," Ragnar announces maybe half an hour after we started our search. He crosses the room to Khazak, and I move to join them. "Thog filed permits to open the factory *three times*, and each time, the council voted to deny it. Really wanted to help his friend, huh?"

"Does it say how they voted?" I don't even know why I'm looking at the paper to be honest.

"No, but your guess is as good as mine," Khazak grumbles. "That same year, the council voted to approve two different measures that restricted where in town certain types of businesses were allowed to operate. This was two years ago. Either the councilman has been planning this for a while now, or he was holding on to Thog for some other reason."

"That's good, right? We can use that to show he has a motive." I feel a little upbeat for once.

"It is still not enough to actually accuse him of anything." Khazak shakes his head. "But it is good information to have." Khazak folds the papers together and hands them to Ragnar. "Take these back to the station to make copies of. I do not want to risk Murbank covering his tracks."

"Aww, by hand?" Ragnar whines. "But the archivist can use a copier-wand."

"She can also tell others what she has made copies of." Khazak fixes him with a look. "It is the only way to be safe."

"Are we stealing those?" Is *Sir* actually gonna break the law?

"*Borrowing*," he clarifies, and I'm not buying it. "We will return them later tonight."

"Wait, what are we going to do?" I just realized he only gave that order to Ragnar.

"*You* will be returning to the station with Deputy Rockfang," he clarifies. *Boooo.* "Though I am not sure anything useful will come of it, I am going to go speak with Mr. Grimrock's family. As they are still grieving his loss, three of us may send the wrong message. I will meet you both back at the station in an hour or two, and we can discuss our next steps."

"Yes, sir."

"Yes, Sir." I nod while Ragnar stuffs the papers into his shirt.

The archivist is just as friendly on our way out, and I can only hope she doesn't get a lot of visitors because she definitely seems like the type to talk someone's ear off. I am glad we got some new info, but I am more than a little antsy for the chance to talk to Ragnar without Khazak's supervision. I have a feeling he'll be a lot more understanding.

We split when we exit the tribal hall, Khazak heading north while we go east. I wait until we are far out of earshot of anyone before turning to Ragnar.

"So... I might have done something really really *really* stupid." Stupid enough that I'm looking over my shoulder right now.

Ragnar narrows his eyes, but nods at an alley on our right, which we both duck into.

"What did you do, David?" Ragnar asks after making sure we're alone.

"I might have, maybe, kinda, sorta...stole Councilman Murbank's keys?" I hold up the keyring with a grimace.

Ragnar's eyes go wide, looking between me and the keys. Then he breaks out into a huge grin. "You did *what?!*"

He doesn't look angry, so I press forward. "It was just...I knew he wasn't going to tell us anything, and I kept thinking about what you were saying about not wanting to give him the chance to hide anything, and after the way the conversation went, I thought there was no *way* he didn't know we were onto him now, so I just sorta...panicked and decided to pick his pocket."

"David, that is *amazing*." Okay, I didn't think he would be pissed off, but I still figured I'd have to convince him to get on board a *little*.

"Really? Because I'm pretty sure Sir is gonna kill me for this." Like *actually* kill, maybe.

"Oh, definitely," he confirms as he takes the keys from me. *Great.* "Which is why you and I are only going to tell him if we find something good after we go over there and search the place."

"Wait, right *now?*" Honestly, if you're still surprised at this point to learn that I didn't think *any* of this through, that's on you. "Does he live alone? Isn't he married or something?"

"Yes, but any time Murbank throws a big event like this, his wife is the one who does the actual planning," he responds confidently, already moving down the alley. "We'll knock on the door when we get there, but I'd bet money she's back in the hall's main ballroom right now, ordering around the crews setting up."

We walk quickly to the southern part of the city. We have some time, but if we want to beat Khazak back to the station, we still need to hurry. We pass by the shipyard on the way, and it's only another few blocks before we reach the councilman's home, obviously in one of the wealthier parts of the city. Just like you'd expect for a man of his station, it's big, though not quite a mansion. A metal gate surrounds his yard, which is filled with fountains and statues depicting orcs in various poses. Behind the house, I can see the wall of the city, acting as a fence for his backyard.

"Wow." It's not that it's unimpressive. There's just something about it that's so...

"Pretentious, right?" Ragnar finishes my thought.

"Very," I agree, the two of us stepping toward the gate.

It's not locked, so we swing it open enough to walk inside and close it behind us. The streets look empty right now, but you never know who might be watching. I make sure to search the windows of the neighboring houses for any faces, and Ragnar is doing the same. He's the one to approach the large wooden doors, giving two quick knocks. We wait a minute before trying again, but there's still no answer.

"See? No one's home." Ragnar grins as he pulls out the keyring. "You and I will be in and out before Murbank even notices his keys are missing."

He sorts through the ring, deciding on which he thinks are house keys. He tries three before we find the right one, the lock clicking open with ease. After one final look around, Ragnar opens the door, and we slip inside, locking the door behind us. We're standing in a large foyer, but it's the next room that really catches my eye.

Murbank's living room—if that's what they're called when they're this big—is *massive*. I think it might be bigger than Khazak's entire house. There's a similar sunken area, this one with *three* couches in front of a very ornate fireplace. Statues dot the sides of the room and artwork lines the walls, and in the back of the room, I can even see a large piano in front of a set of glass doors that lead to the backyard.

"Fuck," I say to no one in particular.

"Yeah, I don't think you get this rich without doing some questionable things." Ragnar steps forward, looking around the room. "Alright, we don't have a ton of time, so we should split up. You take left. I'll go right."

There's a hallway on either side of the room, and another in the back that looks like it leads to a kitchen.

"What are we looking for, anyway?" I ask as I move toward the left hall. "I can't exactly read anything."

"Something that could tie him to the robberies or the bombings," Ragnar tells me from the opposite doorway. "Maybe some of the stuff that's been stolen or a set of black robes. If you see *anything* that might be suspicious, come find me, and I'll check it out."

"Alright, first person to finish comes and finds the other?" I don't wanna be here any longer than we need to.

"Sounds like a plan." Ragnar hits his chest in a half-salute and turns down the hall behind him.

And so begins my search for...whatever it is we're hoping to find here. The hall I start down is a long one, and I pass door after door after door. Some closets, a few bedrooms, and a *lot* of bathrooms. *Is he showing off because his dad invented toilets or something?* I search each room as I pass it, though there isn't a whole lot to look through in the bathrooms and closets, and all the bedrooms look completely unlived in. I don't get the point of having a house with rooms you never use.

Eventually I come to a room that *does* look like it's been used. Some sort of half-bedroom, half-office. There's a decent sized bed against one wall and a desk against the other. A large glass window takes up most of the back wall, and there's a half-open closet next to the desk with a mirror hanging above it. The same pretentious art lines the walls, but a lack of feminine touches makes me think this room is just Murbank's.

The closet is the first thing to get my attention because what do I see out in the open but a set of black robes. A few of them. It's hard to tell if these are the *exact* robes our attackers wore, but it's a good sign, right? Time to search the rest of the room. The bed doesn't tell me anything, except that Murbank likes nice sheets. The desk, however, is covered in papers.

Papers I can't read, of course, but that doesn't stop me from rifling through them. They don't look official, all handwritten without any seals or emblems. From the formatting, I think they might be letters, but it's hard to tell. Just when I'm about to go get Ragnar, something catches my eye.

This paper isn't like the others. There's no writing, just sketches. Sketches of what looks like a bird's claw. The sheet of paper is covered in them, all in different levels of detail, some shaded in, some not, but right dead in the center in solid black, is one that is identical to the one on the burned book and Thog's shoulder. *He designed the symbol himself.*

It's hard to describe the way I'm feeling because as bad as it is to confirm this guy is behind everything terrible that's been happening, I'm a little giddy at the thought that we finally have enough to nail him. Even if this paper of sketches is nothing, I bet there's plenty of incriminating details in these letters.

Gathering the papers together, I make to exit the room when a blur of green in the window stops me. *Wait, Ragnar? Why is he outside, looking in the window?* I hold up the stack of papers and point, but as soon as he sees me, he starts waving frantically. I don't get it. What's wrong?

Right on cue, a noise from the hall behind me answers my question. *Someone's home.* I turn back to the window, but Ragnar is already gone, having the good sense to hide, and I need to follow his lead, fast. Under the bed is the obvious choice, but I don't have time to check for room, so the closet it is. I almost forget to put the papers back, doing my best to spread them around quietly before darting into the closet and hiding in the very back, behind the heavy robes.

Not a second later, Murbank himself stomps into the room. *How did he get inside without his keys?!* From where I'm standing in the closet, I'm just able to see into the room, my body and face *hopefully* obscured by the clothing. He doesn't look happy as he grumbles to himself, and I can see a large dark splotch of something on the front of his purple robes. Can't make out what he's saying, but if I had to guess, I'd go with something about having a shitty day.

He tears off the robe and throws it onto the bed, revealing a simple tan tunic and pants underneath. When he turns to the closet, I have a minor panic attack, barely remembering to hold my breath as he rifles through the clothes hanging to my left. *Fuckfuckfuck, please don't look over here*. I want to (but don't) exhale in relief when he pulls out a similarly colored replacement. Then I notice his wrist.

Covering the inside of his forearm, in dark black ink, is the bird's claw symbol. Same as on Thog's shoulder, same as in the book, same as the sketches on his desk. *Yes!* I'm so excited I could dance, and probably will as soon as he leaves. There's no possible justification he could have for having that tattoo. Now that I think about it, I'm not sure I've ever actually seen him out of his long-sleeved shirts and robes.

But first, I have to get out of here. I watch silently as Murbank pulls on his new robe, straightening out any wrinkles and examining himself in the mirror above the desk. Then he pauses and gives himself a weird look. No, he's giving the *desk* a weird look. *Fuck, the papers!* He reaches a hand out, examining a few and sliding them to the side. Can he tell I went through them?

He wheels around, scanning the room with eyes full of suspicion. He looks at the bed, the desk, the window, the closet. I swear at one point it looks like he's staring straight at me, but a split-second later, it's gone. *That was nothing, right?* Before I have much longer to freak out, he gives the papers on the desk one final glare and exits the room.

I try to listen for when it's safe, but I'm too terrified of exiting the room and immediately running into him because he hasn't left the house yet. I'm just starting to contemplate climbing out the window when another person entering the room makes me freeze. At least until I see that it's Ragnar.

"David? Are you in here?" He's speaking at a normal volume, so I take it to mean that the coast is clear.

"Yeah, right here," I answer as I exit the closet, breathing deeply. "What the hell happened?"

"I don't know." He shakes his head. "I was on the other side of the house but kept getting blocked by locked doors.

I came back to check out the kitchen when I heard the front door unlocking. I ran out the back before anyone saw me. I didn't realize it was Murbank until I watched him leave."

"Ragnar, look." I walk over to the desk and point out the paper with the sketches. "He has this *same* symbol on his wrist, same tattoo as Thog."

His eyes go a little wide in surprise. "Shit. Well, you're gonna want to see this too."

Ragnar leads me out of the room and down the hall, then out the back door. It's fairly sparse, not unlike Khazak's parent's backyard, except for something large and black off in one corner: a carriage, the same one that's almost run me over twice now. No horses though.

"Is this the carriage you keep seeing?" Ragnar asks, walking over to it.

"Yeah. I mean, I think so." I nod, stepping closer.

"That's not all." Ragnar points down to the tracks leading from the carriage into the back wall, the one that is part of the city's wall. When he sticks his hand out to touch it, it goes right through. *Another illusion.* "This is how they've been getting in and out of the city without anyone noticing."

Some trial and error with our hands reveals a hole in the wall more than big enough for the carriage to pass through. The other side of the wall is heavily forested, and I'm sure the added coverage has been a help in keeping their movements a secret.

"So, what do we do now?" I ask, feeling like this is almost *too* good to be true. "I mean, we have more than enough proof, right?"

"We need to find Khazak and tell him everything." He grimaces slightly after saying the name of his best friend and boss. "Hopefully, the info will be enough for him to overlook the way we found it out."

God, I hope he's right.

"You did *what?!*" *Ragnar was wrong, so very, very wrong.* I jump up from my chair to close the door to Khazak's office, not wanting to risk an outburst being heard.

"Just hear us out, sir." Ragnar has his hands out, trying to placate the angry beast sitting across the desk from him. "I know it sounds bad, but now we have *actual* evidence that Murbank is tied to the attacks."

"That you gained by *illegally* breaking into and searching his home!" the orc captain growls. "How could you be so... Why would you steal his keys, David?!"

"I don't know!" I squirm, his attention now squarely on me. "I just panicked when I didn't think we were going to get any more info out of him and grabbed them."

"What was your plan to return them?" He asks point blank, knowing full well I didn't have one.

"Leave them someplace so he'd think he dropped them?" It's not *that* unbelievable.

"And if he realized they were missing before he ever left his office?" *Uhhhhhh…*

"'Man, I'm really bad about losing my keys'?" I shouldn't have risked the joke because it only makes him angrier. "Look, I'm sorry, but he's killed people! And he's going to do it again! We have to do whatever it takes to stop him."

"I understand the way you feel, but this is *not* the way to go about it." He's speaking in that 'I'm not mad—just disappointed' tone of voice. "What if you had been caught? What if he had come home while you were there?"

"Actually..." I *really* don't wanna tell him about this part.

"*What?*" I think a vein on his forehead just started throbbing.

"He came home while we were in the middle of our search," Ragnar answers for me. "But I don't think he saw either of us. Right?"

"...Right." Convincing no one, both sets of eyes stare at me. "Okay, there was a *second* where I thought he might have suspected I was in the room, but it was only a second! Then he left."

Khazak wipes his hands down his face while muttering a curse to himself.

"That's how I saw his tattoo!" Time to bring this back around to the good news. "The bird claw, the same one Thog had, he has it on the inside of his left wrist. All we need to do now is get everyone else to see it."

"And what better place to do that than at the very public event he's throwing in just a few hours?" Ragnar helps me to convince Khazak this is a good thing. "We could end this tonight, sir."

Khazak crosses his arms, staring down at his desk in thought. "I do not like this. It feels too easy. But...I am not sure we have many other options available to us. Meeting with the Grimrock family was completely useless. They only had good things to say about Councilman Murbank."

"So, we're gonna do it? What's the plan?" Forgive me for sounding a little excited.

"Well, you have already convincingly tripped into the man once today. I see no reason not to do it again," Khazak reasons. "You only need to pull back his sleeve this time. We will just make sure you do it in front of several sets of eyes, including mine. That should be more than enough to accuse if not arrest him for the other night's attacks."

"Sounds simple enough, but what do we do until then?" Ragnar asks next.

"Nothing. The event is in a few hours, and we will all need to go home and change. Will you be bringing Nylan?" Khazak shuffles some of the papers on his desk.

"Yeah, he likes these sorts of things and gets mad if I don't." Ragnar nods. That does seem like Ny.

"Then we will not be able to discuss our plans once we are at the event, so I want to make sure we are prepared before we leave."

"Understood, sir." Ragnar nods, standing. "I am going to go make a copy of those papers you wanted and then return them to the archives."

"See that you do. And Deputy, David?" Khazak looks at the both of us.

"Yes, sir?"

"Sir?"

"We are *not* finished discussing your actions today."

I spend the rest of the day feeling anxious, and I'm willing to bet Khazak and Ragnar do, too. I'm so nervous that someone else might notice me acting weird that I don't speak a word to anyone. I barely leave Khazak's office. When it's time for the charity gala, Ragnar gives us a simple goodbye and goes to get ready with Nylan while we head back to Khazak's place to change.

He pulls out some dressy looking clothes for himself, a black collared shirt with buttons up the front and a pair of brown slacks that hug him in all the right places. Not that he's in the mood for any flirting. He pulls out an outfit for me as well, not *as* nice, but it'll do. After a final, brief pep-talk about the plan, we leave the house and make our way back to the tribal hall for the second time today.

Once we arrive, the first thing I do is look for a decent enough place to drop the keys for someone to find. After that, Sir leads us directly to the ballroom—not that I'm sure they even have balls around here. It's a large open room, half-filled with people as well as tables covered in food lining the walls. There's even an ice sculpture. Ragnar and Nylan still haven't arrived, and I don't recognize anyone else, though they are obviously well-off given how nicely they're all dressed.

Our friends don't keep us waiting long, and while I make small talk with Ny, more people arrive, including the councilman himself. On his arm is a young orc woman, her long brown hair shining in the light of the room's torches. They are both dressed similarly, him in flowing purple robes and her in a purple dress. *Must be the wife.* I finish off the food I've been snacking on, eager to get things going.

Keeping Murbank in the corner of my eye, I follow him around the room as he and his wife mingle with the crowd, probably trying to raise support for himself as much as he is donations. He's just so slimy. I make eye-contact with Sir and Ragnar, ready to move into position.

Murbank is currently speaking to a small circle of people, his wife on his right. Khazak and Ragnar move to stand behind the group, Nylan watching me for a moment to wonder why I'm not with them. *Don't worry. I'm on my way.* I cross the room, Murbank and his group on my right. Just when it seems like I'm going to pass him, my leg gives out, and I stumble, tripping and reaching blindly to grab a hold of something—Murbank's sleeve.

I don't fall so hard that he'll be dragged down with me, just enough to pull back his sleeve. I look down in mock surprise to see what I'm grabbing and to come face to face with the tattoo on his arm...that isn't there. *What!?* I stare at the man's blank green wrist, dumbfounded, then lift my head to meet a smug look of satisfaction on his face. Several of the people around us have stopped speaking, and behind him, Khazak and Ragnar are both staring wide-eyed, seeing (or not seeing) the same thing I am.

"Captain, I do believe that is the *second* time your avakesh has tripped today," he says as he removes my hand from his robes. "Perhaps he is not feeling well. Maybe you should take him home."

"I... Yes, I think you may be right, Councilman. I apologize for his clumsiness." Khazak steps forward, caught off guard and doing his best to cover. "Come, David."

Slowly, the people around us resume their conversations, and we don't say another word before leaving. I barely have time to turn and see Nylan watching the two of us even *more* confused when Khazak's hand on my wrist yanks me down the hall and away from the crowd. He's completely silent until we're outside.

"David, I—"

"I don't know what happened. He figured out a way to hide it or something!" *It can't be that hard to cover a tattoo.*

"There is nothing—"

"No! This is bullshit. We're not going home yet, not without proof." Without thinking, I turn and start running south, back toward Murbank's home.

"David, wait!" Khazak shouts from behind me, but I don't stop, just turn to make sure he's still following me.

I keep running, completely out of breath by the time I reach the metal gates. The house is dark. All of them are, most of the residents of this neighborhood likely at the event tonight. *Good.* I open the gate, not waiting for Khazak to say anything, just leading him to the backyard.

"Look, he has the—" *What?! Where is it? Where is the carriage?* I rush over to the corner it was sitting in, finding it completely empty. There aren't even any wheel tracks to speak of. "The black carriage was right here. Really!" Khazak doesn't look convinced. "Okay, well what about this?"

I walk over to the back wall, to the section that is just an illusion, and stick my hand out. *Oww!* I pull my hand back after slamming it into the solid wood of the wall. What the fuck!? I bang against it. "No. *No.* There was a hole here, one big enough for the carriage to get through. He must have moved it or closed it back up or something! I don't know how he did this, but I swear, everything I told you was true. You *have* to believe—"

"I believe you, David." Khazak sighs, head hanging down. "It just does not matter. The councilman knew you were here today. He knows we are onto him, especially after what just happened at the fundraiser."

"We need to get inside. There's papers that could—"

"I just want to go home, David." Khazak holds a hand up to stop me. My mouth opens to argue, but nothing comes out because I know I'm grasping at straws. Murbank beat us, again. That's all I can think about as I exit his property for the final time that day. That and how much worse my punishment for today is probably going to be.

I'm fucked.

Chapter 16

The walk home is quiet, Khazak's form moving stiffly in front of me. He's walking fast though, enough for me to have to jog to keep up with him. He is *really* not happy right now. I think about running off, or maybe just walking slower to buy some time for him to cool off, but I don't think that'll do me any favors.

He opens the front door without a word, stomping inside without even holding it for me. I lock it behind me, and when I turn back, he's already walking toward the bedroom. He hasn't looked at me since Murbank's backyard.

"I'm sorry!" My shouted apology stops him before he goes down the hall. "I know I fucked up. I just thought I—"

"You were not thinking at all!" He finally turns to face me. "If you were, you would not have done something so *unbelievably stupid!* Why would you possibly... I *specifically* warned you that Ragnar would do something irrational like this, and you not only assisted him, you *provided the means to do it! Unprompted!* This is so..." He stops, squeezing his fists together and gritting his teeth before taking a breath. "I do not want to talk about this right now."

He turns and continues walking down the hallway, and I follow. He moves into the bedroom, and from the doorway, I watch as he undresses.

"Don't you... Aren't you going to punish me?" I'm not exactly *asking* for it but, well… being punished means being forgiven. But I guess that would be too easy. I just...really don't like that he's so angry with me.

"Not tonight." He shakes his head. "I am tired and still far too angry. We can talk about it in the morning."

"Oh, okay." I bite my lip, unsure if I should enter the room or not. I remember the last time he was really angry with me. "Should I... Do you want me to sleep in the other room?"

"Not unless that is what you would prefer." He offers me a small smile. I don't *think* he's lying.

"No, not if you don't." I finally step into the room and start to undress myself.

Getting ready for bed isn't any less awkward though, no real talking between us. We both just silently go through the motions before climbing onto the mattress. I'm surprised when I feel his arm wrap around me and pull me back into him, but maybe he just sleeps better with someone else. That's a thing, right?

I wake up from a dreamless sleep early the next morning, alone in bed. This is the first time I've woken up alone in over a month. It feels weird. I can't blame Khazak for not feeling much like cuddling once he was awake.

I'm not sure if we have to work today. If we were still on patrol in the woods, we'd be working through the weekend, but since we switched the rest of our shift, I don't know what that means. It's visiting day at the labor camp, so I hope I can at least do that. Assuming he'll let me go.

I know I should get up and go see what's going on. It just feels like I'm walking into a lion's den. After pulling on some pants (having a serious conversation in a thong is not how I wanna start the day), I carefully open the door and peer my head out. It's quiet, but when I walk farther down the hall,

I see a familiar green body sitting on the couch reading, a mug of coffee on the small table next to him.

"You are awake." He looks up from his book at my entrance. "How did you sleep?"

"Alright, I guess." I shuffle awkwardly on my feet. "What about you?"

"Fine, though when I woke up early, I was unable to return to sleep." Which is why he's up already. He pats the spot on the couch next to him. "Sit. We need to talk."

"I'm really sorry," I blurt out as I take my seat.

"I do not doubt it, but being sorry does little to fix the mess you and Ragnar have made." He sighs, putting down his book. "David, what you did yesterday was reckless. I would like to say I am surprised, but after the attempted jailbreak of your friends, I should have seen this coming. You made *another* impulsive decision without planning or forethought. You broke into Murbank's home without any idea of what you should be looking for, and regardless of the fact that you found something, it does not matter now because you were caught! All of that potential evidence is gone."

"I know! I know." I hang my head low. "I was worried after we talked to him that he was going to do that anyway, and I just couldn't stand the thought of him getting away with what he's been doing any longer."

"It may not matter now." He shakes his head unhappily. "Councilman Murbank is someone who can make things *very* difficult for us. Not even the investigation. I am now worried about my job. If we are right and he is somehow seeking to be reelected to the Tribal Council, I cannot imagine I will be captain for much longer."

"I know. I'm sorry." This is the *second* time I've put Khazak's career in jeopardy. "After learning about what happened with Ny's mom, and seeing how it was getting to him and Ragnar... I'm just so sorry."

"I am dreading returning to the station on Lunaday. Assuming a demand for my resignation is not sitting on my desk as we speak." He sounds dejected.

"What can I... Do you want to punish me now?" I just want to make him feel better.

"Yes, and no," he flip-flops. "You certainly deserve it, seeing as you had no problem disobeying me destroying all of the trust we spent the last month and a half building in a single night." His words make me wince. "However, punishing you will not resolve the situation. There is also the matter of…"

"What?" He's hesitating about something.

"Since we made our 'deal' for you to stay here, your infractions and my punishments have been more on the play side of things—"

"Except that time after I met your family," I helpfully point out.

"You provoked me into doing that," he responds flatly, crossing his arms. *He's right. I did.* "My point is, perhaps it would be better to—"

"What, you don't think I can take it?" I cut him off.

"It is not a contest, David," he answers with a sigh. "You are leaving in two weeks. I just think you would rather not spend those experiencing any more discomfort than necessary."

"That's not the deal we made." I puff out my chest. "I'm a man of my word, Sir. I know you said that it won't fix anything, but…would it help you feel any better?" I leave out that there's a good chance it will also make *me* feel a little better.

"It might be a start... Are you certain, pup?" He's really trying to give me an out here.

"I am, Sir." I nod.

He studies me for a moment. "Alright, then we can get started with the first part before you visit your friends this morning."

"*First* part?" There's going to be multiple?!

"Come with me, please." He stands, crooking two fingers at me as he walks down the hall. I follow him into the bedroom, seeing him rummage through one of his chests.

"Aha, found it!" He stands, holding something shiny and metallic in his hand. "Strip and lay on your back on the bed with your feet hanging over the edge."

On my back? I remove my pants and underwear before following the unexpected order.

"Now I take it you have never seen one of these before, correct?" He steps between my spread legs, holding out whatever is in his hand for me to get a closer look at.

"What is it?" It's definitely metal. It looks like a couple of rings attached to a cylinder. A cylinder that looks a *lot* like a dick, complete with a head.

"A chastity cage." So, it *is* shaped like a dick... Wait, *chastity cage*?!

"And what are you going to do with it?" I eye the contraption warily now that I know what it's for. I've heard of a chastity *belt* before, but mostly as a joke, like what dads say they'd put on their daughters. Which is pretty creepy when you think about it.

"I think you are smart enough to figure that out." With a smirk, I watch him turn a very small key at the top of the cage, allowing him to separate the shaft from the bottom ring. "Of course, you had to pick *yesterday* to pull your stunt."

"What was yesterday?" I don't remember there being anything special other than the fancy event.

"It is more about what *today* is." He sets the shaft of the cage to the side. "It is the 13th of Geminus. Happy birthday, David."

My eyes go wide. *It's my birthday?* I haven't exactly been keeping track of a calendar beyond the day of the week. I guess I knew it was going to happen while I was here. I just didn't think about it. I open my mouth to ask about getting some sort of birthday reprieve from this, but close it when I think about how that would defeat everything else I just said.

"Thank you," I tell him when I realize I haven't said anything for a minute.

"That is all?" He's teasing, but he still sounds surprised at my lack of fight.

"I'm ready for the first part of my punishment, Sir," I reply with a stoic nod.

"Very well." He smiles, and he kneels down, taking a hold of my balls in his left hand while he holds one of the metal rings in his right. "You are twenty-two today, correct?"

"Yes, Sir." This is a weird conversation to have while I'm getting my junk locked in a cage. I inhale sharply when the cold metal touches my skin.

"I had something special planned for you tonight." He slips the ring around both of my balls first.

"You did?" I try and fail to not sound disappointed.

"Do not worry. It is still happening. You will just be in chastity for the duration." He pushes my shaft down, squeezing it through the ring as well. "I see no reason to punish anyone else for your infraction. Except perhaps Ragnar."

He grumbles that last bit, and I am left wondering if their friendship is in danger. Then I get distracted by the feeling of cold metal encasing my dick as the rest of the cage is slipped on. Any growing I was doing because of the handling is gone, which is a good thing because next Khazak connects the shaft to the base ring before pulling out the small key again and locking them together.

"This feels weird." *That's an understatement.* I lean up on my elbows and look down at my encased crotch.

"You will get used to it." He holds out a hand to help me stand. "Or you will not. Either way, it is not coming off until I feel you have earned it."

I spend breakfast squirming in my seat as I try to get used to the cage. It's weird having a solid chunk of metal between my legs. I don't think I realized how squishy my dick was. Khazak is silent while we eat, but his smirk says enough. By the time we're finished, I think I've *mostly* gotten used to it, just in time for my visit to the labor camp.

Khazak lets me go alone this time, saying he needs to prepare for later. I'm not sure if he means for my birthday or the punishment, but I try not to think about it. I'm patted down by the guards once I'm there and brought to an empty table to wait for Adam and Nate. They weren't expecting me this week, so it's the first time they're not here waiting for me.

"It's so good to see you." I hug Adam a little longer than usual.

"It's good to see you, too." Adam takes his seat next to Nate, who is decidedly un-hugged. "Happy birthday."

"Wow, thanks." The mention of my birthday throws me off. "I'm surprised you guys remembered. I didn't."

"There's not a whole thing to do in here besides staring at the calendar." He leans forward, his volume dropping almost to a whisper. "I'm glad you're alright. After the attacks we were all a little worried something might have happened to you. Was this all related to those robberies you were looking into?"

I try to hold in any look of surprise, my eyes darting to the guards watching over the room. I forgot I mentioned that to Liss and Corrine, and of course they would have told

Adam and Nate. And thanks to what I did yesterday, they might have a huge target on their backs now.

"Yes, but don't talk about it. Not to anyone," I whisper after leaning forward myself. "It's not safe."

Adam's eyes go wide as he leans back in his seat, but he says nothing. I'm not sure Nate is even paying attention right now. He's just looking down and fidgeting in his seat a lot.

"I'm okay. I was out in the woods during most of the explosions." I go back to speaking at a normal volume, leaving out the part about the burning building. "Has everything been alright here?"

"Things have been locked down pretty heavily the last few days. Haven't even worked." Adam shrugs. "Was kind of surprised they didn't cancel visiting hours. I guess things are starting to go back to normal."

"What about you?" I nod over at Nate. "You alright?"

"Fine." He rubs at his wrist, not quite making eye contact. "Just want to get out of here."

"Sure..." He seems really anxious or something. "Not much longer. I was actually wondering... You guys are getting paid in here, right?"

"Yeah. Not a lot, but Nate and I ran some numbers." He gives the wizard a little nudge with his shoulder. "Even after they take out what we owe in fines, what we have left over is enough for at least a month's worth of supplies. A month and a half if we stretch it. What about you? Have you been making any money?"

"Yeah." I nod with a smile. "Let's just say we can go a lot longer than a month. I actually started getting some things together. Is there anything that I should start checking shops for?"

My questions brighten Adam's smile in an instant, eager to start talking about strategy.

"Do you think my friends are safe?" The question is out of my mouth as soon as I close the front door.

Khazak is taken aback at my sudden question from his spot on the couch. "What exactly do you mean?"

"After what happened yesterday, if Murbank knows that it was me who broke into his house—"

"Which he most certainly does."

I give a half-hearted glare before finishing my sentence. "—then do you think he might do something to them to get back at me?"

He pauses for a moment to think. "I do not *think* so. They are not exactly a threat to his plans, as far as we know." He pauses, taking a breath, and sighs. "Not that we definitively know what his plans are. I am sorry, David. I wish there was more I could do."

"I just want to protect them." I lean back against the door. "This is all my fault."

"I know things seem bleak, but we will figure this out." Khazak stands and walks over to me, rubbing his hands on my shoulders. "There is nothing we can do about it right now, so best to try and just enjoy your birthday. We have all of tomorrow to discuss our next steps. Sound good?"

"Sounds good, Sir." I nod my head, cracking a small grin.

"Good boy. Now, are you ready for the next part of your punishment?" He cracks a bigger grin.

I groan in response. I also notice that he said "next" and not "last." I hope there's not more. Without waiting for more of an answer, the orc marches me back to the bedroom.

"Strip down to your underwear and bend over the edge of the bed." I'm pushed forward gently when the order is given.

I work quickly, pulling off my shirt before it's fully unbuttoned and kicking off my pants. I want to get this done. A throat clears as I bend over the bed, and I look back to see a thoroughly unimpressed Khazak looking between me and my discarded clothing. With a mumbled "sorry," I pick up and fold my clothes a little more neatly before moving back into position.

"Arms above your head, and I expect them to stay there." A hand touches the small of my back. "Do you need me to get a pair of restraints?"

"No. I can handle it, Sir." He's not mocking me. This is just gonna hurt.

I hold my breath, waiting for the first strike. I wait. And wait. And wa— "*OWW FUCK!*"

I hear a snort of laughter at my outburst. It's not even that it was that hard. It just *really* caught me by surprise. The next strike follows soon after that, then the third, then the fourth... I'm pretty sure he's using a strap, which feels both juvenile and impersonal. I'm not saying I like getting spanked, but I hate it less when he uses his own hands.

"I cannot decide if your actions yesterday were more or less reckless than the attempted jailbreak." *And here comes the lecture.* "On the one hand, the legal consequences would likely be less severe; on the other, *he is a dangerous man we suspect to be responsible for bombing the city.*" He punctuates his sentence with a particularly hard smack.

The strikes start coming faster, but thankfully not any harder. Not that he's being gentle. As the pain and heat in my ass builds, I start to hear myself whimper. My hands are both tight fists, clutching the sheet of the bed to fight the urge to reach behind me, which only gets stronger.

"I am not entirely sure why I am even bothering to punish you, honestly." He doesn't pause the strapping though. "What exactly is the point of agreeing to submit to me if you have no intention of obeying? Especially when it comes to something *so* important."

I don't know, I want to tell him, but even if I could form words right now, he wouldn't want to hear them. I can feel tears starting to well up, and I bury my face into the bed as if that's going to help me hide the effects afterward.

"Do you remember when the wolves attacked, the way you felt when I tried to order you to leave me?" he asks, not pausing long enough for an answer. "Imagine what it would have felt like to learn about it after the fact. To not find out until later how much danger I was in. Now imagine that on top of that, my actions resulted in me putting myself and *everyone I know* in even *more* danger. Because that is exactly what you did!"

"I'm sorry!" I cry out, the grip of my hands on the sheet turning my knuckles white.

"We are supposed to be a team, David! Not just at work, but *always*." He concentrates a few of his strikes toward the bottom of my ass. *Sitting down is gonna suck.* "You do not get to decide to only listen to me when it is convenient! I cannot protect you if I do not know what you are doing!"

"'m sorry!" I yell again into the mattress, not even sure if he can hear me.

The lecture ends, but the strapping continues. After a while, the pain and guilt and tears all start to bleed together, and the next thing I know, there is a dip in the mattress as Sir climbs on next to me, pulling me over to lay face-down across his chest, preventing my poor red ass from touching anything. A gentle hand strokes from my shoulders to my lower back, soft words being whispered into my ears as I come back to my body. A body which is very sore.

"Feeling alright?" The chest I'm lying on rumbles, and I turn my head to meet a pair of brown eyes.

"Other than the obvious," I croak, wiggling my butt in the air.

"Back to your old self already. Good." He smiles warmly, leaning his head forward for a quick kiss. "Then you are ready for the final part of your punishment. Up and bend over with your hands on the bed."

I groan but climb off the orc, hissing when I fail to resist the urge to rub a hand on my ass. Khazak stands, pulling a plug out of the same chest he returns the strap to. He quickly lubes it up and presses it into me, making sure to stop and knead my sore cheeks a little to make me whimper again. Then he leads me out to the living room, where he stands me in a corner that was previously occupied by a pile of pillows.

"Inspection." I don't register the order right away because I'm still trying to figure out why I'm staring at two walls, but slowly I move my hands to clasp the back of my head, legs spreading into position.

Then I hear Khazak sit down on the couch. And do nothing else.

"Are you serious?" I turn to look at the orc like he's out of his mind. He's putting me in *timeout* while he reads a damn book?!

"Do I strike you as someone who jokes around?" He can deny it all he wants, but I *know* I'm rubbing off on him.

"I'm not a kid!" Who tries to make a grown man stand in a corner?!

"Yet your behavior continues to be that of one." He puts the book down and stands. "I am completely serious, David. You are going to stand in the corner with your pretty red ass on display until I am satisfied. Now if you need one, I am happy to get you a gag, but short of an emergency, I do not expect to not hear another word out of you until I say otherwise. Am I understood?"

I open and close my mouth, instead nodding my assent, and I try not to roll my eyes as I turn back to the corner. I move my hands back to my head, and I hear Sir walk back to the couch. Then...nothing. It's silent, other than the occasional sound of a page being turned. Just me and the corner.

At first, I try to use my corner time to think of a new plan to expose Councilman Murbank, but eventually my mind drifts, first to my friends, then to traveling, then to food, and eventually, nothing at all. I'm not sure how long I stand there, but it has to have been at least a couple of hours when Sir's hand on my back gets my attention, just in time for lunch.

I yelp when my butt makes contact with a chair in the kitchen, having forgotten about the strapping *and* plug for a brief moment. Lunch is small, just some grilled salmon on bread, I suspect because of whatever is planned for later. When we're finished eating, he removes the plug but keeps the cage on. I still don't know what's happening, and even though I'm allowed to talk now, I don't bother asking since I know he won't tell me. The rest of the afternoon is quiet, which only makes me feel antsier the more I anticipate what's coming.

There's a knock on the door in the late afternoon, and Khazak opens it to reveal Ragnar and Nylan. Ragnar has a case of what looks like bottles of beer, and Nylan is holding some kind of pie. I can see Ragnar and Khazak sharing an awkward moment, but Ny doesn't seem to notice.

"Happy birthday, David!" He gives me a one-armed hug as he steps inside. "Are we the first ones here?"

"Yes, you are." Khazak shuts the door behind the two of them. "The others should be on their way."

"Then we should drink these now because I did *not* bring enough for everyone." Ragnar comments, making a beeline for the kitchen.

"I know his father probably made something a million times better, but this pie was my mom's recipe, so I hope you like it." Nylan shows me the circular dessert, a golden crust surrounding a sea of bright red fruit.

"Your family's coming?" I turn to ask Khazak.

"That wasn't a surprise, was it, sir?" Nylan bites his lip.

"No, it is alright, Nylan." Khazak shakes his head with a chuckle, helping Ragnar find a bottle opener.

It's his family who shows up next, arms full of even more food and drink. Everyone except his two youngest siblings, who I'm sure had something much better to do. Nylan was right. Rurig did make something: a big two-layer cake that I later learn is a combination of chocolate and coffee. As soon as he's inside, Orlun sticks a hat on me, round and made of leather with a pair of wooden antlers sticking out of either side.

"That makes you 'King of the Hunt,'" he tells me as I adjust it on my head.

"Thank you!" I *think* I have it on straight. "Uh, what am I supposed to do now?"

"What? Nothing. You just wear it." The older orc shrugs.

A few more guests show up after them, first Brull, who very loudly announces his arrival, then some people I know from work: Arik, Orim, Glasha, and Nikka. I'm happy to see all of them, and not just because they all bring me gifts either! Most of it is stuff for traveling, like a new bedroll and knapsack from Khazak's family, or socks from Orim (they're a lot more important than you'd think). Nylan brings me not just the books I asked for, but a few extras he thought I'd like. However, my favorite gift by far comes from Glasha and Nikka: smoke bombs! I've seen Glasha testing them out while training; they're apparently an invention of Nikka's. You flick off a small clay cap and toss it to the ground, and a thick cloud of white smoke fills the area: Perfect for confusing your enemies and escaping.

After the gifts, the drinks start flowing in earnest, and the party really gets started. By which I mean people start to chow down. Rurig went all out, making a lot of fried things, stuff you can eat with your hands. There are some fried venison dumplings, those chicken nuggets I had at the festival, and these tiny little steak sandwiches. Everything is amazing. Have I mentioned how much I'm going to miss the food here? I'm stuffed by the time we're cutting the cake, but I make sure to leave room for a slice of Ny's mom's pie.

"Thish ish really good," I say with a half-full mouth to the elf standing next to me. The filling tastes familiar, like what they stuff in the dar-buk buns. *What did Khazak call that fruit? Some kind of berry? Starts with an S.*

"I'm glad you think so." He grins. "My mom would have liked you, I think."

"I wish I could have met her." If she raised someone like Nylan, she had to be pretty great.

"I remember your mother as a very kind and warm woman." Khazak comes up behind me, cutting his own piece of pie as he talks. "I am sorry I did not get to know her for very long."

"Thank you, sir." Nylan offers us a smile that's only sad for a second. "Since I have you here, can I ask for a favor?"

"What is it, Nylan?" Khazak asks before taking a bite.

"Tomorrow is actually me and my Sir's anniversary." He scans the room for Ragnar, who is over on the couch saying something to Brull. Possibly arguing.

"Congratulations. How long have you guys been together now?" I ask next.

"Eight years." The surprise on my face must show because he follows it up with a "Right?"

"Has it really been that long?" Khazak muses. "I still remember how anxious he was before your first date. As if you had not been our friend for over a decade at that point."

"He was so nervous he almost threw up twice during dinner," Nylan tells me quickly, holding up two fingers.

"What is the favor you wanted to ask?" Khazak redirects things with a chuckle.

"Well, tomorrow is *also* the first night of his patrol week in the forest." He grimaces a little. "Normally, I spend the first night out there with him. Since it's our anniversary, he tried to swap with someone for a different week, but with everything going on, that's not really possible. He's also been so stressed out, even though he's doing everything he can not to let me see it. So, I kind of had a little bit of a late-night picnic planned for the two of us and wanted to know if you would maybe be willing to cover for him tomorrow night, sir? Just for a few hours?"

"We would be happy to, Nylan." Khazak doesn't even hesitate before he answers. "What time should we be there?"

"I was thinking seven? Right around sunset and when we should be getting back from patrol." He sounds really excited, dropping his voice to an unnecessary whisper. "I'm going to take him to Shad'rok Springs."

"Sounds like a great night, Ny." I bump him on his shoulder.

"I am sure he will love that," Khazak agrees.

"Thank you both." Nylan hugs the two of us. "Alright, I was supposed to make him a drink like ten minutes ago so..." He makes a quick grimace that's really more of a grin before moving over to the alcohol.

"That was really nice of you, seeing as you're still mad at Ragnar." The pain in my ass and metal around my dick are reminders of his feelings toward me.

"I would not want to punish Nylan for something his owner did." Khazak takes another bite of pie. "And if I were *that* angry with him, I would not have invited him for tonight's festivities."

I think he's just talking about the party in general, but as the night goes on and guests start to leave, I start to get the feeling that he's got something else planned. Nikka and Glasha are gone, as are Khazak's parents. His siblings Yogik and Ayla are being walked out right now, with Ayla tossing a "you boys have fun" over her shoulder before the door shuts. *What does that mean?*

"Great, now the *real* party can get started," Brull declares before standing and pulling off his shirt.

"Right to the point as always," Khazak says with a chuckle, locking the door and turning to me. "Strip."

I freeze, completely in the dark. Okay, not *completely.* There's only a certain number of reasons Sir would be telling me to strip, and everyone still in this room is someone I've either had sex with or who has seen or heard me having sex—Nylan, Ragnar, Brull, Orim, and Arik—but it's still jarring.

"Are you alright?" I can hear the actual concern in Khazak's question.

"Yes. Sorry, Sir." I shake the spacey feeling from my head and start unbuttoning my shirt. By the time I'm down to just my jockstrap, I can feel everyone's eyes on me.

With a whistle, Brull smacks my ass, making me yelp. "Damn boy, what did you do to earn that?"

I don't answer and neither does Khazak when he steps toward me, turning me around and leading me down the hallway. Instead of going to the bedroom, he opens the door to the side room, and though it's dark, I can see the shape of *something* in one of the corners. After he lights the lanterns in the room, I get a full look at the contraption made of leather, wood, and metal.

There are four tall wooden beams attached at the tops and bottoms by smaller beams that run to the center and cross-cross, forming an X. Hanging from the top of each beam is a chain, which in turn connect to a sort of flat piece of leather that comes up a few inches above my waist. It almost looks like a swing, but not one you could sit on very well.

"What is it?" I ask the obvious question.

"It is called a 'sling.'" He starts walking me to it. "As for what it does, you are about to find out."

"How did you get it in here?" He turns me around so that the leather part is against my back. "This wasn't here before, right?"

"Brull brought it over this morning while you were visiting your friends." He steps closer, bending slightly and putting his hands under my ass. "Grab the chains and lift."

I pull myself up as asked, and Khazak settles me on the leather panel, pushing on my chest gently to lay me out flat. He lifts both my legs, guiding each of my feet through a set of cuffs attached to the chains in front. They're not really restraints, just a place to hold my feet up, which leaves me *very* exposed. I crane my head up to look at my upturned ass.

"I think you are starting to understand its purpose," he tells me with a smirk, and I notice Nylan, Brull, and Orim entering the room behind him, all naked or close to. "Happy birthday, David."

Khazak places the cleansing charm on my belly before he steps back, and Nylan steps forward, dick in hand. In fact, everyone is stroking themselves, Sir included, all looking at my ass. When the plans for the evening finally click in my head, a thrill that's half-nervous and half-excited runs through me. So *that's* what's going on? I've been fucked by more than one person in a night, but six? Can I handle that? I look over to Khazak, who is looking back at me, his eyes hooded over in lust. Guess I am going to find out.

Nylan looks excited as he steps up, though he frowns once he actually reaches me. I realize why when I feel his stomach brushing against my ass. With a grumble, he turns over his shoulder. "Alright, give me the damn box."

With a laugh, Brull bends over and places a small wooden box on the floor, sliding it over to Nylan. The elf moves it into place in front of me before stepping up, grinning when he sees that his crotch is now at target level. Being the only non-orc in the room not on his back, he needs the height boost.

"I've owed you this since the festival," he tells me as he teases me with the head of his dick, already slick with oil.

"You just gonna talk about it shortstack, or—*FUCK*." Ny cuts off my taunt by slamming his dick home.

He's not huge, certainly not as big as one of the orcs, but it's not *nothing*. Thankfully, he doesn't start hammering away, giving me the chance to get used to it, though the look in his eyes is daring me to egg him on again. After a minute, he pulls back and starts to fuck into me slowly. The chains holding up the sling rattle as they move, more so once he picks up speed. His hips hit the backs of my thighs over and over, giving me a quick jolt of pain each time he slaps against my spanked ass. Despite that (*or maybe because of it, shut up*), it feels good. He's hitting my prostate almost dead on at times, and I can feel my dick trying to get hard in the cage. Very different from what I'm used to.

Just as I feel the familiar starts of an orgasm, there's a stutter in Ny's strokes. I look up and see his eyes are closed, and a minute later, he's slamming himself all the way inside of me, moaning low through gritted teeth as I feel him unload. He wraps one of his arms around my leg to steady himself as he rides out his cumshot, sighing happily against my calf when he's finished.

"Happy birthday." The disappointment must show on my face because with a laugh, he says, "Don't worry. I'll be back." With a kiss to my leg, he pulls out, stepping off the box.

"Thanks for opening him up, boy." Brull steps up next, sliding the box away with his foot as he moves between my legs. Not quite satisfied with my position, he grabs my thighs and pulls me forward. "Better."

I can feel the blunt head of his dick prodding between my cheeks, and he reaches down to guide himself as he pushes forward to enter me. I whimper as I'm stretched, much more than Nylan. I can feel the elf's load being forced even deeper inside of me. I'm squirming by the time Brull is fully seated, his generous belly laying over my crotch.

Once he's ready, rather than pull back, he grabs the chains in front, pushing them away and lifting me off of his dick. Once I'm about halfway off (I think), he lets go, and I swing back, his cock sliding right into place. I moan as I'm refilled, and he repeats the action over and over.

"Now hold on. What's that?" Brull reaches down and squeezes the pouch of my jock and the cage within. With a grin, he pulls the fabric to the side, exposing me. "Forget the spanking. What do you do to earn *this*?" He squeezes my balls for emphasis.

Dammit, must have felt it hitting his stomach. I try to think of a reasonable excuse, but the dick currently rearranging my guts is proving to be a difficult distraction, so I just end up staring at him with my mouth half-open.

"Don't worry about it. I'll ask Khazak." He waves off the question, never once slowing down as he pulls me on and off his cock.

Happy for the chance to stop thinking, I let my head fall back against the padded leather as my body is used. Brull's thick length steadily fills me, building up a familiar pressure in my groin that Nylan only got me close to. After a few more minutes of pounding, I finally hit that peak, my ass pulsing all over Brull's cock, something he seems to enjoy a whole lot, judging by the way his dick gets even harder. He spends the new few minutes fucking me through another one before he carefully pulls out.

"Don't wanna cum yet. Unlike certain people, some of us require more than fifteen minutes before we're ready to go again." He eyes Nylan, who's been standing at the back of the room watching since his turn. With a gentle slap to my thigh, Brull exits the room, only to be replaced by Khazak, who I didn't realize had stepped out.

It's Orim who approaches the sling next, though. He's wearing a shy smile, which in turn has *me* feeling a little shy. That's a real talent, being able to look shy and innocent while stroking your dick, especially with someone you've already been inside of. After stepping between them, he rubs both hands lightly up and down my thighs.

I can feel him prodding against my ass, not quite hitting the target. Taking matters into my own hands (*heh*), I reach down to help aim as he presses his hips forward. His head slowly breaches me, and I give a low groan as he pushes the rest inside. I forgot just how thick he is. With a moan of his own, he bottoms out, holding me tightly by my thighs.

Orim fucks much more carefully than Brull or Nylan, the chains holding me up swaying gently in time with his thrusts. I am not sure if this is just his style, or if he's doing it because my bruised butt is on display, and he doesn't want to hurt me, but I don't mind. I have a feeling the night is only getting started, so I'll take my breaks where I can get them.

What's the old saying? Slow and steady...something something. I know it's not "makes David cum," but that's what it's doing right now. Orim slides his hands down my legs to my stomach, then up to my chest, teasing my nipples. I bite my lip when I start getting close, toes curling in the cuffs above my head. I let myself moan out at a normal volume when I cum, pressure releasing once again.

Orim's hands on my chest have me remembering how much he likes that himself, so once I stop squirming, I reach up to do some teasing of my own. I lightly pinch my top's nipples, making him gasp and thrust forward. *Well, shit...* I continue to pinch and squeeze at Orim's chest, driving the orc to fuck me harder. Before long, I have him growling as he slams the full length of his dick in and out of my hole, and with a final grunt, he buries himself, adding his load to Ny's, assuming he and Brull didn't already fuck it out of me.

My hole feels so open right now. Sloppy, even. I can see Khazak eyeing it as he walks toward me, a cup in his hand. He can't help but reach out his free hand to rub at it, making me tighten involuntarily and whimper.

"How are you feeling?" he asks, helping me to drink some of the water he's brought over.

"Great, Sir. Just horny." I reach down and squeeze the stupid cage. I'll say this about prostate orgasms: for as awesome as it is to be able to go over and over and over, you never actually get any less turned on, which normally isn't a bad thing, but with this damn cage on...

"You will thank me for that later. The party is only getting started, and you still have to contend with myself, Arik, and Ragnar, who will be bringing up the rear, so to speak." He smirks at his dumb joke. "Then it is time for round two."

"There are multiple rounds?" *Of course, there are multiple rounds.*

"Do you remember the word I told you to use when you wanted to stop what we were doing on stage during the festival?" He makes sure I finish the water before he lets me answer.

"Uh-huh. Jailbreak." Okay, *maybe* I'm starting to feel a little floaty, too.

"Good boy. If at any point tonight gets to be too much, or you need a break, you use that word, alright?" He hands the empty glass to Nylan, who apparently still hasn't left the room. The others have sort of been coming and going as they watch and wait for their turn.

"Yes, Sir." I nod my head.

"I would have been here sooner, but I wanted to be a good host," he lies with a grin as he rubs the head of his cock against my ass. "I'll have my turn before Arik, at least." Wait, why does he want to make sure he goes before Arik?

I don't get the chance to ask because Sir slams himself home in one long thrust. It almost knocks the wind out of me, forcing some half-yell, half-moan from my lips. With the way everyone is just making themselves at home in my ass, I'm glad I wore that plug so much earlier. Once he's firmly planted inside, he only waits a few seconds before pulling back and repeating the process. He's taking a page out of Bull's book, using the chains to control my movements as much as his own legs.

Of course, the man who's fucked me the most the past few months is able to get me close right away. This is what, number five? And there's gods know how many more coming? With the way Khazak is stroking almost his entire cock in and out of me, it only takes a few more before my leg starts to twitch as I cum dry once again.

Not stopping for a second, Sir pounds away, my hole unable to resist even if it wants to. When my eyes aren't rolling back in my head, I watch his face, his eyes locked down on the place where his dick and my ass meet. It's clear that he's chasing his own orgasm, and the fact that I've had one is purely incidental...which somehow makes everything even hotter and sends me over the edge again. *Fuck.*

I can't really focus much after that because Sir starts fucking faster and faster. I do hear (and feel) him cum with a muted shout a minute later, body shuddering as he adds his cum to the mixture already inside of me. I groan weakly when he stands and slowly extracts himself, bending over to give me a long, languid kiss before pulling away completely.

Things are back in focus when Arik approaches me next. In the dim light, I can make out the twin gold rings piercing his nipples, as well as the numerous dark tattoos covering his chest and stomach. At first, I think he's wearing a jock-strap himself, but then I see the straps aren't fabric, more like a harness for his waist. There's also the matter of the giant fake cock hanging off the end of it. It's dark brown, and detailed, a solid piece of polished wood standing out straight from his crotch.

I look up to ask him what that's about when I notice a pair of scars on his chest, just below his nipples. That makes something in my head click. I *think* I know what's going on, but I'm not sure and don't really know how you ask about that, and it feels like there's a *lot* of potential to come off as rude, and I *holyfuckthatthingishuge.*

"Captain, you owe me a gral!" Arik calls over his shoulder. "He took it no problem."

That may be up for debate, as the more "it" is pushed inside of me, the more I feel like I'm being stretched to my limit. Arik seems to sense this, slowing down while I take a few deep breaths. Patience pays off because a few more deep breaths, and he's all the way in, or at least as deep as my body is gonna allow right now.

"You know what my favorite part of using this is?" Arik nods down toward his "tool." "Unlike the others, I do not get tired after I cum."

My wide eyes stare into his evil ones as he slides back before punching back in fast. I more scream than moan, no longer able to keep my voice down. Grabbing hold of the frame on either side of him, Arik anchors himself as he fucks into me, making me twitch and squirm with every stroke. The more he fucks and massages that wonderful little spot inside of me, the louder and more high-pitched my voice gets.

I cum *five times* in the next fifteen minutes. I think. I know I came that many times. I'm just not sure how long it's been, or what time it is, or that my name is Daniel. Donny? Derrick. Whatever. I'm not sure exactly how Arik's cock works, but he certainly seems to be enjoying himself as much as I have. He came at least twice, or at least put on a very convincing act. It's only after his third that he finally pulls out, wiping the sweat from his brow with one hand.

"He is all yours, Rockfang," Arik tells Ragnar with a smirk and a smack on the ass as he exits. I'm so out of it I didn't even notice him coming into the room.

Rolling his eyes, Ragnar approaches me, as naked as everyone else in his position has been. He is ready to go.

"The captain is lucky I do not mind sloppy seconds. Or sixths," he tells me cockily as he teases my very-open hole with the head of his dick. Though I suspect we both know the *real* reason Khazak relegated him to the last slot. I think about my sore, red ass, which has only been made worse by all of the thighs slapping against it. *This better not be his only punishment.*

I'm not even able to respond, just groan weakly as I'm entered once again. Ragnar doesn't take his time, eager to catch up to the rest of the party goers...who are starting to come back into this room and watch, a few already back to full hardness. *Oh gods, this is my last birthday. This is how I die.*

I'm conscious when Ragnar finally breeds me, but I couldn't tell you how we got there. I know I came, and I can feel his cum leaking out of me, along with everyone else's. But before I can do anything about that, Nylan is pulling his booster-box back into place. He only pauses when Sir tells him to wait, making sure I drink more water before throwing me back to the wolves.

After Nylan cums in me for the second time, everyone else fucks me again as well, though I don't remember the order. At some point, I'm taken out of the sling and moved to the bed, so that the men have access to my mouth as well. The one thing I do remember is Nylan cumming in me two more times before the other tops began to get a little restless, and him a little dick hungry, and he's pulled onto the bed alongside me.

Things get really blurry after that. I know later we moved from the bed to the couch, Ny and I both bent over it side by side, two men behind us and two in front. After a while, there's no keeping track of who's doing what or even what room we're in. It's just a big hot sweaty sex blur.

By the time everyone leaves, it's late, midnight having long since passed. I have a vague recollection of people saying good night, and Khazak closing the door, but it's not until he picks me up to carry me to the bathroom that I start getting lucid. It's a little awkward. Even with our size difference, it's still one grown man carrying another, but he pulls it off, just like he does everything else. *Why did you have to go and screw things up with him again?*

Setting me down on the sink counter, he bends over the tub to turn on the water. Then, while he waits for it to fill up, he stands in front of me, reaching down to unlock the cage and free me. My dick gives a half-hearted attempt to get hard but gives up pretty quickly. I'm too exhausted and fucked out.

Once the large tub is filled with lightly steaming water, Khazak moves me from the sink and helps me to gently sit down in the tub. I hiss when my ass comes into contact with the water, then again when he climbs in behind me and moves me to his lap. The water comes up to around my navel, high enough to cover all of my especially sore bits. Leaning back, Khazak pulls me to lay back against him.

Strong hands work their way down my upper thighs, massaging and stretching the sore muscles. He gently dips between them, and as they move closer to my ass, the touches become lighter, my owner taking my abused flesh into account. Gentle fingers sweep along my crack, and I instinctually spread my legs to give him better access.

"Any pain?" The question is mumbled into my hair as the fingers gently clean away the stickiness it finds on my skin.

"'s sore," I mumble back. "That's all."

"You were wonderful tonight, puppy." The finger leaves me briefly as I watch Khazak slip a bar of soap into his hand. "I am proud to have been able to share you like that with our friends."

I smile, my body feeling warmer as it flushes at the praise. I don't have any more words, content to let Khazak bathe me, using the soap to gently scrub the cum and oil from my body. It stings at times, my muscles beyond sore, but he's as gentle as he can be. Afterward, when he's drying me off with a big fluffy towel, I pull him closer, kissing him gently on the chest before laying my head against it, listening to the beat of his heart.

Then he reattaches the cage before bed, and I'm back to grumbling.

Chapter 17

"When Nylan told my father about his plan, he offered to make the two of them something special." Khazak nudges the basket I'm carrying their food in. "I think he assumed it would be a dessert, not the entire meal."

"Your dad doesn't seem like the type to do anything halfway," I respond.

It's the day after my birthday party, and Khazak and I are walking to the east patrol camp to surprise Ragnar for his and Nylan's anniversary. I've got their picnic, and Khazak is carrying Ragnar's camping supplies on his back. Nylan dropped them off early this morning, sneaking out before his owner woke up, and Rurig brought by the basket of food not long after that. It's early in the evening now, and the sun is just about to start setting, tinting blue sky orange.

It's been a pretty good day, other than waking up with that damn cage on. Do you have any idea what it's like to wake up to the feeling of your dick being squeezed as it tries to grow inside a too-small piece of metal? Not great. Either because or in spite of my whining, he took it off not long after lunch, though the threat of its return still hangs in the air.

Khazak and I spent most of the day coming up with ideas for what we can do to expose Councilman Murbank.

We figure that after he "caught" me in his house, he hid his tattoo, and probably not with makeup. That, plus the repaired hole in the fence that was an illusion makes us figure he has to be using magic to cover his tracks, something that comes up over and over when he's involved. He must have a pretty powerful spellcaster working with him, and sometimes the only thing that can beat magic is stronger magic. The problem is, between the two of us, we don't know many magic users. Khazak asks about Nate, but I'm not confident he's capable enough to help us.

Khazak's ideas are more in line with work. He wants to gather together all the evidence we have—the reports and paperwork, his relationship to Thog and his debt—and present it to Chief Grandtooth to request a formal investigation into Murbank's dealings. The hope is that an investigation would uncover *more* of what he's been up to and force it out in the open.

When I ask what happens if the people working the investigation, or worse, Grandtooth himself, are *already* working with the councilman, I'm met with a sour face and some grumbling about thinking some more. I actually start to consider writing to Mike to see if he can somehow help when I remember that we're headed to the patrol camp tonight—camps that each have a resident mage.

Khazak was hesitant but agreed that it could work. It would just be a matter of figuring out which, if any of them, can be trusted. He thinks that Druid Darkwolf and Shaman Bonespirit are probably safe, but he's unsure of the others, who I haven't even met. Nylan told us last night we'd be going to the east camp, where Bonespirit is stationed, so he seems like our best bet. Now we just need to find a moment to talk to him alone.

"How are you feeling after last night?" I turn my head to see Khazak looking over me.

"Still a little sore, but good." He's asked me that twice already.

"I was worried after I noticed you walking funny this morning," he adds, a sly look on his face.

"And whose fault was that?" It was only for a couple of hours.

He opens his mouth to retort but then lifts his hand and points. Headed toward us, as if he appeared out of nowhere, is Ragnar with Nylan right behind him. I'm glad he looks surprised, because I forgot he'd be able to see us before we saw them, hidden behind the camp's magical camouflage. Magic makes things so confusing sometimes.

"Sir? Is everything alright?" He looks worried to see us. "Did something happen?"

"Good to see you too," I tease.

"I am relieving you of your duties for the rest of the evening, Deputy." Khazak hands over the camping supplies to his friend. "Happy anniversary. Enjoy yourselves."

He looks surprised, but it doesn't take much to get Ragnar on board. "Thank you, sir."

"How much food did your dad make?!" Nylan takes the basket from me, shocked at its weight. "I packed sandwiches and stuff."

"I'll eat them later in the week." Ragnar takes Ny's hand with a smile and leads him away from camp.

"Have fun! Happy anniversary!" I call out as they walk away hand in hand.

Khazak and I resume walking, the camp coming into view once we cross the threshold. It's quiet, seemingly empty except for a few officers. Maybe I'm just imagining things, but a couple of them look more surprised to see us than Ragnar did. The shaman's tent flap is closed, and since none of the other rangers are back yet, this might be our best chance to talk to him until later. As I'm looking at it, the tent opens, and the grey-haired orc steps out.

"Captain? What are you two doing here?" the shaman asks as he approaches.

"Giving Deputy Rockfang the night off for his anniversary." Khazak steps a little closer and lowers his voice slightly. "There is actually something I need to discuss with you in private."

"Of course. Step into my tent." Wu'dag leads Khazak back.

"David, please put our things in the tent while I speak with the shaman," he orders before following the older orc.

Aww. I kinda wanted to talk to him too, but this is less suspicious. Inside the tent, I roll up Ragnar's bedroll and move his stuff to the side while I lay out ours for the night. We didn't really pack, just brought something to sleep on and a change of clothes. Ragnar will be back in the morning, and I'm betting we'll walk back to the city with Nylan since he "won't sleep outside two nights in a row."

I step back outside and stretch my sore limbs. I only recognize one of the three officers currently in the camp. I think his name is Stonearm. The other two I'm not sure, but I can't shake the feeling that they're staring at me oddly, like they're watching me. I look over at the closed tent, hoping Khazak's managing to get the shaman on our side.

"David?" A familiar voice calls out my name as Orim enters the camp behind me, returning from his patrol route.

"Hey!" I didn't realize he'd be out here this week.

"Why are you here?" he asks as he approaches.

"Captain Ironstorm and I are filling in for Deputy Rockfang, so he can spend the night with his avakesh. It's their anniversary." It sounds really formal when I use everyone's titles like that, but I'm *technically* working right now.

"That is very kind of you." I mean, I didn't really have a say in coming out here or not, but if I *did*, I still would have done it for my friends.

We exchange hugs (I've gotten the hang of the whole wrist-clasp orc-hug thing), and then some movement to my side draws my attention. Shaman Bonespirit and Khazak exit his tent together, still talking. After sharing a few more words, Khazak looks for me, then motions with his head toward our own tent.

"What'd he say?" I ask after entering behind him.

"He is sympathetic to our cause, or at least willing to investigate a little further," he shares the good news, voice low. "Tonight, during our watch shift, I am going to lead him to the section of the city wall behind Murbank's home. If magic was used to cover anything up, Bonespirit should be able to detect it."

"Then what do we do?" See how I'm asking before acting? Growth!

"That will depend on what the shaman is able to discover. But I have a good feeling." *That makes one of us.*

I think about sharing my weird feelings about being watched from before, but I'm probably just being paranoid. Not wanting to look odd by spending any more time in our tent, we both exit and take seats by the fire. After Orim, the next ranger back is Hazatin, the dwarf, who is followed by Glasha, then finally Ranger Firedrum, who looks almost put off when she sees me.

"What are you doing here?" she asks, sounding suspicious.

I explain for the tenth time why Khazak and I are here, but her behavior has me second guessing whether or not I was actually being paranoid early. Something is going on, and I need to tell Khazak. The sun has set, so we should be headed back out for our last patrol soon.

"Does anyone know why Boldhammer and Lonespite are not back yet?" Wu'dag asks after the two officers missing from the camp. I need to sync their compass stones with the cap—"

Two arrows whiz past the shaman, landing with a *thunk* in the ground not far from where I'm sitting.

"What the hell?" I, and everyone around me, jump up, searching for the archer responsible. Then two more arrows fly in, followed quickly by a cry of pain as one of them hits their target—Hazatin, who is pierced in the thigh.

"We are under attack!" Khazak cries out, drawing his sword.

More arrows fly in, one hitting Officer Stonearm in the chest and another bouncing off Orim's armor. Of *course*, tonight would be the night Khazak and I decide to skip wearing armor. It was just supposed to be a quiet night! As people try to take cover, I see the shaman slam his walking staff down and begin to chant, his eyes and hands glowing as a fog of white smoke grows around him—and then it abruptly stops, his body slumping to the ground.

Ranger Firedrum stands behind him, blood-covered dagger in hand. I stare at her wide-eyed.

"Tonight is already off to a bad start," she says down to the shaman's crumpled form, wiping the blood off her blade. "We do not need you making it any worse."

"What is the meaning of this?!" Khazak shouts, sword aimed at the murderous orc.

Glasha is near Hazatin, who is having trouble standing with the arrow sticking out of his leg. I'm doing my best to keep my eyes on Firedrum while also trying to search for the archers that are still out in the forest.

"Taking what is rightfully ours." As Firedrum steps over Wu'dag's body, I watch the other two officers move to stand behind her. And then behind her, just beyond the camp's perimeter, is a group of people wearing solid black robes. A dozen at least, barely visible in the darkness. *Oh shit.*

"This is *treason*," Khazak spits at her.

"You're working for him, aren't you?" I ask next. "Councilman Murbank."

Firedrum narrows her eyes at me. "Take out the human."

"No!" I don't even see the arrow coming toward me before Khazak shoulder-checks me out of the way, crying out in pain when it sinks into his arm.

"Khazak!" I do my best to scramble to my feet.

"Take the captain and the human alive. The rest are unimportant," she calls to the group behind her. "Now where did—"

The ground rumbles, strong enough to collapse a few of the tents. Then it sounds like the trees are moving, which seems crazy, but I watch a tree branch swing out of the darkness and slam into one of the officers at Firedrum's side, flinging him into some of the robed crowd behind him. As everyone begins to panic, I look at the ground and see Wu'dag isn't down for the count yet, his eyes glowing.

"Run," is all he says after locking eyes with me before the fire goes out, and everything turns black.

The panicked shouting starts immediately, and I instinctively grab for Khazak next to me. This isn't natural darkness; I can't see *anything.*

"Where are they?! Where is the avakesh?!" An unknown voice calls out. *Why are they after me and Khazak?*

"David, Captain, we must run." *That's Orim.* A hand on my arm pulls me away, and I make sure to pull Khazak along with me. Behind me, I can hear the sounds of a struggle, and I can only hope the other rangers can make it out okay. I try to ignore what I think is the sound of a sword hitting a body and just keep running.

As soon as we are far enough from camp, the world comes back into view, or at least, I can see the vague shapes of trees in the more natural-darkness. Orim is still gripping my arm to guide me, and I've still got a hold of Khazak's... who I am starting to notice is moving slower than the two of us.

"Are you okay?" I turn back in the darkness to ask.

"I think...the arrows...were poisoned," he breathes out slowly. *Fuck.*

"I bet I know what with, too." *What is with this fucking flower?!*

"Distilled poison acts much faster than plant form," Orim explains from the front.

"Are you going to be okay?" I remember the struggle it was trying to move him last time. At least I'm in better shape.

"You should...leave—"

"Nope. Still not an option. Try again." I don't even let him finish his stupid thought.

"But they—"

"David is right, Captain." *Glad someone agrees with me.* "They are looking for you both, which means we must keep you out of their hands."

There's no more arguing after that, though I can just *feel* Khazak's grumpy face glaring at the back of my head. We try to keep moving at our current speed, but once the poison kicks in, we have to slow down considerably. Orim and I move to either side of Khazak to help him, arms over our shoulders, a feat made even more difficult by the fact that I still can't see shit out here.

We're still moving north, at least I think so because of all the hills we're starting to climb. I'm not sure what our plan is. We're just trying to get as far away from them as we can. Just when I think we might be in the clear, Orim's steps stutter, and for just a second, he freezes.

"They are following us." He tries to pick up the pace.

"What?! How?!" Even with better eyesight and hearing, we should've put a good amount of distance between us by now.

"I do not...oh no. My compass stone," he realizes in horror.

"*Fuck*, what do we do? Toss it?" I can't even see where I'd throw it right now.

"It is too late. They are already too close." He sounds torn on something. "You must keep moving while I lead them away."

"What? No, that's as bad as—"

"They are getting closer, David. There is no time." I feel more of Khazak's weight drop on me as Orim steps away from us. "Go."

"Orim, you can't—"

"Go!" he whisper-shouts, and then he's gone. *Fuckfuckfuckfuckfuck.*

I want to chase after him and stop him, but I don't want whatever he does here for us to be in vain. So, I push on and tell myself he'll be okay, that he can handle himself. But I'm still not sure where I'm going or what my plan is. Khazak can barely walk, his movements slow, and I can feel his breathing getting labored. I'm still going north, but the hills are starting to kill me.

Then the sky rumbles.

Fuck. It's hard enough being out here in the dark, but if it starts to rain, I'll be completely blind. Not to mention how much harder it will be for Khazak to move in mud. Now I need to find shelter. Like a cave.

A CAVE! The ruins! I can take us to the temple ruins! We're already headed in that direction, and that would make a great place to hide out from the rain and wait until it's safe. I smile widely in the dark at my stroke of genius, feeling recharged. The trees are already starting to thin out, so I know we're getting close. A distant flash of lightning illuminates the mountain range ahead of us, and I can see where the temple's alcove is.

I breathe a sigh of relief when the cave entrance comes into (a very dark) view. Just in time. There's more thunder as we enter, and I walk us down the long hallway, figuring we'll be safe in the bigger room at the end. I can just hear that piercing noise in my head again when I feel Khazak start to struggle against me, and I panic that it has something to do with the poison.

"Are you okay?" I try to walk us faster; I can put him down once we're in the room.

"David..." he wheezes out, "why was...the cave...open?"

I freeze at Khazak's words, then look back to the entrance, barely visible in the darkness. I didn't even notice. Where were the boulders? Where was the illusion?

Who's already in here?

I'm stuck in place, unsure of whether to keep moving forward or turn back and take our chances in the coming storm. I look back and forth three or four times before something makes the choice for me. Down the hall, the entrance to the temple begins glowing orange as the torches in the room behind it are lit. Robed figures appear in the doorway, slowly approaching us.

Nope!

I turn us right around and start hoofing it back down the way we came in: the forest it is. Just as I turn, lightning cracks through the sky once more, and in the flash of light, I see more hooded figures at the exit, already coming toward us. We're trapped. Pulling Khazak close, I can do nothing but wait for the bastards to finally catch us. But like hell if I'm gonna make this easy on them. Leaning Khazak against the wall, I prepare myself for a fight, pulling out my sword.

"What do we have here?" The first person in robes to exit the room finally reaches us, a familiar voice echoing from under his hood. "You seem to be unable to stop sticking your nose where it does not belong, human."

"Fuck you." I grip my sword handle tightly, daring him to move closer.

"Now now, none of that." The other people in robes gather around him tightly, each drawing their own weapons and caging us in. "I would hate to cause any more death tonight than is necessary."

As the group closes in and my hope fades, all I can think about is what exactly he means by "necessary."

Chapter 18

"Where are they?" Councilman Murbank asks me calmly.

"Have you checked all the bathrooms in your house?" I sneer up at him.

"Again," he tells the orc standing next to me.

I try to brace for the incoming blow, but that's hard to do when your hands are tied behind your back. I cry out as the fist connects with my stomach and the wind is knocked out of me, another orc behind me holding me in place on my knees to make sure I don't move far. I think I taste blood in my mouth.

"Your turn." Murbank walks a few steps to Khazak, who is kneeling next to me.

"Your mother's...bedroom," he wheezes out, and I snort a laugh at his joke, even as he takes another punch for it.

He's asked us both at least a dozen times now, and I'm starting to run out of funny answers. After trapping us in the hall outside, we learned that our hooded friends here were more than a little surprised to see us because apparently I am *not* the avakesh they are looking for. They're after Ragnar and Nylan for some reason, and they've been interrogating us for the last ten minutes to find out where they went. There's at least two dozen people in robes here, all orcs, men and women. I recognize more than a few faces, no one I *really* know, but rangers and officers Khazak and I worked with nonetheless.

"This is growing *very* tiresome, gentlemen," Murbank complains as he saunters back in front of me. "If you just tell me where they are, I can stop all of this."

"Yeah, I know how torture works, asshol—*Oooof!*" I double over after he kicks me in the belly.

"Now, I will ask you again: where are they?"

"What about the barn you met your wife in?" I don't even see the fist flying toward me before it connects with my head. *Definitely taste blood now.* I think he knocked a tooth loose. *Worth it.*

When the ringing in my ears stops (other than the one coming from the pedestal), I hear footsteps down the hall behind us.

"Sir, we have searched the entire area and can find no sign of them." It's Deputy Captain Keenguard—Ragnar was right about her. "Do you want us to try the city?"

"No, they have to be out there somewhere," Murbank responds angrily. "Were any of the other captives forthcoming?"

"No, they only know that the captain and human were filling in for them for the night, not where they went." As she talks, there's more shuffling behind me, and I watch as Glasha, Ranger Hazatin, and Officer Stonearm are brought in by more orcs in robes. Glasha is forced to her knees next to Khazak and me, but Hazatin and Stonearm are just dumped on the floor. I can't tell, but I hope they're not dead, just unconscious, poison no doubt coursing through their bodies. I'm surprised Khazak is still able to speak at all.

"Where's everyone else?" I demand, thinking about Orim and Wu'dag and anyone else they've attacked.

I get a slap across the face in response. "You are not the one asking questions here. *Where are they?*"

"Are you *sure* you looked in all your bath*OOOFFF*." I take another fist to the stomach, and as I'm bent over in pain, something in me finally snaps, and I let out a laugh.

"I am losing my patience with these games, human." Murbank paces before stopping in front of me again. "The longer you draw this out, the more I will have to hurt you."

"Okay, okay, okay. I'll tell you. C'mere." I speak low, encouraging Murbank to lean in close, just a little. "They're right behind you," I whisper, before I start to laugh again, not stopping even when I take another punch to the jaw. *At least he can't hit as hard.*

"Are preparations *still* not finished? We do not have all night!" a new voice criticizes the man in front of me. A voice I know. I swing my head around to see someone else in robes entering the room.

"I am afraid we ran into a problem when our targets left camp early," Murbank explains, cleaning some of my blood from his hand with a handkerchief. "We have captured their replacements, but they will not tell us where they have gone."

"You are never going to get anywhere with that one, not like that," the figure pulls his hood back to reveal the dark red hair of Advocate Naruk Redwish.

"You have *got* to be fucking kidding." I start to laugh again, sounding even more unhinged. Of *course*, this asshole has a part in this.

"You two know each other?" Murbank looks between the two of us.

"Know each other? I wouldn't even *be* here right now if it weren't for this asshole." My words immediately make Murbank eye Redwish suspiciously.

"Is that true?" It seems like these two already might not trust each other all that much, which gives me an idea.

"Hardly, I represented him and his friends after they—"

"Oh no! If this dickhead hadn't tricked me into challenging Captain Ironstorm to a fight, I'd be sitting in a jail cell right now, not out here in the middle of the fucking forest." The more I can get them to argue, the more I can stall them to give help time to arrive. "*Neither* of us would be here right now if it wasn't for him."

Murbank stares at Redwish disdainfully, and the red-haired orc only rolls his eyes in return.

"Are you honestly going to let this *urchin* manipulate you like that?" Redwish steps closer, before turning to look at both me and Khazak. "The only reason he challenged the captain is because of a pathetic hero complex. He would happily throw himself on a sword if he thought it would protect his friends." He pulls a knife from his pocket, then moves to stand behind Khazak in place of the guard. Pulling Khazak's head back roughly, he exposes his neck before holding the knife to Khazak's throat. "No, to get information out of this one you need only threaten someone he cares about."

My heart skips a beat, and on instinct, I try to stand. "Let him go!"

"See? Pathetic," he says to Murbank before turning back to me. "Now where are they?"

"Fuck you!" I spit with venom, regretting it the instant I see Redwish press the knife into Khazak's neck.

"Ah ah ah! Any more of that, and I will bleed him out right here in front of you," he threatens coolly. "We have plenty more hostages after this one. You would not want to be responsible for any *more* deaths tonight, do you?"

I'm stuck staring in silence for what feels like forever. If I tell them, they could catch Nylan and Ragnar, but if I don't... I watch as Redwish presses the knife down harder, a small trickle of blood leaking down Khazak's skin.

"Fine!" I shout before my head drops down in defeat. "Shad'rok Springs."

"See? Much easier." Redwish releases Khazak, pushing him to the floor before wiping the knife on his robe. Right away, the guy that was previously holding Khazak steps forward to straighten him back on his knees.

"Keenguard, Firedrum," Murbank calls as he steps toward the temple entrance, hands already glowing with dark energy as he works a spell. A second later, two black horses form, seemingly from nothing more than shadows. Fuck, *he's* the wizard? He's the one doing all the actual dirty work?! At least I know where the horses went now. "Go. Find them and bring them back quickly."

The two women each grab one of the horse's reins and walk them out of the cave. Of the faces I've recognized, those two are definitely the most capable fighters here. Probably overkill for Nylan, but Ragnar might put up a decent fight. The distant sound of thunder cracking gives me hope that they may have already abandoned the springs when they saw the rain coming. Maybe they're already home.

"What do you want with Ragnar and Nylan?" I ask Murbank, both to figure out his plan and stall him while I try to think of something.

"Why would we tell you that?" Redwish answers for him, then turns to their robed lackeys and nods at Khazak. "Beat him."

Immediately, three of them rush forward and begin punching and kicking Khazak's prone form.

"Stop! Get off of him!" I struggle to get free and help before staring at Redwish with fury. "What the fuck!? Why are you doing this?!"

"Ay! The boy told you what he knows!" adds Glasha, also struggling with her captor to my right.

He strides over to me quickly, yanking my hair back roughly. "Because you do not seem to understand that you are not in control here." Hand still gripping my hair, he forces me to watch as Khazak is beaten.

"Enough," Murbank stops them a few minutes later, and Redwish releases me.

I watch Khazak crumple to the ground when he's released, no longer a threat. I try again to move over to him, but I'm held firmly in place. He's still breathing, but just barely. There's blood in the corner of his mouth, and he hasn't opened his eyes again yet. When he finally does, he tries to stand, only to be grabbed and forced to his knees at my side once again. *At least he's conscious.*

"I'm sorry," I tell him, though if it's for getting him hurt or telling them our friend's location, I'm not sure.

"Do not blame...yourself for...the failings...of others..." he wheezes out, still looking at Redwish and Murbank with venom.

"Perhaps you are right. I see no need to be cruel. Afterall, you are about to witness something glorious: the Order of Zeus's ascent to godhood." Satisfied, Murbank turns to advance on me, and I see Redwish over his shoulder rolling his eyes. *Well, that's interesting...*

"What the hell is 'Order of Zeus?'" Besides having something to do with the temple, *duh.*

"It is this group of dedicated men and women around you, my dear boy." Murbank straightens himself as he talks like a proud father. "Men and women of our city who understand that it is our destiny to achieve greatness. And after tonight, we will be unstoppable."

He stares at me, smirking, and I stare back, confused. What is he talking about? We're in a cave.

"Do you know what this place is?" He finally asks when he's done basking in my confusion, still smirking.

"A temple? To Zeus?" It's in the name.

"Very good, but it is so much more than that." Murbank points to one of the room's walls. "The murals that line the temple, have you ever read them?"

I look at one of the murals he's pointing at, confused. "...No?"

"They tell the legends of Olympian heroes and demigods." He begins walking around the room, pointing at different murals as he speaks. "Perseus, Atalanta, Caeneus, Penthesilea... all mortals, all granted unbelievable strength by the gods. Gods the ancient elves communed with using this very temple."

I *think* I've heard the name Perseus before, but the rest are a mystery. As is his plan—what the hell does this have to do with staying on the council?! "...Okay? So what? You're gonna start praying and…what, ask them to make you a councilman again?"

"Hardly," Murbank replies after snorting, walking toward the raised platform at the room's center. "Do you know what this altar was originally used for? The magic that is contained within?"

"No..." I know I'm not smart, but he's acting like I'm missing something obvious. He also *really* likes hearing himself talk. "I thought it didn't do anything."

"Of course, that is what the official report was made to say. Both the city and the elves did not want to risk the public learning its true purpose, lest someone try to use it for themselves." Murbank walks around the altar, staring at the lead box at its center. "You see, this altar is a conduit to the astral plane. The ancient elves used this to commune with the gods and receive their blessings."

"Fairytales and rumors?!" Glasha growls out to the entire room. "You have all elected to commit treason over *fairytales and rumors?!*"

"They are so much more than rumors, Ranger Silentfang." Murbank shakes his head in her direction. "It was my father who pushed for the temple to be investigated. After he learned of its true power, he became obsessed with it. It was not until he shared the information with me and started the Order that we were finally able to discover how to utilize the altar's power for ourselves." He pauses, staring at me like he's waiting for me to ask for more.

"How did you do that?" I can't help but roll my eyes as I ask.

"Do you know what Olympian altars are traditionally used for?" He pauses, putting both hands on the pedestal.

I shake my head. I'm really starting to get annoyed with all the questions he *knows* I don't have the answer to.

"Sacrifice." He grins creepily.

The word sits in my head for a minute before my eyes go wide at the implication. "Oh my god, you started a cult."

"Cult is such an ugly word." He feigns being wounded. "I am only doing what the gods intended, what the temple was built for. They left us all the necessary tools."

He pauses, bending over to pick up something that was leaning against the back of the altar: a sword still in its scabbard. The leather making it up is rough and tattered—it looks ancient. The grey metal of the handle shines brightly in the light of the room, despite being wrapped in the same old-looking leather. *The sword. That must be what they stole from the vault.*

"What are you going to do with that?" I don't know why I ask; I already know.

"Finish what I started with my father twenty years ago." He pulls the sword from the scabbard slowly, leaning the leather case against the altar again when he's finished. It's a one-hander, but it's still pretty large, bigger than any sword I've wielded. The blade is wide, curving at one end almost like a scimitar. The metal shines brightly in the light of the room. "This sword is enchanted with many spells of its own, but one in particular works to activate the conduit in the altar. It only requires the proper catalyst—blood."

"Technically, it requires a life," Redwish corrects Murbank. "One that is sacrificed through bloodletting."

"So why Ragnar and Nylan?" The way they're talking about this like it's nothing is fucking creepy. "Why wait twenty fucking years to do this?!"

"It is simple my boy: elf magic requires elf blood," he answers casually. "My father and I attempted to prove that twenty years ago. It was simple enough to manipulate Warhunter into starting his pathetic little rebellion, which gave us the cover we needed to begin our *real* work. It took weeks to uncover how the altar worked and move everything into place, but we did it. Then that bitch of an elf decided she would rather sacrifice herself than be a part of something great and destroyed everything we worked for. The order lost so many brothers and sisters that day. My father was ready to give up, but I knew I just needed to be patient and the opportunity would present itself once again."

"I'm sorry, *attempted to prove?*" I ask, my mind still stuck on one of the first things he said. "You don't even *know* that this is going to work?!"

"We have tested it with human and orc blood." He shrugs. "I told father not to bother. It obviously needed to be an elf, but he still insisted on trying. We had to wait for the right moment to—"

"Actually, Councilman, I myself have been wondering why you have been so insistent that we use *this* elf in particular." Redwish steps toward the older orc, sounding skeptical. "There are dozens of elves in the area. We could have had this finished *months* ago. Years even."

"Where is the poetry in that?" Murbank lays the sword back against the altar. "Twenty years ago, that elf destroyed my father's work! She sacrificed herself to wipe out our movement, and tonight I will sacrifice her son to restore it."

"*Poetry?*" Redwish's voice goes icy. "You are telling me that I have been stuck in this backwater hellhole for over a year now because of your obsession with damned *poetry?!*"

"I think you may want to watch your tone, Brother Redwish. I would like to remind you that we had been prepared for this two months ago before someone facilitated and encouraged the city's ranger captain to agree to a public battle on top of the vault we were to break into later that night!" Murbank is almost shouting now. "I had the plans in place to retrieve the sword for *months*, and you ruined them in a matter of hours! Luckily, I always have a backup plan, even if it did require far more force than I would have cared to use."

"You are right—the fact that after eight months you *still* did not possess one of the most important components for your plan should have been more than enough to indicate to that you have no idea what you are doing!" Redwish starts shouting himself. "And I would like to remind *you* that the only reason this little shit and his friends were able to enter the temple to begin with is because your *cult* left the entrance wide open for them to find in the first place!"

He points over at the "little shit," who is me. That does explain why we were able to find the place and get inside so easily. This is perfect though, exactly what I was hoping for. The longer I can get them to argue with each other, the more time I have to think of a plan. Which so far isn't going so well.

"Who do you think you are to speak to me this way?" Murbank growls, stepping into Redwish's space.

"Well, I do not know what else to call bunch of fanatical zealots tattooing bird claws all over their bodies!" They're standing so close they're almost touching. "Have you been *trying* to get us found out, or are you—"

Redwish stops speaking, turning his head toward the tunnel entrance. Several orcs, including Murbank copy him, and a second later, I hear it myself—horse hooves coming our way. *Dammit.* My stomach is in my chest as I struggle to turn to see if the rangers came back empty handed or not.

"Wonderful." Redwish breathes a sigh of relief, and my heart sinks. "Now, could we please get started?"

To my left, I watch a dark horse led by Deputy Captain Keenguard come into view, a bound Nylan thrown over the saddle on his stomach, hands behind his back. Keenguard pulls him off and forces him to stand, the horse dissipating into a puff of smoke with a hiss. There's a similar noise behind me, and then Ragnar is forced to his knees on my left next to Glasha.

"Let go of him!" Ragnar struggles in Firedrum's grasp. He looks bad, covered in small cuts, his eye swollen and his lip split and bleeding. He and Nylan are only half dressed, so I can assume they were probably caught by surprise. I hear the distant rumble of thunder, and I curse the rain for not starting sooner. I feel awful. *This is my fault.*

"Sir." Keenguard pushes Nylan toward Murbank. "We caught them not far from the springs. It seems they were heading back to the campsite but became...distracted."

"I suppose we should be thankful for that." Nylan looks terrified as Murbank inspects him.

"I said LET HIM GO!" Ragnar roars and breaks out of Firedrum's hold, only to be tackled to the floor a moment later.

"Get him under control, Captain." Murbank directs the order at Keenguard, apparently having already decided on Khazak's replacement.

Keenguard helps Firedrum wrestle Ragnar to the ground, giving him a few well-placed punches to subdue him.

"Stop it! Please!" Nylan cries out. "What do you want from us? I told you, our families don't have any money."

"What you are here for is so much more important than material possessions," says the very rich man who uses debt to blackmail people. "No, my boy. You are here to finish what was started twenty years ago as your mother was meant to do before you."

"What are you talking about?" He sounds as confused as he does scared. "I'm not... I can't use magic like she did. I don't know about any of that stuff, I swear."

"Of course, you do not." Murbank strokes Nylan's face creepily. "But you will bleed just the same."

At Murbank's words, Nylan panics and turns to run but is immediately grabbed by Redwish.

"This is insane! You don't even know this is going to work!" It's my turn to shout. "He's not even a full elf! He's half!"

"Which is why we have Deputy Rockfang here as well," Murbank replies smoothly. "Two halves make a whole, do they not?"

"Oh, okay. So, you're like, *crazy* crazy." I mean the cult alone should have been a giveaway, but I guess I was still hoping he could be reasoned with.

"Enough of this," Redwish complains before shoving Nylan back toward Murbank. "Can we *please* move things along? We do not have all night."

"Brother Redwish is right." Murbank sighs as he takes a hold of Nylan and moves to the altar. "Everyone, to your positions."

Around us, all of the cult members move to stand in a half circle around the altar, all except for the four holding me and the three still-conscious rangers in place. I can see Keenguard looking on proudly from one side of the lineup while Redwish looks more skeptical on the opposite. Murbank climbs the steps to the altar, pulling a struggling Nylan behind him.

"We tried...everything...we could." I hear Khazak struggle to tell Ragnar on his other end.

"I am so sorry, Ragnar." I try to apologize as I watch in horror as my friend is about to be sacrificed to some insane plot.

"I'm right here baby!" Ragnar shouts, trying to comfort his lover. He sounds so defeated.

"Captain, if you would not mind clearing the altar." Murbank nods at the lead box covering the altar's basin.

At its mention, I become aware of the annoying piercing sound once again, the one that I've been mostly successful in ignoring while all this has gone on. I watch Keenguard pull out her weapon, and I shut my eyes tightly as she swings, terrified that whatever is released is going to make my head hurt so much worse. If it doesn't explode.

I hear the sound of metal on metal and something shattering, and a second later, the ringing is gone, something else in its place. Something that sounds like speaking, or maybe whispering. Multiple voices, I think, but I can't even tell if they're in the same language. I open my eyes, watching Keenguard finish removing the remains of the lead box. I look at the faces of everyone else carefully, looking for some indication that I'm not the only one hearing this, but I see nothing. *What the hell is going on?*

Murbank reaches for the sword, and I start to struggle again. I can't let this happen. I can't let Nylan die like this! But the orc behind me is strong, and he gives me a solid punch to the head to settle me. *Fuck, that hurt.* I try to reach my hands up to rub my head, but they are of course still tied behind my back. In frustration, I flail my arms, trying to summon the strength to rip apart the rope binding them, but it's no use. Then my hands brush over something in my back pocket.

Holy shit. It's one of Glasha and Nikka's smoke bombs.

They never searched Khazak or me after they captured us. After mentally cursing myself for not noticing it earlier, I try to quickly come up with a plan, Keenguard already moving back into position with the others. Nylan and Murbank are on the side of the platform closest to us, facing away towards the giant mural of Zeus, while the rest of the cult is on the opposite, watching. The only things between us and the hallway out are the four cult members holding us. As Murbank raises the sword, I start moving.

"Do whatever it takes to clear a path to the exit!" I yell to Glasha, Ragnar, and Khazak before tossing the bomb on the floor behind me.

As smoke and confusion fills the air, I turn and headbutt the orc behind me right in the groin, making him double over in pain. Glasha and Ragnar catch on quickly and do the same, minus the headbutt, while Khazak elects to throw his body weight on his. After a well-placed knee to the forehead, I turn to charge at Murbank on the raised platform. The rest of the cult can see us, but Murbank can't, and I'm a lot faster than they are. I body slam the bastard from behind, knocking him stomach-first into the altar.

"Run Ny!" I shout to the elf, who is off before I can even finish. *Good boy.*

I'm tackled from the side and pushed to the ground, and as I look toward the smoke, all I can see are the shapes of a few bodies struggling. *Please have gotten away.*

"*Yar'ku ti'na-she!*" I hear Murbank's voice shout to my left and a gust of wind blows through the room, clearing out the smoke.

I see Firedrum and the other two traitors struggling with Glasha and Ragnar, but no sign of Nylan. *Yes!*

"After him. Now!" Murbank shouts at a few of the cult members off to the side, two of which immediately rush down the hallway. Gods, please let Nylan be a fast runner.

As all the orcs around me begin to argue amongst themselves, I can't help but smile. I completely fucked up their plan. No matter what else happens, as long as Nylan gets away, someone will be able to stop them. The rest of the city will know about this.

"I suppose you think this is funny." I look up to see Redwish glaring down at me angrily.

"Kinda, yeah." I nod, mocking him even from my spot on the floor of the platform.

He grabs me from the orc holding me to the ground, yanking me to my feet, and even I have to admit that he's a lot stronger than he looks. The altar is in front of me and the temple entrance to my right. Right next to it, the whispering sounds coming from the basin are even louder, but I still can't understand them.

"I have had quite enough of you interfering with my plans." Redwish spins me around to face him.

I open my mouth for a comeback, but I'm cut off by a sharp pain in my chest. I look down. *Oh.*

I didn't even see him grab the sword.

"NO!" someone screams.

Blood pools around the weapon in my chest, dark red meeting shining steel. As quickly as it entered, the sword is pulled back out, blood pouring from the wound and staining my dark blue shirt almost black. Blood fills my mouth when I try to draw in a breath, and I struggle to keep standing, gripping the altar behind me tightly. I try to move but only manage to turn myself around and collapse on top of it.

More people are yelling, and as the edge of my vision blurs, I see Khazak. He's struggling, crying, trying to say something, but I can't hear him. I can't hear anything over the whispering. When did it get so loud? The light in the room is fading. I try to reach for him, but my limbs are too weak. I can't breathe. It's so cold. *Heh, he's gonna be so mad at me for this.*

I'm sorry...

...I don't want to go...

...I love you...

It's dark. At least I think it's dark. I can't actually see anything. Or feel anything, or hear anything, or—Oh fuck, am I dead? I can't move my body... Actually, I'm not sure I have a body anymore. I'm not cold. I'm not hot. I'm not anything. Is this death? Just...nothingness, forever?

[Amused Male Voice: "Well, that took long enough."]

I hear someone talking, only not out loud. Like it's in my head.

[Confident Female Voice: "You can't rush prophecy."]

Another voice.

[Cocky Male Voice: "Well you can, it just doesn't usually end well."]

How many people are here?

[Soft Female Voice: "And we are certain this is the correct one?"]

I try to answer but can't figure out how to make any sounds.

[Confident Female Voice: "Yes. There was always a chance it could have been either of them, but it's been clear for some time it would be him."]

I give up on trying to talk.

[Disdainful Male Voice: "I still say we would've been better off with the other one."]

Well, that feels rude.

[Amused Male Voice: "I thought he still had like, six or seven years to go?"]

[Cocky Male Voice: "No, not *that* other one."]

[Sultry Female Voice: "I dunno. He's definitely the cuter one."]

Thank you, disembodied voice.

[Sultry Female Voice: "And you know I'm a sucker for a good love story."]

[Curt Female Voice: "Seeing as this is who we prepared for, I think we should be grateful."]

[Proud Male Voice: "He's plenty strong. I'm not even sure I'd know what to do with his brother."]

Brother?

[Defensive Male Voice: "He would have been just as strong, simply in different ways. Have you known my line to be weak?"]

Who are these people?

[Disdainful Male Voice: "Are we certain you want to do this, brother? He called you a drama queen."]

Wait, I know these people?

[Haughty Female Voice: "He's not wrong."]

I think that's the tenth voice I've heard now.

[Defensive Male Voice: "Excuse me?"]

[Cocky Male Voice and Curt Female Voice: "He's not." "He's not."]

Those are definitely siblings.

[Exasperated Male Voice: "Can we move things along? It's a pain in the ass getting up here, and we really don't have a lot of time."]

We don't?

[Defensive Male Voice: "Yes, yes. Is everyone ready?"]

No! I still don't know what's going on!

[Wise Female Voice: "Is this truly the only option?"]

[Defensive Male Voice: "You know that it is, sister."]

[Wise Female Voice: "He just has such a difficult journey ahead of him."]

...I do?

[Defensive Male Voice: "A journey he will not be making alone."]

[Cocky Male Voice: "Good thing too. I have a feeling this one is going to need help with control. At least he already likes being kept on a tight leash."]

[Curt Female Voice: "Yes, I'd say we lucked out with his large green master, as long as he actually does what he's *supposed* to."]

Khazak?

[Exasperated Male Voice: "Neither of them is going to be doing anything if we don't speed this the fuck up and send him back already!"]

[Confused Male Voice: "Why am I here, exactly?"]

[Defensive Male Voice: "Because this only works with all of us. Now everyone be quiet and concentrate. We haven't done this in millennia."]

[Amused Male Voice: "It's just like riding a bike."]

As the voices continue to speak, warmth starts to flow through my not-body. What are they doing?

[Haughty Female Voice: "You've never ridden a bike. Now shut up and focus. We need to...wait, who's doing that?"]

[Proud Male Voice: "Just giving the kid a little jump-start for when he gets back. He's gonna need it."]

[Soft Female Voice: "Will it be enough?"]

The darkness gets brighter, first to a grey, and then to solid white, but I still cannot see anything.

[Defensive Male Voice: "It's going to have to be because we are out of time. We must send him back now."]

I can feel the energy coursing through me, enveloping me, charging me. Then it's as if everything begins to fade again.

Wait! I still don't understand! What was all this? Who are you? What am I supposed to do?

My eyes focus on the stone walls of the temple as I come to. My body feels tight, like it's overflowing with energy. And strength. And *rage*. I push myself up from the altar and scan the room. Maybe two dozen threats, if that. The room is silent, all eyes on me as I bend to reach my weapon on the floor. The same one used to kill me. The Harpe.

They don't see me coming. I don't give them the chance. I leap across the room, pinning the first person in robes I see to the wall and driving my sword directly into their stomach. The screaming starts immediately, everyone around me panicking. All except the bastard currently bleeding out at my feet. I turn and look for my next target.

I rush toward the next nearest set of robes, not even stopping to give the owner a chance to defend herself. As I continue my attack, all around me the people start to scatter. Some draw their own weapons, but many more flee out of the cave entrance. I'm not worried. It will be simple enough to track them once I am finished here.

I cut my way through the remaining cult members quickly. The coppery smell of blood is thick in the air as I turn to face the three left standing. They're certainly the strongest, two warriors and a mage, but they'll fall to my blade the same as everyone else.

"What the hell is he?!" one of the warriors asks aloud.

"Is it not obvious? The spell worked," the wizard replies. "He has been blessed by the gods."

"Why is he attacking?" The other warrior asks as she points her sword in my direction. *A threat.* "Why did the gods bless him and not us?!"

"I do not—"

I leap at the warrior with her sword aimed at me. She does her best to block my blows, but I can tell it's a struggle. She may be larger than I am, but I'm stronger, a fact I can tell shocks her. I knock the blade from her hand and ready my killing blow when I feel the air behind me ripple and turn just in time to catch the sword of the other warrior.

This one is stronger than the first, and she strikes repeatedly with her sword, quickly putting me on the defensive. I meet her blade with mine each time, shrugging the force of her blows off like they're nothing. I watch her anger build with each attack until I finally see an opening and strike, my sword sinking into her midsection before her body crumples to the ground.

"Enough!" I turn and see the wizard holding a knife to the throat of my *sýzygos*, my *kýrios*, my master. "You will drop your blade and then you—"

Seeing red, I rush across the room, I knock away the knife and slamng the wizard into the wall behind him hard enough to crack the stone. Then I fling him across the room, watching him stumble to his feet after tumbling across the ground. He looks terrified, his hands shaking as he begins casting a spell, lightning crackling in the air around him. *Good.*

I come toward him slowly, and he flings his hands in my direction, sending two crackling arcs flying straight at me. I hold the Harpe out in front of me, absorbing the magical energy into its metal. A look of shock on the wizard's face is all he has time for before I leap at him and knock him to the floor once more. He looks up at me in anger as I approach.

"You cannot—!" he starts to spit.

I sink my sword down into his chest, the blade piercing through flesh and bone until it hits the floor beneath him. I release the sword's stored lightning, the wizard's body convulsing as I return his spell to him by force. When I finally remove the weapon, he is still, other than the smoke rising from his overcooked corpse.

Satisfied, I turn to look for the remaining warrior, but it appears she has fled, along with any remaining survivors. No matter, I will have plenty of time to hunt them down later. I see a few of my allies still standing, watching me with a mixture of fear and worry. But they are not who I am concerned with.

Rushing back to my master's side, I check his neck for any damage from the knife, finding only a thin red line. My hands clench into fists. *The one who did this already escaped.* My master is breathing, staring at me half-conscious and confused. I need to get him out of here. I look up to see my allies now standing between us and the exit, eyeing me warily.

"David?" the male says to me. "Can you hear me?"

I tilt my head at the question.

"Are you sure he's in there?" the female asks.

"You saw how he defended the captain. He has to be." He does not sound sure of himself.

They look suspicious as they move closer. They both pick up weapons discarded on the ground, and I immediately lift my sword and snarl. *What are they getting at?* My growling makes them both freeze, dropping the weapons back to the floor. No longer trusting them, I begin to pace back and forth in front of my master, watching the two carefully. They need to get out of my way. *Now.*

"What the hell was that?" It's the man's turn to ask.

"He does not trust us." The woman shakes her head.

"But he *knows* us." He sounds incredulous.

"I told you—I do not think he is all there." She shakes her head again.

"How are we supposed to get everyone help if he won't let us get near them?" He's getting frustrated.

"We need him to calm down." She holds her hands up to me in surrender.

I don't have time for this! Just as I ready to drop into an attack stance, shuffling behind me makes me turn around.

"David," my master croaks out from his spot on the floor. Khazak croaks out. *Wait, who?* "It is...okay. I am...okay."

I watch him on the floor, one arm reaching for me. It's like he and the rest of the world are coming back into focus. I shake my head, hearing the sword clatter to the ground at my side. What... What happened? I look around the room and see Ragnar and Glasha watching me, frightened. I see some of our friends bound and unconscious against one of the walls. And the bodies. So many bodies. So much blood.

What did I do?

"Khazak?" I barely have time to look at him before I feel myself falling, and everything fades to black once more.

Chapter 19

*I*t's dark, and I am once again in the forest. This is all *so familiar, and I'm not surprised when the large black wolf comes slinking toward me, the two others right behind it. As its red eyes lock onto mine, I stand my ground. I'm not afraid of these things anymore. Still, it's hard not to feel nervous when it crouches to attack, or panic when it leaps at me. Just as I expect to feel its jaws connecting with my flesh, there's a flash of light and a crack of thunder, and the only ones flinching are the wolves. They look on in anger as the bright light surrounds me, snarling as they return to the forest from where they came.*

"Nngh... You better fucking run..." I mumble, waking from my dream.

"David?" A concerned voice on my left asks. "He is awake!"

"Oh my god, really?"

"I *told* you he would be alright!"

"Why are you all yelling?" I open my eyes just enough to make out a green shaped blur before I close them again. The light in the room is way too bright.

"Why are we..." Khazak laughs before reaching out and squeezing my arm. "We are just happy you are okay."

"Why wouldn't I...?" My eyes finally adjust to the room, and I realize I'm not at home. I'm lying alone in a huge bed with all my friends crowded around me. Like, everyone: Adam and the rest of my team, Ragnar and Nylan, some of Khazak's family, the other rangers. *What?* "Where are we?"

"The healer's clinic," he answers for me, looking concerned. "David... Do you remember what happened in the forest? In the temple?"

"No, what—"

"David, you've been asleep for *five* days." Adam says on my right. "They said you *died.*"

As soon as the word is out of his mouth, the memories flood back. Covering for Ragnar in the forest. Getting attacked at the campsite by other rangers. Finding Murbank and his cult in the temple ruins. Rescuing Nylan and getting a giant sword through my chest as a thank you. I quickly look down, surprised to see it unbandaged. Instead, down the center of my chest, right over my heart, is a jagged, golden colored scar. It stretches from below my collarbone to right under my rib cage.

"What is this?" I run my fingers over the scar, unsure of why I'm not feeling *any* pain. "Five days? What happened?"

"I would like to see if I can figure that out myself," a new voice from behind the crowd answers, bodies parting to make room for who I assume is the healer. "But first, I am going to need *everyone* except the captain and the two of you to exit the room." She points at Adam and Corrine with two fingers.

With some minor bellyaching, the rest of my friends, orc and non-orc alike, file out of the room.

"David, this is Doctor Brightmarsh," Khazak introduces me to the woman now standing at the side of my bed. She's dressed nicely, wearing a cloak over a more formal shirt and pants.

"I am glad to see you awake," the doctor tells me. "How are you feeling?"

"Alright, I guess." Physically, at least.

"That is good." She gives me a small smile. "You have been unconscious for some time. Your friends have been very concerned for you. These two are the leader and healer of the group you are traveling with, correct?" She indicates Adam and Corrine again.

"Yes..." The way she wants to be sure the two of them are here is making me nervous. "Am I okay?"

"Short of being unconscious and the appearance of this scar, I was unable to find anything amiss," the doctor looks at me skeptically. "You seem to be in perfect physical health."

"I mean, something *definitely* happened to me." *Right?*

"No, David. I really mean *perfect* health. I cannot find *anything* wrong with you. No injuries, not a single scratch. Even this scar..." She hovers her fingers over the gold skin on my chest. "Normally, scar tissue is weaker than the tissue it has replaced. Magic cannot heal it without first removing the old tissue. But this scar? It appears to be just as strong and healthy as the rest of your skin."

"What about his internal injuries?" Corrine asks, her voice sounding a little hoarse, and I notice that it looks like she's been crying.

"As with his skin, I can find absolutely nothing wrong with his bones, muscles, or organs." Doctor Brightmarsh touches my shoulder. "You have a smaller, matching golden scar on your back, and I presume your internal injuries look similar."

"I'll continue to monitor him like you asked, just to be on the safe side," Corrine tells the doctor.

"Thank you. I know it may not be possible to take his full vitals while traveling. Just do what you are able," the doctor replies.

"Since she's the team healer, the doctor wanted Corrine to keep an eye on you once we start traveling again," Adam tells me after seeing my confusion. "Turns out there's a lot more to healing than just magic. She actually knows *a lot* about medical stuff."

"Got it." *Still don't like being talked about like I'm not here.*

"Now, David, I know you have been through something traumatic, but we still do not know what actually happened." The doctor touches my shoulder again. "Do you think you could walk us through what you remember of the events from five nights ago?"

"Uh, yeah. Okay." I nod slowly, nerves already rising. "I remember being attacked at the camp and running, then trying to hide in the temple and getting captured. They tried to beat the info of us, caught Nylan and Ragnar, and then I used a smoke bomb to start a fight. I remember Nylan getting away and then I..." I can still feel the sword sinking into my chest. The way everything got so cold. The loud whispering. "I died. Wait, do you remember when I told you about the ringing noise in the temple I kept hearing?" I ask everyone but the doctor.

"Yes. You told me about that. but in the confusion and stress of the bombings, we completely forgot to follow up. Did it happen again?" Khazak asks, concerned.

"At first, but when they finally removed the lead box covering the altar, it changed." I'm probably going to sound crazy. "It turned into whispering."

"Whispering? Actual voices?" Corrine is *very* interested. "Could you hear what they were saying?"

"Kind of? I couldn't really understand any of it." *Could barely even hear it, at first.* "But when I was dying, it got louder. And then..." Wait, *did* something else happen after that? "I guess I came back to life."

"*Very* curious." The doctor is just as interested but still clueless like the rest of us. "What can you remember about that?"

"It was weird. I *knew* I had died, but it was like I didn't care." I remember how I stood up and just started...doing things. "I was still in control, but there was something else driving me. Like I had a mission, pushing me forward. But it was all emotion. I remember feeling angry—*so* angry, and I just started to—" I cut myself off, unable to continue as the violence I caused flashes through my head. "I don't remember what happened after that or passing out."

"After hearing some of the other survivors' accounts, I initially suspected some sort of possession, but I was able to rule that out fairly quickly." I try to ignore that she used the word *survivor*. "I've brought in additional spellcasters of all types, but none have been able to determine exactly what was done to you. We know there was a spell, and that it has magically altered you in some way during, or perhaps because of, your revival. Your magical aura has grown *extremely* bright."

"I don't understand. How does someone just come back to life?" This doesn't feel real.

"Magical resurrections *are* possible." I look at the doctor, confused. *They are?*

"They've actually been pretty well documented," Corrine adds.

"Yes, but unfortunately none of the details of *your* resurrection match up with any of those," the doctor offers with a frown. "There is not a magic user powerful enough for something like that within five-hundred miles of the city, perhaps even farther. I am at a complete loss as to how this cult managed to pull off what they did. Captain, would you mind filling in the rest?"

"Of course," Khazak answers with a nod. "We had been in the temple for at least an hour. I was feeling the effects of the poison *and* the beating, so I was sluggish and unfocused." Khazak looks directly at me next. "When you set off the smoke bomb, Glasha, Ragnar, and I attacked our guards while you ran for Murbank. You jumped onto him, which freed Nylan and allowed him to escape." He pauses, looking down. "Then I watched as Redwish picked you up and ran you through with the sword."

"That sword, correct?" The doctor points to a corner of the room, and leaning against it is the old looking scabbard, metal hilt shining in the light of the room. Something about seeing it here, having it so close, makes the bottom of my stomach drop out.

"Yes." Khazak nods stiffly, swallowing thickly. "He pulled the sword out of your chest, and you fell onto the altar as you bled out. I saw the life drain from your eyes, and then..."

"What?" I can remember this, when things started to go dark, but after that... "What happened?"

"First, the storm outside seemed to grow even stronger." He's able to look at me again. "The wind was howling through the cave tunnel, and the lightning and thunder became more frequent, louder. Then it was as if the mountain itself had been struck. The whole room started shaking as a bolt of lightning came down *through* the temple ceiling and struck your body. It was terrifying, but I couldn't look away as your body convulsed. Then it stopped, and you were still. Until you were not."

"I was already starting to fade, all the energy and adrenaline drained from my body. But then you clutched the altar and stood up," Khazak continues. "At first, I did not understand what I was seeing. Then I was just happy that you were still alive. But something was off. You were not talking and your eyes looked dark, unfocused. Until you looked at one of the cult members. Then all I could see in your eyes was fury. Even after you...stopped them, you were still not acting like yourself. It was only when I was able to get your attention that I saw for just a moment that you were back, right before you passed out, and we brought you here."

I'm speechless when he finishes, but when no one says anything, I press forward. "So, we still don't really know what happened to me?"

"Though it may sound far-fetched, the simplest answer is that whatever the group was attempting to accomplish worked." Kind of surprised it's a *doctor* saying this. "Unfortunately, we do not have a way of truly knowing."

"So, I'm 'blessed' by the gods?" Sure doesn't fucking feel like it.

"We are going to figure this out, David," Khazak tries to reassure me. "While you were recovering, I spoke with the remaining members of the Tribal Council. Murbank was correct about the city having more information regarding the temple, but it is not much. They intentionally asked the elves to keep it secret to prevent something like this from happening. We may not know what they really discovered twenty years ago, but we know who does, and your friends have already been discussing your travel plans for what to do next."

"Yeah! We're gonna figure this out together, David," Corrine tells me cheerfully before turning to the doctor. "Would it be alright if he started seeing visitors?"

"Yes, I think that would be fine, but only two at a time other than the captain, please." She holds up two fingers, then looks at me. "I would like to keep you here a bit longer, just to be sure that everything is alright before releasing you."

"Got it." I nod. "Thank you." It's not her fault we don't know what's going on.

As soon as the healer is gone, Corrine nearly throws herself at me to hug me, already crying again.

"It's so good to see you guys," I say after she's finally composed herself. "How are you even here right now?"

"Aside from you almost dying? Turns out our former lawyer wasn't actually a lawyer *and* was the one who stabbed you." *Good point.*

"After your apparent resurrection, Redwish was one of the first ones to leave the temple in the chaos that followed." Khazak sighs unhappily. "We were able to catch most of the others, but unfortunately not him. We searched his home and found it nearly empty, and it appears he may have forged his entire identity. We are not even sure Naruk Redwish is his real name."

"So, because of that, they released us and a few of his other defendants early," Adam finishes explaining.

"Considering we *definitely* did the thing we were accused of, I think we got pretty lucky," Corrine adds with a sniffle after fixing her hair.

"Seriously." It's so great to see them like this and not cuffed behind a table.

"What about you?" Adam asks, concerned. "Are you alright?"

"I guess?" I *feel* fine. "Other than this gnarly scar."

"We don't mean physically, David." Corrine touches my arm gently.

"...I don't really know." For so many different reasons.

"We're here for you, David," Adam assures me. "We're going to figure this out."

"Yes, we are! Pákannon is only a five day walk from here, so if we leave in the next couple of days, we should arrive around a week from now!"

"The friends you've made while we've been locked up have been *really* helpful." Adam looks at Khazak with a smile. "We've been staying with Captain Ironstorm's family since yesterday. They're letting us crash there until we leave. His sister already helped figure out the fastest path from here to Pákannon and then from there to Manamequohi."

"How did you say that so easily?" I look at Adam, half-surprised and half-annoyed.

"What? Manamequohi?" Corrine asks and my look moves to her.

"Whatever," I grumble and cross my arms. "I'm glad Ayla was able to help. Khazak's family is great."

"They've all been so nice," Corrine agrees, smiling at Khazak.

"Some of the rangers told us about where to find some decent weapons and armor, and that Nylan guy offered to show us around the marketplace later today," Adam adds.

"That's great." I try to sound sincere and not nervous about what Nylan may inadvertently reveal about how I've been spending my time here.

"As long as they let you out soon, we figure we'll be on our way in a day or two." Adam grins, and it's hard to not smile back.

"Yeah, I guess it's time to go." With Murbank dead and his plot out in the open, there's not any reason for me to stay.

"Rest up, okay?" Corrine says while hugging me again. "We are just *so* happy you are alright."

After Adam and Corrine leave, I expect Liss and Nate to be next. Instead, a sobbing Nylan jumps halfway onto my bed to hug me tightly, Ragnar entering behind him.

"I'm s-so happy y-you're okay!" he cries into my neck. "You got stabbed a-and then d-died and it w-was all because of me! I w-was so worried you w-weren't gonna wake up and—"

"Ny, it's okay. I'm okay." I hug the half-elf tighter as he chokes up. "I'm glad *you're* alright. That's all I cared about."

"David, I don't know how I can thank you," Ragnar manages to tell me over his crying boy. "If you hadn't risked your life like that to save him... Just, thank you, so much."

"I didn't even think about it." I release Nylan, now only sniffling instead of sobbing. "I just wanted to protect my friend."

"The ranger force is in shambles right now." Ragnar shakes his head. "Almost half of the cult was made up of rangers and officers. Everyone is demoralized and suspicious of everyone else potentially being a traitor. The people in the city are furious with the council *and* Chief Grandtooth for letting this happen on their watch. Half of them are suspected of being traitors themselves."

"We apprehended Keenguard hiding in the forest with several of the other cult members. It has been easier than anticipated getting them to talk. What happened in the temple seems to have shaken them," Khazak adds, leaving out that I'm the thing they're probably afraid of. "We were able to locate where Murbank had moved the black carriage, which was housing the missing supplies."

"Finding out Murbank was a wizard was a surprise. Even to his wife, she claims." Ragnar sighs. "But at least it explains how he was able to get away with all of this for so long without anyone suspecting. We even found out he and the cult are the ones responsible for all the patches of Ralor's crown that have been popping up in the forest."

"We have already started to root out other people in the department." Khazak sounds more confident. "Considering the small amount of us we know for a fact are not compromised, it will take some time. But with the main issues resolved, you are free to leave the city like we originally planned."

"Yeah, I guess you're right." I smile, but inside I feel a stab of regret. I don't have a reason to stay anymore. In fact, I have a very good reason to go. "Now I just need to try and figure out the rest of this shit."

"I might be able to help with that." Nylan blows his nose into a tissue Ragnar hands him. "I have family in Pákannon where the archaeology group came from. Plus, my dad *led* the expedition with my mom, so if anyone knows about the temple, it's him. I wrote letters to both places."

"I know your friends are already talking about that being your first stop," Ragnar adds before turning his head when a throat is cleared. "And they are waiting for their turn next. Come on, boy. We'll be back." With a smile and another hug, the couple leaves the room.

Liss and Nate are next. Liss is her normal gruff self, but I can tell she missed me. Even Nate seems happy to see me. Or happy to be out of jail, at least. Next comes Glasha and Arik, and then Hazatin and Stonearm, all of whom look recovered from the ordeal themselves. They're friendly, but I can't help but feel like they're looking at me funny. Like they're afraid of me too. Khazak's family is next, even Brull, but I can't help but notice one glaring omission. One I'm worried to ask about.

"Hey, do you mind if me and Khazak talk alone for a bit?" I ask Brull, our conversation having veered into small-talk territory. *I need a break.*

"Of course! Feel better, pup." The larger orc gives my thigh a light squeeze. "Make sure you come see me before you leave to say goodbye, alright?"

"I will, I promise." I nod with a smile as he exits.

Once Brull's out of the room and we're alone, I can relax a little more, and I feel Khazak do the same.

"I cannot even begin to tell you how scared I was." Khazak pulls a chair closer to the bed so he can sit, never letting go of the hand he started holding once my friends left the room. "Grief, then anger, and then *shock* when you were alive again. I thought I had lost you, and I never... I am just so happy that you are still here."

"I was pretty worried about you, too." My eyes go to his throat where Redwish held the knife. "I am glad you're okay too." I squeeze his hand, my mind lingering on the question I am afraid to ask. "Where's... Where's Orim?"

"David, I am so sorry." Khazak sags in his seat. "Orim and Shaman Bonespirit did not make it out of the forest."

"No..." It feels like the wind is knocked out of me. "I shouldn't have let him go off on his own like that. If he had just stayed with us, he might still——"

"You cannot think that way, David." Khazak moves quickly to swat that thought down. "You are *not* the people who killed him. You are not the reason he is dead. None of this was your fault."

"He was my friend..." Apparently, I can't do much more than state the obvious right now, my vision blurring as I tear up. Then, since I'm a glutton for punishment, I ask the other question that scares me. "How... How many people did I kill?"

He hesitates to answer. "David, I am not sure——"

"*Please*. Just tell me." It's hard to not let my voice crack. "I can still see it. I can hear the screams. I can still *smell* it. So much blood... Don't... Don't make me try to count it on my own. Please."

"...Eleven," he finally tells me.

"*Fuck*." The wind is knocked out of me again. I knew that I would probably kill someone someday, but never so many, not all at once. Not like this.

"David, you were not in control——"

"Except I told you that I was." I can't even look at him. "I remember all of it. I remember feeling angry. *So* angry. That they had hurt you, that they had tried to kill Nylan. For everything. Even after I stopped them, when Glasha and Ragnar were trying to talk to me, I couldn't turn it off. It was like I couldn't hear them. All I could think was that I needed to protect you, and they were in my way, and if they wouldn't move, I——"

"*Ah!*" Khazak pulls his hand out of mine with a hiss after I squeeze too hard.

"I'm sorry." I pull away from him entirely. *What is wrong with me?*

"It is alright." He quickly retakes my hand, pulling me back into his space. "Even if you *were* aware of what was happening, something else was still the cause of your actions."

The mention of *something else* draws my attention back to the deadly weapon in the corner of the room. "Why is that thing here?" I point.

"After I spoke with the council, it was decided that given it's relation to the events, the sword should go with you." Khazak nods at the sword in question. "It is now yours."

"I don't want it." Even looking at it makes me uncomfortable.

"I understand why you feel distressed with its presence." He offers me a sad smile. "But it is without a doubt connected to whatever happened to you in the temple. It could be the key to solving it. You do not have to use it, but you do need to take it with you."

I know he's right, but I don't want him to be. I don't ever wanna see that thing again. "Do you think I could just be alone for a little while?"

"Of course." I expect a flash of hurt to cross his face, but there's just understanding. "I am going to go find you some food. I will be back a little later. Please, try not to wallow or allow yourself to feel guilty about this. Despite how terrible your actions might seem, they still saved us. If you had not been there, Nylan and Ragnar might be dead. We all could be." With a final hand squeeze, he stands, puts his chair back against the wall, and exits the room.

I know he said not to, but as soon as I'm alone, I spend the first twenty or so minutes wallowing. I just can't stop thinking about it, no matter how hard I try. Getting attacked at the camp, running through the forest at night, the "interrogation" in the temple... I can feel the anger starting to rise up in me again, and I have to take a few deep breaths to calm down. When the flashes of violence start popping in, I wish I had something to distract me.

The doctor comes back in at some point to run some tests: heart rate, breathing, that sort of thing. Just making sure I'm still healthy. About an hour after he left, Khazak returns with food *and* Nylan, who it turns out is impossible to feel sad around. He spends lunch distracting me with horror stories from work, followed by reading me some of his favorite and most ridiculous romance novel passages. During the rest of the afternoon, my other friends pop in and out, and the doctor runs her tests again until finally, just before sunset, she lets me go home.

We end up grabbing dinner with my friends at Rurig's restaurant, *Bauzi'kro*, before going home. Rurig isn't working tonight, but the food's still great. It's actually nice to just sit down and have a meal with my friends, something I didn't realize I would miss. I forget about my problems for a little while and just laugh and joke around. Before we leave, we make plans to meet up in the afternoon tomorrow for one last round of shopping before we leave the next morning.

You'd think that after spending almost five full days asleep, I'd be full of energy, but after dinner, all I want to do is go home. I feel drained, and on top of that, not terribly sexy, but seeing as we only have maybe 36 hours left, I feel bad asking Khazak if he'd just read to me while we sit on the couch together. He doesn't look disappointed if he was hoping for more, and as he recounts the tale of Khazak Steelrun to me, I nod off against his chest.

A public funeral is held the following morning for Orim, Wu'dag, and the other victims of the Order's attacks. It's a somber affair, a small procession of rangers followed by High Priest Bhok leading a prayer. I don't bother trying to hold in my tears. All I can think about is how my friend should still be here. That and how much I'm going to enjoy hunting down Redwish and making him pay for this.

After the funeral, Orim's family is holding a *trakul*, which is basically a wake, but more cheerful. People are still crying, but it's accompanied with smiles and laughter as everyone shares stories from Orim's life. I learn about the first time he went fishing from his father (he tripped and fell in the river), how afraid he was of horses when he was little from his mother (he would *literally* hide under her skirt when they got too close), and his terrible first date as a teenager from his older brother (he thought he was stood up, but he was at the wrong restaurant). Even translated, hearing these stories makes me smile. They also make me sad that he didn't get the chance to tell me any of them himself. That he won't get to make anymore.

I have a few hours before I need to meet my friends, so we head home around noon. I'm full from all the food they had at the wake, so all I really wanna do is relax. I don't say this, but I also want to get in as much alone time with Khazak as I can. This is our last day and night together. When I ask if he'll read to me more, he just smiles and pulls me into him on the couch. I find myself trying to memorize the sound of his voice, afraid it will be the last I hear it.

Eventually, it's time to go, and with a frown, I get dressed so I can meet with my friends. I eye the sword—the *Harpe* is what I called it during my rampage—sitting in the corner of the room with hesitation. I really wish I didn't have to bring that thing, but Khazak's right, it's definitely connected to all this. I bring my shortsword, so I can find a second one that will balance with it well, but I'm happy to leave this one here for now.

Before I meet my friends in the marketplace, there's one stop we need to make: Brull. It's not that I don't want the man around my team, it's that I don't want my team aware of Brull's shop or what he sells. The door to the store is open when Khazak and I get there, only a single customer inside browsing. When Brull sees us enter, he walks around the counter and hugs me hard enough to lift me off the ground.

"I am gonna miss you, pup," the orc tells me while squeezing the life out of me.

"I'll miss you too, sir," I reply when I can breathe again.

"I believe this is yours." He pushes a small cloth bag into my hand, and when I open it, I am greeted with the sight of the puppy tail plug I wore on stage.

"Thank you, sir." I blush as I squeeze the small bag into my pocket. I'll have to make sure I hide that *really* well. I'm not sure I could bring myself to get rid of it.

"You better come back to visit." He pokes me in the chest. "At least for the next festival."

"I will. I promise." I nod. I'm going to try, at least.

There's some small talk after that, but I know I'm just stalling, so I finally say my goodbyes. Just as I turn to leave, expecting Khazak to follow, he stops me.

"I think you should go and meet with your friends alone." He gives me a sad smile. "You will be preparing for your journey, and I would only get in the way. Besides, you likely want to start getting back into the mindset of being a team, right?"

"Yeah, right." I try not to sound disappointed at his dismissal.

"I will see you afterward at my parents', alright?" He steps close and runs his hand through my hair.

"I'll see you there, Sir." Fuck, I'm even gonna miss calling him "Sir."

I find my friends in the marketplace easily enough, the group of humans sticking out like a sore thumb. Everyone's happy to see me, and unlike some of the rangers, they don't seem scared. They all look the same as yesterday, except for Liss who has gotten a haircut. Rather than redyeing her hair black, she seems to have had all of it cut off, leaving her with a head of short red hair styled almost like mine.

"Alright, first I want to make sure we're all clear on what we're doing." Adam is the responsible one, as always. "Five days ago, David was killed and then resurrected through an ancient magical ritual. The only two places we know with information on that ritual are Pákannon, which is a five-day walk north-northeast, and Manamequohi, which is a two-week hike from there. I say we hit both places and gather all the info we can. Any objections?"

"Nope!"

"No."

"Nah."

"I guess not." It feels weird to be the focus of our group's activity. "But there's something else we need to do to: find Redwish. He'll know more about what happened to me, *and* he needs to be held responsible for his hand in all of this."

"Alright, tracking down our skeezy former lawyer is added to the list," Adam says with a grin, and it's damn hard not to grin back. "Let's get stocked up because we leave in the morning!"

The first thing we look at are food and rations. It's only a five-day journey, and I've learned a few of hunting and fishing tricks while on patrol with Khazak, but it's still good to stay prepared, so we get enough for a full week. Mostly jerky, but we also find some things like nuts and dried fruit. I insist on buying, something the group reluctantly agrees to. I also convince them to let me grab us a few collapsible fishing poles. Then I try to buy Adam a brand-new sword, and he quickly turns me down and tries to assure me that I have nothing to make up for. So no, not gonna be able to get rid of my guilt that easily.

After the rations, we take care of the rest of our supply and equipment needs. Weapons are sharpened, armor is repaired, and new clothes are bought. I finally pick up that second sword and I even grab a bow to practice hunting with. It's really interesting watching how my friends each handle their purchases. Adam is as patient and respectful as always, and it sounds like he actually picked up a little of the language while in jail, maybe even more than I have. Liss is more silent with a lot of pointing and holding up fingers to count. Corrine uses her hands a lot when she speaks too, though I'm not sure it's actually helping, and Nate just tries talking louder, at least until he gets his answer shouted right back to him. *I missed these guys.*

When we're finished, the afternoon is long over and all of us are starving, which means it's time to head to the Ironstorm residence. I am fully expecting the massive feast Rurig has prepared for us when we get there. What I'm not expecting is for almost *everyone* else I know in the city to be here too. Work and otherwise. While I'm happy to see them all, it also means there's a lot more opportunities for my friends to discover more about what I've been up to while they've been gone.

There are way too many people to keep in one room, and everyone sits down wherever they'd like once they've piled their food onto a plate, table or not. That makes it even harder to try to keep an eye on everyone. Eventually, after downing a few beers, I manage to calm down. *Everything will be fine. You're leaving tomorrow. Try to enjoy this.*

"For hardened criminals, your friends have been excellent house guests, David," Ayla jokes, grouped in a corner with me, Nylan, and Ragnar. "The brunette has been a little squirrely, but honestly, my parents have loved having them here."

"The blonde isn't bad to look at, either," Nylan adds.

"He does seem like your type." Ragnar looks over at Adam, currently talking with Arik and Glasha. "Tall, handsome—"

"Arms that could pop my head like an overripe melon," Nylan finishes, ignoring the way Ragnar rolls his eyes. "It's going to be weird not having you around anymore, David. I've gotten used to having someone who knows what it's like dealing with all this." He gestures between him and Ragnar.

"You're pushing it, boy," Ragnar warns.

"...Sorry, Sir." Nylan stretches up to kiss his owner on the cheek. "I'm just really gonna miss you, David."

"I'm going to miss you too, Ny. All of you." I take a moment to think about what I want to say without getting too sappy. "I know I didn't end up here under the best pretenses, but it's honestly been amazing. You guys have taught me so much stuff, about myself, about the world... Even with all the bad, I'm not sure I would have done anything differently. I'm going to miss this place a lot."

Suddenly, my arms are full of a sobbing half-elf. "You have to promise to keep in touch. You can't just forget about us or never visit or—"

"Ny, I'm *literally* leaving to go meet with your father. There's no way you won't hear from me again," I try to reassure the guy sobbing into my chest. "I'd never be able to forget about you."

"I don't think you're the only one to feel that way," Ayla says while Nylan composes himself. "I know I have not been around very much, but I cannot remember the last time I saw my brother this happy. He normally takes everything so seriously, but since I've been home, I swear it's like he's ten years younger. He makes *jokes* now. I can only imagine how much he's going to take it once you are gone."

I look over at Khazak, who's standing with Corrine and Nikka, feeling the heat rise in my face as Ayla's words sink in. I tell myself it's just the beer.

Later, after most of the other guests have left, Khazak and I make our excuses to head home ourselves. I half-expect my teammates to wonder why I'm not sleeping here with them, but even with the open beds they have, I'm pretty sure Adam and Nate are still sleeping on couches, so I have the excuse of wanting a real bed if I needed it.

As Khazak and I walk home, for once devoid of left-overs, I feel one of his hands reach over and slowly envelop mine. We walk the rest of the way hand in hand in silence, his thumb stroking mine. I'm smiling, and I know he is too, but there's a feeling of melancholy hanging in the air. This is our last night together.

We don't stop holding hands until Khazak has to unlock the front door. We enter quietly, lingering in the living room, neither of us sure what we want to say.

"David—"

"Khazak—"

After some chuckling, he finally goes first. "I just wanted you to know what these past few months have meant to me." He takes both of my hands in his as he talks. "Despite the circumstances that led to us meeting, and the last few days notwithstanding, I have really treasured our time together. I can only hope when you look back on this, it is not the ways I hurt you that you focus on. I am so sorry for that."

"I keep telling you there's nothing to apologize for." *My turn.* "Thank you for being so patient with me, even though I kept screwing things up over and over. And over. You've taken care of me in a lot of ways you didn't have to. I'm sorry I didn't make things easy on you. I... I..." *Say it.* "I'm really going to miss you."

"I am going to miss you too, David." Strong orc arms pull me in for a hug.

I wrap my arms around him, and we stand there, holding each other. I can feel the sadness start to overtake me, the water in my eyes welling up, but it's not until I hear him sniffle that I realize he's crying too. Still no words, but his hold tightens, just a little. I'm not sure how long we stand there, but I'm not ready to pull away until my eyes are dry.

"So, I know it's late," *and we both just got done crying,* "but since it's our last night together, and I was wondering if we could—"

"Bedroom and strip." I'm given the three-word order before my mouth is captured in a hungry kiss.

I'm moving as soon as I'm released, pulling my shirt off on my way down the hall. I can feel Sir's heavy footsteps right behind me, and when we enter, I go straight to the bed. I finish undressing while I watch him light the bedroom's lantern before rummaging through his chests, pants drooping at his waist. When he stands back up, he's holding a pair of leather cuffs connected by a chain. He finishes stripping and climbs on the bed to stalk over me.

As he kisses me again, he uses his free hand to pin one of mine above my head. Forgetting about everything except his mouth on mine, I make a questioning noise when I feel the first cuff attaching to my wrist. Never releasing my mouth, he pulls up my other wrist. The second cuff is attached, and an experimental tug reveals the chain is threaded through the headboard.

He's still kissing me, his tongue thick in my mouth. I want more, trying to memorize the way he tastes, as weird as that may sound. I whine when we break apart, feeling him chuckle as he moves to my neck, sucking bites into the sensitive skin. I tilt my head back to give him more room, biting my lip as he moves down my collarbone, then my chest, and then my stomach.

I feel the familiar press of the charm against me as Khazak moves between my legs, spreading them wide and pushing them back. Of course, he avoids my cock and moves straight to my ass. That sounded like a complaint; it's not. At least I'm not wondering whether or not I can touch myself.

I shudder when I feel his mouth on my thigh, moving down to where the skin meets my groin. My hands curl into useless fists, squirming when his beard tickles me as he continues to bite. I breathe a sigh of relief when he finally moves to his real target, warm tongue swiping across my hole. The swiping soon turns into poking, and my toes curl when I feel him finally breach me, pushing in as deep as he can go.

Sir eats my hole like it was a prisoner's last meal, leaving my ass feeling wet and sloppy whenever he pulls away to breathe. His tongue fucks me hard and fast, spearing and spreading me as much as he can with nothing more than his hands to lift and hold me open. I find myself whining when he finally pulls away for good, settling me back on the bed and kneeling between my legs.

I feel the oil covered finger against my spit-slick hole next. *When did he grab that?* Doesn't matter—finger one pushes in deep and is quickly joined by a second as Khazak pumps them in and out of me. When they're pressed in all the way, he scissors them apart, making me gasp and squirm even more before they're removed.

The next thing to enter me is Sir's cock, *finally*. I can feel myself being stretched even farther; his dick so much bigger than two fingers. I'm glad that there's still just the smallest hint of a sting. I want to remember as much of this as I can later. Bruises, hickeys, all of it. I wrap my legs around his waist when he finally bottoms out, pulling him into me.

Stroking his hands from my chest down to my sides, he holds me gently by the waist while pulling his hips back, pushing back into me slowly. I try to use my legs and urge him to go faster, but he's content to move at his own pace, stroking his hands over my body as does.

"*Ta sra'tor pik'qa avakesh vaz'ka sap,*" he whispers almost reverently. "*Ta ril'pa ta yee to'vash. Alak tiu.*"

I don't know what he's saying, but it feels like I understand him nonetheless. I struggle in vain to reach him, lifting my head from the mattress and pulling at the chain with my hands. My efforts are rewarded when Khazak lifts my legs from his waist, bending me in half as he leans down to kiss me. Still buried to the hilt, he starts snapping his hips even faster, making sure to hit *all* the right spots.

He growls into my mouth when my hole flutters against him, both of us knowing what's coming. I grip onto the chain holding my wrists together tightly in both hands when I feel my hole starting to contract, and I cry into Sir's open mouth as I cum on his cock for the first time tonight. Never slowing down, he grips me tightly by both shoulders, holding me steady while he drives himself in and out.

Happy to continue at this speed and pace, my senses are filled with nothing but Khazak. His weight pressing down on me, the way he smells, the taste of him in my mouth. He's kissing me so deeply, it's like he's trying to consume me. I feel the same need, like it's not enough. I need more. I struggle to follow when he breaks us apart again and cry out when he pulls out completely and I'm empty.

I don't get the chance to voice my complaints. I'm quickly flipped onto my stomach, the chain at my wrists tightening as it twists with me. Strong green hands lift my hips, holding my ass in position as Sir quickly sinks back inside me. The sudden intrusion nearly makes me shout, but I hold back, not wanting to give him any reason to stop. *I need more.* He's pounding me at an almost punishing pace, his hips roughly slapping against my ass each time. The sound of smacking becomes almost rhythmic, and it's like I sink into a trance. When he starts to spank me, it's almost too much. *Almost.*

"Harder," I beg. "Harder, please. I need it." *I need your marks. I need to wear them long after I'm gone.* "Please."

It works, my master taking pity on me, smacking my ass harder and harder as he fucks me. It hurts, but the knowledge that I'll be able to see the marks and feel the bruises for days only pushes me closer to that edge again. It only takes a few more spanks before I have my second orgasm, my hole spasming around his cock as it pistons in and out, never pausing.

Only when he gets close himself do his movements stutter, and with a tight grip on my hips, he slams forward, burying himself to the hilt. I feel the familiar pulse of his cock as he unloads, and happy as I am to know I'll be able to carry part of him around with me, the knowledge that it may be the last time has the melancholy returning.

Carefully slipping out of me, Khazak uncuffs my hands, gently rubbing my sore wrists as he settles me against him. We are both sticky and sweaty, but I don't think either of us wants to wash any of this off, not right now. For now, he just holds me, taking one of my hands in his and splaying our fingers together, the gentle flicker of the lantern's flame highlighting the sweat-covered curves of his body.

I'm going to miss this so much.

"Alak tiu," I hear Khazak whisper against my neck, just before sleep overtakes me.

Chapter 20

I dream that I'm flying over the ocean again, only this *time the waters are quiet, the skies clear. I can feel the cool breeze against my face, my body, my wings. I feel calm. Free. The sun is shining brightly, high above the clouds. The longer I fly, the brighter it seems to grow. Then, off in the distance, I can see land appearing just over the horizon, right before everything fades to white.*

I wake up early in the morning. After spending two and a half months here, I've learned how to tell time in this room by the light of the sun, a skill that will no longer be useful after today. Normally, I'd be happy to let Khazak sleep in a little longer, but seeing as we only have a few hours left together, I don't stop myself from reaching out for him.

I nuzzle my face into his chest, inhaling his scent, still trying to memorize as much of him as I can. I feel him stir, but he doesn't move other than to stroke a hand down my back. Neither of us speaks, content to hold each other silently in the dark room.

Eventually, he does pull back slightly, watching me as he strokes a hand down my face. He's wearing the barest hint of a smile, but it's drowned out by the sadness coming off the rest of him in waves. I know I need to get up, get the day started, get ready to meet my friends and leave. But I can't. Not yet.

"Can... Can we pretend?" I ask into his chest, hands still trying to pull us closer. "Just for a little while longer?"

There's a flash of something in his eyes—hurt, understanding, lust?—but I don't ponder it for long. With a gentle nod of his head, he leans forward to capture my mouth. I close my eyes out of habit, leaning forward against his lips. I eagerly open my mouth when I feel his tongue seeking entrance, and Khazak rolls me onto my back, climbing over me as he deepens our kiss.

My hands roam all over his back and neck, reveling in the way his weight feels on top of me. Our morning erections grind as he ruts himself against me. One of his hands moves to my hair, tugging gently and letting him change the angle of our kiss as he desires. His other hand slides down my side, cupping my cheek gently as it spreads me, inching closer to my hole.

The finger is gentle, checking for any damage, and to see how slick I am from the night before. My hands tighten on his shoulders as he breaches me, and I hold back a small whimper of pain, not wanting to risk anything that might stop him. All while never breaking our kiss, still holding me close.

Satisfied that I'm still prepared, I feel his precum-slick cockhead rubbing along my ass, guided by his hand. Pulling back for just a moment, Khazak brings his hand up to his mouth, spitting into his palm and slicking it over himself. Wet cock against my hole, he pushes down until he finally breaches me, making the both of us gasp as our mouths meet again.

His hips start slow, the bed softly creaking as he slides in and out of my body. The lack of real lube feels a little rough, and the angle is awkward, but I don't care. I want more. I don't want this to stop because when we stop, everything is over, all of this ends, and we both have to go back to our regular lives. Whatever those even are anymore.

It does have to end eventually, though. Sir starts to thrust faster, and stronger, and after only a few more, he pushes in deep, holding himself steady while a familiar warmth spreads through my lower body as I'm bred. I wrap my legs around his waist, not ready for the moment to be over. We lay there together, still attached, breathing against each other's skin, holding each other tightly.

Wordlessly, Khazak lifts himself from his position atop me, his now-soft cock slipping out of me. My hole twitches in response, and I silently bask in the soreness of my body. *I hope it lasts for days.* Looking up, I meet Khazak's gaze in the dim morning light, his hand reaching out to stroke a thumb down my face. He leans forward to kiss me again, and I feel so many different emotions coming through—hope, sadness, longing—that I have to wonder if I'm not projecting my own as he wordlessly helps me from the bed.

We clean up together in the bathroom in silence. I know I should probably shower, that it will be my last hot shower for gods know how long, but the thought of scrubbing away the last of Khazak on my body makes me stop cold. *I'm going crazy.*

I gather my things together while Khazak works on cooking something for breakfast. I finished packing yesterday, but I search through everything one more time, just to make sure that I don't forget something. As I go through the chests in the bedroom, I find myself pulling out some of his clothes and smelling them. *I'm really glad he's in the kitchen right now.*

By the time my bag and weapons are in a neat pile by the door, Khazak is finished with breakfast. I wasn't really paying attention before, but now I notice the familiar smells in the air: coffee and bacon. I'm not surprised when Khazak bypasses the table in the kitchen, pulling me onto the couch and over his lap. I would have never thought it possible to feel both joy and sadness while being hand fed pieces of bacon, but here we are.

When my belly is full and the coffee has gotten my brain working, it's almost time to go. We are meeting my friends at the north gate, the closest one to our next destination. Even though I've got everything together, I still feel myself dragging things along, trying to milk every last second I have here. Stupid, I know.

I strap on my pack and swords (of which I am now carrying *three*) when I can't delay things any further. Khazak looks me over, making sure I'm dressed for the journey, and then triple-checks that I'm not leaving anything. At a certain point, it feels like we're *both* stalling, standing near the front door in silence.

"Well, I suppose it is time for you to leave." He tucks some hair behind my ear—I'm gonna need another haircut soon.

"Yeah, I guess it is." I nod sadly, watching him reach for the door.

I give the house one last look after we exit. This place has been my home for the last two months. It's weird to think I might not be back here to see it again. At least not for a long time. I can't help but feel the same about a lot of the places we pass on our walk: the station, the marketplace, the Hall of Honor in the distance. This place made such an impact on me in such a short time, and the rest of the world doesn't even know it exists.

Khazak and I exchange glances as we walk north together. I keep finding myself wanting to reach out and take his hand, but anytime I do, I get a flash of worry that my friends might see, and my arm remains stiff by my side.

Maybe he can read my mind, or maybe he just notices the turmoil on my face, but Khazak reaches a hand out to my shoulder, squeezing gently.

Eventually, the north gate comes into view along with the rest of the wall. As we get closer, I notice the small crowd gathered around its base: all of my friends and Khazak's family. I knew we'd be getting a send-off, but again, I didn't expect it to be this big. This is everyone from the going away party last night.

"There you are!" Adam calls to me as I approach. "We were starting to wonder if you'd decided to stay."

"Can't get rid of me that easily," I half-joke back.

"You sure?" Liss adds snarkily.

It feels good to be back with my team. It also feels weird to have everyone here right now staring at me, so let's get these goodbyes going, so we can get out of here. I go to Arik, Glasha, and Nikka first, giving each of my former coworkers a hug. Arik can't help himself and reaches down to pinch my ass, but Nikka pushes a small bag into my hand after her and Glasha's turn.

"More smoke bombs," she tells me. "They saved lives before, and they will do it again."

"Thank you, Nikka." I reach behind me to tuck the bag into one of my pack's pouches. "It was really great working with you all."

"You too, David," Glasha answers with a smile. "Certainly kept things interesting."

I hug Brull next, who is sure to whisper a few dirty things in my ear about what I can do on the road to keep myself busy before moving on to Khazak's family. While Orlun gives us a nice pep talk about our journey, Rurig hands us a basket of food for the road. Jarek, Ayla, and Yogik all wish us well, and even Ursza and Ignatz give me a hug goodbye.

"It's not fair," Nylan cries when it's his turn. "You only just got here and now you're leaving."

"I know! I'm sorry. I'm the worst," I try to console the half-elf. "But you know this isn't the last you'll hear from me."

"You know you've always got a home here with us, David." It's Ragnar, hugging both me and Nylan together. "A job too, even if you like to bend the rules a little." He winks. *Like he doesn't.* "But really...I can't thank you enough for saving my Ny. For saving everyone."

I shake my head at the half-orc. "I know you'd do the same." *Speaking of...*

I turn to face my final goodbye. The person responsible for knocking me out, capturing, and enslaving me. The person who I wanted nothing more than to hate at the start of all this. The person who for the past two months has been one of the most patient and kind men I have ever met.

How am I supposed to say goodbye?

"I guess this is it." I stand in front of him, ignoring the fact that all eyes are on the two of us right now.

"I suppose so." A sad smile. "Only one thing left to do."

Reaching into his pocket, Khazak pulls out a small key. Then, reaching forward into my shirt, he pulls out my collar. I've gotten so used to wearing it that I almost forgot about it. Holding the padlock in his hand, he slides the key in and turns, the lock opening with a *click*. Sliding the chain off my neck, he gathers it in his hand, meeting the two ends of the chain again and closing the lock once more.

"I want you to keep this." He places the chain collar in my hand. "To remember me by."

"I couldn't forget you if I wanted to." I lean forward to wrap my arms around him in a hug. "Thank you. For everything. You've done so much for me, and I..." *Say it, dammit. TELL HIM!* "...I'm just really going to miss this place and you." *Coward.*

"I am going to miss you too." His voice rumbles in my ear, and I can only squeeze him tighter.

We stand there holding each other for a while, probably way too long, but I just can't bring myself to end it. Ending it means leaving, and I just want to stay. I keep hoping for something to happen, for Khazak to ask me, hell, *order* me to. Anything to keep me here. But of course he doesn't. He can't.

"What about the uh," I point back and forth between us after we finally release each other, "rest of the avakesh thing. The paperwork?" *Sad wood.*

"I will take care of signing the papers to release you myself," he assures me. "No need to worry."

"Great," I lie.

The two of us finished, Khazak signals to the guards to open the gates. With a final wave to everyone, the five of us gather together, ready to leave. I can't bring myself to make eye contact with anyone, my vision already starting to blur as the water builds up.

"What, you gonna miss your—OWW!" Nate doubles over after taking my fist to his stomach.

"That's for getting us in this fucking mess in the first place."

I move in front, leading my team out of the city gates. If anyone else notices me crying, they don't say anything.

We make pretty good time that first day. It's hard at first to not constantly look back at the city as it fades from sight, but the farther away we are, the easier it gets. It takes us a few hours, but once we're far enough northeast of the city, we find the trail we're looking for and make a brief stop to eat the sandwiches Rurig packed for us for lunch. Then it is right back to walking.

We stop to set up camp a couple of hours before sunset, just on the outskirts of a forest. Normally, we would push a little farther, but seeing as this is more walking than most of us have done in months, we could use the break. There's a river nearby, so after we get the tents up and start a fire, Adam and I grab the fishing poles and try to catch some dinner.

We don't really need it, we have more than enough rations, plus more food from Rurig, but I haven't been able to see my best friend one-on-one in months. We find a good spot, throw our lines in the water, and just talk. There's a little bit of awkwardness, only for a second, and then it's gone and we're like two friends who just got back from separate long trips. Adam tells me stories about his time in the work camp and the people he met there, and I tell him about some of the work I did with the rangers. It must be at least an hour before we start hitting on anything serious.

"So, what was it like?" Adam asks after a lull in the conversation. "Dying."

"Scary," I answer after thinking about it for a moment. "Because you know it's happening, and you know you can't stop it. I remember feeling sad too. Sad about the things I wouldn't get to do." *That you still didn't do when you came back.*

"When they first told us what happened to you, we didn't really believe them." Adam looks over to me. "Not until we saw the scar, and even then... Dying and being brought back to life? I needed to hear it from you before it really sunk in."

"I don't blame you. I still don't really believe it myself." I'm not sure I know who or what I really am right now. "What if there's something wrong with me?"

"We'll figure it out because we're a team." He nudges me in the shoulder. "You know, not to ignore how dark and fucked up everything has been for the two months, but...we have a real goal now. An *actual* mission."

"A mission that doesn't pay." *Aren't I so helpful?*

"We'll figure it out," he repeats himself. "Remember what we said at the start of the year? We came out here because we wanted to explore the world and discover something amazing. And now we're doing it man. That's pretty fucking cool."

"I guess you're right." Adam has a way of turning anything into a positive. "Just would have been nice if it didn't require me dying."

"Yeah, you pulled the short straw there, I guess." Adam chuckles. "So... You wanna talk about Captain Ironstorm and why you keep touching that necklace in your pocket?"

I freeze at Adam's question, though when I glance over at him, he's giving no indication that he's asked me anything remotely interesting. He looks downright bored. Still, I release the collar and pull my hand out of my pocket. I didn't even realize I was doing that.

"I, uh..." *Fuck, stop stammering.* "Why don't you tell me what you guys heard, and I can fill in the blanks?"

"Okay, yeah." Adam doesn't look all that surprised by my answer. "Well, Corrine and Nate told us about you challenging him to the fight. It wasn't until later that we found out the whole thing ended in sex."

My face heats up, and I can't bring myself to look over at Adam.

"It scared us since it sounded like you were being forced, but then a couple of the guards threw us some taunts about how much you liked it." *Assholes.* "We were still pretty worried until we saw you the day of the trial. You seemed okay, and Ironstorm—Khazak—didn't seem like a monster, so we didn't really know what to think. After we were released, when you were still unconscious, he wouldn't leave the side of your bed. Even when he *had* to, he always made sure someone else was there in case you woke up. I don't think I even saw him eating or sleeping all that much."

"He did all that?" The info causes a burst of warmth in my chest.

"Yeah." Adam nods. "It seemed like you guys had gotten pretty close."

"We did, eventually." I take a deep breath before I start. "Everything you heard was basically true, even the forced part. The thing is, that ritual I challenged him to hasn't been used to solve criminal issues in like, decades. It's used by *couples* already in relationships. Information Redwish kept from me, while at the same time telling Khazak I *did* know, trying to convince him to accept."

"Why'd he do that?" Adam asks. "Do you think it was part of their plans in the temple?"

"No, they weren't expecting me to be out there that night." I shake my head. "I think he just thought it was funny."

"Asshole." Adam's cursing makes me smirk.

"Agreed," I continue, nodding. "The first few days were rough. He did not make things easy for me, and I fought him at every turn, but eventually they settled down, and we found some sort of mutual respect. At least until... Do you remember your last night in the jail cell before being moved to the labor camp? When I came to see you in the middle of the night?"

"Oh yeah, what the hell was that about?" Adam looks confused. "I thought I dreamed that."

"Well, I was sorta...trying to break you guys out." I duck my head sheepishly.

"What?!" Adam booms out with a laugh. "You did *what?*"

"So first, I drugged Khazak with some hypnograss and stole his keys." Adam's eyes go wide. "Then I climbed the wall around the jail—which they rigged with alarms now, by the way—and tried to get you out of the cell. Except you had been moved to a cell inside days before. I got caught right after that, and that's when I was brought in for that late night visit. I wanted proof that you were all okay."

"Well, I appreciate the thought," he chuckles, "but I can't imagine that worked out well for you."

"Yeah, he was *pissed*. We had a huge fight." I grimace, remembering the next day. "But it got us to actually talk about stuff, which is when we figured out that we had both been tricked by Redwish. He felt *so* terrible—still does—but after some more talking, we came to an agreement for the rest of my stay. And then, like you said, we...got close." I pause, feeling bashful again. "I swear, it wasn't that I was trying to hide something from everyone, or at least I didn't *want* to hide anything, but I was worried about what everyone would think, and it's not like there was ever a good time to—"

"David, hey." Adam's hand on my arm stops my nervous rambling. "It's okay. I get it. You're not the only one who's *gotten close* with another guy."

What? I have to look over at Adam three times before I'm sure I heard him correctly.

"Remember Rich Fullbrush?" I nod in response. Rich was a former schoolmate and knight-in-training who I thought was going to kiss me, right before he threw up all over my shoes. "Once, during a party, when he was *really* drunk, he kissed me."

"I *knew* it," I whisper.

"It made me realize it didn't really matter to me if the person I was kissing was a man or a woman," he finishes, scrunching up his face. "It also tasted like he just got done throwing up."

"Gross." I avoid gloating about the fact that his vomit-flavored mouth means Rich tried to kiss me first...for now. "With the way everything went down, it was like I couldn't avoid or ignore it anymore. I just had to accept it. Then, because everyone I knew was far away or in jail, it was like I got to be this whole other person. Someone who didn't have to worry about what anyone else would think."

"The longer things went on, the easier it was," I continue, reaching into my pocket and pulling out the collar, looking at the engraving on the lock. "He had this custom-made for me. It showed that he owned me, but also that we were...close." My voice drops to a whisper, afraid it might crack. "I think I might be in love with him."

"Woah." Adam straightens at my revelation. "That's... Maybe when we finish with all this, we can go back. Maybe even soon."

"Yeah, maybe." I nod, both of us knowing it probably won't be that easy. "Thanks for talking to me, man. I really missed having you around."

"Ditto, bro." He nudges my shoulder with his. "Alright, I don't think we're catching anything, and it's getting dark. Let's head back."

We fold up our rods and pack up, making the short walk back to where our camp is. The sun is almost down, but the fire is plenty bright, and we don't even have to use it for cooking! I help Corrine pass out the jerky and some plums. I figured we could enjoy a day or two of fresh fruit before we have to move on to the dried stuff. Weren't cheap, either.

Just as I go to sit down on the ground, something rustling in the bushes has everyone on alert. Weapons are grabbed, and we quickly move into a circle formation on the other side of the fire, watching the shrubs carefully. Could be nothing, could be bandits, could even be a wild boar.

What I am *not* expecting is an orc, both hands held out in front of him.

Khazak?

"I was beginning to worry I would not catch up with you."

I immediately drop my swords to my side and start walking toward him. "What are you doing—"

"Not so fast." Adam's hand on the back of my armor pulls me back. "What *are* you doing here?"

"Well, seeing as you are all unfamiliar with the area, I could not help but think your group might benefit from having a guide." He eyes everyone else's still raised weapons with a cocked eyebrow. "Perhaps you could all lower your weapons so we can discuss and avoid a repeat of our first meeting."

"Sorry." Adam finally sheaths his sword, and the rest of the group relaxes, but he still doesn't release me. "Well, we only bought enough supplies for the five of us, and you know we can't afford to pay you, right?" *What? I bought a ton of extra rations.*

"That is alright. I have brought enough supplies for myself, and payment is not what I am after." He gestures to the bag on his back.

"Well, I'm pretty sure I know what you *are* after, so... let's negotiate." I quickly look at Adam, confused. *Negotiate what?* "Besides being a guide, what else can you bring to the group?"

"I am an excellent hunter. Which actually connects to one of my stipulations." Khazak settles his gaze on me, instantly making me blush. "David was borderline under-weight when I met him, and I have spent the last two months helping to strengthen him back. I want to ensure that does not happen again, even if that means I need to hunt for his food myself. I would also be happy to pass along some of my hunting skills to rest of you."

"That seems fair. Though for the record, that wasn't our fault." He's right. In those early days, when we were *really* broke, we split everything evenly five ways. "But we are talking about giving you my best friend here, so what else you got?"

I stare at Adam slack jawed, though I'm not sure if it's because of the negotiation, or because he's talking about *trading away his best friend like it's nothing.* To our left, I can hear Liss try and fail to hold in a laugh. Adam's gaze doesn't waver from Khazak, not bothering to look over at me.

"Well, I could point out that it is *very* obvious that none of you are from around here." Khazak circles a finger in the air. "Not only would you have a translator, simply having a local on the team may make it easier for others to trust you. Or at least, I stand a better chance of noticing if someone is trying to deceive us."

"Good point." I see Adam cock his head to the side for a second, apparently accepting the answer. "Alright, you're in. David, go to the nice man." Adam pats me on the back before pushing me toward the orc.

I half-glare at Adam, but the smile I am unable to hide takes out all the bite. "I'm going, but not because you told me to."

I don't stop to say anything yet, just grab Khazak by the wrist and pull him into the forest so we can talk away from everyone. I'm consciously ignoring the fact that basically the entire group knows about this now. I'll deal with that later. Once we're far enough away, I stop and finally turn to face him.

"David, I—"

"I love you," I blurt out. "I'm sorry. I wanted to say it before, but I was scared and—"

"I love you too." That's more than enough to cut me off. "I wanted to tell you as well. I did, in a way... *Alak tiu.*"

"Well, that's very helpful." I can't even snark very well, taking hold of both of his hands while also noting the way to say "I love you" in Atasi. "How are you here?"

"It was not easy. I tried to move as fast as I could, but I was actually starting to get worried I would not find you until—"

"No! I mean your family, your house, your *job*." I poke him in the chest. "You have a entire life."

"After you left, it no longer felt like I did." He cups the back of my head, stroking my ear. "I asked Ayla to look after my home. I thought that might give her more of a reason to stay. That and not living with our parents."

I laugh and ignore the fact that I'm pretty sure my eyes are starting to water. "What about the rangers?"

"I resigned." He shrugs, smirking like it was nothing. "I spoke with Ragnar and left a letter of recommendation naming him as my replacement. I felt terrible leaving in the middle of so much turmoil, but I did not have a choice."

"He understood?" They are literally in the middle of investigating their *entire* force for traitors.

"He and Nylan were the first ones to encourage me to chase after you." That sounds like Nylan for sure. "And he swore it was not just so he could take my job."

"That's... Wait, what about the paperwork stuff?" I pull back to look at him. "Did you sign the papers to release me?"

"I, uh..." It's too dark to see him blush, but I can feel it. "I may have forgotten to before leaving."

"Forgot?" I question his motive.

"...It will just be so much easier when we come back to visit this way." *Oh my god*. I laugh.

"Uh-huh. Sure." I'm not even mad about it. "Guess that means you need to put this back on me." I pull my collar out of my pocket for the second time tonight.

"I suppose I do." Reaching into his shirt collar, Khazak pulls out a thin silver chain from around his neck where the key to my collar now hangs. *That's new. We kinda match now.* Opening the lock, the cool metal wraps around me, thick green hands sealing it with a click. I take comfort in the familiar weight around my neck, Khazak admiring his work in the dim light.

"You're... You're really coming with us?" It still doesn't feel real.

"I am really coming with you." He pulls me close, so our bodies are flush. "Wherever your journey leads, I want to be there."

"Khaz..." I wrap my arms around his neck, trying to crowd him even more. "I really thought I was going to lose you."

"Well, I do not know who this 'Khaz' is, but I can assure you, puppy, I am not going anywhere." I laugh into his chest, too happy to give him a hard time.

Pulling back, green eyes stare into chocolate-brown just before pink lips meet green, and for the first time in months, it feels like I'm home.

The story of David and Khazak will continue
in the next chapter of *Steel & Thunder!*

About the Author

Dominic N. Ashen is an author and avid reader, with a heavy focus on gay, BDSM-themed erotica. After spending his youth in search of books with characters who were more like himself–queer ones, specifically–he decided to start creating some of his own. His stories star queer protagonists, most often gay and bisexual men, and feature heavy themes of dominance, submission, and all sorts of kink. Dominic loves the fantasy, sci-fi, and horror genres, with a penchant for writing longer stories where he is able to weave in the sex and kink right alongside the plot.

dominicashen.com

patreon.com/dominicashen

facebook.com/dom.n.ashen

instagram.com/dom.n.ashen

twitter.com/DomNAshen

HONEY CUMMINGS

Sleeping with Sasquatch
Cuddling with Chupacabra
Naked with New
Jersey Devil
Laying with the Lady in Blue
Wanton Woman in White
Beating it with Bloody Mary

Beau and Professor
Bestialora

The Goat's Gruff
Goldie and Her
Three Beards
Pied Piper's Pipe
Princess Pea's Bed
Pinocchio and the
Blow Up Doll
Jack's Beanstalk
Curses & Crushes

FANTASY/PARANORMAL ROMANCE

BLAISE RAMSAY
Through The Black Mirror
The City of Nightmares
The Astral Tower
The Lost Book of
the Old Blood
Shadow of the Dark Witch
Chamber of the Dead God

BEAU LAKE
The Beast Beside Me
The Beast Within Me

VALERIE WILLIS
Cedric: The
Demonic Knight
Romasanta: Father of
Werewolves

The Oracle: Keeper of the
Gaea's Gate
Artemis: Eye of Gaea
King Incubus: A New Reign

J.M. PAQUETTE
Klauden's Ring
Solyn's Body
The Inbetween
Hannah's Heart
Call Me Forth
Invite Me In

V.C. WILLIS
Prince's Priest
Priest's Assassin

4HORSEMENPUBLICATIONS.COM